Love's Last Call

Beth Matthews

Copyright © 2014

Published by EDW Books.

Original Copyright 2014. Elizabeth Walker

Edited by LaRee Bryant.
lbryant316@aol.com

Cover art by Fiona Jayde.
http://fionajaydemedia.com/

Contact the author: beth.matthews.books@gmail.com

www.bethmatthewsbooks.com

ISBN-10: 0996009973
ISBN-13: 978-0-9960099-7-3

For Sarah at UCB.
She helped me put me back together.

ACKNOWLEDGMENTS

First and foremost, I have to acknowledge Biaggio. Without him I would never have had the idea to write this book. Thank you, Biaggio, for the stories and the fact-checking and, of course, for loving me. Most importantly, thank you for teaching me the difference between a headlock, a Full Nelson, and a Half Nelson. I should be utterly lost without you.

Thanks to Mom, Val, Evan, and the cats for various acts of love, support, and/or distraction as the case may be.

Thank you to all my friends who helped troubleshoot the title (especially Sam and Nathan). Thank you to Ashley Brunts who came up with the name Jezebel's. Thank you to my editor, LaRee Bryant, who helped give me a boost when I needed it. Thank you to Fiona Jayde for another beautiful cover. (And this time it was relatively painless!) ;P

Thank you to the folks on the Marie Force Yahoo group for their generosity in sharing their knowledge.

Lastly, if you've made it this far, thank you for reading my book.

Chapter One

Sweet Christ on a bike, Lucy hated St. Patrick's Day at the bar.

Dodging a crowd of braying frat boys, she re-adjusted her hold on a tray of Jell-O shots. St. Patrick's Day meant a huge mob, mostly from UCLA. Every drunken college kid, seemingly within a hundred miles, had packed the place from wall to wall. Almost three hundred sweating, stinking, immature cavemen swilling cheap beer and leaving crap tips as they groped her. All packed into one bar.

Oh, joy. Oh, rapture.

As a shot girl for The World Famous Jezebel's Bar & Lounge, part of her job description included wearing skimpy clothing, and tonight she was in top form. The bar hosted a St. Patrick's Day theme night every year so, of course, all the shot girls had to wear something appropriate for the occasion. Wonder of wonders, Lucy had managed to find a "Sexy Leprechaun" outfit online. Her top was low, her skirt was short, and her grandmother would have died to see her dressed this way.

A perfect outfit, in other words, to help her hawk the noxious test tubes and Jell-O shots on her tray. Outfits like this paid her community college tuition.

3

A table of frat boys signaled to her and, with a sigh, she stretched her lips into an unfelt smile and battered her way through the crowd. When she got to their table, she set her tray down and bestowed a flirty smirk on the group at large. "Hello, boys. Interested in some shots?"

The frat boys, all five of them, laughed like this was the height of wit. She kept her smile pinned in place and waited.

One guy slapped money on the table as he gave her a lascivious once-over. "Test tubes all around, gorgeous."

"All right then." She stuffed the money down the cleavage of her shamrock-patterned bustier then fished out a shot from her tray. "Who's first?"

More laughter and back-slapping followed, but, at last, the one who had paid volunteered. He was chubby and stank of sweat. She pushed him into his seat and set one high heel on his chair so he could get an eyeful of her cleavage as she bent over. One of the other kids at the table tilted over to look up her skirt, but she always wore shorts underneath her outfits. She was desperate, not stupid.

Resuming her business, she lifted her patron's hands to her waist and was gratified when they actually stayed there. The kid tipped his head back and she poured the alcohol down his throat. He crinkled his nose as he swallowed, and she climbed off him.

The next one in line grabbed her wrist, leering as he tugged her nearer. "Want to see my Lucky Charms, baby?"

So original. Ignoring his remark, she quickly served the rest of the table in the same way, and only one tried to cop a feel. Mr. Lucky Charms. She laughed and flicked his hands away from her ass. "Sorry, that's not on the menu tonight." *Or ever.* At least he'd spared her the "magically delicious" tag-line that other guys had used.

"Ah, come on, blondie." He made to grab for her again, but she twisted away.

"Well, unless you guys want some more…?" she asked once she stood at a safe distance.

The frat boys grimaced as one man and even the guy who'd been trying to score waved that offer away. Dollar shots were not, as a rule, the tastiest drinks on earth.

"Happy St. Paddy's Day, boys." She waited a beat then, as Mr. Lucky Charms ogled her again, she slid away. "Holler if you want more shots."

She stalked off, pounding the floor with each angry step. Cheap bastards. If they groped her she should at least get a tip. *Guy probably decided the grope* was *my tip.* She hoisted her tray onto her hip and scouted the bar for more likely prospects.

A table of three guys waved her over and she went. The biggest one gave her a thorough once-over then licked his lips. "Hey, sugar, want to see where I've hidden my Lucky Charms?"

With a supreme effort of will, Lucy managed not to groan. *It's gonna be a long night…*

***

It is going to be a long night. Norm fisted his hands on his thighs and flopped against the passenger seat as traffic, despite his own fervent wishes to the contrary, continued to inch along. But then, the universe never was very accommodating.

Norm's roommate, Zack, swore gently as he drove, stamping his foot on the accelerator when traffic picked up, then thumping his foot on the brake when traffic

5

slowed to a crawl twenty feet later. Cars clogged the streets and half-drunk pedestrians in green risked their lives careening through traffic to get to the other side.

Why did the party girl cross the road?

To get to the good booze, of course.

Norm glanced at the dashboard clock. Six minutes until his shift started. He fussed with the collar on his bowling shirt, smoothing his palm over the "Jezebel's" logo on his right breast pocket. The shirt's fabric was stiff and laced with that distinctive new clothes smell. Lifting his sleeve to his nose, he winced as he also caught the faint scent of diesel too. This was one of the perils of bumming rides from Zack: Norm ended up smelling like a gas can.

Hopefully, Norm's own car would weather this latest trip to the mechanic without needing to be put down. Of course, Norm didn't know yet how he would pay the mechanic's bill when he was still in the hole to Zack for rent money. Nervous energy popped inside Norm, like oil sizzling in a hot pan, and he yanked again at his shirt collar. *Please, let this job work out.*

"You nervous?"

He glanced over at Zack then shook his head. "What's to be nervous about?" Even as Norm said the words, his gut coiled with sick tension. *I'm an idiot. There's no way I can do this job.* But he *had* to do this job. His employment prospects had crumbled to this or working fast food at a theme park.

Zack's old Mercedes continued creeping down the busy streets of Hollywood. Norm scanned the curb for somewhere Zack could park to let him out. Five minutes until his shift. Trying to drum the anxiety out of his body, Norm tapped his foot against the ragged carpet of the car.

"I feel so proud." Zack's voice went all mock-quivery, as if he were about to cry. "Like I'm sending my kid off to kindergarten or something. This is definitely the best career opportunity you've ever had."

"For me? Or for you and your drinking problem?" *Four minutes.*

"For me, of course." Zack darted him a sideways glance and tightened his fists on the steering wheel. "I understand none of the other jobs were really your cuppa, man, but we're treading a thin line here. I can't cover another month of rent on my own."

Norm gusted out a deep breath. "I understand, Zack. I'll pay you back out of my first paycheck from the bar." *And I'll just sell my body or something to pay the mechanic's bills for my car.* Tension clotted underneath Norm's sternum, and he pressed a fist there to ease the ache.

Violently pink neon flashed "Jezebel's" across the windshield and Norm pointed. "There's the bar. Hey, there's a space--someone just pulled out."

Zack jerked the wheel hard over and rolled to a stop by the curb in front of Jezebel's.

"Thanks. I should be off at two." Norm pushed his door open and climbed out.

"Later, Bates." Zack gave a small salute then drove away, shoving the nose of his beat-up, brownish Benz into the flow of traffic. Much honking ensued, but Zack got his way and the Benz rolled on, always the winner in these automotive gladiatorial contests.

Norm turned toward Jezebel's. His new place of employment. And his very last hope.

He'd only been here once before for his interview, during daylight hours when the bar was wan and empty, all

7

Jezebel's mystique ruined by the harsh revelations of daylight. But now night's gentle glow had restored the bar its allure. Ghosted by light from other neon signs, the huge picture windows out front showed the place packed with people, a throbbing crush that swayed back and forth like a cresting green wave.

He tugged the heavy wooden door open and stepped inside. The laces on his Converse started glowing from a black light above his head. Music filtered down the short corridor. The bar had a live band playing most nights, and they took requests from the crowd in a fish bowl. Tonight a brunette on piano led the band with two guys on guitar accompanying her in a cover version of "My Sharona."

A small podium/desk hybrid sat right inside the front door, manned by a burly black guy in a Jezebel's shirt like Norm's. The door guard began to say one thing then his gaze dipped to Norm's shirt pocket and he changed whatever it was into a smile instead. "You must be the new guy."

"Yeah, I'm--"

But the bouncer had already snatched at a small phone hidden by a rise in the desk. "Hank? Yeah. New guy's here…OK."

Norm's fellow bouncer hung up then glanced at a point over Norm's shoulder.

Am I invisible?

Then a cold gust of air at his back told him that customers had come in and he was blocking their way. He edged sideways, but the corridor couldn't comfortably accommodate him, the podium, the other bouncer, and the four drunken college girls who tottered in. The feminine press of bodies should have been pleasant, but they all reeked of sweat and booze. One of the girls, a brunette with big teeth, quickly had her ID checked, paid her cover, and wobbled past. She took two steps then tripped on her heels.

Norm reacted a beat too to catch her, and all he caught was a dusting of sweat as her length of damp hair extensions whipped past his arms. The girl landed in a spill on the floor, and her friends all giggled.

He started forward to help, but the girls edged past him and hoisted their friend up. The girl who'd done the face-plant shot him a look over her shoulder once she was upright. "Hey, Stretch, buy me a drink later?" This set off another round of giggles from her friends as they towed the brunette inside the bar.

Norm swallowed, that familiar prickle of unease in his gut flaring to a full-fledged ache. *What have I gotten myself into?*

"You get used to it." The other bouncer slid sideways to greet the next group of patrons staggering through the door.

Before Norm could really weigh the idea of bolting for the street, he recognized the bar manager, Hank, approaching him. A big guy, dark-haired, thirtyish, Hank had skin that was either deeply tanned or naturally dark, and, though he stood a few inches shorter than Norm, Hank was massive with muscles--the epitome of the burly bouncer type--everything Norm was not. Except tall. Norm had tall covered. Norm had enough tall to go around.

He shook Hank's hand when the other man offered it.

9

"Welcome to Jezebel's," the manager said. When Hank dropped Norm's hand, the bar manager smoothly transitioned into a glance at his watch. "You're on time. Early even. Already you are an improvement over the last guy." He leaned past Norm to speak to the bouncer taking cover, "Ben, you seen Eddie?" The other man shook his head. "Fucking slacker," Hank murmured then unexpectedly slapped Norm hard on the shoulder. "Come on, newbie, I'll show you the place." Hank waved his hand at Norm in a *come-along* gesture and plunged headfirst into the teeming mass of people, leaving Norm no other option but to follow.

Hank yelled over the crowd as he led the tour, shoving his way through and pointing to the various positions the bouncers occupied on the floor. Norm staggered along, trying to soak up as much info as possible while simultaneously trying to avoid running into people-- and he kept failing terribly at both.

Hank was scarier than most of the bar patrons, though, so...*what are a few bumps and bruises?*

The bar's layout valued the proliferation of small tables for drinks over any kind of dance floor, or even room to move. This did not, however, stop people from trying to dance, or trying to maneuver between the bar and tables. The set-up uncomfortably reminded Norm of a net full of freshly caught fish, all of them flailing and flapping, trying to get someplace else. *Swim down, people. Honestly.*

The small stage for the band was built against one edge of the picture window so any passersby on the street, when trying to see into the club, could observe half of the excited crowd inside through the window, and half of the band members' asses and sound equipment.

Jezebel's heart itself, the bar, bloomed immediately across from the stage, stretching from one wall to another, with a highly-polished wooden top. Mirrors were mounted against the back wall which added depth to the room and made it appear as if Jezebel's stocked twice as much booze as they really did.

People swarmed over the bar, like sharks on a feeding frenzy of particularly good chum. Hank invested most of his man power in the bar, staffing that activity hub with a half dozen people all hopping around taking orders, mixing drinks, ringing up orders, closing tabs. Norm grew tired just watching that hive of activity.

Once Hank had shown Norm the back room and thereby completed The Grand Tour, he stationed Norm with him at one of the side doors. "Watch the floor and if anything looks bad, step in. Follow my lead for now."

Hank's "lead" at that moment entailed standing very tall by the door, crossing his arms over his chest and continually surveying the bar with an air of quiet menace.

Trying to ape Hank's vibe, Norm drew himself up to his full height to enhance the effect, but the pose didn't feel right. Norm didn't have Hank's bulk to pull off the whole menace thing.

After several minutes of zero conversation from Hank, Norm switched to people watching, which was part of his job, after all.

Gradually, he noticed the infamous Jezebel's shot girls weaving through the crowd hawking their wares. Each of the half dozen or so girls was pretty, and each had a great body clad in a truly revealing green outfit.

One girl in particular caught Norm's eye. Short and blonde, this girl wore one of the few St. Patty's Day outfits that might have taken any effort to construct: a sexy leprechaun. Something that first seemed a bit of an oxymoron.

An unexpected flush of excitement surged through Norm when she weaved his way. '*O brave new world that has such people in it*'. She hadn't seen him; that the tide of the crowd nudged her in his direction was simple coincidence but still, the tingle of anticipation zipped through him. From a purely aesthetic sense of appreciation, he wouldn't mind a closer glimpse of *her*.

Hank stirred beside him, and Norm managed to tear his gaze away from the girl to face his new boss.

The bar manager quirked one eyebrow and leaned into Norm, bellowing to be heard over the piano player, "I realized I forgot to mention the number one rule at Jezebel's."

Norm waited, but when Hank didn't continue he rose to the bait. "What is it?"

"Staff can't date each other. *Especially* bouncers and shot girls."

If you have a strict no-dating rule for employees, you can't then imply the rule's not so strict unless you're a shot girl and a bouncer. Norm bit his tongue on this unwise reply and nodded instead.

Hank gave Norm's shoulder a stinging pat. "I'm going to walk the floor. Make sure nobody sneaks any lit cigarettes in from the patio."

Hank stalked off, and Norm hissed out a relieved breath. Wow, Hank was wound tight. *I peek at a pretty girl for two minutes, and the guy has to go reading some deep significance into it.*

But a prickle of disquiet began, and rapidly doubled, as Norm found his head turning again to follow the little blonde's progress through the bar. Something about her drew his eye back and back and back again. Maybe it was the impish grin she gave her customers or maybe her silly leprechaun costume, which indicated to him a certain amount of creativity and humor. Or maybe--

He stopped, a chill shooting through him. *This is my first night, I really need this job, there's only one rule in this place...and I'm already thinking of breaking it.*

Chapter Two

After only half an hour, Lucy had emptied half her tray. *Doing good business tonight.* She'd maximized her opportunities on the bar side of Jezebel's and so she wandered toward the band side. One of the other shot girls, the voluptuous redhead Ronnie, approached and leaned in to be heard over the music. "How you doing tonight, Luce?"

"OK." She'd sold lots of shots, but there hadn't been too many good tips as yet. As a shot girl, she got a small percentage for every drink sold but she preferred obscenely big tips.

Ronnie jerked her chin toward the table Lucy had just vacated. "Did the buff one hit on you? He is gor-gee-ous."

If you like a dumb ass on steroids. Lucy grimaced. "He tried to grope my boob, in fact."

Ronnie widened her eyes, her voice honeyed with satisfaction, and a smirk played over her generous mouth. "Well, that's a promising start."

Lucy groaned low in her throat, and waved her friend's words away. "Do *not* try and fix me up with another drunken frat boy. Not tonight." *Not ever.*

Ronnie *tsk*ed and adjusted her shot tray as someone brushed against her from behind. In the swirling mass of bar patrons the two of them blocked the natural flow of traffic. "You don't know what you're missing, honey."

Lucy rolled her eyes. Sometimes she wondered if she stayed with her loser boyfriends longer than necessary just so she wouldn't have to deal with Ronnie's matchmaking. The bossy redhead always hustled up a man every time Lucy remained single longer than five minutes. Slowly backing away, Lucy cried out in an overly dramatic tone, "Go on without me, Ronnie, save yourself."

Ronnie laughed and whirled away to seek her next conquest--customer, that is. Lucy walked backwards one more step; a tactical mistake as the mass of the crowd heaved and a tipsy co-ed in a green bowler hat knocked into her. Lucy bobbled her tray and it slid out of her grasp. She watched in horror, feeling the world slow as her tray of shots crashed to the floor.

The crowd recoiled from the mess, falling silent for a moment, then someone let out a low, drunken, "*Buuummer!*" that could be heard even over Mia the piano player's Maroon 5 medley.

Bummer indeed. The test tubes were plastic but the booze was all over the floor and all over Lucy's black thigh-highs. The scent of the alcohol burned her nose, making her eyes water.

She stood there for a long moment, frustration stiffening the muscles in her body. Every minute it took cleaning this up and getting another shot tray filled was money out of her pocket. Money she couldn't afford to lose. "*Fuck,*" she snarled in a low voice, with feeling. Letting her breath out through her teeth, she turned to see if she could signal someone to bring her a broom.

15

She blinked as someone she didn't recognize knelt and began grabbing at the plastic test tubes on the floor. *A customer?* But then he straightened from his crouching position to hand up a cluster of shots to her and she caught sight of the black Jezebel's shirt which all the bouncers had to wear. *The new guy.* Hank had mentioned he'd hired someone at the staff meeting last week, and now here was the newbie. In the flesh.

Lucy kept peeking at the newbie as he snatched at test tubes, but getting a clear glimpse became a challenge as the crush of the bar kept shifting and bumping into her. She did notice he landed on the skinny side of things, lankier than most of the bouncers, but his arms were well defined with dense, corded muscles. He grabbed the last tube and straightened to his feet. And as he did he just seemed to keep going. Glancing toward his face, she had to stare up and up and *up.*

She was five-three and a half in her bare feet, not the tallest of women, but even with her insanely high heels on, he made her feel like a freaking shrimp. He had to be at least six-three, maybe six-four. Even if he lacked the bulk of the other bouncers, his height alone carried a nice intimidation factor. He *loomed* over a person.

She tucked her damp, now empty test tube tray against her side with one hand and extended the other to shake his. "Hi, I'm Lucy York. You must be the new bouncer."

He gripped her palm in a quick, firm shake. His hands were big with long, slightly callused fingers, his skin only slightly damp from the spilled booze. "Norm Keane."

Norm? She stifled a snicker. "As in 'Norman'?"

He nodded sheepishly. "Norm's fine, though."

What were his parents thinking? Although the name did fit him: a quintessential geek-type with his lanky form, a head of shaggy brown hair growing past his ears, a large nose with a slightly crooked bridge, and a pair of deep-set, toffee brown eyes. *Puppy dog eyes,* she thought with an inner laugh. Soulful eyes and sweet somehow, not least for the fact that the whole time she'd been standing there he'd kept his gaze fastened on her face--and not on what was surely a fantastic bird's eye view of her cleavage.

Hank, the bar owner, manager, head bouncer and King of Everything at Jezebel's, pushed his way toward Lucy, aggressively shoving frat boys aside when they hampered his progress.

At Hank's approach Norm swallowed and straightened, making himself even more ridiculously tall. The new bouncer tried to settle a stern glare over his nervousness, which only succeeded in making his face twitch. Lucy had to hide another chuckle; Norm had every right to be jumpy on his first day, especially with a boss as intimidating as Hank could be. Hank crossed over and cast a quick look of displeasure between the two of them. "What happened?"

Lucy fought an urge to stick her tongue out and snap Hank away from his DEFCON Five intensity. It wouldn't work anyway. "I dropped my tray. Norm was helping me pick all the tubes up. I tried to signal for a broom but no one came."

"Yeah, I had to send a bar-back home puking so they're in the weeds." Hank stepped toward her then recoiled, holding his shirt collar over his nose and mouth. Glancing down, she remembered she was soaked in cheap booze. Her nose, ever adaptable, had already stopped sending that particular signal to her brain. She glanced over at Norm, but apparently he didn't mind standing upwind of her.

Hank shuffled away. "Clean yourself up, Luce. Norm, since the bar is short-handed, go with and help get her tray refilled. Hurry up. We need all fucking hands on deck here." With that, Hank whirled away, no doubt to put out another fire elsewhere in the bar.

Lucy snorted. "I swear the day Hank cracks a joke at work we better watch for the Four Horsemen."

Norm gave a small, nervous laugh.

She grinned and gestured for him to follow her. "This way to the back room."

They were halfway through the crowd, Norm taking point and parting the Red Sea for her--or at least the Drunk Sea--when someone grabbed her by the elbow and hauled her toward one of the tables. She whirled to find herself facing Mr. Lucky Charms III, the buff guy Ronnie had picked out for her. He raked his eyes down her form, lingering on her legs. "Off to find your pot of gold?" He wiggled his eyebrows. "I could go with you, then maybe we'd both get lucky."

Don't offend the customers. Hank had drilled the mantra into her head until his voice looped through all on its own unprompted. She stretched her face into a smile and gently plucked her elbow free from his grip, but her skin throbbed from the echo of his hand. Either he was too drunk to control his grip or this guy liked things rough. Fantastic.

Norm had swum his way back to her against the tide. "You OK?" His fingertip ghosted over the green material of her jacket shoulder. His looming presence at her back was oddly comforting. Especially when Lucky Charms stared up and up and *up* at Norm then, without another word or glance, scooted around on his stool to face away from her.

Lucy beamed at Norm in gratitude, then blinked as his face split into an almost incandescent grin in response. Something tilted, wobbling in her stomach. She shook her head, reassessing her first opinion of his appearance. Norm might be a total geek, but that didn't mean he wasn't cute. Especially when he smiled.

Lucy stopped walking, unease sweeping in like clinging seaweed with the tide of that thought. Hank's Number One, Non-Negotiable, Break this Rule and Die Edict was: **No Dating**. Staff in the bar were *not* allowed to date each other. Too messy. And Hank didn't like messy in his bar.

Between one stride and the next, one thought to the next, she was laughing at herself. *Overreact much? You think Norm's cute. In a* geeky *way, even. Nothing to have a panic attack about.* The realization had been startling, but just because her lady parts were coming out of hibernation, that didn't mean Norm had anything to do with it.

Though he did seem like a nice change from the local Neanderthal population.

But there was no reason in the world to believe she would even want to date this guy. Or that he would want to date her. Swallowing unease, Lucy ducked into the back room, Norm at her heels.

***

I have to ask her out. Norm felt like he'd been hit upside the head with a two-by-four--*in the good way*--simply from looking at her.

19

He scoffed. Yeah, she was cute, but that didn't mean they would have anything in common. The exterior of a woman wasn't everything. *And*, his brain drew special emphasis to this next point, *have you already forgotten Hank's so edifying lecture about not dating shot girls? You don't need to be fired your first night for the sake of a good pair of legs.*

Lucy pushed open the door to the back room, the muscles in her calves tensing as she stalked forward in her high, high heels. Norm blinked, his mouth going dry. *What about for the sake of a great pair of legs?* He wiped a hand over his face as he followed her into the back room.

But then Lucy plopped onto the leather couch, kicked off her heels, and began slowly peeling away the black thigh-highs.

Norm blinked again. *Is this a surprise seduction? Did I wander into a porno and someone forgot to tell me?* "Uh…"

She glanced up, then shook her head and paused with one stocking half-rolled down. "Right, I forgot you don't know how to make the shots." She stood in her stockinged feet and pulled a few mostly empty bottles out of the storage room along with an empty pitcher. Her test tube tray she dumped in the sink. The soiled test tubes she dumped in the trash; they were so cheap it wasn't worth the time to wash them. Then she grabbed a stack of three trays pre-filled with empty test tubes and she placed them on the counter across from the couch along with the other things. "Pour all the bottles into the pitcher. Mix well. Pour into test tubes."

"Three trays?"

"We'll probably need more. Might as well make them now so they're ready to go when we need them. Especially if we're missing a bar-back."

He set to work and she flopped onto the couch to finish with her stockings, which were probably being discarded because they'd received the brunt of the spilled booze shower. Displaying great strength of will, he kept his back to her as she cleaned up, but the whole time his body remained instinctively tensed. *Get a grip, Norman.*

But Lucy was just the kind of girl that made a guy's brains implode into mush. Petite and sweet, Lucy had a compact, trim figure, long blonde hair that glinted like spun silver even in the dim bar lights and the biggest, prettiest pair of dark blue eyes. Her face was heart-shaped with a small pointed chin, a Cupid's bow of a mouth and a modest, vaguely button-esque nose. Lucy combined the wholesome beauty of the girl next door with the curvy body of a wanton nymph.

Please, let her be more wanton than wholesome.

Also, her leprechaun outfit was *epic*. Under her bright green, twin-tailed coat, she wore a white bustier with a shamrock pattern which hugged her pert breasts to perfection. A short, *short* black skirt with a gold belt buckle served to emphasize the curves of her legs. As if they weren't noticeable enough all on their own. And she topped the whole outfit off with a jaunty green top hat already shedding its heavy coating of glitter down her back and onto the floor.

He liked the effort she'd invested in the outfit. Most of the other shot girls had thrown on revealing green dresses, but Lucy had put thought into her St. Patty's Day outfit. It showed an attention to detail, an enthusiasm he could appreciate and, maybe, a sense of humor too. And, of all the assets a woman could possess, a sense of humor was the sexiest.

21

He winced, annoyed with himself all over again. *Stop it, Norman. Stop it. At this rate Zack will be your sugar daddy forever. Or you'll have to move back in with Mom and Dad. You don't want that, do you?* The idea of trying to cram his adult life back into the tiny confines of his childhood bedroom, of having to share a house with his family again, with his incredibly judgmental father again, had him nearly shuddering with horror.

"Does that happen often?" he asked while he poured and mixed, poured and mixed, hoping conversation might distract him from his thoughts.

"What?"

"The bad pick-up lines?"

"Oh, yes. All the time. I even keep a diary where I write down the best ones from the evening."

"Reeeeally?" He glanced over his shoulder at her, raising one eyebrow in challenge. "Do you know any more St. Patrick's Day ones?"

"Prepare to be amazed." She pushed to her feet, her thigh highs discarded, her bare legs smooth and gleaming as she sidled close to him in her heels. He tensed in reaction, unsure what was happening and more excited by her nearness than he should be.

Lucy pressed close to his side, wetting her lips and thereby sending all the blood in his body careening southwards. "I haven't got four leaves, but if you pluck me, baby, I'll give you luck."

He barked out a startled laugh and she giggled, more like herself for a flash. Next instant, the vixen mask slid into place and she was fake-hitting on him again. "How would you like to help put the Irish Spring back into my step?"

22

"Guys have actually used these on you?"

"Oh, yes." Letting the sex kitten act fall away, she retreated a step, giving him back his personal space whether he wanted it or not.

"May I apologize for the utter stupidity so prevalent in my half of the species?" he said.

"Accepted." Her pretty pink lips curled up. In the brighter light of the office, he noticed a tiny beauty mark above her lip on the left side, impossible to see unless you were right next to her. He twitched, uncomfortably aware of how close she was to him, and how much closer still he would like her to be.

She crossed her arms and tapped her lips with one finger. "Let's see, what are some other good ones?"

"I want to play too." Anything to get his mind off her lips.

She laughed in surprise then graciously motioned for him to take the floor.

He cleared his throat then leaned down, fake leering at her, doing his best imitation of the drunken patrons he'd been observing all night. "Do you have a little Irish in you? Would you like some?"

"Everyone knows that one."

"So we get points for originality here?"

"Always."

A few *original* ideas popped into his head but he shoved them aside. His competitive spirit had been stirred; he had to exert himself now.

Finally, after a long moment of sorting through common Irish themes, inspiration struck. He straightened and adopted a purposefully horrible fake Irish brogue. "*Ach*, Lassie, you must help me. It's your ancestral dooty."

Playing along, Lucy replied, "What do I have to do?"

"Drive the snake out of my pants." Norm's face heated as he said it, but a surprised peal of laughter burst from Lucy and banished his embarrassment. *Great laugh.* High and light, with a hint of a giggle. Yet another row on the inventory of her awesomeness.

"My turn." She faced him, laying her palm flat over his on the counter. "I've got a pot of gold hidden up my skirt…wanna follow the rainbow and see it?"

Norm leaned close and dropped his voice to a frantic whisper. "If you don't sleep with me, then the leprechauns have already won."

She burst out in another crescendo of laughter, slapping a hand over her mouth as she glanced at the office door. But no one burst in from the club proper to bust them for fake-flirting, if that's what she was worried about.

He had finally filled all the test tubes with the mixture. Curious, he took one off the top tray and knocked the drink back. The flavor, sickly fruity but with a strong alcoholic kick, made him gag. He coughed and glanced at the three racks of test tubes he'd prepared then gazed at Lucy in despair. "I screwed up somehow. These shots taste like ass. I'm sorry."

"*Norm.*" She said it 'Nooo-*orm*', dragged out into two long, vaguely annoyed, vaguely amused syllables.

He'd never liked the sound of his own name more.

Lucy shook her head as she slid the top tray out and lifted it. "The shots *always* taste like ass. If you're buying test tube shots the point isn't the taste, the point is to get the hit from the alcohol and to have a hot girl wriggling in your lap."

24

"Oh."

She shook her head, casting him a quick glance that made him feel like a sheltered little lamb. "That's why we shot girls have to dress this way. To compensate for the bad booze. Otherwise no one would buy these things."

The phone in his back pocket buzzed, thankfully saving him from any rash action--like trying to kiss Lucy. Or propose marriage. He glanced at the phone's screen: **Srry Bates. Picked up shift. Can u get another ride?**

He let out a grunt of annoyance and pocketed his phone. "Crap." Zack needed the work; they both needed to work as much as possible to get them out of the money pit which Norm's prolonged unemployment had dug. But hitting up one of Norm's new co-workers for a ride on his first night made his gut tighten with discomfort. Norm hated being the guy who didn't have his shit together. And, at the rate he was going, drooling after Lucy, risking this job, he might never have his shit together again.

"What's up?" Lucy asked.

"Ah, my car's in the shop so my roommate planned to take me home, but now he can't. So now I'm screwed." Norm beamed at her to show he wasn't too upset about the whole thing. No need to dump on Lucy with his problems.

"I can drive you."

Yes. "No. It's OK. I'll figure out a ride. I can ask one of the other bouncers or something." Being alone with Lucy was far too appealing, which meant it was far too dangerous.

She raised both her eyebrows. "But I'm offering."

"Right."

Her expression made it clear that if he kept refusing she would think he didn't like her or something. He was trapped between good manners and his own good sense telling him that alone time with Lucy was a bad idea. *Crap.* "That would be great, Lucy. Thank you. I…can give you gas money if you want." *And then not eat for a day or two.* He winced inwardly.

"No, Norm. Jeez. Consider this your welcome to Jezebel's, OK?"

Shaking off his inner disquiet, Norm widened his eyes, letting his voice go unnaturally high. "You mean I can officially consider myself a member of the tribe?"

"Sure. We'll pencil you in for your initiation rites tomorrow." She leaned close and, utterly deadpan, said, "Don't worry. The bleeding usually stops after a few hours."

"And then I'll *finally* be a man."

She bit her lip to keep from laughing as she slid her tray off the counter again and stepped toward the door. "I'll find you when I'm off?"

"Works for me. Thank you, Lucy." *And I hope I don't regret this.*

"Better get back out there then." Her voice sounded odd. Hesitant? Reluctant?

Yeah, right. Feeling delusional tonight, are we, Norman?

She reached for the door, but he beat her to the portal, moving to open it for her.

This maneuver, however, only meant that instead of getting points for being a gentleman, he got smacked in the face when the door burst open.

Chapter Three

Norm recoiled and cradled his throbbing face as an Amazonian redhead pushed into the room. The new shot girl was zaftig, curvy in the full, bouncing hourglass style pioneered by Jayne Mansfield, but she had a very young face oddly discordant with her bombshell figure. She couldn't be much older than twenty-one.

"Ugh," the redhead groaned, utterly oblivious to Norm as she raked a hand through her bright hair, mussing her ponytail. "I hate having red hair on St. Patrick's Day." She shoved an empty shot tray onto the counter so hard the serving dish slid and hit the wall. "If I hear one more comment about my drapes matching my carpet tonight someone will *die*."

Lucy hurriedly placed her full tray onto the counter and rushed toward Norm. "Are you all right?" Her cool hands prodded the sore spot on his face and a wash of happiness coursed through him.

Pathetic, Norman. But, in that moment, he didn't have it in him to resist.

He glanced at the redhead, scared he would do something stupid if he both looked at and touched Lucy at the same time. Red wore a green Irish peasant-girl outfit with a lace up bodice, shamrocks around the hem of her

27

short skirt and, most persistently eye catching of all, two large, shiny shamrock patches were sewn onto her white blouse, strategically placed right over her nipples. With her full DDD+ breasts the effect was…startling. Mesmerizing and horrifying at once. Like gazing into the Eye of Sauron.

The redhead leaned on the counter, giving Norm a dry glance. "I'm Ronnie. You must be the new guy."

"Norm." He nodded hello.

Ronnie let out a snort of amusement at his name. "Aren't you kinda scrawny for a bouncer?"

He flinched, but instantly recovered his equilibrium when Lucy glared at Ronnie on his behalf. Lucy glanced over Ronnie's bright green village girl ensemble and scoffed. "And how did Hank like your outfit?"

Ronnie smirked. "Oh, he hates it."

"You know, a smart woman wouldn't antagonize her boss," Lucy said.

"A smart boss wouldn't criticize the methods by which I make him a fuckton of money," Ronnie replied.

"Fair enough."

Ronnie grabbed one of the trays and bumped the office door open with her butt. "Speaking of Hank, he sent me over here to say he wants both your asses on the floor. *Now.*"

Norm's stomach dropped. How long had he been back here with Lucy? Not nearly long enough--yet way too long when he needed so desperately to make a good impression on his boss and keep this freaking job.

"Crud." Echoing his thoughts, Lucy dashed away and grabbed her tray.

Ronnie bent to examine herself in the computer desktop monitor. "Luce, have you seen Jenna anywhere? I haven't seen her on the floor for a while."

"Nope." Lucy hustled to get her shot tray in order. Norm hurriedly held the door open for her again, and she cast him a grateful look. Glancing between him and Ronnie, Lucy's face screwed up in steely resolve, her voice deepening as she said, "'Once more into the breach, dear friends.'"

"Here we go again." Ronnie stalked past him, disappearing into the green mob on the floor.

Lucy left him with a quick, parting wave as she hurried after Ronnie. Following the blonde's progress through the bar, his gut flipped. Pretty and petite. Kind and clever. *And she quotes Shakespeare.*

He banged his head against the doorjamb, idly hoping that would cure his insanity.

She turned back to flash him a tentative grin and his gut did that elated, sick, swooping thing again. *Oh, I am in trouble.*

He needed this job. She was off-limits and way out of his league. Even if they *were* allowed to date she wasn't likely to be interested.

And yet he could only helplessly beam after her, even as he knew he'd just canon-balled into a pit of emotional quicksand he wasn't likely to pull himself out of anytime soon. He tugged his phone from his pocket to text Zack back: **Dont worry about the ride. Im covered.**

"'Follow your spirit,'" he murmured to himself, watching Lucy, "'and upon this charge cry *God for Harry, England, and Saint George!*'" With a skip in his step, and a

29

reckless joy in his heart, Norm plunged back onto the floor, more eager than ever for his shift to be over.

***

"What were you doing with the newbie in the backroom for so long?"

Lucy jumped at the sound of Hank's voice and forced her gaze to stay locked on the money she was counting even as her nerves jangled. She'd been asking herself the same thing all night, but that didn't mean she wanted Hank asking her. "Norm was helping me refill the shot trays." True enough, but that didn't begin to cover the stimulating, fun banter they'd exchanged, the giddy troupe of butterflies that had wheeled through her belly all the rest of the night.

"Luce," Hank's voice rumbled low, that familiar thread of concern running deep. "You know I can't cut you any slack on the rules here in the bar, right? The rest of the staff won't stand for that."

She scoffed and finally did look at him, but only to glare. "Is that what you think of me? That I'd want special treatment? That I'd betray your trust like that?" After all the years they'd known each other, Hank should understand her better. She wasn't about to harm him or his beloved business for the sake of a cute guy she'd just met.

"You still need me to come by and fix that light bulb in your apartment?" Hank asked after a moment, his tone light.

Recognizing the olive branch, Lucy glanced at him as she finished counting her money and sadly shook her head. "Thanks, but not this weekend. I've got to finish that stupid essay for English, and you know I can't do English with any distractions."

He chuckled. "OK, let me know a good time. Is the bathroom sink draining better?"

"It's draining. That's all I care about." She finished counting the last of her ones. Too many ones, she never wanted to see that particular brand of currency again--or at least not until tomorrow night.

Hank perched on the arm of the couch, dropping his voice so the others in the back room wouldn't hear. "What's wrong, Luce? You've been weird lately. Not just tonight."

She restrained a sigh. Hank was exactly like a big brother to her. Demanding. Overprotective. Sweet. Which is exactly why she had to obey the bar rules more stringently than anyone else. So no whiff of favoritism could touch him. "I'm just worried about the essay."

His mouth tipped up in one corner. "Right. Your key to transferring to a four year."

"I can't screw this class up. Not with one semester left."

He waved that away. "OK, you pick a time and let me know when I should come over with the step ladder." He clasped Lucy's shoulder then wandered away to hassle some of the other shot girls who were gossiping and, therefore, taking too long to count their money.

Emotion prickled in Lucy's throat. Hank had been good to her, more than a boss, better than a friend. What would she do without him if she ever quit this place? And what would she do if she made it into Berkeley? Her stomach knotted at the idea of moving so far away. Being so alone. *Again*.

Ronnie dropped onto the beat-up old couch beside her. "You want to grab a bite at that all-night diner in

31

Burbank? Me, Eddie, Mia, Jenna, and probably some of the others are going."

"Can't. I'm giving the new guy a ride home. His car's busted." She didn't *want* to tell anyone, but driving off alone with a stranger without telling someone didn't seem like the greatest idea either. Norm seemed fine, though.

More than fine actually--he seemed *great*. So much so that she didn't even know what she'd been thinking to make that offer. She'd never liked playing with fire as a kid, so why invite a box of matches to ride home with her now?

Ronnie must haved read something in her face because she raised both bright red eyebrows at Lucy. "Ooooh."

"It's nothing."

Ronnie rolled a shoulder in a *we'll see* kind of way. "Text me when you're home safe?"

"Will do."

"Or...you could come out with us and ditch the new guy."

"Ronnie, I can't. I have to go home and work on my English assignment."

At that, Ronnie shot to her feet, as if English homework were a communicable disease. Ronnie had dropped out her first semester of college, and never looked back yet as far as Lucy could see. "Call my cell if you change your mind."

Lucy waved assent as she checked the time on her own phone. Hastily, she pushed to her feet to race toward the parking lot.

In the parking lot, she bundled herself up in a musty coat she dug out of the backseat and hunkered in her car waiting for Norm to emerge. Trying to dry her clammy palms, she smoothed her hands down the front of her coat. She was just giving the new guy a ride home. Nothing unseemly. She flexed her hands on the steering wheel. Nope. Nothing at all.

Soon enough, Norm bounded out the back door. She waved the car window and he started over, his long legs eating up the ground as he strode toward her car. She reached over to unlock the passenger door for him. Her car was old as dirt and, though she loved it with an affection most people reserved for their children, her ride didn't have any of those new fangled car features like, oh, automatic locks or power windows.

Norm opened the side door and poked his head in, his gaze roaming over her car with something approaching awe. "Is this a 1964 *Mustang*?"

She grinned, pleased to have her baby admired. "Yup. Get in, Norman. It's been a long night. I'm tired."

He began to climb in, but first he had to stop and scoop up the pile of her textbooks she'd forgotten were there.

"Here." She reached over to take and throw the books in the backseat, but Norm held onto them, keeping the stack in his lap as he peered at the covers with interest. He managed to fold all of his long, loose-limbed body into her car. The cold, empty air that had surrounded her when she'd sat alone was filled at once with his big, warm self instead.

Now she was alone with him again, Lucy's body hummed with nervous energy. *I shouldn't have offered him the ride.* She had to hold the line, and she would, but something about Norm made her wonder what the other

33

side of that line might look like. *Don't*. Lucy started the car. "Which way?"

"Take the 134 East."

Lucy pulled out of the parking lot, driving the familiar route to the freeway on-ramp in auto-pilot.

Norm leaned down, squinting to read her textbook covers in the dark. "Linear Algebra? Multivariable calculus?" He shuddered as he cracked the spine on her Calc textbook and flipped through the pages, glancing at problems in the dim light of the car. "Yeesh. I'm getting ill just reading these problems. I'd probably barf if someone actually asked me to solve one."

"It's fun."

Norm gaped at her.

She chuckled. "Not a math guy?"

"By no stretch of the imagination."

She shook her head as she flicked on the radio, idly hoping she hadn't left it on an embarrassing station. She glanced at the numbers on the radio tuner: classic rock. That should be safe. Whatever the last song had been finished in an energetic crescendo of guitar then the opening chords of "Faithfully" by Journey came on.

Steve Perry's soft rock vocals soothed her while her car hummed along the freeway, and she mouthed the lyrics along with good ol' Steve. Working at a bar with a lounge singer and a high population of college kids as customers, she'd become intimately familiar with "Don't Stop Believin'" so it was a little refreshing to hear a *different* Journey song.

Lip-syncing along to "Faithfully", her chest tightened with a bittersweet ache. She could sympathize with Steve singing about sleeping alone because she was sure as hell sleeping alone that night. And every night for the foreseeable future.

She didn't have time to date. Between school during the day, homework, college planning, and moonlighting as a shot girl, pretty much every moment of her day was spoken for.

For some reason, though, the old "no time" refrain echoed hollowly inside her tonight. Steve's lyrics were too resonant, too true, his voice practically vibrating through her body as he sang about the lover he'd left behind, the lonely nights. Lucy didn't even have anyone to leave behind, anyone to miss.

But it was fine. She nodded to herself, trying to screw the idea to some sticking place where she could believe it. The road rolled away beneath her car, empty of other people, dark but for the yellow lines speeding by, and Norm sat beside her, the sound of him gently flipping pages soft, reassuring.

She'd be alone tonight, but she wasn't alone now, and there was comfort in that. *Wouldn't it be nice to have someone for keeps, for forever? Someone faithful and sweet and funny?*

She glanced over at Norm, and he lowered her textbook, casting her a quick, shy smile. The music went on, its lyrics sinking little hooks into her soul until she finally had to get stern with herself. *You're lonely. It's not Norm specifically. You want someone, and he's the nearest warm male body.*

Finally, *finally*, "Faithfully" wrapped up, with Steve belting out his eternal devotion to his lady, and Lucy let out a slow breath to release her tension.

A run of commercials began, and Norm shifted half-sideways in his seat so he could face her. She tensed,

35

hoping he wouldn't flirt with her or ask her out or do anything else to tempt her resolve.

When all he asked was, "What are the textbooks for?" she sagged in relief.

"I'm in community college, finishing my IGETC."

"I-get-see?"

"Inter-segmental General Education Transfer Curriculum."

"Sounds painful."

She laughed. "I'm almost done and I'm, hopefully, transferring to a four year school as a junior in the fall. Depending on what schools I get into."

"That's great. What's your major?"

"Mechanical engineering."

"Ahhh." He hefted the textbooks. "Hence the Linear Multivariable Math of Doom?"

"Yeah."

"Take this exit," he said. "So, why is the bar called 'Jezebel's'?"

She tilted her head sideways to consider the question as her car glided down the freeway off-ramp. "Well, she is the patron saint of false prophets and fallen women." She passed a hand over her body to emphasize her revealing clothing, like a lovely assistant on a game show gesturing to all the Fabulous Prizes.

"You're a fallen woman, then?" he said.

"Oh, yeah, *loooong* time ago. I've fallen and I can't get up."

"Turn here. I don't think she was a saint."

Lucy spun the wheel over to make the right. "Jezebel?"

"Didn't a bunch of politicians throw her out a window or something?"

"Yeah." All of the shot girls were intimately familiar with at least the rough sketch of Jezebel's narrative. Lucy shook her head in dark amusement as she remembered her favorite part of the story. "You know she got herself all gussied up first before they killed her?"

"Well, sure. I mean, you don't want to have bad hair for your defenestration."

"For your...who with the *wha*?"

"*Hem*." Norm cleared his throat and assumed a dry, didactic tone as he said, "Defenestration. From the Latin 'de' for 'down and away from' and 'fenestra' for 'window or opening'."

"So, defen-whosis is a fancy way of saying she got tossed out a window?"

"Yup." Norm pointed to a tall brown apartment building on a block blooming with apartment buildings. "This is my place."

She pulled her car over. "Hey, you're better than one of those word-a-day calendars."

"And I dare you to use defenestration in a sentence today."

"Maybe later." She waited, edgy, as Norm made no move to get out. He had his hand poised on the door handle, but his shoulders were tense. He cast a quick glance at her, opening his mouth, his face pale with nervousness.

He's going to ask me out. Her breath caught--with nerves, with regret, but with excitement too. As bad an idea as getting involved with Norm was, some part of her wanted to say yes. She held her breath as she sat with

37

Norm, poised with him in the odd tableau--waiting for him to move even as he waited for her to do something. She tipped forward, raising her eyebrows in gentle encouragement. "Norm?"

"Lucy..." Swallowing, he looked away from her then fumbled for the door handle, making dull clunking noises against the metal. Finally, the door popped open with a small *scree* as the bottom caught against the curve. Lucy winced and Norm recoiled. He heaved himself out of the seat and stalked away, clutching her textbooks. As she opened her mouth to call to him, he whipped around and tossed the books onto the passenger seat, leaning forward to say, "Thanks for the ride."

"You're welcome. See you at the staff meeting tomorrow. Good night."

"Drive safe." Norm's shoulders slumped as he padded away.

Lucy lingered to make sure he got into the apartment building OK. But then, even when he'd disappeared inside, another moment passed before she shoved her car into gear. She huffed out a breath, unsure whether she would have said yes or no if he had mustered the nerve to ask her out.

Some things are better not to know. She drove onto the freeway, heading home to her empty apartment and her waiting mountain of homework.

Chapter Four

The next day, Norm's car was finally released from the shop with a clean bill of health. Fortunately, he had enough to cover the repairs, but his meager savings account was now wiped out. His first Jezebel's paycheck couldn't come soon enough.

Norm drove himself from the mechanic's to Jezebel's for the staff meeting. He arrived way too early, but for his second day on the job he wanted to make a good impression. Especially since he hadn't made the best impression on his first day by drooling over Lucy.

Norm was obscenely early for the meeting, but Hank could already be found leaning on the stage with a clipboard, reading over his notes.

More pleasantly, Lucy sat at one of the booths in the far corner, bent over a textbook, pencil in hand as she worked her way through a Math Problem of Doom.

She wore a plain gray sweater buttoned to her collarbone and a pair of dark blue jeans. Her hair was pulled into a ponytail tied with a yellow ribbon and her bangs fell in wispy lines against her face. She had her full-on shot girl makeup applied already: heavy eyeliner, false eyelashes and bright, bright red lips. The contrast between her wholesome outfit and her femme fatale makeup was a

39

charming mix to Nom, and he had a hard time looking away.

Hank stirred and Norm gave a guilty start. Busted. Again. But Hank only gave Norm a small, acknowledging nod before looking back to his notes. Norm hesitated, gazing between Lucy and Hank, feeling as if a shoe were hovering over his head ready to drop. *Hank and Lucy?*

Granted, she might just be obsessively punctual like Norm, but she seemed settled at her booth and, when Norm had walked in, the silence between Hank and Lucy had been warm, companionable. So...did Hank not want Norm dating shot girls or did Hank not want him dating *that* shot girl?

Lucy didn't put off vibes like she was spoken for but Norm had known--and, unfortunately, dated--girls who liked to keep their relationship status as murky as possible. What was the wisest course of action here?

Lucy glanced up and smiled at him. He managed to keep his own expression to a mere grin and not the full-on, high-wattage smile that wanted to erupt. Anyway, bad manners to sit somewhere else when he and Lucy were the only ones there. He slid into the other side of her booth.

Content to bask in her presence, and not wanting to distract her from her homework, or annoy Hank, Norm tugged out his own notebook and began scribbling notes. A great idea for a short story had come to him in the shower, and he hadn't yet managed to get the plot idea down on paper.

Lucy startled him when she tapped her pencil against his notebook. "What are you working on?"

Norm froze and carefully slid his arms to cover his work in progress. "Huh? Oh. Um. Nothing."

"Oh. OK." She sat back, her face falling as she refocused on her math.

Crap. "No. It's not--" He took a breath while she watched him, her eyebrows raised in confusion. "All right, I'm sure you already suspect I'm the biggest geek on the planet, and if I tell you what I'm working on it'll only confirm your suspicions."

She raised both her eyebrows, giving him a challenging glance from under her lush black lashes.

He sighed. "It's a science fiction story. I'm a writer. I write science fiction and fantasy." He squeezed his eyes shut, stalling the moment when he would have to see the horror and pity on her face. "I want to be Neil Gaiman when I grow up."

"Who doesn't?"

He opened his eyes and gaped at her. He'd never met a girl who'd read Neil Gaiman before. Well, maybe he had and they hadn't admitted it. His last girlfriend had been a fan of cozy mysteries and utterly disdained anything even resembling magic or aliens. "You've read Neil Gaiman?"

"I *adore* Neil Gaiman." Lucy leaned forward. "And, for that matter, you are not the only one with some hardcore geek credentials, my friend. I'll have you know I dressed up as Princess Leia for Halloween three years in a row in high school."

God, that's hot. He bit the response back and instead leaned away, draping his arm over the booth edge as he arched a skeptical eyebrow. "Yeah, but it's sexy when girls are geeks. You don't have to hide your nerdy side the way guys do."

"Me reading Neil Gaiman and having a Star Wars obsession is sexy?"

41

"Um, *yeah*."

She gazed at her textbook, lifting her pencil. "I'll remember to bring my *American Gods* paperback tomorrow then."

Was she flirting with him? Norm took a quick breath then dove off the deep end. "Maybe if you play your cards right, I'll let you borrow my TaunTaun sleeping bag sometime."

Lucy dropped her pencil and made no show of disinterest now; her eyes were fairly shining with covetousness. "You have that? *Ohmigod.* The one with the lightsaber zipper and the TaunTaun guts?"

The avid look on her face was hotter for Norm even than her leprechaun outfit had been the night before. He crossed his arms, assuming the posture of a man of infinite bounty. "The very same."

"That's hot." She managed to keep her face straight for one long moment before her gaze met Norm's, then they both burst out laughing. She cast a quick glance Hank's way then covered her mouth with one hand, muffling her laughter.

Norm's own amusement died at the gesture. She was flirting with him, but she didn't want Hank to know? Boss or boyfriend? And how could Norm ask for that clarification when the question itself would betray his own interest in her?

And, anyway, whether Hank was boss or boyfriend, Norm was already playing with fire. Hank had made it clear Norm was supposed to stay away from Lucy.

Yeah, Norm wasn't doing too good with Jezebel's Rule #1 so far.

Lucy bit her lip and settled her features into a more serious expression. "So, if you're a writer, you're good at English Lit stuff, right? Essays and the like?"

"It was my major in college."

She blinked at him, like he'd admitted to a brief stint as the Emperor of China. "You went to college?"

"Yup. Graduated and everything."

"Then why--" She broke off and bit her lip.

"Am I working at the bar?" He finished for her, totally unembarrassed. "Well, the economy for one. But, also, I got out with my shiny new English degree and didn't have any idea what I wanted to do. Not in the real world. I didn't want to commit to some soul-sucking job in the rat race. I didn't want to spend thousands more dollars in grad school either preparing me for a career in academia I wasn't sure I wanted. So I decided to take at least a year or two to explore my options."

"And the bar is your option?"

"One of them. I attended college straight out of high school without catching my breath, and I wanted some time to breathe once I got out."

"And the noxious air of the bar is so good for your lungs. All that pungent man-smell and day-old vomit." She took a deep breath then let it out on a satisfied, "*Ahhh.*"

"So young to be so jaded."

"Hey, babe, I am all of two and twenty years old. I've seen some things."

Before he let himself think too much, he tilted forward and tweaked her long ponytail tied with its yellow ribbon. "Ah, yes. You embody the image of a world-weary pessimist."

43

She pressed her elbows onto the table, angling toward him with sudden intensity. "Would you read one of my essays for me? Just to tell me if I'm on the right track, catch any grammar mistakes, you know? I'm about to finish at my community college, but I saved the class to fulfill my English requirement until this last semester because, well, because I'm *stupid*. And a procrastinator. English is not my strong suit."

"But you speak it so well."

She poked his arm. "You know what I mean. I'm no good at analytical stuff. I like math and tinkering and problem solving. And I like reading, but for fun, not picking apart every last punctuation mark. Sometimes a penis joke is just a penis joke."

"I don't know. Some of Shakespeare's penis jokes can get pretty intricate."

"Math and science I do OK, but if I don't pass this class my transfer to a four year school will be delayed a whole semester, and I won't be able to go to Berkeley even if I get in because they don't allow spring transfers and--"

He lifted a hand to cut off her flow of half-panicked babble. "Lucy, I'm happy to help." More than happy. Getting closer to her was a bad idea, but he didn't care. He'd never been smart about women anyway. And his nearly empty bank account became a distant worry while bathing in the warmth of Lucy's company.

"Great," she said. "Thank you. Do you want to grab a bite after the meeting?"

Was she asking him out? His heart squeezed with hope.

As if reading his mind, she leaned away from him and plastered a polite but distant smile on her face. "So we can

44

talk about my assignment and you can read my essay draft."

He fought hard to hide his disappointment and chirped out, "Sounds great."

"Hey, Norm, can I just ask: why Jezebel's?"

He blinked at the non-sequitor. "I was working at a bookstore, but the place went bankrupt and closed down. I have to eat and pay my half of the rent, so when I saw Hank's ad on craigslist I dragged myself down here. Me as a bouncer seemed a bit of a long shot, but I begged and Hank said yes."

"Begged?"

Norm tipped his hand in a so-so gesture. "Asked nicely. I get the impression you guys go through a lot of bouncers?" *Which is why a scrawny beanpole like me had a shot.*

She rolled her big blue eyes heavenward. "God, yes. It's as bad as the Defense Against the Dark Arts position. Actually, most of the staff has a high turnover. Bouncers are just the worst. Working in a bar can be hard, you know? The hours interfere with the rest of your life. You're spilled on and stepped on and hit on and sometimes, if you're a bouncer, actually hit. It's not an easy job. But, for some reason, lately we keep hemorrhaging bouncers. They fall asleep half way through their shift and Hank fires them. They steal the good booze and Hank fires them. They get an acting gig and they quit. Their girlfriend visits the bar, takes one look at Ronnie and orders the guy to quit--"

"Won't be a problem for me. I'm footloose and fancy free."

Her eyes crinkled at the corners with pleasure. "Fancy free, huh?"

45

"Oh, yeah." He tweaked his shirt collar to demonstrate. "Fancy, right?"

Lucy laughed.

He loved making her laugh, and decided, whatever the risks, that he would try to make it happen as often as possible. "What about you? How long have you been working at the infamous house of fallen women and false prophets?"

"Since I turned twenty-one." She leaned forward, her face serious, her voice earnest. "It's a great place to work. As much as I bitch about Jezebel's, I make good money, and work doesn't interfere with school. And Hank might not seem like it, but he is really sweet."

Hank, perhaps hearing his name, chose that moment to gaze at them sitting together in the booth. His brow furrowed, and Lucy recoiled in her seat. When Hank looked away to refocus on his notes for the meeting, she bit her lip. "OK, maybe I exaggerate the sweetness. But Hank's a good guy. He's done a lot for me."

Huh. Hardly the way one would speak about a boyfriend. Her sentiments sounded more...sisterly. He hoped.

Norm craned around as a bustle of voices filled the bar. The main door opened and a crowd of employees shuffled in together, taking seats at the tables clustered before Hank and the stage.

"Better go down." Lucy flipped her textbook closed, sandwiching her notebook and pencil in between the book's pages. She stuffed everything into a black backpack spotted with rainbow colored polka dots. In the cluster of half dozen buttons on her backpack, there was a simple black one with "HAN SHOT FIRST" in bold white letters.

A woman after my own heart.

Norm, entranced and attracted by this tangible sign of geekery, realized he was helpless to resist her--whatever his financial difficulties. He followed her to the seating area for the meeting, feeling like one of the hypnotized rats trailing after the Pied Piper, doomed and elated all at once.

***

After the meeting broke up, Lucy led Norm down the boulevard, smiling up at him as he took in the various storefronts and other clubs. After the third store they passed carrying huge vinyl leather boots with seven-inch heels in the window, he asked her, "Are we in Drag Queen Heaven and someone forgot to tell me?"

She gave a small skip and tossed her ponytail, laughing at him, enjoying his bemusement more than she probably should. "It's Hollywood, babe. Doesn't pay to be understated here."

"Right." He resumed his window browsing just as they passed a head shop with a bong as tall as him. Norm blinked and quickly moved on. Lucy chuckled to herself. *Norm is shaping up to be quite the innocent.* She stopped as they neared their intended destination. Lucy planted her feet and lifted her hands to gesture at the restaurant's sign with a big, "Ta-da!"

Norm took a long moment to just beam at her before he looked where she was indicating. Her face heated in a blush under his admiring regard.

When he finally gazed at the restaurant he burst out laughing. "'The Dogs of War'? There's a hot dog place named after a Shakespeare quote?"

"It's Hollywood, we got all kinds here." She held the door open for him. "You're an English lit dork so I took a chance you were a Shakespeare nerd too."

"Oh, I am."

"Also, they make good hot dogs."

He passed in front of her into the small, cool interior of the hot dog shop and she followed, taking a moment to admire his surprisingly nice butt. Something about the way Norm carried himself made him seem like he wasn't fit, but when she scrutinized his body she noticed the well defined state of his shoulders, the wiry muscles in his arms. His so-pattable ass.

She blinked and stopped studying the seat of Norm's nicely fitted black pants. The fact he'd slid into one of the booths and snagged a menu helped.

Despite the literary name, the Dogs' décor had a generic, vintage diner feel with red vinyl seats and small, 50s style juke-boxes on each table. The tables had clear tops with photos inside.

He set his menu aside and bent closer to examine the table. "What are these?"

"You know how most local businesses sponsor kiddie soccer teams and high school football?"

"Yeah."

"The owner of the Dogs feels like sports get enough attention, so he sponsors the arts." She pointed to the pictures, which were all Western themed, then pointed to the bright red flyer in one corner. The poster had "Romeo and Juliet the Western" written out in an old-fashioned stagecoach font and surrounded by a rope lasso in the shape of a heart. "All the tables have pictures from local school productions the Dogs helped sponsor." She drew

Norm's attention to the shot of Tybalt costumed as a gunslinger, all in black, with Juliet's Nurse draped over him, dressed as a saloon girl.

"Wow."

Lucy snagged her menu, unreasonably delighted that her lunch choice had so pleased him. Something about Norm's goofy grin set a hook in her stomach and pulled.

You're not here for that. She swallowed. Right. Homework help. Lunch was supposed to be payback for his assistance.

This. Was. Not. A. Date.

He glanced up from his menu. "The 'Much Ado About Nothing Dog'?"

"That's their basic hot dog. No frills."

"The 'Et Tu, Brute Salad'? Hmm." He dropped his voice to a conspiratorial whisper. "Their menu puns could use some work."

After admiring the good and not so good Shakespeare references on his menu, he eventually settled on the Two Gentlemen of Verona Combo which came with a drink and two chili dogs. Lucy, not being a freakishly-tall, man-type person, got a Much Ado.

Norm lifted his first chili dog to his mouth then stopped as she grabbed the ketchup to douse her own food. She paused with the bright red bottle poised over her dinner. "It's not polite to stare."

He blinked and his hotdog almost mirrored the expression as a dollop of chili splattered against the grease paper lining his basket. "You put *ketchup* on your hot dogs?"

"Yes."

"Sacrilege."

Elbows perched on the table, she cocked her head to one side as she let out a slow, "*Ohhhh.*"

"What?"

"You're a food snob." She flashed him her perkiest smile the chewed with slow, seductive relish, slitting her eyes closed in pleasure. "*Mmmm.*"

When she'd swallowed and opened her eyes again, he was staring at her with his mouth open, the chili off his hot dog sliding into the basket. He cleared his throat. "Can you do that again?"

She laughed. "Eat your hot dogs, Norman."

"Yes, ma'am."

She laughed to herself, then froze in horror. She was doing it again. Letting Norm get to her, letting herself...what? *Like him.* Too much. She set her hot dog into her basket, the grease paper crinkling loudly. "Well, I better get my paper out so you have time to read it before we have to go back to work." She unzipped her backpack and fished out her latest essay. As she slid the papers to Norm, she forced herself not to care about the way his face had fallen.

He swallowed his latest bite of chili dog, carefully wiped his hands with a heavy duty napkin, then lifted her paper. She took a few bites of her hot dog while he read, but the food had gone tasteless in her mouth, like chewing ash. She had had to shut down their flirting, but maybe she shouldn't have been so abrupt about it.

He finished his second chili dog and her paper at about the same time. He slurped a gulp of his drink then faced her, clasping his hands on the table in a business-like manner. "It's good. Where I think you can improve is in the basic structure, and maybe smoothing out some of the language." He slid the small writing notebook from his pants' pocket and swiped the pen from there to make notes, giving her suggestions for where she could tweak the writing, move things to make the paper stronger.

When he was done she stared at him wide-eyed. He was so sharp, so meticulous. Norm's edits made her paper a thousand times stronger. "You are good at this."

He tucked his pen away along with his notebook, his face expressionless, shuttered. She winced internally to have hurt his feelings and silently vowed to stay away. If she couldn't keep him at a safe distance without hurting him, if she couldn't be his friend without sending these stupid mixed signals, then she'd do better not to spend alone time with him at all.

He slid the pages to her, and she snatched them up, clutching his notes to her like the precious thing they were. "Thank you. Really."

"No problem." He fished his phone out of his pocket to check the time, then signaled the waitress for the check. "We should get back to Jezebel's. You need to change before your shift, right?"

Lucy swallowed and nodded. She didn't want to go back, didn't want to adopt her chirpy shot girl façade. She would have loved to stay at the Dogs of War and chat with Norm some more, maybe snap him out of the bad mood she'd put him in. If only she didn't work with him.

But that idea was too dangerous to entertain, so she pushed it to the back of her skull and reached for the plastic tray with their check.

When she tried to pull the check toward herself Norm rested his hand over the tray. "Lucy, I'll get it."

"No way. This meal was my bribe for you to help me with my homework."

"I didn't need a bribe to help you."

"Norman." She frowned and pursed her lips, glowering at him. She pointed one finger at her own face. "This is my Stern Face. Do you want to argue with the Stern Face?"

He raised one eyebrow, watching her, and she fought to hold the Stern Face and not bust out laughing.

At last, he eased back. "You're right. No one wants to square up against the Stern Face." With that, he lifted his hand from where it had been covering hers. Lucy tried not to notice how her skin missed the warmth where his hand had been.

As she tossed cash down and picked her backpack up, Norm stood too, towering over her. He tapped one finger on the check and caught her eye. "I'm paying next time."

There won't be a next time. The Much Ado dog grew heavier in her stomach, leaving a sour taste at the back of her throat. But she nodded. "Yup. Next time."

They were mostly silent walking to the bar. When they pushed through the doors at Jezebel's someone popped out and made her jump in surprise.

Hank started forward and she panted, pressing her hand over her heart in a vain effort to calm her pulse. "Jeez, Hank."

"What?"

After a beat, she noticed solid warmth pressed against her back. Norm. She'd been leaning on Norm the whole long minute she'd been trying to catch her breath. Hastily, she stepped away with a murmured, "Sorry."

Hank crooked his finger at her and jerked his chin toward the back room. "Wanna talk to you."

She swallowed and trailed after Hank. "Thanks again, Norm," she said without turning as she walked away. Watching Hank's broad shoulders, listening to the dull thump of his boots, was like trailing after some black-masked executioner. The whole long walk to the back room she kept thinking, *I haven't done anything wrong. I'm not guilty. Not guilty.* And yet her guilty conscience throbbed with each reluctant step she took.

Hank led her to the office and closed the door with a click. She sank onto the couch while he propped his hip on the edge of the desk. "You OK, Luce?"

"Stressed about school but…" She shrugged.

"You still seem distracted. Off."

Guilty? "I'm not. I'm fine."

"Are you seeing that guy again? Bryan?"

She was so relieved she let out a laughing scoff. "Bryan? No, Hank, no. That was over five months ago. And we only dated a month or so anyway." And she hadn't dated anyone since that rather lukewarm association. No wonder she was ogling Norm. She was overdue.

"Good. Because he was bad for you."

Lucy pressed her teeth together to hold back an annoyed growl. "Did it ever occur to you that who I date isn't your business?"

"I've been watching out for you for a while now. It's a hard habit to break, kid."

Hank *had* looked out for her, supported her, cared about her when there was no one left in the world who did. How did she disengage from that pattern of support?

53

How did she say to him, OK, Hank, time to let the little bird leave the nest?

"Lucy?"

She blinked. "Right. No, I'm fine. No looming love disasters on the horizon."

Even as she said the words, Norm's goofy-sweet smile flashed through her mind. She hissed her breath out between her teeth, more determined than ever to avoid Norm. For her own good. *And* his.

Chapter Five

After her not-date with Norm at the Dogs of War, Lucy managed pretty well to stick to her resolve to avoid him. It wasn't hard. Hank liked to keep the new guys close during their first couple weeks. For all she could tell, Norm was doing all right at bouncing and settling in well to his new job. She couldn't know for sure because she hadn't said much more to him than "hello" and "goodbye" in the last week.

Now things were basically back to normal: Another day. Another dollar. Another revealing shot girl outfit. Tonight it was her Jezebel's uniform: a pair of insanely snug short shorts and a skin-tight, black tank with the Jezebel's logo blazing in red across her boobs. Some of the girls--*Ronnie*--filled the tank top better than others. And some of the girls--*Jenna*--liked to roll their tops up to the bottom of their bras to show their flat abs.

Out of a desire to stand a fighting chance, Lucy had cut a slit in the neck of her tank to show her meager cleavage to better advantage, and she rolled her shirt to her waist to flash her belly button.

She'd also put on a pair of high red heels that made her feel sexy simply seeing them, and tied her ponytail with a jaunty red ribbon. The shoes were higher than she

55

usually wore, and, only an hour into her shift, her toes were already pinched. The price women everywhere paid for sexiness, and the price she, as Sweet Little Lucy, had to pay to compete with the sex bombs she worked with.

Wanting to best Ronnie's sales, Lucy hunted for likely prospects to sell shots to, but she kept getting distracted when her gaze crossed with Norm's. He stood across the bar, shadowing Hank on the floor again. Lucy wheeled at once to stay away from that section. No point in encouraging Norm. No point in ogling him either.

She nudged between a pair of sorority girls. Zeroing in on a promising cluster of guys a few tables over, Lucy elbowed her way toward them, teetering unsteadily in her heels.

A customer shifted as Lucy passed, and Lucy over-balanced, tottering backward into space until she half-fell into someone's arms.

Miraculously, she managed to hold her tray steady so only a bit of the alcohol spilled across the tray to trickle over her wrist. She wheeled to thank whoever had caught her and her heart gave a small thump of excitement as she had to gaze up and up and *up* past several feet of lean male torso clad in a Jezebel's shirt until..."Hello, Norm."

Seeing him again in his element as a bouncer, she wasn't quite sure why he'd been hired. What had Ronnie called Norm? Scrawny? That was harsh, he was wiry rather than scrawny, but still, he didn't exactly have the classic silhouette of a Jezebel's bouncer.

It's probably the way he looms. Muscle wasn't everything in a bouncer, after all. Sometimes a guy had to be able to see over the crowd to find any stray shot girls caught in the undertow.

She stared up at him for a long moment. Too long a moment. She gazed into his soft brown eyes and jiggled her head to clear it. *This is a bad idea.*

Pinning a cocky smirk on her face, she brazened the moment out, covering over her very real--and very inconvenient--attraction to him with a bout of fake flirting. Playfully, she raked her gaze over him head to toe, doing her best to imitate her customers. "Well, someone get a glass. I just found me a *taaaaall* drink of water." She cocked her hip and one eyebrow in challenge, hoping he'd rise to the bait and not ask why she'd shunned him all week.

He hesitated but then, sliding neatly into his role, his gaze locked with hers. "Is the sun coming up? Or is that you lighting up my world?"

She narrowed her eyes, getting into the game. "Your eyes are bluer than the Atlantic Ocean and, baby, I'm lost at sea."

He snorted in amusement. "They're brown."

I noticed. "I get extra points for ineptitude then."

"Damn. I need something good." He stroked his chin then pouted his lips into his best imitation of the Drunken Frat Boy Smolder. "You must be from Hiroshima cuz, baby, you're da bomb."

"Ugh. Inept and offensive. Double points. Although, a gentleman at the last table did use the infamous shoes pick-up line."

"Shoes?"

She cast a quick glance at Norm's shoes. Red Converse like the Tenth Doctor. The geek footwear of choice. She snapped her head all the way back to meet Norm's eyes again. "Nice shoes." She paused for a beat and then, "Wanna fuck?"

57

Norm smothered a laugh against one fist. "Wow. I can't top that. Clearly, *that* dude is the winner of Worst Pick-Up Line for tonight."

"I don't know. The Hiroshima one was pretty bad."

He preened. "I try." He studied her shoes, and she tried not to fidget. "Those *are* nice shoes."

"Ronnie says shoes like these are classified as 'Come-Fuck-Me Heels,' and I get what I'm asking for when I wear them and guys proposition me."

"No comment."

She soft-punched him on the arm. Flirting--well, *fake* flirting, with Norm was fun, and relaxing, but she'd spent too much time chatting. Every minute she spent chatting with him was a minute she didn't make money. Which was, after all, the name of the game.

Norm must have seen some sign of her weary thoughts flitting across her face, because his happy expression faltered. He touched her shoulder. "You OK?"

She stiffened her cheeks in a false, cheery smile. "Thanks for stopping me from falling on my ass. Getting up again in these heels is a bitch." She cocked one leg to display for him her wickedly tall red Mary Janes, and felt a small flush bloom when Norm's eyes lingered ever so slightly on her legs. Long enough to be a compliment but not long enough for the look to morph into a leer. After these few years working in a bar, she had learned the difference between the two, and how to appreciate that difference.

"Well, you win this round of Bad Pick-Up Lines," she said, "but I'm gunning for you." She brushed past him and caught the clean smell of soap on his skin and the detergent from his shirt. She took a deep breath, hoarding the smell in her sense memory to act as a buffer against the next sweaty drunk she'd have to climb over.

With a quick mental slap, Lucy jerked herself back into Business Mode. Now was not the time to be copping a sniff. No matter how good Norm smelled.

One of her patrons frantically summoned her to his side with an upraised twenty. She straightened her spine and sauntered over to the twenty dollar bill. Only three more hours of this then she could go home to her math problems. She groaned inwardly. *You know your life sucks when calculus homework is your greatest source of pleasure.*

***

Norm watched Lucy teeter away, mentally scolding himself even as he did. When it came to Lucy he'd known he never had a shot. Hank or no. Stupid anti-dating rule or no. Out of his league didn't begin to cover the obstacles. She was Princess Leia and he was the swamp monster from Dagobah.

Thank God he'd never become so totally lost to good sense as to ask her out. That would have been the best and fastest way to betray himself to her as a hopeless, delusional, maybe even creepy loser in one easy step.

Just as well. He did *not* want to get fired for dating her. He was just beginning to claw his way out of the money pit, and endangering his steady income for a great pair of legs was the height of stupidity. He normally left that kind of thing up to his roommate Zack.

Once the crowd had swallowed Lucy up, hiding her from sight, Norm forced himself to reassume his post against the wall. Looming. That was his job. Leaning against the wall and projecting an air of quiet intimidation. Like Hank.

59

I should be more like Hank. Hank didn't lust after the shot girls. Hank stuck to business. Hank might as well have been made of stone for all that anything--like a pretty shot girl--could faze him, or deter him from his job.

Norm blinked. *It probably sucks to be Hank.*

Norm was supposed to watch the crowd for signs of trouble. And looming, of course, all the time keeping up with the looming. What was the good of having a six foot four bean pole if he didn't loom, after all?

But Norm had a hard time keeping his eyes off Lucy. The shot girl uniform was preposterous in its skimpiness, and yet sexy beyond belief, appealing to the lowest common denominator in every heterosexual man in the room. Him included.

Tearing his gaze away from Lucy, Norm re-focused his attention on Table #4 and the squad of drunks occupying it. All five of them had been a shade too loud, too rowdy the entire night, and they had Norm's spidey senses tingling. Well, if he *had* spidey senses, they'd have been tingling.

As the Drunk Squad lured Lucy over to their table the whatever-senses shrieked into high alert, making Norm's nerve endings fire all along his arms and legs. One of the guys waved a couple bills like a flag of surrender over his head, and Norm's teeth ground together with a friction that made his jaw ache.

He forced himself to stay put as Lucy approached Table #4, home to Lord Jack-Ass and his squad of boozy men. Her smile stayed on, but the tension around her mouth and eyes displayed for anyone who cared to notice that she was forcing herself to look happy.

Norm kept his eye fastened on Lord Jack-Ass and his posse until she'd safely fled their orbit and skittered toward another group. With Lucy removed from the reach of the drunks at Table #4, Norm checked on the other shot girls to get a general feel for the vibe of the bar.

Everything was loud, the crowd boisterous, but nothing out of hand. All the other shot girls were safe and sound, wandering the floor hawking their wares. Norm swiftly passed from studying the other shot girls to checking on Lucy once more.

She was in the corner with the one guy who hadn't come tonight with a pack of friends. This guy was older too, and he'd chosen the table booth in the corner, more shadowed and private than the rest of the bar. This was supposed to be another bouncer's section but Norm didn't see the guy, Eddie, anywhere. *Great.* Scanning for Eddie's spiky blond hair, Norm slowly waded into the pulsing crowd toward the corner booth, ready if Lucy needed help. Not because he had a crush on her. Nope. Not at all.

As Lucy's voice rose above the boom of the chatter of the crowd, he increased his pace. He couldn't make out the words, but the general tone sounded like *"Hands off!"*

One of the other bouncers was also wading in toward Lucy from the other side. *Shit.* His second week and Norm already had a notion that a Two Bouncer Problem was not good.

He redoubled his pace and pushed two frat boys aside before he finally got a good view of the situation. Mr. Corner Booth held Lucy in his lap, his hands clutching her waist while she fought against his death grope. Norm burst forward, red rage blanking out his vision.

61

Skidding to a halt at the booth, he towered over the guy. Lucy jerked her head up, and all the fear and tension leaked out of her pale face, washed away with relief. Norm drew himself up, his gut clenching with nerves. He wanted to deserve Lucy's trust in him.

He jerked his chin at Mr. Corner Booth. "OK, lady's all done. Time to let her go, buddy."

"Nah. She's a nice little lapful." The jerk squeezed Lucy so hard that she let out a squeak of pain.

Lucy shoved the guy's hands off her waist, and Norm rushed in to seize the moment. He scooped her free of the guy's lap with one hand under her knees and the other behind her shoulders, basically hauling her up and over the table to safety. As Norm lifted her, Lucy's feet knocked over one of the six almost empty glasses on the table, spilling the booze in the guy's lap.

Lucy was light as Norm carried her, her body compact as he swung her free of the table then back down to the floor. She caught her breath and blinked up at him, her mouth open in an adorable 'O' of surprise. He released her waist, in no way wanting to emulate Mr. Grabby Hands here. Norm bent to stare her full in the face. "You OK?"

She gave a small nod.

"Good." He whipped away from her, shielding her from the jerk with the bulk of his own body. Time to deal with the King of the Douchebags. Still braced with anger, Norm faced the groper in the booth. "All right, time to call it a night--"

The man lurched to his feet, revealing himself to be about five-six. His lap was stained with the spilled alcohol, his face red with rage and drink. Ignoring Norm, Mr.

Corner Booth dodged past him to get at Lucy and actually managed to catch her wrist.

Norm stepped between them as the drunk pulled. Lucy collided with Norm's back, all of her softness squishing against him for one lovely moment. He grabbed the drunk's wrist to stop him yanking at Lucy anymore. "*This is ridicu--*"

Norm never finished the sentence. The pint-sized jerk was spry, and in one smooth move he swung his free hand to punch Norm in the face.

The hit clipped Norm's chin, and the throbbing echo of pain there beat in time with his already intense anger. "*You little shit!*" Gritting his teeth, Norm curled his hands into fists, jerking his arm back to return the blow.

"Norm, *don't!*"

Lucy's voice slid like a hot brand through his brain. He readjusted the momentum of his punch and swung his whole body behind the drunk to get him into a Full Nelson instead. As Norm's arms settled into the familiar position and the drunk ineffectively flailed to break free, satisfaction rushed through Norm. He was an older brother; he defied any sawed-off little pervert to break one of his holds.

Hank and Ben, a massive African American bouncer, arrived and relieved Norm of his burden, hauling the kicking, thrashing drunk toward the door.

Someone tapped Norm on the shoulder and he wheeled, grinning, expecting to see Lucy standing there.

He found himself facing the mirror image of the man they'd just evicted. "What the *hell* are you doing to my brother, asshole?"

This one's punch hit with a lot more accuracy.

63

Chapter Six

I got decked by an oompa loompa.
Twice.
I'll never live this down.
They're probably writing my pink slip right now...
 Shit. Shit. Shit.

The bullet train of Norm's speeding thoughts was swift but repetitive, like a toy circus train with all the painted animals circling a ten-foot track. Over and over and over and...

Shit.

He let his head fall against the musky couch in the bar's break room/counting room/office suite. He pressed the first aid ice pack to his swelling eye and contemplated his options for finding new gainful employment. Having reviewed said prospects (i.e. none), he came to one conclusion: Not promising.

I haven't even started repaying Zack yet. And the car ate my savings.

Shit. Shit. Shit.

When the office door creaked open he jumped in surprise, then straightened to attention as Lucy sidled into the room. "I brought you this." She lifted a bottle of imported beer. The good stuff. "I got special dispensation from Hank."

Norm swallowed, his body heating with awareness that this was the first time he'd been alone with her all week. *Pathetic*, his brain piped up. Norm managed to greet Lucy almost normally as he said, "You are a treasure among womankind."

"That's what all the guys say."

He reached for the beer, and his fingers brushed hers against the smooth glass of the bottle. A jolt of excitement zipped through him which he firmly slapped down. He would be out of his mind to make a move on her tonight after everything.

Although, since he was probably fired from his bouncer job, Rule #1 wasn't an issue anymore. Still, it seemed logical that being groped by a drunken asshole didn't put women into the romantic mood. *Time to drown my sorrows then.* Norm used the table end to pop the top off his beer and took a long drink.

Lucy rolled the desk chair over and sat across from him.

He tried not to twitch under her gaze, but she had the most beautiful dark blue eyes he'd ever seen, large and clear. A wing of black Cleopatra liner accented them at the corners, but the makeup was half smudged on the right side.

How easy it would be to slide his hand along the creamy expanse of her cheek and brush the smudge of black away with the tip of his thumb. *You'd only smear it and make it worse, numbskull.* But his brain was on a roll, and didn't want to stop the fantasy machine...he'd cradle her cheek, her skin warm and soft under his hand, then he

65

might let his fingers linger there and trace that too-tempting beauty mark above her lip.

She clasped her hands on her legs and twisted her fingers, appearing as nervous and keyed up as he felt. But that couldn't be right. Why would she be nervous? "You're a real gentleman, Norman Keane. You know?"

He lifted his beer in a toast then sipped, watching her over the edge of the bottle. *What's going on?*

Her face softened, and she reached forward to catch his hand, wrapping her fingers over his and squeezing. "Are you all right?"

"My eye's all right. I'm wracking my brain for where my next job's coming from."

"Next job? You're quitting?"

"I suppose I could. Save my pride and all that."

She sucked in a breath through her teeth then let the air out on a huff. "You think Hank will fire you for this? It's not your fault that guy sucker-punched you."

"The first or the second time?" Norm winced. Sucker indeed.

Lucy, *all sympathy*, rolled her eyes. "It happens. Drunken idiots are going to take a swing at you. Comes with being a bouncer. But management doesn't fire the bouncers for it. Besides, you handled yourself like a pro. That was one hell of a hold you got him into."

He raised his bottle in another mock toast. "To younger brothers. Who knew they'd teach me such useful skills?" He didn't know whether to be relieved or devastated that his job was safe. *Rent money. Food money. No Lucy.* He took another pull of his beer.

"Norman, this is not a big deal. It would have been if you'd hit him back--"

"Which I almost did." He flinched again, remembering. Assault and battery charges in two easy steps.

"But you didn't."

"Thanks to you."

She waved that away. "Even Hank's been decked a time or two. The only thing that could get you fired is pouting about it."

He oozed into the couch cushions to avoid her glare. "I am not pouting."

"Oh?"

"I'm licking my wounds."

She laughed. "OK, tough guy, do what you gotta do." She stood, and Norm instinctively stood up with her. At his gesture of chivalry, her eyes sparked with wry humor. "Thank you for charging to my rescue tonight." She slipped her arms around his waist in a hug.

He froze, going rigid for one long moment before he returned the embrace. Her body was soft and warm against him. The scent of her shampoo drifted up, something sweet and vaguely fruity. Norm tried to stay cool, to treat this as the friendly hug she meant it to be, but his reluctant body disobeyed and held on to her just a beat too long.

She stirred against him, pulling gently away, but then--maybe because she sensed something--she tipped her head back to meet his eyes. "Norm?" Her voice was light, questioning, and...hopeful?

He swallowed and started to release her.

She caught her breath, and, her face going slightly pink, she eased closer to Norm until her breasts pushed against his chest. She grasped at his shoulders, her hands tugging his body closer. Appearing worried but

67

determined, she bit her bottom lip as her gaze flicked to his lips.

A frisson of awareness zipped through him, making all his nerve endings explode like fireworks. He gulped again, the pulse of his blood thumping in his ear as he tightened his arms around her shoulders.

Her lips were near, close enough that her breath stirred on his cheek, but then she gave a small jolt and recoiled from him.

He reared back, a flush flaming across his face as hot and painful as if he'd been slapped. *Stupid.* He didn't know how he could have misread this situation so badly--*ever heard of wishful thinking, dumb ass?*--but his mouth was already stuttering out an apology, his voice anguished to his own ears. "I'm sorry. I didn't--I wasn't--"

She shook her head, chuckling, one arm cranked across her chest and over her shoulder, patting at a place on her shirt. At last she glared at him, her face half exasperated, half amused. "The ice bag, Norm. You pressed the ice against my shoulder."

"Fuck." He collapsed all the way down onto the couch, letting his skull thunk painfully against the top.

"Norm?"

He pinched his eyes closed.

"Norm."

He shook his head, the refrain of *Doomed. Doomed*, echoing like the roll of a foghorn warning ships away from the cliffs. But the warning was too late, he'd run aground, all hands lost, and now he was toast. *Damn, I'm so distraught I'm mixing metaphors.*

"*Norm.*" A hint of annoyance edged her clear, light voice this time and, for all that he was a foot taller than her, the quiet menace there caught his attention. He tipped his head off the couch and stared at her.

She stood, hands on her hips, pissed off but incredibly sexy in her shot girl outfit and those blood red "Come-Fuck-Me" heels. Balancing herself with one hand on his shoulder, she leaned in. With herculean effort, he refrained from admiring the epic view of her cleavage this position presented.

And yet he was only human. After what was probably far too brief a moment of restraint, he let his gaze drift down for a glimpse at the swell of her perky breasts pushing against the slit cut in her tank. When he gazed again at her face, she had one eyebrow raised in amused irony.

"I'm sorry," he said. "But I'm only human. Fallible. Weak."

She chuckled and tipped her head in understanding then she swallowed, her gaze flicking over his face, her expression heart-breakingly vulnerable. "So am I."

He blinked, his heart swelling two Grinch sizes too large, making his chest ache. *Did she just say what I hope she said?*

Feeling very daring, he brushed his hand along the bare skin at her waist where her tank was rolled up. "Really? Maybe we should help each other out with that." He carefully tensed his hand, the skin of her waist supple, soft, and under the urging from his fingers she leaned ever so slightly nearer to him.

A horrid rising hope pressed on his chest again. Norm knew he wasn't much to look at: too skinny, goofy, awkward as hell. But he'd invested time in developing other skills, and he *knew* he was a damn good kisser. Now if Lucy would only let him...

Her ponytail fell over her shoulder as she leaned over, the hair slithering in a golden spill along her tank. He eased his hand up slowly, and she caught her breath. He tweaked the red ribbon in her hair, then, swallowing his nervousness, knit his fingers through her ponytail. "Have I ever told you how much I love your attention to detail?" Circling his thumb on the skin of her neck, he tickled behind her ear. She shivered and eased closer, so gently she barely moved at all, but Norm felt it, felt her body's almost subliminal acceptance of his touch. She bit her bottom lip, her gaze dropping to his mouth before her eyelids fluttered closed. He caught his breath.

But instead of leaning in, she leaned away, her breath gusting out of her in a long sigh to stir against his cheek. He let his hand fall, the soft flax of her hair sliding through his grip.

She shook her head, like she was trying to clear her thoughts, then stared at a space to the right of his feet. "We can't." Pain crossed her face as she said the words. A nice sop to his ego but not much of a consolation prize as things went. "Believe me when I say that our dating is a *bad idea*. Shot girls and bouncers can't date." Her voice softened. "I'm really flattered. If things were different--"

"Don't. Say it." He tipped his head to the side in a cajoling, conciliating way even as he wailed like a baby on the inside. "Please."

"Right." She straightened, her face tense, then wheeled away toward the door.

As she stood poised in the entrance, he lifted the beer to her in salute. "Thanks for this."

"No problem."

"Tell Hank I'll be out in a few minutes. See you, Lucy."

"Yeah." She eased the door closed, returning to the floor.

Gritting his teeth, he slumped onto the couch, wondering if the beer or the ice bag--maybe both--could ease the sting of this latest rejection.

Chapter Seven

After closing that night, Lucy sat counting out in the back room, making neat stacks on the desk of twenties, tens, fives, and ones. Unfortunately, the ones pile was a lot higher than the twenties. Her feet ached from the Mary Janes, she'd lost her red hair ribbon somewhere and--now she was sitting instead of running around after drunks--her skimpy uniform left her distinctly chilled. And then there was the Norm Problem...

She couldn't stop remembering that near-miss kiss. *What was I thinking?* Norm was incredibly sweet and adorable. A-*dork*-able even. And it had been sexy as hell when he lifted her over the table earlier, all of his corded muscles wrapped around her, protecting her.

But Hank hated when he caught bouncers and shot girls *flirting*, let alone dating or anything else. And he'd specifically warned her that he wouldn't make exceptions for her. If she crossed the line he would fire her. And, as much as Lucy's job could annoy her at times, she did love Jezebel's; loved the place, loved the people. Anyway, she needed her job to pay for community college. And rent. And, oh yeah, other luxuries like food and soap.

So Norm was out of the question. Best not to think about his long, graceful hands, the ropey muscles in his arms, the pale brown of his eyes, the sweet vulnerability of his smile--

Briskly, she entered the total of her money minus her cut on her cash out sheet, stacked the money into a clump then popped to her feet to find Hank.

As she reached for the office door it swung open, and she barely ducked away in time to avoid a broken nose. Ronnie poked her head in. "Done with the desk?"

"Yup."

Ronnie's black stilettos made the floor ring as she stomped over to the chair then dropped her five-ten, voluptuous frame to sit. Slapping her money pouch down, Ronnie yanked the cash out in a big chunk.

A tingle of satisfaction warmed Lucy when she realized her stack of bills for the night was bigger than Ronnie's. *Sometimes short and sweet does win the race.* Humming to herself, she whirled away, ready to find Hank so she could hand off her cash and get the hell home.

"Pretty interesting tonight." Ronnie's voice was husky from her last smoke break. "You and the new guy."

Lucy stopped, her hand curled around the door frame and, for some reason, she felt short of breath, like she'd been kicked. "Me and Norm? Ronnie, *what*?"

Ronnie whipped one acid green fingernail out to separate her bills, carefully laying them on the desk one by one. Her moves were all over-careful, too deliberate, and her eyes never met Lucy's. "I'm saying watch yourself, Luce. You were in here with the newbie for awhile. Hank didn't like it."

Lucy's face flamed hot, the sensation burning up her neck like a pot of water boiling over. "I came back here with *Norm* because I wanted to thank him for getting

73

punched in the face for me. If Hank wants to read more into my actions than that, well, then he can screw himself."

"Duly noted." At the sound of Hank's distinctive baritone, Lucy froze.

After a long, tense moment she wheeled on one heel, beaming with maniacal cheer. "Hank! Just the man I wanted. Here's my take."

He tucked the cash into the small bank bag under his arm. She forced herself to stay still as Hank raised an eyebrow at her, inviting her to repeat to his face what she believed she'd been saying behind his back.

Ah, screw it. She crossed her arms, mirroring his posture, and tipped her chin up as high as she could, standing tall in her heels--well, *taller.* "Hank, here's the thing, I understand the no dating rule. Dating a bouncer would be messy and things could go south quick. Some customer gets too friendly. My boyfriend the bouncer freaks out and punches the customer. Or something. Then you're in trouble. The bar's in trouble. And me and my bouncer boyfriend would be out of our jobs. But," she lifted one finger to emphasize her point, "that is *not* what's happening between me and Norm. I wanted to thank him for…I don't know, going above and beyond the call of duty. None of your other bouncers have ever charged to my rescue like that."

Ronnie snickered. "All that was missing was the white horse and some armor."

Lucy refrained from casting a death glare at the redhead, and kept her gaze trained on Hank.

His dark eyebrow stayed cocked and dubious.

Chewing her lip, the words leaving a sharp bitterness in her mouth, she said, "Seriously, Hank, does Norm even look like someone I would date?" *Desperate times...*

Hank snorted but at last gave a small nod. "Fine. You're a good shot girl, Luce. And Norm could shape up to be an OK bouncer." He leaned close, smelling of sweat and booze like everybody else in the bar after a night of work. "But," he lifted one finger for emphasis, mimicking her earlier gesture exactly, "remember, if I get even a hint something's happening between you two then someone is going out on their ass." He shot her a glare. "And if I decide you lied to me guess who that will be, Luce?"

"Fair enough."

"So no more beers in the back room, Blondie." Ronnie smirked as she counted her money. The redhead always did love it when someone besides her was on Hank's shit list. Particularly if that someone was Lucy. Just a part of the not-always-so-friendly friendly competition between the two shot girls.

Hank wheeled toward the desk. "Hey, Ronnie, are you counting that money or inspecting it for fingerprints? Stop slacking off so I can get my ass home."

Ronnie shrunk into her seat and began flicking through her money faster, her lips moving as she counted to herself, a line between her brows.

Lucy tiptoed toward the exit, more than ready to go home.

"Drive safe, kid," Hank said. "Night."

"Night." She closed the office door behind her and started toward the lockers to grab her coat and purse. She froze when Norm pushed away from the wall where he'd

75

been leaning--and listening--and hurriedly stalked away from her, his shoulders braced with tension.

He heard me. No…

All the air in her lungs seemed to be sucked up and pulled along behind him until her chest actually hurt. Lucy cast an uncertain glance at the office door. She whipped her head toward Norm, but he was already all the way down the corridor and almost out the street door. She hesitated, torn, poised on the balls of her feet--

Ah, screw Hank. And then, gasping in a huge whoosh of breath, she raced down the hallway after Norm.

Her heels clacked hard against the linoleum of the floor. A sickening dose of adrenaline laced her pulse, and she teetered on her heels as she ran. *Please, don't let me fall and break an ankle.* She pushed against the back door, but it stuck, so she put her shoulder to the metal and shoved until the damn door finally fell open, nearly dropping her to the ground outside.

Norm's legs were longer, but he hadn't actually *run* away from her so Lucy managed to catch him just as he reached for his car door.

She stopped a few feet away, panting, one hand pressed to a stitch in her side, her feet vibrating with pain for making them run in the Mary Janes. "*Norm, wait.*"

He released his door handle but kept his body half-turned from her and shook his head, soft brown hair falling over his eyes. "It's fine. Go back inside."

His voice was absolutely flat, and the sound stung, sending a cold blast through her body. "No. I need to apologize."

"For what?" The words were half-swallowed, like he'd said them through his teeth.

Seeming to respond to the ice in his tone, the wind increased, burrowing underneath the cotton of her shirt to make her shiver. "I know you heard me. What I said about you. I didn't mean it." She puffed out her breath, and the air steamed white. "You heard Hank. He said he'd fire us if we start anything. You just got this job, you don't want to lose it already, do you? I'm trying to keep Hank off my back. And yours."

"Well, thanks." He pressed his palms against the car door and shook his head. "Don't worry. I got the message loud and clear. I'm not gonna bother you again. I may not look it, but I'm not so desperate I pine after women who find me repugnant."

She stalked over to him, her heels picking divots out of the gravel in the lot with each furious stride. When she got close enough, he finally glanced at her, frowning, and she punched him on the arm. "You freaking drama queen." She stepped closer and dropped her voice. "I almost let you kiss me, you idiot. At work too. Right under Hank's nose."

One corner of his mouth reluctantly quirked upwards, then his eyes fell to her bare skin, which was undoubtedly popping with goose bumps. "You came out here without a coat?" He shrugged off his Dickies jacket and dropped it over her bare shoulders.

The jacket was warm from his body and smelled like him, soap and detergent with a hint of some spicy cologne that tickled at her nostrils, daring her to take another sniff. She hugged his jacket to her body, her skin sucking up his leftover warmth. "And if that didn't show you I absolutely do not think you're repulsive--"

"Repugnant."

77

"Whatever. If *that* didn't show you I find you attractive then you have your head stuffed farther up your ass than Hank does."

"And that's saying something."

To keep from smiling, she bit her bottom lip. Norm moved closer, his body casting a shadow over hers, his face haloed by the streetlamp behind him. The warmth coming off his body was very tempting, a magnet tugging her closer.

She forced herself to step away from the heated circle of his arms. "OK. So. We've established I lied to Hank and you are not, despite what you might believe, repugnant--" She was babbling, but stemming the flow became impossible. If she kept her lips moving then they couldn't be misappropriated for...anything else. "--and if things were different I would totally have let you kiss me. But they aren't and we can't so: Friends?" Panicky with nerves and clumsy with cold, she stuck her hand out for a handshake but almost punched him in the stomach because her body was moving too stiffly.

He stepped away, shaking his head. "Wait. You lost me."

"Which part?"

"The no kissing part. I *like* you, Lucy." He rested his hands gently on her arms, his thumb whispering over the material of his jacket.

And, if I let myself, I could like you too. She put one hand on his chest, pressing her fingers over his heart, feeling his pulse accelerate beneath the fabric of his black t-shirt. The nearness of him stirred something low and urgent in her gut even as she said, "No. I'm sorry."

"Friends or nothing?"

"That's right." She raised her chin, trying to appear firm and determined. Inside, she wrestled with temptation--and temptation had her pinned to the mat.

Norm narrowed his eyes. "I choose option C."

"*Norm.*" The word came out a long wail, half-annoyed, half-beseeching. "There is no third option--"

"Friends then, on one condition." He hissed in a breath through his teeth and held it for a long moment. Then he blew the air out and leaned closer, his voice a rough whisper. "Let me kiss you, Lucy."

Her body flashed hot then cold then hot all over again, like a series of geologic events rewriting the landscape of her heart. Continents shifted. Mountains formed. The earth moved. She shook her head, her ponytail jiggling against her neck where the hair was pinned by his jacket's collar. "That is a monumentally bad idea."

"No, hear me out: one kiss. That's all. Aren't you, you know, curious?"

Yes. After their moment in the office, she'd spent the whole night wondering what that missed kiss could have been like.

"We'll kiss once," he said. "Just to, you know, get it out of our systems."

She hesitated, waiting to see if he was playing her somehow. Then, rolling her shoulders to relax, she tipped her chin up in her most business-like manner and let her eyes drift closed. "OK, but no tong--"

She didn't get the rest of the sentence out. He swooped in, covering her mouth with his, kissing her hard.

His lips were incredibly soft and warm, but firm as he traced the line of her mouth. His lips tenderly brushing

79

over hers sent a jolt of pure desire slamming through her body, making her all bright and tingly. *So that's what a lightning strike feels like.*

The ache of her loneliness rose up, swelling like a lump at the back of her throat. Norm was hot but gentle, eager for her and so close. Looming deliciously near. How easy to surrender to this stupid attraction, to salve her loneliness for even just tonight with him.

Lucy froze, and she pressed her hand to his chest, pushing him away. He shifted under the pressure, slowly, reluctantly moving away from her. A small sound of disappointment escaped his throat to vibrate against the barrier of her closed lips.

This was it, the one moment she had where she could stop this stupidity in its tracks. She felt herself teetering, toppling, like that moment in a dream where you fall forever before you jolt awake. *Time to wake up then, Lucy...*

Only she didn't. Lucy let herself fall.

After a moment, before she could make herself pull away, she had coaxed his lips apart and gently brushed the tip of his tongue with hers. Throbbing heat swirled in her gut at that brief contact. Throwing her arms around his neck, she deepened the kiss again, massaging his tongue with hers, enticing him back into her mouth.

With a groan of pleasure, he slanted his mouth to fit more closely to hers and snugged that long, lean body against her too, pressing her back against his car.

If Norm is this good with his mouth, what will he be like in bed? She slid her hands into his hair to keep him from escaping and grinned against his mouth to find how soft his hair was, silky and cool. His lips were as soft as his hair, his mouth hot and urgent, and the slow stroke of his tongue against hers made her veins itch with desire until she wanted to climb into his skin.

He skimmed one hand inside the confines of the jacket, and brushed his fingertips over her bare stomach, leaving a trail of prickling awareness that seared her with longing. *More. More.* She shivered against his hand and arched to meet the touch, wanting to push against him, to feel her body tight against his, wanting his hands on her *everywhere.* Just then he slid his hand off her hip, moving to cup her ass and hold her tight against him. She caught her breath, excited and nervous, heat pulsing between her legs.

Someone fumbled with the bar's back door, thumping at it from inside as Lucy had done, sending up a loud bang like cannon fire.

A small "*no*" of disappointment ghosted from Lucy's mouth before she could stop it. She wheeled away from him and pressed a hand to her mouth, closing her eyes.

The cold wash of reality tumbled ice through her veins. She breathed into her palm, trying to catch her breath, trying to recover from the cascade of heat and lust and emotion that Norm's kiss had sparked inside her.

I want him. The call was a small cry from somewhere deep in her chest, hollering into the abyss of her heart, trying to make her listen.

She clenched her teeth, flexing the muscle in her jaw. The tension of her teeth grinding together finally snapped her into something resembling normal. She let her hand fall away from her mouth, breathing slowly again. Norm got under her skin, sure, making her twitch with wanting him, but that didn't mean she had to give in.

Lucy stalked toward her own car. She reached for her door handle then stopped and froze. *My stuff is inside.*

81

Going back inside Jezebel's felt far more harrowing than it should, but the part she truly dreaded was facing Hank. Especially because, for the second time that night, she'd conspicuously spent way too much alone time with Norm. *Crap.*

Pivoting on one heel, she headed for the bar but stopped short before crossing into the streetlight beam. Worriedly, she patted at her face. *I hope I didn't have enough lipstick left for Norm to smear.* The back door finally banged all the way open, and Ronnie stepped over the threshold, picking her way across the gravel parking lot in her stilettos.

Lucy gave her a distracted nod. "Forgot my purse inside. Night, Ronnie."

Ronnie shook her head, casting a speaking glance between Lucy and Norm. Norm wasn't helping smooth the situation as he stayed frozen, leaning against his car and staring off shell-shocked into space.

"Night you two." Ronnie climbed into her car without further editorial comment and drove away.

Lucy shook her head and redoubled her pace for the bar door.

"Lucy." Gravel crunched as Norm approached from behind. He caught for her hand but she jerked away, keeping her back to him.

"You got your kiss, Norm. Now it's over." That sounded so cold, so dismissive. Like the kiss hadn't totally mind-fucked her in the most orgasmic way possible. She half-turned over her shoulder, letting anguish leak into her voice, so he could hear, so he could *know* how important this was, that she wasn't blowing him off for kicks. "I'm sorry, but I can't lose this job."

Still facing away from him, not wanting to see his expression, she nearly yanked the door hard enough to rip the thing off its hinges. For once the damn door didn't stick. Savage with satisfaction, she pounded inside to get her things.

After grabbing her purse and coat she circled back to the parking lot, Norm's jacket draped over her arm. She was half-hoping, half-afraid he'd waited for her. She didn't know what she'd say, but still, she wanted him to be there.

Unfortunately, by the time she returned to the parking lot Norm was already gone, a great empty spot where his car had been.

Good. Fine. Fabulous. One less thing to worry about.

She fingered the stiff material of his jacket and fought a fierce urge to see if the fabric still smelled like him. Letting out a *tsk* of disgust with herself, she flung the jacket onto her backseat.

***

"And how was your day, dear?" Zack asked when Norm entered the apartment that night.

Norm dropped his house keys on the coffee table and flopped onto their moth-eaten old couch. *Amazing. Frustrating. Painful.* He lifted one shoulder in a shrug.

"Your brother--"

"Which one?"

"Truman. He texted me because you don't reply quickly enough to your email, I guess. Wants you to read his latest article before he shows it your father."

Great. More English homework. "I'll email Tru tomorrow."

83

"And your dad so kindly mailed you more of those brochures for Masters programs." Zack gestured vaguely over his head toward the kitchen counter.

Because I needed one more bad thing piled on top of this already shit-tastic day. Norm crossed to the counter where his mail was stacked. He pulled out the two letters he needed and a Netflix envelope, then shoved the five glossy college brochure packets deep into the garbage, punching them down with much greater force than necessary.

"Oh, and Mom called. Wanted to remind you about her birthday."

"You know, she isn't actually *your* mother," Norm snapped as he stomped out of the kitchen.

"Yeah, but I like your mom better than mine." Perhaps reading Norm's tone, Zack finally glanced away from the late night showing of *Doctor Who* on BBC America to look at him. He immediately did a double take. "*Dude.* What happened to your eye?"

It took Norm a long minute to figure out what he was talking about. In the aftermath of that earth-shattering kiss with Lucy, he'd forgotten all about being punched. "I got decked fighting a horny midget off one of the shot girls."

Zack snorted into his beer bottle as he sipped.

Norm dropped onto the couch then leaned back and let the evil aliens' plan for world domination flow over him, relishing the good Doctor's skill as he bustled about thwarting evil robots, saving the universe.

How nice to have an easy life like that. Where things were black and white. Good. Evil. Yes means yes. No means no. And where responding to a kiss by nearly crawling on top of you meant the girl was interested and not playing some complex mind-game. *What the hell is Lucy's deal anyway?*

"Was she cute?"

"*Hmm?*" Norm pretended absorption in *Doctor Who* even though both he and Zack had most of the show memorized.

Zack leaned over, forcing Norm to look away from the TV. "The shot girl. Was she hot? I went to Jezebel's once. There's this redhead with big--" Zack mimed two watermelons in front of his chest.

"That's Ronnie."

"Could you set me up with her?"

Norm gaped at him. "*Ronnie?* Zack, she's sexy as hell, sure, but she is one of the scariest girls I've ever met. A real man-eater. Like...in the literal sense." *And why would anyone lust after Ronnie while Lucy's around?*

"Who'd you get decked for then?"

Norm hesitated, catching his breath. "Lucy."

"Lucy, eh? And was she properly grateful for your chivalry?"

Norm wallowed up from the couch and stalked toward his bedroom. "Good night."

"Bates, is that a yes or a no?"

"It's a 'bouncers and shot girls can't date so it doesn't matter how grateful she is'."

"Oh. That sucks. I was hoping for your sake that was one of the bouncer perks."

"Well, it's not."

"Maybe some of the hot customers will throw themselves at you. You need to get laid. It's been awhile, right? Like *months*. Not since the last girlfriend?"

85

Norm hissed his breath out through his teeth. Usually he liked his roommate, but just now, if Zack said one more thing, Norm was ready to deck him.

Zack set his beer on the table and stood. "Hey, you OK?"

Norm deflated, his annoyance evaporating. "Tired." He pushed his bedroom door open. "Good night, Zack."

"Night, Bates."

Norm stripped to his boxers and pancaked backwards onto his sheets, staring at his pocked stucco ceiling. It was after 3 a.m., he should be exhausted, but his head buzzed a mile a minute. And mostly what his mind buzzed with was Lucy. *Lucy. Lucy. Lucy.* Thoughts of kissing her. Of how she'd kissed him back...

Of how she'd totally rejected him and hop-scotched across his heart. Repeatedly.

Maybe he *should* start checking out other girls.

***

Norm was spared having to see Lucy the next night. Shot girls didn't come in during the early part of the week, he discovered, usually from Sunday to Wednesday. Which meant Norm had a little under a week to mull over the kiss in the parking lot before he would see Lucy again.

She was worried about her job, he was too, but chemistry like theirs didn't come by every day. If he could talk to her, maybe convince her to talk to Hank with him. There had to be a way. Hank, despite the tough guy persona, was not a total asshole.

If Norm was being honest with himself, he couldn't quite believe he'd kissed Lucy. *Lucy.* And she'd kissed him *back.* Kissed him back and blown his brains out with lust.

Finally Thursday, Dollar Beer Night, rolled around again, and the shot girls were back. Dollar Beer Night basically translated into College Night, because college kids more than anyone loved cheap booze.

In honor of the latest big budget, over-hyped comic book movie, the theme of the night was superheroes, which meant the shot girls had to go all out. Any bar staff who wanted to play along could, as long as their outfit didn't interfere with their duties. Two of the bartenders were dressed as The Wonder Twins, and one of the other bouncers, Ben, had shown up as a very buff Spiderman. Hank had, unsurprisingly, refrained from participating. Norm, unsure how far out the non-shot girl members of the staff were allowed to go, had also refrained from dressing up. Mostly.

He manned the front door, taking cover charge, checking ID, and stamping hands for re-entry. The task was by turns mind-numbingly boring and incredibly fast-paced, depending on the ebb and flow of people wanting to get in the door of The World Famous Jezebel's Bar & Lounge.

No matter what the flow of traffic, Norm kept himself poised and anxious waiting for Lucy to arrive. If he could, he wanted to talk to her alone before her shift. See if they could hash out some compromise on the no-kissing thing.

And, of course, being a true guy born and bred--and a devout geek into the bargain--Norm really, *really* wanted to see what sexy superhero she'd dressed as.

An hour into his shift, Lucy hadn't arrived, and he felt like one big exposed nerve ending, bracing himself every time someone walked in the door. Finally, during one of

87

the lulls, he slid the schedule out from under the cash box. His heart sank. Lucy was only scheduled for a five hour shift. She wouldn't be in for *two more hours*.

The first rush of the evening had passed and there probably wouldn't be another one until right about when Lucy had to clock in. Just in time to keep him from having any chance to talk to her.

"Crap." His desires flouted, he whipped out the paperback he'd stuffed in his pocket. He was allowed to read in between customers since he had to stay chained to the front door.

People trickled in for the next few hours, with a small rush at nine, but then nothing for twenty minutes. So he was thoroughly engrossed in Neil Gaiman's latest fantasy novel when someone tapped the book cover to get his attention, making him jump. But the newcomer was only Ronnie.

"Hi, Ronnie." He glanced back to his paperback then blinked and looked again.

Ronnie's full hourglass figure was always worth a second glance. But that night it probably warranted a third. Apparently, the superhero theme had spoken to her soul because she had gone all out in a killer Poison Ivy costume. Little plastic ivy leaves molded lovingly to her curves in a strapless bustier one piece. Thigh-high green boots encased her legs, and green opera gloves covered her arms to the elbow. She even wore green lipstick. The costume was Ronnie's soul made reality, the perfect combination of danger and sex appeal.

She cast him an amused glance from under her eyelashes. "Like the costume then, newbie?"

"You are going to make a *lot* of money tonight."

"Here's hoping."

"Oh, Christ, Ronnie." Hank's annoyed voice made them both turn.

Norm frowned at that clear annoyance, always confused by the weird dynamic between Hank and Ronnie.

"Like it?" Ronnie smirked and sidled toward Hank, wiggling her hips suggestively.

"Superheroes, Ronnie. *Heroes*," he enunciated the word slowly, like Ronnie was an idiot, and a notch formed between his eyebrows.

What is Hank's problem?

Ronnie made a *moue* of distaste. "There aren't any good redheaded superheroes."

Hank rubbed his forehead. "Mary Jane Watson."

Ronnie wrinkled her nose. "She's a superhero's *girlfriend.*"

Provoked, Norm huffed out, "Jean Grey."

"She's a doormat."

"What about when she's Phoenix?"

Cool disdain settled over Ronnie's beautiful face. "Absolute psycho."

"That's only really in her *Dark* Phoenix incarnation," Lucy said from the doorway.

At the sound of Lucy's voice, Norm whipped to face her. She wore a long peacoat so he couldn't see her superhero outfit, but she was gorgeous anyway, her hair loose in a long cascade down her back.

"You know superheroes?" He beamed at her, unbearably turned on by this new revelation. A girl who looked like Lucy was a rare find, but a girl who looked like Lucy and quoted Shakespeare and read Neil Gaiman *and*

89

knew her superheroes, well, that was just bordering on perfection.

She slid him a small smile, and stuffed her hands into her coat pockets. "Some. And I used to watch the X-Men animated show on Fox when I was a kid."

Hank growled in the back of his throat and whipped away, storming into the bar proper. "Geeks. I'm employing a bar full of geeks."

Ronnie gazed after Hank for a long minute, seeming suddenly wilted, then she shook her head, straightened her shoulders and vamped her way into the bar, the redheaded vixen once more.

Norm paused, arrested by the sight of Ronnie appearing, even momentarily, as anything other than a cast-iron sex kitten. But, despite the mystery of Hank and Ronnie, he hurriedly whirled back so Lucy wouldn't decide he was leering after the redhead. Ronnie was nice to watch, of course, but for him there was no competition when Lucy was in the room. He knit his hands together on the podium and gazed at Lucy with interest. "So, are you in Secret Identity Mode, or can I ask which superhero you are?"

In response, Lucy thumbed open the buttons on her coat, and Norm finally noticed her bright red boots.

Which superheroes wear red boots? The Flash. Wonder Woman. But that didn't narrow the field too much. In the land of sexy costumes, where outfits were rarely accurate, she could be anyone from Elektra to Iron Man. *Elektra would be hot.*

Lucy finally yanked her coat all the way off, revealing an adorable and, actually, fairly accurate Supergirl costume.

But this is OK too. Norm blinked, all the blood rushing to his lower extremities. The blue top was long sleeved but low-cut in a square neck across her breasts, which were perfectly emphasized by the giant Super-S symbol in the middle of her chest. The top was cropped just under her breasts, leaving her midriff bare. He'd never had a thing for bellies before, but he could easily develop a fascination for Lucy's. She had a great stomach, flat but still soft and feminine; no rock hard six packs there.

Her skirt was bright red and shiny with a gold waistband, and the hem hit her mid-thigh, almost dowdy among shot girls. Her outfit suited her personality the way Ronnie's had suited hers. But where Ronnie was all poison barbs and sex on a stick, Lucy had the wholesome physical appeal of the girl next door mixed with her bright, All American gumption, and all of it together drove Norm crazy with lust.

Lucy set her coat on the counter then twirled for him, making her short red cape unfurl behind her. Raising one eyebrow, she pursed her lips in a sexy pout. "I'm one of the last survivors of the planet Krypton. Care to help out an endangered species?"

God, yes. Norm bit back this first response. The bad pick-up lines game. Right. Because they were *friends.* And he'd seem like a bad sport if he didn't play along. He narrowed his eyes at her, sending her the cheesiest of cheesy smolders as he slowly unbuttoned his Jezebel's bowling shirt. She watched him, tapping one booted foot impatiently.

At last, all buttons undone, he grabbed each side of his shirt and whipped it open like a street flasher to reveal his plain black shirt with a screen-print of the yellow

91

Batman logo on his chest. He dropped his voice to an action hero growl, gravelly and low, and said, "*I'm Batman.*"

Lucy waited, head cocked to the side. After a moment, she laughed and shook her head. "That's it?"

"He's *Batman.* Does he need good game? He just shows up and the panties drop."

"Fair point." Lucy grinned, but her eyes were tense at the corners and she stepped close to him, crowding the podium as she lowered her voice. "About last week--"

He lifted his hand to stop her mid-word and leaned over the podium, covering her hand with his. "Lucy, I want to talk to you about this, but here and now is not the best time. For one thing, Hank's hovering, and also your shift's about to start so we'd have to rush. I know a good hot dog place near here. Can't we go there after work and hash things out? There *has* to be a way we can make this work."

Gently, she pulled her hand out from under his and picked her coat off the podium. Her blonde hair glinted in the black light by the door as she shook her head. "I've decided. Last week was fantastic, but it is *not* going to happen again."

Norm winced but nodded. He was a gentleman. If the lady said no then he would back off. He forced a shaky smile onto his face while inside he howled with disappointment. "If that's what you want."

"It is." She swallowed and passed the podium to head inside. But, before stepping into the club proper, she glanced over her shoulder. "Have a good night."

"You too."

She walked away and Norm slumped on his stool. So that was it.

Who knew being a bouncer came with so many job hazards? Getting punched in the face was one thing, having his heart squeezed to a pulp seemed excessive. Norm slapped his hand on the paperback and slid it off the podium, cracking the spine open so forcefully he marveled that he hadn't ripped the book in half.

Chapter Eight

Lucy spent the rest of the night with the image of Norm's hurt face superimposed over her eyelids. Was she being stupid pushing him away like this? She rolled her eyes at herself. OK. Yes. But *how* stupid?

Her brain didn't have an answer for that, so she forced the question to the back of her mind and refocused on work. One of the other shot girls, Jenna, went AWOL for over an hour, which left Lucy and Ronnie in the weeds with too many eager customers and not enough hot girls to serve them drinks. Jenna wasn't usually a flake, so Lucy and Ronnie covered for her to Hank.

Although, when Jenna reappeared with her lipstick smudged, her dark hair mussed, her eyes clearly glowing from the aftershocks of lust, Lucy bristled with annoyance. *Why am I working double-time so she can sneak off to tryst with the customers?* Still, Lucy was sort of happy to stay busy, to have work consume any spare brain power she might otherwise have used for mooning over Norm.

Lots of the usual bad, ill-formulated pick-up lines got thrown her way, taking the form of superhero puns involving rescuing pussy from trees, and many inquiries and/or offers regarding her X-ray vision. Lucy couldn't wait to get away and take a shower, but the shot girls had made big bucks so she was among the last of the Jezebel's crew to leave. She finished counting her money *finally*, grabbed her coat and shoved her way out the back door. Halfway to her Mustang, she noticed one car left in the parking lot besides Hank's.

Norm. She swallowed. So he had waited her out. Something prickled through her, a strange cocktail of pleasure and annoyance. No wonder she kept sending Norm such mixed signals when her own brain didn't even know what she wanted.

Norm popped open his car door and his long, wiry body unfurled for her. Heat pooled low in her gut, and suddenly she didn't feel so confused anymore. She strode toward him, her brain abuzz with conflicting ideas for what she should say. But, before she could say anything, Norm called out, "Hey, can you jump me?"

Well, that was crude. Still, abrupt delivery or not, Lucy was tempted--*The things that man can do with his mouth*--and she redoubled her pace toward him, tingles starting under her skin.

But then he held aloft a set of jumper cables and she stopped, her body sagging with disappointment. Car trouble. He hadn't been waiting for her at all. His stupid car wouldn't start. She only stood there for a brief moment of distress before she managed to collect herself. "Sure!" She crossed back to drive her car closer to his in the parking lot.

He already had the cables out and his own hood popped by the time she pulled in next to him and got out. Gazing at her, the two pairs of crocodile clips in each of his hands, abject terror filled his face.

She stifled a knowing chuckle. Ah. Norm had the jumper cables but he clearly had no idea what to *do* with them. She reached for the clips. "Here, let me. I took auto shop in high school."

"No, no, the car's dirty. You'll screw up your costume. Tell me what to do."

"Explaining everything to you will take twice as long as just letting me do it in the first place."

He hesitated, clasping the clips closer to his body, as if scared she would snatch them away.

She let out a growl of annoyance then, remembering how she was dressed, she placed her hands on her hips and stuck out her chest so the red cape caught the wind and whipped out behind her. "Norm, trust me. Superman is my brother--"

"Cousin."

"Whatever. I can leap tall buildings in a single bound, I'm faster than a speeding bullet, yada, yada." He grinned at her posturing and she tipped her head to the side, making her voice cajoling, "I can handle a jumpstart."

"OK. But use the jumper cables, all right? I'm not sure my battery can handle the power of your laser vision." He handed one set of the clips over which she attached to his battery then she popped her own hood and leaned over to attach the other pair. As she bent over the engine, a gust of air flipped her skirt up, flattening the fabric against her back. Heat pulsed into her cheeks, even though she was wearing shorts underneath. The shorts covered everything worth seeing, but having your skirt blow up was still dead embarrassing.

As she straightened and faced Norm, her face burning with mortification, he tipped his head to the side, staring contemplatively at the moon. "You know, it just occurred to me how impractical a skirt is for flying."

She choked on a laugh, and he wheeled to his own car and slid into the driver's seat. She followed suit and started her car.

Nothing happened. She futzed about for a few minutes, connecting and reconnecting the cables, but Norm's old Toyota remained lifeless. At last, after half an hour of trying, she slumped in her driver's seat, and called out, "Are you sure the problem was the battery?"

"No." He let his head fall against his own steering wheel with an audible *whump*.

"Wasn't this in the shop a few weeks ago?"

"Yes.'

"Fire your mechanic." She hauled herself out of her own driver's seat again. Time was catching up with her. Her body was sluggish with the yearning for sleep, and she had to keep covering her mouth to stifle jaw-cracking yawns.

He didn't appear much better when he leaned away from his steering wheel. The light off the street lamp cast dark shadows over the hollows of his face, and his eyes drooped, half-lidded with fatigue.

"Come on," she said. "I'll drive you home."

He waved that away. "I'll call Triple A. I should have done that anyway instead of holding you hostage."

Irritation flared through Lucy and, because she was so tired, she was a lot less polite than she might have been otherwise. "Norm, it's 3 a.m. and even if you are nine feet tall and fairly strong I'm not leaving you here alone to be kidnapped and--and sold into white slavery. So, if you feel

97

such guilt about keeping me here then don't waste anymore of my time arguing about this, *okaaay*?"

"*Yes, ma'am.*" He snapped off a quick salute, climbed out of his car and into the Mustang. His eyes were crinkled with amusement.

She plopped into the driver's seat and cranked the heater. Something crunched under Norm as he sat, and he yanked out a set of Xeroxed pages from beneath his butt. "Hey, 'The Cats of Ulthar.'" He blinked in confusion. "Which math class has you reading H.P. Lovecraft?"

"It's for that English class you helped me with." She started the car and rolled out of the parking lot.

"Oh, this is a great short story, you know."

"What happens?"

"Well--" He broke off, frowning. "Actually, a bunch of housecats eat some people."

"Cheerful."

"They had it coming."

She snorted out a laugh.

"Seriously, though, if you like Neil Gaiman I bet you'd dig H.P. Lovecraft. Do you have to write an essay on this?"

She groaned. "Yes, and we're being quizzed to prove we read the story. Which I haven't yet. Good to know about the house cats. I hate writing essays."

"It's really not that bad."

"To you. You *like* English."

"You make it sound like some weird sexual perversion."

"Close enough."

He leaned his head against the seat and closed his eyes. "Tell me, how does a girl like you--"

"Like me?"

"Blonde. Beautiful. Dainty—"

"Dainty is a fun word. I love your big vocabulary," she purred the words out, teasing him.

He twitched and cleared his throat. "Anyway, how does a girl like you come to take auto shop?"

"It was the closest thing to an engineering class my high school offered. That was partly why I began a robotics club my junior year."

"Robotics Club?"

"We had to design and build a competitive robot, less than 120 pounds, capable of both autonomous and remote controlled action that could complete a series of assigned tasks and games."

"You did that. .in high school?"

"Yeah. Lots of schools have teams. All over the country. All over the world. I read the other day there's a new one for local kids to make a solar powered boat."

"Ah, let me rephrase: you built a *working* robot in high school--"

"Lots of kids build robots as hobbies these days. We live in the future, Norman."

He knit his hands in his lap and turned to her with a brisk, businesslike manner. "Tell me, do you have a timetable laid out for your world domination yet? And, if so, are you taking applications for minions?" She giggled and he fell against the car seat, shaking his head in apparent wonder. "And you're working at a bar," he murmured.

"Hey, I had a couple bad years after high school. And Hank helped me. I owe him."

Norm held his hands high in surrender and apology. "I'm sorry. Not my business."

"No," she growled. Then, casting a glance his way, she softened, trying to keep her voice from sounding too defensive. "Anyway, I'm not staying at Jezebel's forever. I'm transferring to a four year school this fall."

"Do you know where yet?"

"A state school, probably CSULA. I do want to keep working at the bar to help pay for school, but..."

"But?"

"I applied to UC Berkeley, but the commute from there to Jezebel's is a bit long."

"Is Berkeley your top choice?"

Her belly fluttered at the idea of attending Berkeley, the best Public University in the country with one of the top undergraduate engineering programs. *Don't think about it.* Lucy had learned not to get her hopes up.

She gritted her teeth and faced Norm. "Yeah, but Berkeley is also the last of the California schools to send acceptance letters. Because they want to drive their prospective students *crazy*. So I won't know until next month." She clenched her hands around the steering wheel.

A short silence fell and then, "You built a freaking robot when you were seventeen?"

She cast him an uncertain glance. "Um, sixteen."

Norm's grin only widened, and, so far from being intimidated or put off by her brains, it became clear he was *more* attracted to her because of them. He reached over and gave her shoulder a friendly pat. "Berkeley is nuts if they don't take you." He sat back then said, almost as an afterthought, "I'm glad."

"Glad?"

He scratched at his neck, looking uncomfortable. "That, you know, you're not in for the long haul at Jezebel's."

"Hey, pal, *you* work at Jezebel's."

"Yeah, but I'm a no good slacker bum who will never amount to anything, whereas *you* are clearly destined for great things." His words were light, joking, but his tone was sincere, vehement even.

How long had it been since someone had believed in her like this? How long had it been since a man had even noticed there was more to her than a revealing outfit?

She glanced at him and he flashed her one of those heart-breakingly vulnerable grins of his, so goofy and sweet. Something flipped in her gut with a heady whoosh that reverberated through her whole body. She swallowed and darted a questioning look his way. "I'm destined for great things?"

"Yes "

She wanted to say something sincere, heartfelt, to let him know how much she appreciated his faith. But the quiet certainty in his voice unnerved her to no end, making her fidget in the driver's seat. *I'm such a screw-up. I don't deserve this.* She swallowed then forced a smile onto her face. "Great things like dominating the world with my army of high-powered robot warriors?"

His smile fell a notch, but he recovered enough to tease her back. "*Tsh.* See, I knew a twisted heart of darkness lurked behind that angelic façade."

Oh, Norm. Why did he have to be so a-dork-able? Distracted by him and frustrated, she pulled over in front

101

of his building hard enough that she dinged her front wheel against the curb.

Norm jerked and sat there blinking. "Are you all right?"

She tossed him a bright nod that didn't feel remotely genuine.

He eased back in his seat, releasing the car handle. "You want to come in, and I can make you a quick coffee to get you home safe? You're in the totally opposite direction, right? Long drive?"

"It's not that faaa--" A jaw cracking yawn interrupted her, and lasted so long that, by the time she was done, her eyes watered. She sat in her seat for a long moment, her body so weary from contemplating the turn of her ignition key that all she wanted was to drop her head down and sob.

"OK. That's it." Norm's voice right beside her made her jump.

While she'd been sitting there, a breath away from fatigued collapse, Norm had gotten out and circled to her side of the car. He tugged her door open and hunkered down so he didn't loom. "Come inside. Drink some coffee. You are not in any condition to drive home right now."

She pressed her skull against the head rest and had to agree with him. Apart from her total, bone deep exhaustion, the idea of going into Norm's apartment had a powerful appeal--which suddenly made going inside seem like a bad idea, after all.

She tensed, torn between staying and going. But another yawn broke her focus and finally made her decision for her. She reached out a hand, and he grabbed her fingers to help her out of the car. Snatching her bag up, she slung the duffel over her shoulder.

Somehow, as she trailed after Norm to his third floor apartment, she kept holding on to him. His hand was warm and dry, his long fingers curling around hers, totally covering her hand like some kind of protective casing.

Finally, they reached his apartment and he pushed the weather-beaten old door open. She braced herself as she stepped inside. Single guys living without regular feminine influence usually had pretty scary apartments. Lucy only hoped that Norm and his roommate were well mannered enough to keep their porn hidden.

Norm let her go inside ahead of him, but he stood taut with tension behind her. Craning his neck, she guessed he was doing a frantic last minute check to make sure nothing truly heinous lay out in the open.

The front door let onto the living room, which was fairly spacious for a not-so-great apartment. The TV was immediately across from the door, and beside the couch sat a scarred coffee table cluttered with comic books, notepads, pens, and an old can of root beer.

She lifted the hem of her red cape. "Can I borrow your bathroom to transform into my secret identity? I wanted to change at the bar but I forgot."

He pointed down a narrow hallway. "Bathroom's last door at the end. I apologize in advance for the state of it."

"Well, if I don't reappear in an hour, send the search party." She wandered down the hallway, passing a large hall closet with long gray curtains that half-concealed several shelves of cleaning supplies and comic books. Were these Norm's secret vices? Cleaning and comic books?

103

Like the rest of his apartment, the bathroom was passably clean, especially for two single straight guys. There was shampoo, bar soap. No loofas. A normal amount of hair product, although she suspected *that* was the roommate's. With ladylike restraint, she abstained from peeking into the medicine cabinet. Although she doubted the cabinet held any delicious mysteries since on the bathroom counter--right next to the hand soap--sat a big jar full to the brim with condoms. Something twinged inside her; it might have been jealousy. Did Norm really have that much sex?

Maybe they were his roommate's. But then why would they be in one of the common areas in the apartment?

Shaking her head, she skinned free of her Supergirl costume and used a towel from her bag to wipe her body down before she changed clothes. She rifled through the bag once more then dropped it in aggravation. Shoes. She'd left her sensible shoes by the front door of her apartment. She stared in disgust at the red-heeled boots then appraisingly at her socks. Which was worse? Sore feet or showing Norm her silly novelty socks?

Eventually, she padded back into the living room, red boots safely tucked into her bag, silly novelty socks displayed loud and proud. She paused en route to the living room, standing in the short hallway and watching Norm. His counter and stove were on opposite sides of the narrow kitchen, and he puttered about, sandwiched between the two, lifting a bag of coffee easily down from a top shelf. A shelf she was too short even to see.

His gaze roved over her outfit: a black v-neck t-shirt and light blue sweats. Not exactly fashionable. Sometimes she felt like she didn't know how to dress if she wasn't dressed as a sexy shot girl. But he seemed to have no strong feelings about her clothing as he glanced away, measuring out the grounds.

The rich smell of the coffee, the sight of him in the kitchen, cheerful and humming--heck, even her silly socks sinking into his carpet--all of it blended together into a perfect moment that struck Lucy as homey. Comfort food for her soul.

Norm caught her gaze and jerked his head toward the living room. "If you go sit on the couch I'll have coffee for you in no time." His polite smile, his careful words broke the moment for her. Where she had felt warm and safe, Norm appeared only harried and awkward.

Lucy snapped herself free of her reverie and craned around to see where he'd pointed. She blinked in baffled horror at his butt-ugly orange couch that the wall had mostly hidden before. She padded to the living room and eased herself down, scared she might sink into the squashy cushions and never be heard from again.

Norm futzed about in the kitchen, clanking and running water. Lucy rose and pursued her feminine duty, engaging in a mild snoop of the living room. The walls were painted that dull white color every cheap apartment defaults to, but Norm or his roommate had spiced the walls up with posters, one on each side of the TV. The poster on the right had all the main characters from Neil Gaiman's *Sandman* comics hanging out together by a fountain: a lot of old gods, fairies, witches, and monsters partying together, drinking champagne.

The one bracketing the other side of the TV first seemed like a rock band poster, but when she stepped closer she recognized the *Star Wars* theme. In the poster, Han and Luke rocked out on their guitars. Leia--in torn plaid pants--hollered into the microphone like a punk space princess. And Chewie wailed on the drums like the total bad-ass he was. *Dear Norm. You have to love a man who can fly his geek flag this high.*

She trailed back to the couch and gratefully sank into its quicksand-like softness. Curling her feet under her, partly to conceal her stupid socks, she leaned against one arm of the couch, pillowing her head on the arm rest. She let her eyes drift closed. *Just for a minute…*

***

Lucy had fallen silent in the living room, and Norm ducked around the kitchen wall to peer at her. "Sugar? Milk?" he called, rattling dishes in the sink to wake her if she'd already drifted off. Lucy in his apartment was stressful enough. Lucy asleep on his couch might give him a heart attack. The sheer stress of trying act calm when every nerve ending he had was vibrating with anxiety just might be enough to make him keel over.

"Lots of milk, little bit of sugar, please." Her voice was thick, somewhat distant, like her brain was already far, far away.

Uh-oh. Fading fast. He yanked the coffee off and slopped some into one of his mugs. He doused the drink with milk and sugar then hustled into the living room and clanked her steaming mug in front of her. "Here you go."

She twitched and blinked her eyes open, pushing herself to a full sitting position with a small groan. He sank onto the opposite end of the couch, flinging his arm over the back, trying to appear relaxed, unfazed.

Lifting the coffee to take a sip, she paused and glanced at the mug, then her mouth fell open in surprise.

Norm winced and closed his eyes. He'd grabbed a clean mug out of the cabinet without checking it. *Lord, please strike me dead now if I just handed her Zack's "*I Heart Titties*" mug.* Granted, ol' Zack had bought the mug at a breast cancer rally with his sister. Still, a mug like that was hardly part of the tone Norm wanted to set with Lucy.

"*Phoebus?*" she gasped, eyes wide.

Relieved, Norm let his breath out through his teeth and twirled the mug to glance at the design: a circular decal with a stylized, gold-embossed chariot pulled by three horses made out of flames. The name "Phoebus" was emblazoned across the mug in bold red letters. Phoebus was a new space telescope, the latest project to emerge out of the prestigious Manning Flight Research Laboratory.

"Where'd you get the mug?" She leaned forward, her feet tucked under her, her long tangle of hair falling over her shoulder. "Do you know someone who worked on the mission?" Her voice sounded breathy, excited.

Right. She's an engineering nerd. He sank into the couch, stretching his feet out underneath the coffee table. "My brother works there in the contracts department. He likes to buy all of us a mission patch or sticker for everything that comes off the lab, but I told him I liked the logo design for the Phoebus mission a lot, so he got me a mug."

"Wow." She scooted the mug so the design faced her again. "That must be so cool to work there. Even as an office drone. To contribute even in some small way to the human exploration of space."

He tipped his head to the side. "Makes paperwork and filing sound almost appealing."

She took a sip then leaned against the couch, her eyes drifting closed. She resembled an angel, one crafted out of spun sugar by some master confectionary. "You were right, I can barely keep my eyes open, but the coffee should help."

"Least I can do," he said. "Thank you for going so far out of your way to get me home."

"Well." Her voice was thick with sleep, a low, raspy bedroom drawl that made the hair on Norm's neck prickle. "You're one of us."

"'Us?'" He let his head fall against the back of the couch too, closing his eyes to ease some of their throbbing tiredness.

"At Jezebel's."

Norm winced. *Jezebel's.* No escaping the damn place. No escaping the fact that Lucy had chosen the bar over pursuing any kind of *anything* with him. And certainly no escaping the fact he needed his stupid job as much as she did hers. So he really should've been working harder to get her off of his couch.

But the lazy, languid warmth in her eyes had worked voodoo on him, turning him into a zombie with no will of his own. No desire but to lie on the couch beside her, to be warmed and soothed by her closeness. *You're an idiot*, he thought, but without much venom.

"We take care of our own at Jezebel's." Her voice sounded more muffled, like she had snuggled into the couch cushions.

He could understand that; at the moment the couch cushions were trying to suck him into their insidious comfort too. "Does that mean I'm a fallen woman?"

108

She gave a little gurgle, and Norm half sat up, cracking one eye open. Her eyess fluttered open at the same time to meet his gaze. "You can be a false prophet if you want."

"Oh, good. I'd look terrible in high heels."

She gave that small sleepy gurgle of laughter again, making his chest ache with wanting her. But he stayed glued to his half of the couch even as she settled more firmly into hers, stretching her legs out so one of her sock-clad feet brushed his thigh, making him jump. Which she was too sleepy to notice.

He glanced down and choked back a surprised laugh; her socks were plain black with poufy-haired Albert Einstein heads ranging all over them. He glanced up, but Lucy had her eyes closed. She would never know he had discovered her secret.

"You'd look like Godzilla in high heels," she continued in that same muzzy, faraway voice. "If there was ever a man who didn't need to be taller it is you, Norman."

He'd never liked his name before. *Norman.* Norm was one of those names parents gave their kids never thinking of the hell they were condemning them to. But something about the affectionate, teasing way Lucy said it, like his full name was a private, delicious joke between the two of them...well, he could get used to that.

He snorted to himself. So much for throwing in the towel where Lucy was concerned. Clearly, he was as attracted to her as he'd always been with no cure in sight. Though he could stop pursuing her like she'd asked. Just because his crush lingered didn't mean he had to keep bugging her about it and risking both their jobs.

109

His mind wandered, a lazy hamster rolling in its wheel until his own thoughts were foggy, disjointed with sleep. A long moment passed before he realized Lucy's breathing had slowed to a deep, regular rhythm.

"Lucy." He kept his voice low. "Are you awake?"

He managed to force one eye open. Lucy was passed out cold at the end of the couch, her hands pillowed under her cheek as she snored softly, like a door mouse with a deviated septum. Beautiful.

He mustered his cells for the herculean effort of rising and walking into the bedroom. He would have offered the bed to Lucy and taken the couch. Now that she'd passed out, though, letting her sleep in peace seemed the best option. He reached up and flicked the living room lights off for her.

The dark was lovely. Lulling. He let his eyes flutter closed again. *I'm just resting them...I'm so freaking tired...I'm just...going to...rest my eyes...for one...more minute...*

Chapter Nine

Lucy slowly came awake, stretching just to feel her muscles move, trying to push out some of the syrupy lethargy that weighed her down. Under her clothes her skin felt clammy, and the underwire on her bra dug into her ribs. *Why did I sleep in my clothes?* She blinked, muzzy, then remembered why she was sleeping on the ugliest couch in creation.

This couch, she groaned inwardly with an ecstatic delight. The thing wasn't much to look at on first view, but man, the couch really was the height of comfort. So much so, she was half-tempted to slide down and get the rest of her interrupted beauty sleep.

Norm stirred and she froze, scared she might have woken him up with all her fidgeting. His breathing remained low and even, though, signaling sleep.

She watched him for a moment. Shaggy brown hair mussed from sleep, tufts stuck up in back from where he'd rubbed his head against the couch while he slept. Her fingers prickled with the memory of raking through that soft, thick hair of his, and an urge seized her to lean forward and tangle her fingers in his hair.

It was amazing how many things became possible in the dark and quiet of the night.

111

Before she quite knew what she was doing, she tilted onto her palms, crawling forward on the couch. She perched over Norm, her arms braced against the couch, her face inches from his.

Leaning forward, she feathered the ghost of a kiss over his cheek, the stubble on his face tickling against her lips. She remembered how tender and soft his lips were from their last kiss but she had never noticed before how nicely shaped his mouth was. His lower lip was slightly full without being too large, his upper lip a small but perfectly shaped Cupid's bow. No fair a man being so sweet and such a good kisser. No fair at all.

She wet her lips then dipped her head and brushed her mouth against his.

It was the barest touch, a mere tingle against the skin of her mouth to tell her she'd made contact at all. Yet a strong surge of emotion exploded inside her, spreading from the epicenter of her mouth.

He flinched beneath her, startling awake, his eyes snapping open to lock on hers. She froze above him but didn't move away. Her breath sounded quick, shallow to her own ears. "Norm." The word was the barest gasp from her mouth, the breath of a plea.

He searched her face, his brows drawing together in a small frown, a grimace almost of pain. "What are you doing?"

In answer, she brushed her mouth over his again, gentle and testing, more an insinuation of a kiss.

His hand came up, cradling her face, his fingers grazing over the skin of her cheekbone, making her shiver. He pushed up, rising to her mouth but stopping short of returning her kiss. "You're driving me crazy," he murmured, close enough so she could feel his lips moving against hers. "Lucy, what do you want from me? I'm getting whiplash here."

The vibrato of pain in his voice nicked at her. What must these past weeks have felt like from his perspective? Mixed signals. Mind games? She leaned back but traced the line of his jaw, the pad of her thumb rasping against his stubble. "I've really screwed this up, huh?"

He tipped his head to the side, encouraging without committing to anything.

She moved farther away, her knees brushing his thighs. He draped his arms across the back of the couch, and his hands clenched in the loose fabric there. Maybe to keep himself from reaching for her?

She raked her fingers through her hair, confused and frustrated. "Maybe this can be like the kiss. Scratch the itch. Satisfy our curiosity. Get it out of our systems?"

"I didn't get it out of my system with the kiss." He sounded wistful.

Lucy sighed. "Jezebel's means a lot to me, Norm. It's not just a job. I don't want to jeopardize that. That's why I've been blowing so hot and cold. But I am crazy about you." She met his gaze finally, willing him to believe her, to see her sincerity. Yet, even as she said the words, her gut clenched with dread. "But we shouldn't risk our jobs for a fling. However hot our chemistry is."

He tipped forward, sitting up on the couch to thread his fingers into her hair.

I should leave. Stick to the avoidance strategy. But his body was warm and hard and right there. *I should leave.* But she only leaned into his touch.

113

"Right," he said with brisk, business-like efficiency. "I don't want a *fling*. I want the whole hog."

"Am I *the hog* in this scenario?"

His face softened, and he nibbled gently at her jaw, working his way toward her ear. He nipped her earlobe and made her shiver. "I want to really be with you, Lucy. Dating. Romance. The whole--everything." He sat back, and cradled her face in both his hands, like Indiana Jones with the Holy Grail. His brown eyes bored into hers, darkening to a burnt toffee as his voice lowered with desire. "And, for the record, I'd risk a lot more than my stupid job for a chance to be close to you." He peeled back her shirt, which was already pretty low cut, and pressed his mouth against her neck, biting softly.

"More?" She tilted her neck to give him better access.

"Much more?" he murmured, sounding like he was willing to haggle or something.

Laughing, she yanked him away from her neck by a fistful of his hair. She narrowed her eyes at him, ruthless now. "How much?"

He pushed the puppy dogs eyes onto full Pitiful Mode, clearly trying to scam her. "Lots?"

"Can you quantify that more specifically?" She lifted her legs, moving to straddle his lap.

His hands slipped to her waist, tugging her closer, pushing at the hem of her shirt until his fingers tickled against her bare stomach. "I'd risk my entire comic book collection."

"Hmmm…"

"And my TaunTaun sleeping bag."

She bit her lip to keep from smiling. "Huh."

His hands slid from her waist to cradle her shoulder blades, tugging her closer to him. He nuzzled under her chin, the softness of his hair dusting at her skin. "And my heart."

She eased back to gape at him with a small "Wow," of astonishment. Then she tipped her head to the side and shook it. "Corny, Norman." She leaned close, wrapping her arms around his neck, yanking him nearer. "Cute but, *tch*, a leetle corny."

"Did it work anyway?"

"OK." She swallowed, equal parts nervous and excited.

"OK as in yes?"

"Yes," she whispered. Then, as his tentative smile blossomed into a goofy grin, she yelled, "Yes!" and kissed him hard on the mouth.

He kissed her back, the wicked stroke of his tongue coaxing a moan out of her against her will. Slowly, he bent her back across the couch, the weight of his body covering her in the most delicious way. She let her legs fall wide so he could fit closer to her. He got the memo, and pushed her deeper into the couch, his erection pressing against her through their clothes. She arched against that hardness, her panties already wet.

The hollering from inside her rib cage began again. *I want him.* All of him. Everywhere. *Now.* She peeled off his Jezebel's shirt and threw that over her head. The Batman shirt went next, her fingers clawing for the hem, and she ruthlessly dragged that over his head, tugging hard when it got stuck. That garment too flew over the side of the couch until she had access to his bare skin.

115

His body was beautiful, slim and long, all the lines of his muscles well-defined and hard beneath her fingers without being bulky. "You've been holding out on me, hiding this body under baggy t-shirts. *Tsk tsk.*"

"I was on the swim team in high school. I like to do laps." His voice had become a tight gasp, like he had to force the words out, and she smirked to hear such a palpable sign of his arousal. She kissed his mouth again, digging her fingers into his hair, holding his head to keep his lips fastened to hers while she sucked and nibbled and tasted him.

He moaned and stroked up her stomach under the hem of her shirt, tickling over her rib cage until at last he moved to fondle her breast through the bra.

Her face heated. He had to realize it was padded. Yet he made no complaints as he deftly kneaded and stroked her over the bra, her nipples pebbling in arousal. Obviously, her Norm was a man who knew how to handle a breast. Not one of those boob squeezers who liked to honk a woman's chest like breasts were bicycle horns.

He eased away from her kiss and tugged gently at her shirt. "May I?"

In answer, she whipped her own shirt over her head, tossing it to pile with his clothes somewhere on the other side of the coffee table. Being so exposed, Lucy prickled with nervous tension, a thousand hot, tiny pinpricks. Swallowing her nerves, she sat up and undid her own bra. She let the garment slowly fall away.

Pushing him onto his back again, she climbed on top. As she straddled his lap his taut, gorgeous body pressed to hers, hard against soft, and a particularly insistent thread of desire would all through her. The heat and wetness between her legs pulsed with need. Trying to ease some of that urgency, she rocked against him, rubbing her core against the bulge in his jeans. He closed his eyes and bit his lip, his head falling back as she moved against him. "God, *Lucy.*" His voice was strained, inarticulate with need. And for a man of words like Norm that was high compliment indeed.

She pushed him deeper into the couch, rubbing and rocking against him through the layers of their clothing. What was it about fooling around with clothes on that made the activity extra naughty, extra exciting? He put one hand behind her back, angling her down and leaning up himself to suck one of her nipples into his mouth. She groaned and gripped his head, holding him to her breast. He licked and sucked then rolled her nipple lightly between his teeth, making her cry out in pleasure at the sweet pain. "*Fuck.* That feels good."

Her panties were thoroughly soaked, the heat between her legs a steady throbbing, as regular and insistent as her heartbeat, but aching and empty. Her skin itched; her veins crackled with light, sparking between her eyes, and she increased her rhythm, grinding against him rough and fast. He increased the pressure with his mouth. Her own movements and the sweet scrape of his teeth combined to jerk on the thread inside her until it snapped and she shook with the force of her own orgasm.

The world blacked out, and a lovely tremor passed through her, leaving her muscles warm and loose in its wake. She sat there, riding the wave, still straddling him as she rolled through the aftershocks of her climax. She shivered and at last blinked her eyes open. "Damn."

117

He hauled her toward him and kissed her mouth, catching her lower lip and nipping at it gently.

She pushed him tenderly away with one hand poised on his chest. "Want to show me your bedroom?"

His lips spread wide in that charming, bright, utterly a-*dork*-able grin. "Hell yeah."

Chapter Ten

Norm rolled Lucy off himself in one easy motion and shot to his feet, bedroom bound. He tugged her along behind him, her breasts still bare as she laughed and skipped to keep up. Her foot caught on her bag and she knocked it over sideways. In a wonderful show of enthusiasm, she hopped the spilled contents and jogged to follow him.

Unable to resist her, he pushed her against the hallway wall, covering her mouth in a kiss, sinking his tongue into the sweetness of her mouth. She moaned, her tongue massaging against his, and arched so her peaked nipples brushed his chest. His dick twitched in appreciation, painfully hard after the bout of dry humping on the couch.

He eased away from the wall, kissing her hungrily, walking backwards and praying he didn't fall as they stumbled together toward his bedroom. He kicked his door open and, mouth and tongue firmly twined with Lucy's, he pushed her down so she fell onto his mattress, all her delightful curves bouncing. He reached behind to flip the light switch up.

"Are you leaving those on?" she asked.

"All the better to see you with, my dear." He stood, hovering at the edge of the bed, his leg between her knees, and admired her for a heart-stopping moment. Her body was slim but soft, her breasts rosy-tipped, the perfect handful each. She propped herself on her elbows and bit her lip, shooting him a naughty glance from under her lashes. Then, ever so slowly, she slid her hands down her body, over her breasts, along her rib cage then finally all the way to the waistband of her sweats. Norm tensed, catching his breath, just watching, his dick throbbing with wanting her.

She slid sweats and underwear off together at the same time, slowly down her legs until the garments were a pool of fabric at his feet. He stayed frozen in place as she sat all the way up, her face eye level with his torso and slowly fumbled with his belt buckle. He closed his eyes, tilting his head back, trying to focus as singly as he could on the sensation of Lucy's hands working at the button on his pants. She slid his zipper down, peeling the fabric back and over his hips then hooking her fingers into the elastic of his boxers. Carefully, she tugged the underwear over his hips, his erection springing free as the material dropped away.

He opened his eyes and stared at her for a long, incredulous minute as the boxers fell. Lucy. Naked. In his bed. He swallowed again as the sweet ache in his chest spread until his body trembled. She gave him the small, wicked smirk again and curled her fingers around his cock, stroking until he had to bat her hands away or risk coming right then and there.

He leaned down to kiss her on the mouth. "Hold that thought." Naked, he sprinted into the bathroom to fish a condom out of the jar they kept on the counter by the hand soap. Rubber in hand, he took one step toward the bedroom, hesitated, then reached back and grabbed a handful of condoms instead of just the one. Norm was nothing if not an optimist.

He bolted to the bedroom and dropped his stash on the bedside table.

Lucy laughed. "Ambitious."

"Hell, yes." He plucked a condom free of the pile, tore the foil and hurriedly spread its length over himself. He surged toward the bed then stopped as he noticed Lucy still had her socks on. He pointed imperiously. "Those. Off. I can't do this with Albert watching me."

She giggled and did as ordered, peeling her Einstein socks over her feet and tossing poor Albert away. Norm removed his own sensible white socks at the same time, idly hoping his feet didn't stink.

And then his mind was blanked out of all considerations but Lucy. He climbed onto the bed, moving to hover over her, propping himself on his elbows. She let her legs fall open beneath him, her face soft, her eyes heavy-lidded with arousal. He bent to taste her lips then eased away only far enough to say, "You're beautiful, Lucy."

Her skin flushed, a pretty rose tinting her complexion, and he skimmed his hand down the silk of her skin to cup her pussy. "Ready?" She nodded, and he parted her folds to slide a finger into her. She was gratifyingly wet already so he slid his finger out and away. She gasped as he nudged the tip of himself inside her. Groaning, he hesitated a brief moment, but she bit her lip

121

and arched to force more of him inside herself. "Norm," she whispered.

He complied to the plea in her voice and, in one smooth stroke, pushed all the way into her, a moan of pleasure breaking from his throat. *Perfect.* Being inside her, surrounded by her, was nearly enough to make him come his brains out right there. He stayed still for a moment, savoring the feel of her, not just where they were joined, but where their bodies pressed together. She slid her tongue in his mouth, insistent, roughly passionate, and he began to move, easing in and out, the friction of their bodies together making his veins crackle.

She moaned and writhed underneath him, pressing toward him, pushing her back off the bed, doing things with her hips that tugged insistently on his own pleasure, coaxing a swirling flurry of sensation from inside him. Her legs wrapped around his hips, and she dug the heels of her feet into his ass, drawing him in deeper.

He increased his tempo, rolling his hips against her, thrusting in and out hard enough that his headboard thumped rhythmically against the wall. Her eyes squeezed closed as she moaned, low and loud. Her face became a study in ecstasy he couldn't tear his eyes away from, a portrait of beauty he wanted to memorize, to sear into his brain so he'd never, never forget the look of passion on her, the pleasure he was giving her with his body.

She tensed beneath him, her breath catching. Her body twisted and writhed beneath him in, apparently, her second orgasm of the night. He pinned her hips to the bed with his hands and pounded into her as she continued to shudder beneath him. His own body was coiled, everything in him taut and straining until at last he broke and really did come his brains out inside her. He collapsed, too drained even to support himself, idly hoping he hadn't squash her.

Her hands hugged his waist, wrapping him in a firm hug. She dropped a kiss onto his ear and rubbed her cheek against the top of his head. He closed his eyes, his heart swelling with a pleasant ache at these small gestures of affection. Finally, she bucked beneath him, which he took as code for "Now, you're squashing me, bub." He eased off her but didn't pull out; he liked being inside her too much.

She kissed the tip of his too long nose. "You fuck like a champion."

He propped himself on one elbow and used his other hand to pluck a tendril of hair from her face. "I aim to please. Or I guess I fuck to please. Or am pleased to fuck. Or something."

She giggled then tugged him closer for a quick, smacking kiss. He rolled off her and disposed of the condom while she tiptoed to the bathroom. While she was gone, he flopped stomach down on the bed, burying his face in the pillow which now smelled like Lucy. Soft, sweet, beautiful, sexy, delicious Lucy. He stretched, all his muscles warm and loose after this, the best sex of his life. The best sex of his life, and he'd been with Lucy. *Lucy*. He laughed and shook his head, still half-worried he'd wake up to find this had all been one fantastic, Technicolor, 3-D wonderland of a wet dream.

But then Lucy bounced onto the bed and crawled over him, falling against his body so the softness of her front pressed all along the contours of his back.

"Are you a blanket?" he asked over his shoulder, conversationally.

"I can be." She nuzzled at his skin, her hair tickling along his spine and making him shiver with happiness. *Lucy. Lucy.* Her name was an ecstatic song, zipping down his veins, echoing in his heart. "Luce" meant light, and Lucy had brightness and beauty enough to light the whole world with.

She pressed another kiss to the skin of his shoulder then smoothed her palm softly over the spot like she was rubbing it in. "You're amazing, you know?"

Some tremor in her voice, a hint of fragility, made him roll over and draw her into the nook of his shoulder. "You OK?"

"I'm just worried about how we can hide this at work."

At her words, ice water trickled into his veins. "Do we have to hide it?"

"For now." She looked over, probably because of the way he'd tensed against her as the warm afterglow leached out of him. "Oh, Norm, only at work. I promise. I don't want to hide you, but I don't want Hank to know and fire us."

"What's the deal with you and Hank anyway?" He stroked her arm, staring at the delicate lines of her collarbone because he couldn't bear to watch her face.

"Hank and I are friends. Always have been. Always will be."

"But…"

"But?" Her cheeks were pink, flushed from the sex, and her mouth was a ripe cherry, lips swollen from his kisses. Hard to believe in that moment that there could be anyone else.

He threaded his fingers into her hair, his stomach fisting into lumps as he tried to articulate his worries. "He doesn't treat you like the other shot girls. Doesn't talk to you the same way. He's warmer. More affectionate."

As she dipped her head, avoiding eye contact, his stomach gave a sickening swoop.

She wet her lips and began speaking, the words tumbling from her in fits and starts. "Hank and I have a long history. I...I was having a hard time after high school. I was suddenly all on my own trying to support myself, and I'd never even had a job."

What could have happened to throw Lucy alone into the world like that? What happened to your family? But, clearly, since she hadn't gone into that, the topic was not up for discussion tonight.

She folded her arms on his stomach and rested her chin on one forearm, her side pressed all along Norm's side in a closeness that was pure comfort to him during this difficult conversation. "So," she continued, "I was twenty-one with no job experience, no degree and no real skills. I met Hank right about that time. He--" She broke off and her gaze darted to meet Norm's before dropping away. "He had a younger sister. She died a few months before he met me. I think...I think he started taking care of me, helping me, because he couldn't save her, you know?"

"How'd she die?" he asked, keeping his voice soft, gentle.

"Cancer. We met at a support group." She bit her bottom lip, letting out a shuddering breath before she met

125

his gaze square on, hurriedly riding over any questions he might have asked her about cancer support groups. "Hank's become my family, Norm. He took me to live with his aunt until I could afford a place and gave me the shot girl job when I was old enough. He helped me so I could find my feet again. He saved me. I can't even imagine where I would be if I'd never met him."

Pure love resonated in her voice, and admiration and pride, and it stung to have her talk so warmly about another man--*a, let's face it, much more attractive man*--right after Norm had been with her. Hank clearly had a powerful hold on her heart. Even if their relationship was as platonic as she said, Norm might have difficulty competing with that kind of history.

He traced the lines of her face, her high cheekbones, the swell of her lip, the tiny beauty mark that always tempted him to kiss her. "If he's your family, why can't you tell him about us? Doesn't he want you to be happy?"

She let out a noise halfway between a grunt and groan then studied Norm from under her lashes, somehow shy and apologetic. "He never likes the guys I date. He *really* won't like me dating a bouncer. Hank didn't make that rule to be a sadist." She cradled his cheek, and he instinctively tilted his head, like a house cat butting into someone's hand, begging to be petted.

She continued as her thumb traced circles along the stubble on his face, "A few years ago the rules were more lax, and he let a shot girl date a bouncer. A customer grabbed her ass one night. It wasn't even a particularly heinous grope, but her boyfriend the bouncer lost his shit and beat the hell out of the guy before Hank and the others could pull him off. The customer sued and Hank

126

nearly lost the bar. He doesn't want a repeat of that ever again so he asks people to find their romance outside work. I mean, Hank nearly lost everything because of a jealous boyfriend. Considering what we deal with, asking people not to date each other at the bar is totally reasonable."

With all of Lucy's beautiful, warm nakedness against him the rule sounded pretty fucking unreasonable to Norm. He caught the hand touching his face and lifted her fingers away, clutching them gently. "You agree with Hank, but you want to date me on the down-low?"

She shifted closer, her breasts rubbing against his chest in a way he would have appreciated much more before this whole conversation began. "Yes. Because I know you can control yourself if you see someone groping me. And I know you won't mind keeping this a secret, just for a little while?"

"OK." Even as he agreed, his whole body prickled with stinging, nervous adrenaline.

Is this a bad idea? He'd never had a secret relationship before and didn't particularly want one now, but the lying would only be when they were at the bar. And, if this was the only way to have Lucy…He coaxed her close for a kiss, tasting her with a fierce desperation as he tried to remind himself why he was agreeing to this disastrous plan. As she kissed him back, her hair tumbling in a sleek fall of gold, the idea seemed slightly less problematic.

"Do you have to be anywhere today before work?" She raised one eyebrow in wicked invitation.

Today was--well, now it was past five a.m., today was Friday. Which meant he didn't have work until seven p.m. He had to buy groceries, but, if Lucy was suggesting what

127

he thought she was suggesting, he could put that off. Who needs food? "I don't have to go anywhere until I clock in at seven."

She climbed onto him, tangling her legs with his and rubbing his calf with the arch of her foot. "Do you have any reason to get out of this bed before then?"

In answer, he rolled to pin her beneath him. "No, ma'am."

Chapter Eleven

After two more rounds of deliciously athletic sex, Lucy conked out and Norm soon followed her. They slept twined together until the early afternoon. He woke first and left her curled in his bed, her hair like a spill of sunlight on his pillow, the curves of her body lush and edible-looking all tangled in his sheets.

He slipped on his boxers and padded to the kitchen, his stomach howling for food after so many hours of such intense--and damned fantastic--physical exertion. Lucy was small, but she had the sexual appetite of a bull elephant.

As Norm popped open the fridge to forage for a snack, he waved hello to Zack. Gradually, Norm became aware of Zack's fixed and incredulous gaze. Irritated, Norm glanced away from the fridge. "*What?*"

"Were you mauled on your way home from work?"

"Huh?"

"Your *neck*, man."

Norm patted self-consciously at his neck then grinned in memory of Lucy's hot, sweet mouth on the skin there, nipping and biting. *I must have a hickey. A hickey from Lucy.*

Now Zack was grinning too. "I wondered when I came home and found that." He jerked his chin toward the dining room, and Norm craned over to see Lucy's

129

Supergirl costume draped neatly over the back of one of their chairs.

Zack was still smirking, highly amused and ironic. "Is Batgirl coming by later for a threesome? Can I get in on it?"

"Zack."

"Did she show you her secret identity?"

"*Zack*--"

"Bates, please, tell me you didn't nail the redhead because if you *did* I may expire from jealousy."

"He didn't nail the redhead."

Norm froze and even Zack tensed beside him at the sound of Lucy's voice. Norm slowly twisted, Zack mirroring him, to face her in the kitchen doorway.

She was delectable, her hair mussed with sleep, her face fresh-scrubbed and prettily pink. She'd thrown on his Batman shirt from yesterday and a pair of his boxers which left a lot of her long, lovely legs bare. Amazing a woman so short could have such killer legs.

One corner of her mouth curled with mischief as she met Norm's eyes, and, just like that, he was hard again. He turned toward Zack. "Zack, don't you have an elsewhere to be?"

Zack, fortunately as quick as he was obnoxious, edged away. "Yeah." He scraped his keys off the kitchen counter and bounded past Lucy. He paused in the doorway and extended his hand. "I'm the roommate. Zack."

"I'm the superhero. Lucy."

"Pleasure." Zack pumped her hand once, quickly, then dropped it and jogged for the front door. He paused on the threshold to toss off a quick salute to Norm. Then he faced Lucy and, beaming like the handsome village idiot, said, "You make sure to get your money's worth out of him, Lucy. Even if it takes all day. We run a first-rate establishment here Satisfaction guaranteed." With that, he slammed the door and locked them in.

Norm shook his head, dropping his forehead to press it against the refrigerator. "Sorry about that. He pays half the rent so I have to let him into the apartment. Even if he isn't house-broken."

Lucy let out a gurgle of laughter. "Do I get breakfast with my sexual ravishing, or is that extra?"

He grabbed her for a hug, propping his chin on top of her head, the fruity smell off her hair like ambrosia. "Angel, you get whatever you want."

"Pancakes?" she asked with a high, wistful note in her voice.

"Done."

"Did he call you 'Bates'?"

Norm rolled his eyes. "An affectionate nickname. Ever see *Psycho*?"

She winced. "Ah."

"Good morning, by the way."

"Morning." Her voice sounded soft, kind of shy. She tucked herself closer to his body, her arms twining around his waist.

He tucked his hand under her chin then gently tipped her face up. He wet his lips, nervous. "Any regrets?"

She looked up at once, her eyes shining with happiness. "No regrets. Of any kind."

He let his breath out and dropped a kiss on her lips. He'd meant the contact to be brief, chaste even, but she

131

opened her mouth against his, and he found himself falling into her, backing her against the fridge.

When he briefly came up for air, she gave him a little push. "Nuh-uh, babe. You promised me pancakes."

He stole one more kiss then eased away from her. "Fair enough." Reluctantly, he set about assembling everything he would need for pancakes: box of mix from the cabinets, eggs and milk from the fridge, vegetable oil, a bowl, a spoon, and a skillet from the drawer beneath their oven. And, his secret weapon, the small brown bottle of vanilla extract.

As he assembled all these ingredients on the counter, he happened to glance over at her. Her arms were folded over her chest, her mouth pursed. Both expressions suggested to him a fairly hostile attitude for someone about to get a homemade breakfast. "Make a lot of pancakes for overnight guests?" she asked.

He froze, squinting his eyes in concentration as his brain fumbled for the best answer to this decidedly perilous question. "Noooo. Zack does. Not me. I *never* make pancakes." He dropped the pancake mix and crossed to her, caressing her hair. "I've been saving all my pancakes for you."

She giggled and dropped her forehead to his chest. "I haven't had *pancakes* in awhile either."

He laughed, cheered by this information, and gave her another squeeze which crushed all the softness of her against him in the most enjoyable of ways. Forcing himself to let go, he resumed the all important task of pancake preparation.

She retreated to the "dining room," sliding out a chair and sitting cross-legged with her legs all contorted to fit on the seat.

When he had a platter full of golden brown pancakes he set them, the syrup, and two plates with silverware on the table. "Milk or O.J.?"

"O.J., please."

He poured two tall glasses of orange juice and finally slid into his own seat at the table.

She was slowly twirling her glass in circles, studying the condensation rings on the wood. "*Zack* has lots of lady friends?"

Tugging her fingers away from the glass, he squeezed her hand. "Zack has lots of lady friends. And me? I have none. Zero. Zilch. I was contemplating the monastery before you came along."

She poked him. "Well, now you have one."

"And I am a one lady friend kind of man. Especially after she's had my pancakes."

Lucy, apparently satisfied at last on the lady friend question, scooped a bite of pancakes onto her fork. "And they are quite good pancakes." She winked and finally tried his *other* pancakes. Chewing, she made a small hum of pleasure in the back of her throat. After she'd swallowed, she gaped at him. "How'd you get so good at making these?"

"I used to cook them for my younger brothers on the weekends. My parents would bribe me with cash to do it so they could sleep in." *My* dad *would bribe me so we wouldn't bother him.* Irritation at this remembered neglect flared briefly inside him, but he pushed the feeling aside, shoveling up another warm bite of pancake. He had no

133

taste for contemplating his dad that morning. Not with Lucy glowing so beautifully in front of him.

"That pancake thing's pretty smart." She poured about a gallon of syrup then spread it on the pancakes with her fork. *Hell of a sweet tooth.* The slow, graceful motions of her fingers made Norm formulate several interesting ideas for what else one could do with maple syrup. Later.

He reached for the butter, to keep himself from reaching for Lucy. "Yeah, but that's probably why I ended up with one brother who's more than a decade younger than me. Tommy turned twelve this year."

"Do your parents live in SoCal?"

"Yup. They're in the house I grew up in, over in Santa Clarita." He forked up a mouthful of pancakes and jerked his chin toward her. "What about you? Your family from around here?"

Her face immediately fell; somehow he had managed to ask the wrong question. With a pang, he remembered her subtle allusions to being all alone from the night before. And cancer support groups.

He dropped his fork with a clatter against his plate and reached for her hand. "Never mind. You don't have to tell me." All that lovely, golden warmth and happiness, and he'd managed to eradicate it with one question. That took skill. "Lucy?"

She poked at the spongy tops of her pancakes, spearing them with her fork, then examining the holes like she was some kind of hole-y pancake inspector. At last, she sucked in a breath and met his gaze. "My mom left when I was a kid, and my dad raised me. He passed away a few years ago."

Norm cleared his throat, taking a stab in the dark. "Cancer?"

She nodded once, stiffly.

He sat there for a long minute, tongue-tied. "I'm sorry, Lucy." Judging by the raw pain etched into her face, "a few years ago" probably meant within the last two to three years. Right before she turned twenty-one, for example? More pieces of her past slotted into place for him, and his heart ached for her.

She continued poking at her pancakes, even taking a mouthful and chewing mechanically, but clearly her heart wasn't in it. Working his way through his own stack, he still kept an eye on her. The sad, shuttered look on her face made morbid curiosity scratch away at him. Exactly how long ago had her dad passed away? And how soon after that earth-shattering event had she met Hank and adopted him as her new family?

After a few more half-hearted bites, Lucy rallied and glanced at him, smiling shakily. Her expression wasn't convincing, but the *effort* was sincere if not the emotion, so he let it slide. "So, how many siblings do you have?"

Unfortunately, he had a mouth full of sticky, buttery pancake when she opened this so-promising conversational gambit. Chewing swiftly, he clasped his fork between thumb and pointer finger and held the other three fingers up as he swallowed. "Three younger brothers," he got out at last. "The other two, Truman and Hunter, are closer to me in age."

She cocked her head to the side, startled. "Norman, Truman, Hunter and...*Tommy*?"

"My parents named us after the male founders of the New Journalism literary movement from the sixties and

135

seventies." His voice came out a low, mechanical drone. This explanation he had made many a time before, and, surprisingly, it never got more exciting for him. "It was my dad's idea."

"Ah. You come from a family of literature geeks. It's genetic."

"Seems like."

"So, Truman is after Truman Capote? Hunter for Hunter S. Thompson? Norman for..."

He sucked in a breath, his insides knotting. If Batman's identity was an automatic panty-dropper, then Norm's namesake was whatever the opposite of that was. Panty-upper? Other lady friends had not handled this revelation well. Hysterical laughing. Mockery. Abject horror. Letting his breath out on a long sigh, shoulders tense, he murmured, "Norman Mailer." As soon as the words left his mouth, he leaned forward to watch Lucy's reaction...

Which was to fork up another mouthful of pancake and turn to him with interest before taking the bite. "Huh. And Tommy? How'd he get so lucky to have a normal name?"

Relaxing into his seat now the horrible truth was out-- and it hadn't been so horrible--he set his fork down, clasping his hands. "The only one left from New Journalism was Tom Wolfe."

"Four boys." She whistled. "Have your parents heard of that crazy, new-fangled thing called birth control?"

"They were both only children growing up, lonely, so they wanted a big family." He remained unsure where he himself stood on the Kids Question. He wanted some, but four, he knew from personal experience--especially any poor schmucks cursed with four *boys*--could be a bit excessive.

"Then I can see where they're coming from, I guess." She shook her head. "That's one of those typical grass is greener kind of things, isn't it? People from small families want huge ones. People from huge families want small ones."

"I guess." He didn't have to think hard to guess which kind Lucy had come from, or which kind she wanted. *Or has made for herself.* The crew of Jezebel's flashed into his mind.

"Hey." Her slow drawl made him glance over. She tossed the hair out of her face, narrowing her eyes in a way that would have had him blushing if it hadn't made him so horny. She crooked one finger, beckoning him to her with a glint in her eyes. "Come here. Zack's right. I want to get my *full* money's worth."

Clearly, the time for pancakes had passed.

"Satisfaction guaranteed." In one smooth move, he scooped her up by the waist and settled her over his shoulder. She squealed adorably and giggled, a featherweight of delectable squishiness pressing into his shoulder as he bounded to the bedroom.

"This is really sexy, by the way," she said in a conversational tone.

His insides warmed. He knew he wasn't much to look at, but he *could* carry a woman to his bed. He even knew what to do with her once he got her there.

He lifted her off his shoulder and tossed her on the bed so she bounced high once then plopped spread eagled on his mattress. He yanked the borrowed boxers off her then tugged the Batman t-shirt over her head, loving the way her golden hair cascaded free from the t-shirt neck. Mostly, though, loving that he had her beautiful body in his bed.

She pulled him to her by the elastic waist of his boxers. "You won't be needing these. Today is a day for nakedness." She tugged them down with one efficient yank and Norm covered her with his body, falling into her warmth.

And he did his level best over the next several hours to make sure she did, indeed, get her imaginary money's worth out of him. And to make sure she forgot, at least for a short while, all the things that had made her so wistful at the breakfast table.

Chapter Twelve

Lucy was pleased to find Norm was as inventive a lover as he was inventive at creating horrible pick-up lines. While basking in the afterglow of another mind-blowing round of sex, a sense of utter rightness settled over her, like concrete hardening into a sidewalk. *I'm glad I did this.* She'd been half-asleep and maybe slightly crazy with lust when she'd propositioned him, but, come what may at work with Hank, she didn't--*couldn't* regret spending this time with Norm.

He'd stretched out on the bed and she'd draped her legs over him and snuggled her chest against his arm. She traced one fingertip down his long nose, and his mouth curled up.

He appeared impossibly tall all stretched out on the bed beneath her, his body long and taut and delicious with the finely etched lines of his swimming muscles. He occupied so much more space than her, and an absurd sense of accomplishment spread through her--that she had so thoroughly loved such a very big man. For all the world like she'd climbed Everest or something.

His hands traced her legs to her feet and he bent upwards, examining her toes as his magic fingers kneaded out the knots her superhero boots had left. She flopped

139

onto the mattress, humming with pleasure at his caresses. Good hands. Great lips. Great…everything.

His fingers tickled, running over the tops of her toes, and she instinctively bucked away, but he held her foot firmly, capturing it.

"You have weird toes," he remarked, not tickling anymore but gently pressing his thumb into her heel, making her want to keel over and drool with pleasure.

"What's wrong with my toes?" she asked lightly, too blissed out to be offended.

"They're tiny mousey toes. Here." The bed creaked as he lifted one of his lengthy, hairy legs high to present her with a better view of his oversized feet and toes.

She glanced indifferently at his toes, then fell onto the mattress, her body sated, her mind half-foggy with sleep. "They're toes, Norman. What? It's not like I have an extra one."

"Well, no, but most people, their second toe is longer than their big toe. Not yours. Your toes all line up in a nice diagonal. And they're so little."

She pushed onto one elbow and gave him a narrow-eyed glare, fighting to keep a straight face. "Do you have a foot fetish I should know about?"

"With feet like these, angel, I might get one."

She kicked her foot free from his grasp and rolled away, giggling. "A guy at the bar once offered me twenty bucks for five minutes of sucking on my toes. With an option to earn more."

"Nasty." He captured her foot again, resuming his massage. "Still, that's not bad money."

She laughed, playing along. "I know. I'm walking on a gold mine, and I didn't even know it." She flexed her toes to demonstrate.

His expression turned mischievous and he took a firmer hold on her foot. "This little piggy--"

"Norm!" She gasped, trying to twist free as he tickled her. Never one to play fair, she slid her hand down to fondle the impressive package between his legs.

He dropped her feet and raised his hands high in surrender. "You fight dirty, lady." He didn't sound too displeased about this revelation, though.

"Hmm. And what about your assets?" She rubbed the length of his rapidly hardening cock. "With endowments like these you could earn a pretty penny too."

He grabbed her shoulders, gathering her to him in a kiss. Her hand stayed pressed between their bodies, and a lovely new erection started, hard and hot against her palm. He hugged her closer until her breasts flattened against his chest, his hair there tickling her skin. As the kiss continued, the stroke of his tongue in her mouth made her body go limp and languid with sudden heat, tension coiling between her legs.

He broke away after a long moment to grin against her mouth, stealing nibbling kisses as he spoke. "Oh, I thought you knew. Zack's my pimp. He's coming back here any minute with your bill." He gripped her ass, holding her against the swell of his newly minted erection. "Don't forget to tip your server."

But just when things were getting *really* promising, he glanced up. "Crap. It's nearly five."

She craned around to see for herself, disappointed and disbelieving. The red numbers on the digital clock

141

glared at her, malevolent and accusatory, the Scarlet Letter of appliances. "Drat."

He kissed her again then rolled off the bed, shuffling through their piled clothes on the floor. "I need to do something about my car. Which I had totally forgotten about until this moment. You are one hell of a distraction, lady." He cast her a steamy glare from under his brows that left her longing to pull all that appetizing man-hunk back into bed with her. She hadn't had sex in a while, and she hadn't had *good* sex in even longer and she'd never had *great* sex--until now.

She slithered to the side of the bed and watched him dress. "I could check under the hood, if you want. I took auto shop, remember?"

"What if what's wrong with my car goes beyond high school auto-shop?"

She pushed herself all the way to a sitting position, and was gratified as Norm's eyes stayed glued to the bounce of her breasts the whole time. "I built a '64 Mustang. I can probably at least get a rough idea what's wrong with your car. Now that it's not four a.m. and pitch dark, and now that I'm back to my secret identity."

"*You* built the Mustang?"

She swallowed, uneasy as memories stirred. "Yeah. With my dad."

"Oh." Norm's face became carefully blank, and she didn't know whether to be gratified or annoyed.

Nettled, she plucked the Batman t-shirt out of his hands and slipped it over her own head. She continued the story, determined to show him that she wasn't the fragile buttercup he suspected her of being. "One summer he bought a body kit and we built the car from the ground up.

Bumper to tail lights. He knew I liked building things, I never had enough projects to keep me busy over the summer, and he wanted to get me a car. So: build my own car."

"Perfect solution."

"But we didn't exactly know what we were doing so, in consequence, the old girl has broken down a lot. Fixing her was fun--"

Norm scoffed out a laugh.

"*So*, over the years I got more and more into cars in general. I have become *intimately* acquainted with everything that can and will go wrong with an automobile. Your crappy old Toyota—"

"*Hey.*"

"--should be a piece of cake."

"OK." He raised an eyebrow, and tugged at the collar of the Batman shirt, his knuckles brushing the sensitive skin of her throat. "Do I get my shirt back?"

"Nope. I'm stealing this shirt to forever remind me of the night I stole your virtue."

"*Tch.* You don't fool me. You just want to run around town fighting crime dressed as a giant bat." He crossed to his dresser and slipped on a fresh gray shirt. When he wheeled back, she dropped her eyes to read the writing on the front: *SAVE THE CLOCK TOWER, The Hill Valley Preservation Society.* At sight of the *Back to the Future* reference she let out a squeal of fan-girlish delight.

She sidled to the edge of the bed on her knees and yanked him closer by a fistful of his t-shirt. "I might have to steal your virtue again so I can take that shirt too."

143

His hand cradled the back of her head, drawing her forward until his breath stirred against her cheek. "Are you using me for my body or my t-shirt collection?"

"Can't I do both?"

He kissed her again and, quickly enough, they had *both* lost their shirts.

***

They finally managed to haul themselves out of bed after another hour. Lucy slid into her light blue sweats, and nabbed Norm's Batman t-shirt. She didn't pause to examine why.

Norm texted Zack to make sure he could get a ride to work, leaving Lucy free to run home and change, thereby avoiding anything resembling a walk of shame. After all, her battered old sweats and Norm's Batman t-shirt wouldn't exactly rake in the tips. But she hated to leave Norm, hated to leave the intimate bubble they'd created for themselves.

Alone in her car, driving home, her body throbbed with the lack of him, missing his warmth or his solidness or his smell or maybe just the sound of him breathing next to her. Whatever the feeling was, she remained twitchy the whole drive, and it wasn't until she'd parked that she realized she'd never even bothered to flip the radio on. She'd driven the whole way in total silence.

Running a quick shower, she took a moment to safely stow her pilfered Batman shirt. She folded it then hugged the square of fabric to her chest. Dipping her head, she caught that lovely clean scent of Norm's, spicy and male and delicious.

She'd been hugging the t-shirt for five minutes before she snapped out of her trance. Hurriedly, she shoved the garment into her bureau then slammed the drawer closed. *Stupid.* They'd had a marathon bout of, well, frankly fabulous sex but that did *not* mean she had to get all gooey over him. She hadn't even had a real date with him yet.

Nodding sharply at this homegrown wisdom, she stalked away from the bureau and changed into her shot girl uniform--less than ideal for playing mechanic, but she didn't have time to change twice before work. Applying her makeup at record speed, she was out the door in good time to have enough light left to examine Norm's car.

***

"You and Supergirl, huh?"

This was one of the perils of bumming rides from Zack: his incurable nosiness. That and the so-lovely aroma of diesel which permeated every corner of his roommate's battered old Benz. "What can I say? I'm her Kryptonite."

"Come on, Bates, don't hold out."

"A gentleman doesn't kiss and tell."

"Good thing there are none in this car. And you can skip over the kissing part. Tell me about the rest of it."

"All I will say is that I appreciated you double-timing it out of the apartment this morning."

"A man needs privacy to bake pancakes." Zack cleared his throat and darted an uneasy glance at Norm. "So, Bates, your car...do you need me to front you some cash?"

Norm stirred in his seat, restraining a frustrated groan. Yes, he could use another loan, but damned if he'd take anymore of Zack's money. Bad enough Norm hadn't been able to make rent last month, making Zack pay for his car was not in the cards. "No, Zack, I'll ask my dad for help if the repair bill is too much."

145

His roommate winced, shaking his head with startling forcefulness. "*No*, Bates. Then he'll think he owns your ass. He'll make you go back to school. Make you stop writing."

Norm tried to laugh, to seem unconcerned, but his blood still chilled at the idea of giving his dad any kind of power over his life.

Zack's hands were fisted, white-knuckling around the wheel, and his voice was almost shaking with anger on Norm's behalf. "You showed him one story and his criticism was enough to make you quit writing for a *decade--*"

Potboiler trash. Sourness coated Norm's throat at the memory, and his father's voice echoed in his head. *Why are you writing this trash, Norman?* "I was *ten*. He doesn't have that kind of influence over me anymore."

"Give him half a chance and he'll grind you into the spitting image of himself. Look what happened to Truman." For once, Zack's face was set, his grin gone, his voice totally serious. "You're my buddy, Norm. And it's only money."

Norm cleared his throat and glanced away. "Thanks. I'll let you know. But, honestly, for right now I'm OK." He forced a smile onto his face to reassure Zack.

His statement was true after a fashion. Norm would be totally OK--until he saw the mechanic's latest bill for resuscitating his old clunker. Still, even with the money worries and the family worries and everything else on his plate, he wasn't sorry about what had happened with Lucy.

Zack drove into the Jezebel's parking lot. "Ah, Supergirl."

Norm peered eagerly out the window, his eyes gathering in the sight of her to burn away the chill of his discussion with Zack.

Lucy was leaning against her cherry red Mustang, and Norm admired the car with new eyes, knowing Lucy had built and maintained every square inch of that machine with her beautiful hands.

She had on a pair of gray sweats over her Jezebel's short shorts, and--a curl of warmth coiled in his belly--she was wearing the Dickies jacket he'd loaned her over her tank top. He cast a cursory "Thanks" Zack's way and hopped out of the car, Lucy-bound.

As the Benz's engine shut down and a car door slammed, Norm stopped and wheeled. Zack smirked at him from across the top of the Benz, his usual self once more. "I think I'll do some reconnaissance on your bar tonight, Bates."

Norm gaped, horrified. "You're staying?"

"*Hey*." Zack angrily tapped the rusted car top with his keys. "Let's get a little gratitude here for the chauffeur. And don't make it sound like I said I wanted to watch you pee or something. It's a *bar*. I'm already all the way down here. I figure I might as well hang out. I liked it here last time, after all."

The gravel crunching behind him made Norm about-face to see Lucy. She smiled as she approached them, but the expression was stiff, her eyes pinched at the corners. "Hello again, Zack."

Norm cast his roommate a dark glower, trying to psychically project the warning: *Behave.*

147

Zack made a quick, conciliating gesture with his palm. *No worries*. He tipped the brim of an imaginary cowboy hat Lucy's way. "Ma'am."

She snorted at the joke and shook her head. "I'm sorry, but you can't park here. This is only for employees. But it's early enough there might be street parking."

Zack swung his car door open, and some of the tension leaked out of Norm. Zack was great, his best friend, but Zack's sense of humor when it came to Norm and the women he dated could sometimes be…Not helpful, was probably the politest way to phrase it. Cock-blocking might be a bit more on the nose. Zack didn't usually like the girls Norm dated but, God willing, Zack seemed to like Lucy so far.

"Any good restaurants round here?" Zack asked. "It's too early for booze, and I got kicked out of my kitchen today before I could eat." He wiggled his eyebrows at Norm, and Norm rolled his eyes heavenward. "I'll grab dinner somewhere nearby then swing by later for a beer." He wheeled toward Norm in a big, arm-flailing turn. "*OK*, Norman?"

"Yeah. Sorry. Try Dogs of War down the block. Good chili dogs."

"Great." Zack disappeared into his car then popped out again, gazing eagerly back and forth between Norm and Lucy. "Hey, as a friend of the bar, do I get some kind of discount on drinks?"

"I'll talk to the bartenders." Norm waved him off, feeling like every precious moment of his alone-time with Lucy was sliding away, sands through the hour glass or something.

"Thanks for the tip, Bates. See you, Supergirl. Let me know if you need any help saving the world later." With that, Zack at last dove back into the Benz and drove away.

As Zack drove off, Norm sauntered over to Lucy, raking his eyes over her in the Drunken Douchebag leer. "If I had a nickel for every time I saw someone as beautiful as you then, sweetheart, I'd have five cents." He was rewarded for his play-acting when she let out a giggle and stepped closer to him for a quick 'hello' hug. Not as good as a 'hello' kiss, but he would take what he could get.

She jerked her chin at the dust trail left by Zack's exit. "Will he always call me 'Supergirl'?"

"It's a safe assumption. He's been calling me 'Bates' for twelve years."

"He was making Hitchcock references when he was eleven?"

"Ten. Zack had a thing for horror movies. Not Hitchcock specifically, per se." Norm caught her hand and ran his thumb over the soft skin there.

"I suppose I should be grateful he's not calling me *Mrs.* Bates or something."

Norm shuddered. "God, *don't* say that in front of him. Something sick and twisted like that would exactly suit his sense of humor. I'm just glad that nickname hasn't occurred to him yet."

She'd already applied that thick coating of makeup she wore at the bar. Smoky eye shadow fanned out from her eyelids, and she'd done that little tail of eyeliner too, which made the blue of her irises pop beautifully against the paleness of her skin. Her lips were a pouting bright red, and she'd darkened the beauty mark above her mouth that drove him crazy.

149

She looked like a vixen, Marilyn Monroe's kid sister. "You got your war paint back on," he murmured.

She was beautiful, of course, but she always seemed hard-edged to him when she was dressed this way, like she was wearing armor. And since he'd now seen her fresh-scrubbed, her lips plump from his kisses, her hair a tangle on his pillow--it was harder to feel enthusiastic about what he recognized now as her work façade.

Made up or not, Norm's lips tingled with wanting to kiss her and muss that bright, bright red lipstick. He settled for pressing the pad of his thumb gently to her lower lip, brushing over its softness.

She flinched away. "Norm," she said, casting a wary glance toward the back door of the bar.

"Right." He dropped his hand, and tried not to curl into a big ball of pain after she recoiled from him. *I have to remember she won't do that anywhere but at work.* But it was hard to remember when it hurt so much to see her pull away. Harder still to remember why she had to recoil from him at all. Ever. "Sorry. I forgot we're in Undercover Mode." His voice came out stiff, monotone. He cleared his throat.

Brows pulling together in concern, she sighed. "Oh, Norm. It's just that if people see us together they'll figure it out. Hank will figure it out and fire us. Can't you tell when two people have slept together?"

"Honestly, I don't worry about that too much." After having such free access to all of Lucy's sweet self a few hours ago, finding the great wall of China stretching between them, not just cock-blocking but blocking *all* contact, just sucked balls on an epic scale that could be seen from space. He jerked his chin toward his Toyota.

"Want me to pop the hood? I probably need to go in for my shift soon."

Her face fell, and he winced. *I am a total shit.*

She glanced over again, bright eyes lighting her face. "Hey, want to hear my favorite pick-up line?"

Recognizing this as a white flag of truce, he tucked his hands in his pockets and leaned against his poor Toyota. "Sure."

She gave a small toss of her head to tousle her hair then planted her arms akimbo on her hips. Apparently in position, she met his eyes with a piercing bedroom smolder as she purred out, "What winks and fucks like a tiger?"

He blinked, and in the moment it took him to process the question, she began winking, so fast and spasmodically she appeared to be having a seizure. He burst out laughing, both at the joke and her outrageous face. She giggled and the gravel crunched beneath her feet as she picked her way next to him in her heels. Together, they leaned companionably against the car while still leaving enough room for Jesus between them.

He wiped laugh-tears from his eyes. "That *is* a good one. So good, in fact, *I'll* sleep with you." He winked.

She bit back a snicker and shook her head. Then, frowning, she reached up to tug at the collar of his Jezebel's shirt. Her fingers tickling at the back of his neck had him squirming, but this might be the only touching he got all night so he endured. "What are you doing?"

She eased away and batted her eyes. "Checking the tag to see if you were made in heaven, babe."

"Oh, really?"

"Actually, I'm fixing your collar to hide the hickey better."

Just like that his buzz died a quick and violent death. He dodged away from her hands. "Why? The hickey doesn't have 'Made by Lucy York' stamped on it."

She winced and leaned her head against his car, staring at the overcast sky. "Norm, is this going to work?"

It was like someone had transformed his guts to lead. "Lucy?"

"It's just if we fight every time we have to work together..." She didn't finish, didn't seem able to, only turned her head slightly against the car roof to meet his gaze.

Norm rolled his body toward her, but managed to stop himself from reaching for her. "Yes. Lucy. Yes. It'll work. I'm sorry. Going from warm afterglow to cold shoulder was just a little difficult."

Her brows knit together in guilt. "I'm *sorry*--"

"No. It's my fault. Really. You explained last night, and I didn't absorb the information properly, I guess. It's fine. I'm fine. We're fine." And now he couldn't keep from touching her, but he limited himself to a small brush against the fabric of his jacket over her arm.

"OK," her voice was small, sad, but she smiled as she pushed away from the Toyota. She jerked her head toward the car. "Pop the hood for me, I need to check your engine."

"I thought you already did this morning." He winked. "Norman."

He recognized the Stern Face and immediately scrambled to obey because, as he had already learned, you did not fuck with the Stern Face.

She slid the jacket off and tossed it into the backseat of the Mustang. Norm tried not to conflate himself and his jacket; just because she'd so carelessly tossed the one aside didn't mean she'd do the same to the other.

Lucy bent over his car, her head disappearing into the Toyota like a lion-tamer into the man-eater's mouth. "You better go inside. It's almost seven. Leave me your key?"

"All right. Um, the guy last time said he fixed something with the transmission. Maybe check there." He tossed his car key to her, and she caught it one-handed. Norm started inside then whipped back around. "See you after?"

"At the very least I'll have to give you a ride home if I can't get this clunker going."

Running late, he had to be satisfied with that, although her response left a lot to be desired. Besides her.

As he shoved his way through the stubborn bar door, his insides squirmed in uneasiness. He liked Lucy. A lot. And this morning he'd believed their budding romance would weather this work hiccup. *Or maybe it's a* hickey-*up*.

Yet now, hurting after the minor rejections of the parking lot, he wasn't sure how much of this secrecy stuff he could take. Discretion he could get behind, but having Lucy flinch away every time he tried to touch her, having Lucy pretend she didn't like him, pretend she didn't even find him attractive?

How was Norm supposed to deal with that without going crazy?

153

Chapter Thirteen

That whole night at work Lucy felt like a performer in a precarious high wire act, only *she* was the wire, wound too tight between a rock and a hard place, ready to snap at any moment.

In the cool dimness of the bar, surrounded by her friends and under Hank's watchful eye, her glowing certainty of the morning had frozen into a hard lump of dread. So much of her life was wrapped up in this bar, woven through the fabric of Jezebel's. These people were her family, and if she kept going with Norm then she could lose all that, could lose the only family she had left.

Norm was working the patio door, which meant she had to pass by him several times throughout the night. Each time he tried to catch her eye and sneak her secret glances. Instead of calming her, or reassuring her, his actions just stressed her right the fuck out.

Hank was big, not stupid, and connecting the fresh hickey on Norm's neck with Lucy's mouth wouldn't take a genius if Norm kept giving her the bedroom eyes every ten seconds. Finally, fed up, she shot Norm a quick, burning glare and made a small cutting gesture with her hand to say, *Enough, Norman*.

He got the message after that because he stopped making eye contact at all. This was worse for her peace of mind. Before he'd been playful, flirtatious, now he was subdued and looming in the doorway like a stiffed-back Lurch. There had to be some way to balance keeping her job safe and making Norm happy.

And if there isn't? What will you do then? She pushed that thought hurriedly away, even as her stomach writhed.

Later, Ronnie stopped her as she was coming out of the back room with a fresh tray of shots. "Have you seen Eddie? Hank needs him."

Lucy shook her head and tried to move past, but Ronnie blocked her path. "Hey." The redhead jerked her chin in the general direction of the bar proper. "What did he do?"

Lucy blinked in confusion, antsy to be back on the floor making money. "Eddie?"

"The newbie. You've been a total bitch to him all night. What did he do?" Ronnie leaned close, her voice going low in excitement. "And, as your friend, should I be mad at him too?"

Lucy opened her mouth, once, twice, then snapped her lips closed. She sucked at lying. Why did she think this was a good idea? Pushing past the other shot girl, Lucy called casually over her shoulder, "Oh, have I been a bitch? I guess I'll have to watch it tonight. Just that time of the month. Norm didn't do anything." *Except complicate the hell out of my life.*

Ronnie clacked behind her, her heels loud and forceful, like an accusatory cuff to the head. "Yeah but you're only being bitchy to *him*."

Crap. Lucy rushed for the safe anonymity of the crush on the floor and popped onto her tiptoes, teetering precariously in her Come-Fuck-Me Heels. "Oh, Table Five is hollering for blood. Or shots. 'Scuse me." She beat a hasty retreat, nervous sweat pinning her tank to her spine. *Please, God, distract Ronnie with something shiny so she forgets all about me.*

An hour or so passed. After emerging from a particularly generous, and grabby, group of frat boys, Lucy scanned the bar for more prospects then stopped. She found herself awash in gratitude for the speed with which her prayer had been answered. Norm's roommate Zack had one of the corner booths, and Ronnie was crawling over him, giving him shot after shot, making a lot of money and maybe a love connection. Or at least a lust connection.

Zack was tall, dark and well-built. Also ridiculously pretty, which did nothing for Lucy but apparently pushed all of Ronnie's buttons. Lucy frowned as the redhead tossed the third shot in as many minutes down Zack's throat. Their test tubes weren't particularly strong but, at the rate he was going, someone would have to pour him into his car. And then drive the car for him. *Hell.*

Not my problem right now. Norm was a standup guy and had probably kept a weather eye on his inebriated roommate. Her head turned in his direction, but she stopped herself in time. Looking for Norm was inviting trouble, and she didn't need that when she was supposed to be earning her livelihood.

The rest of the night she tried to work the section as far away as possible from Norm. The less contact she had with him, the less chance she had to hurt his feelings. She winced. *The nicest, most wonderful guy I've ever met and, boy, am I fucking things up so far.*

***

When the worst shift of Lucy's life was finally over--and this was even counting the night she'd been propositioned by foot fetish guy--she sat in the back room alone, counting out. As the office door popped open, she jumped in surprise and wasn't very reassured when Hank stepped into the room. "Hey, kid." He perched his large form on the edge of the couch, and she had to tilt back in the office chair to meet his eyes.

"What's up, Hank?"

"The new guy."

"Norm?" She fought an instinctive urge to swallow, but if Hank had caught on, a nervous gulp at this moment would hardly help.

"I noticed you seemed to shut him down tonight. Is he bothering you? Should I talk to him?"

She finally swallowed, but it was a relieved laugh instead of her nervous spit. "Oh no. It's fine. He's harmless, and I'm sure he got the message tonight and won't bother me again. I remember the no dating rule even if he can't. Besides, didn't you see that hickey? Norm's been getting some good lovin' somewhere. He's probably ju--just chatting me up to pass the time. Working the patio door's not very exciting, you know." She clamped her jaw to make herself shut up. If she kept babbling like this she'd give everything away.

Hank gave her a narrow-eyed glare, and she fought to remain absolutely still. Which might have been suspicious, but not as bad as throwing herself on the floor and confessing everything--her first impulse when he gave her

157

the fish eye like this. After a long moment, he eased away and nodded toward her pile of cash on the desk. "You done?"

She entered the last few numbers on her sheet, then handed him the whole pile. "Night, Hank."

"Night, kid. Drive safe."

Her heart squeezed as she stepped out of the office. Hank had been a good boss, but he'd been a good friend to her too. Whether the no dating rule was stupid or not, by violating his rule she knew she'd betrayed Hank's trust.

After changing into her sweats, she grabbed her bag and headed into the bar proper. Eddie, the second newest bouncer, had his head bent low as he chatted to Jenna in a booth while Ben muscled in on their fake-flirting, sleepily resting his bald head on Jenna's shoulder. The brunette shot girl only laughed and glutted on all the male attention.

They signaled Lucy over but she waved and sidestepped them to reach Norm. He was leaning on the long wooden bar next to Zack and talking in a low voice to his roommate. Zack, it seemed, was good and knackered.

Norm glanced over at the sound of her approach. "Oh, hi, Lucy. Thanks for the ride offer, but I need to drive Zack home. Friend of the bar discount did him in. That or all the shots he bought off Ronnie tonight." Norm's voice was pleasant, friendly, and totally distant. Like he was talking to some casual acquaintance he barely knew and not the woman he'd been inside only a few hours ago. The bar was empty except for the trio at the table, Hank in the office, and the last, lone bar-back wiping the counter on the other end of the bar.

"Oh. OK." Lucy sidled closer to Norm and dropped her voice. "I'll follow you home then in my own car?"

Norm didn't glance at her, keeping his gaze focused on Zack as his roommate slowly oozed into an almost liquid state, spreading himself across the bar surface. "Nah. You probably have homework and stuff you have to get to," Norm said, equally low-voiced but in that same oh-so-pleasantly distant tone.

She'd hoped she could make amends for cold shouldering him at work by sleeping on his shoulder that night. Apparently not. "Well, yeah, I have homework but-"

"And I wouldn't want to *bother* you again." His gaze was cool as he met hers.

Crap. Why did the man always have to be within hearing distance when she said stupid shit like that? More than that, why could he never, never see that she didn't mean it? She pressed her hand flat to the bar and leaned close to his ear, quieting her voice to a livid whisper. "You *know* why I said that, and you also know I didn't mean it. And if you *don't* know that after last night then you're an idiot. I'm trying to keep both our jobs safe. What is so wrong about that?" She stepped away, feeling guilty and mad too, but he grabbed her by the elbow.

"*Lucy.*"

The bar-back glanced over, glaring hard at Norm; Eddie and Ben also perked up in their booth, watching this exchange. Lucy flinched, getting some small inkling now why Norm was so hurt. With her disinformation campaign, she was painting him as the bad guy who wouldn't leave her alone. A classification he didn't deserve. She'd started this. She'd pulled the trigger on their relationship, but Norm was getting all the backlash for her choice.

Norm slid the other guys a glance then jerked his head at Zack's sprawling form. "Lucy, could you help me get Zack to his car? I can haul his useless carcass, but if you could manage the coats and keys it'd be a help."

As she bent to scoop the garments up, he leaned in and whispered, "*I'm sorry.*"

"Me too." Lucy nodded and a surreptitious grin flashed over his face, then Norm bent and hauled Zack to his feet, slinging his friend's arm around his shoulder as Norm half-dragged-half-walked him out the bar. She called a goodnight to the others then followed Norm out the front door and down the block. He stopped in front of the old Mercedes Benz which appeared to be held together only by its rust spots and sheer stubbornness.

Lucy had been too distracted with Norm earlier in the evening to notice Zack's car but now, in the gentle glow of moonlight, she realized exactly how big a piece of shit the car was.

Norm must have caught her look because he flipped her an ironic nod. "A classic."

"Oh. Uh-huh," she said with mock brightness.

Norm laughed then gave a small grunt of exertion as he stuffed Zack's body into the backseat and buckled him in. Zack immediately keeled over sideways, stretching out on the seat and humming something under his breath. Norm stepped away and dusted his hands in a gesture of completion. "Well, at least if he yaks we're in his car."

She stood there with him for a moment, popping her ankle in nervousness, a habit she thought she'd kicked in junior high. "Can I come over tonight?"

Norm sighed, which wasn't promising. "Zack's probably about to boot in the backseat, and I'll need to

160

hover over him all night. He can be a pain in the ass but I'd rather not let him die from alcohol poisoning. Casa de Norman won't be too romantic tonight."

She stepped close, brushing his arm, the most intimate gesture she would allow herself this close to Jezebel's. "I don't care. I want to be with you."

Norm hesitated then reached over to cover her hand with his. "OK." He jerked his chin toward the Benz. "Hop in and I'll drive you to your car. Save you the walk."

"All right."

Things were obviously tense between them, but not irreparable. Lucy clung to that hope later as she made the drive to Norm's house, keeping the Benz's taillights in her sight all the way up.

***

Back at his apartment, Lucy helped Norm get Zack's inert body into bed. Norm slapped Zack's cheeks to rouse him. Zack blinked his eyes open and his face split in a sappy drunk's grin. "Buddy. Thanks for the discount." He burped.

"*Zaaack*." Norm reached down and brandished the bucket he kept in the apartment for mopping the floors. A rare instance where his neat-freakishness had come in handy. Norm jerked Zack's face toward him. "*Zack*. I am leaving the bucket right here by the side of the bed. You feel sick: it is Right. Here." Norm gave the plastic bucket a pat then carefully set it within easy reach of the bed.

He made sure Zack was propped on his side and not his back then Norm padded to the kitchen. Lucy already stood there with a collection of stuff gathered in her arms. She held each thing up as she passed it to him. "Gatorade for the dehydration." She'd snagged two bottles, clearly a

161

woman who took her rehydration seriously. "Crackers usually help me with nausea in the morning." The sharp edges of the column of saltines dug into his skin as she pressed the crackers and sports drinks against his chest. "Also, have you guys ever tried taking an extra multi-B vitamin before bed? It helps me." She handed him the vitamins last, pills rattling hollowly as she stuffed the bottle into the crook of his arm.

He gaped at her, astounded by the breadth of her hangover knowledge.

Observing his surprise, she snorted, raising an eyebrow. "I work in a bar, I've had a wild night myself a time or two, and I'm a fallen woman."

"Right." *Duh, Norman.*

"If you can get at least some of that into him before he falls asleep he'll probably feel more human in the morning."

"It *is* morning. And he's already dead to the world. I'll try, though." He slightly lifted his armful of hangover remedies. "Thank you. If you want to, um, crash on my bed that's fine. I'll probably be awake with Zack for a while."

She blinked and a flush fanned across the pale skin of her neck to dot her cheeks. "Oh. Right."

He groaned, tired, achy and more than a little depressed. Their second night together and he was already sending her to bed alone.

She whirled away, her padded feet shushing across his carpet.

Screw it. He dropped his armful of stuff on the kitchen counter and chased after her as the vitamin bottle spun to the floor with a loud clatter. He held her by the forearm and pulled her to him, catching her mouth in a long kiss. She moaned and melted against him, her arms twining around his neck, her body pressing close to his in a way that told him, yes, no matter what she'd said before, the lady definitely was *not* bothered by him. He laughed against her mouth and eased away, bending to press his forehead to hers. "I'm sorry I was a stupid ass at the bar tonight."

"I'm sorry I was an unfeeling bitch."

"Truce?"

"Yes, please."

He trailed his lips down her jaw then lower to the sweet spot on her neck that made her breath hitch when he kissed there. Her fingers dug into his shoulders as he licked then nibbled lightly at the tender skin of her neck.

"We should get you into bed, too," she said, her voice thready and uneven. "Way past your bedtime, isn't it?"

"Will you tuck me in?"

"I'll even help you put on your pajamas."

"And I'll make sure you don't have any." He slanted his mouth against hers again as she gave a breathless laugh. The tip of her tongue licked into his mouth. Only a handful of hours had passed since he'd last been inside her, but even that seemed like too long ago. Still kissing her, he backed her down the hall toward his bedroom, past Zack's door and through his own.

Norm flopped her onto his bed, and was all ready to begin the really fun part, when the sound of retching from next door reached his ears.

"Shit." He let the hem of Lucy's tank fall into place and cast her an apologetic glance. "I have to check on him. I'm sorry." He sank onto the mattress to give her a goodbye kiss, but the sounds from next door got louder, so he sprang away and rushed out.

Zack was indeed having an incident. Fortunately, he was sober enough to get to the bucket in time. Norm waited for him to finish then hoisted Zack up by the elbow, coaxing him toward the bathroom. Norm had expected Lucy to stay safe in the bedroom, but she appeared at Zack's other side, right on the front lines with Norm as they shuffled his roommate off to worship at the shrine of the porcelain god. She helped arrange Zack in a comfortable position against the toilet.

Norm eased away, leaning against the door frame, his face burning with embarrassment. Not exactly the romantic interlude he'd been hoping for. "I'm sorry about all this. I swear, we are not party guys. I think the discounted drinks were just too much of a temptation for him."

Nicola scoffed. "Ronnie more likely. She was bouncing on his lap all night, milking him for every penny he had." She slapped Zack gently on the shoulder. "You poor sap."

Zack moaned. "Never again."

Lucy laughed and Zack's head lolled down, his hair falling into the danger zone. She plucked her hair band free of her ponytail and the golden cascade tumbled over her shoulders. Wrapping the hair band around her wrist, she reached forward and deftly smoothed Zack's overlong, wavy brown hair into a small ponytail at the nape of his neck. Guys never worried about holding each other's hair, but Lucy thought of everything.

Norm writhed against the door, folding and unfolding his arms, unable to find any position that could accommodate the depth of his embarrassment. "I'm sorry about this. You can cut out, Lucy."

"Norm, I work in a bar. I've dealt with this before. Besides, I'm not sure I got my money's worth this morning."

"I can offer you a full refund." Zack half-raised his head, smiling dopily. "Or store credit."

Lucy grinned and shoved his head back down. "Norm will do me fine."

"Yes, I will."

A long beat stretched and the words seemed to echo in the room. Norm slapped a hand over his mouth, his face on fire, actually burning now with his mortification.

Lucy's mouth fell open in an O of pure shock then she burst out laughing. "I can't believe you said that!"

Zack snickered from the toilet, and Norm kicked the bottom of his roommate's foot to shut him up. Shaking his head, Norm held his hands in front him, palms up in supplication. "I'm sorry. You--you bring out the perv in me. Or you slipped me something Freudian." He widened his eyes, grasping for one last straw. "Would you believe I was playing the crappy pick-up lines game?"

Zack's head wallowed upwards from its porcelain pillow and he shot Norm a disgusted scowl. "'You bring out the perv in me'? Smooth, Bates. Real smooth. Be still my fucking heart."

"Says the man with his head in a toilet," Norm shot back.

"I'm not trying to get in Supergirl's panties. I don't poach. I'm trying to give you helpful advice."

"Again: *says the man with his head in a toilet.*"

165

"Boys, boys." Lucy held her hands up, hastily motioning for peace. She leaned closer to Zack, patting his shoulder. "Are you feeling OK, Zack? Do you think you're done?"

Zack blinked and leaned away. "Maybe."

"Try drinking this." She passed him one of the Gatorades she'd apparently grabbed before checking on them in the bathroom.

Zack slowly drank, and everyone in the room held their breath as he swallowed, Norm especially because he was on clean-up duty. Zack managed to drink half the bottle then handed the Gatorade to Lucy. She screwed the cap on and set the bottle aside, then began a flow of warm, idle chatter that had Norm's head bobbing sleepily even though he was standing. Zack was half-unconscious even on the cold, hard floor of their bathroom.

After a few more minutes poised over his least favorite deity, Zack proclaimed, "I think I'm done. I'm feeling almost sober." Lucy made him finish the Gatorade, take the B-vitamin and eat a handful of crackers, then Norm hauled his roommate's drunken ass to his bedroom and placed a fresh just-in-case bowl by the bed. Lucy hovered close by, ready to help. With Zack finally settled, Norm and Lucy trudged the few feet to his bedroom in a surprisingly companionable silence.

I'm glad she was here. Not only because he planned to do numerous immoral things to her later, but because she was really comforting to have around.

Any of his old girlfriends would have bailed the moment he had to pour Drunk Zack into the Benz, but Lucy stuck in there. Lucy was loyal and dauntless and helpful. Hell, Lucy even bantered with drunkards when there was imminent vomit on the horizon.

Norm's heart twinged as she stripped in his bedroom, exposing the supple lines of her body. Her movements were slow--not sluggish exactly, she was too poised for that--but, despite the languid grace of her limbs, her movements betrayed she was obviously as exhausted as him. No immorality tonight then.

He pulled out one of his well-worn old shirts as well as a pair of boxers and tossed them to her. She skinned into his clothes, seeming fragile and young, like a China doll dressed in a grown man's castoffs. She slid under his covers and was asleep in moments, snoring that soft mousey snore of hers.

A fierce urge to protect and cherish her swamped him, submerging him to the tiptop of his outrageously high head in a rush of feeling for her. Lucy was magnificent, nothing so dull as perfect, but sharp and funny and sassy and sexy and--and Norm was falling harder and harder for her with each passing hour.

He slid under the covers in his work clothes, and she curled against him, soft and warm, her breath tickling against his neck as she settled into the curve of his shoulder. No doubt about it: Lucy was a keeper.

Yeah, so now you just have to figure out a way that she'll let you keep her.

Shaking his head in disgust with himself, Norm snuggled closer to Lucy. He had her for the moment, and the moment would have to be enough.

Chapter Fourteen

Lucy woke to the gentle scribble of pen on paper. She blinked her eyes open and stretched, her hand sliding over an empty mattress beside her. She eased onto her elbow, peering over the plush mountain of Norm's striped comforter.

He sat a few feet away, bare-assed naked in his computer chair. Hunching forward, he squinted at a fat stack of paper with the intensity of a neurosurgeon repairing damaged synapses. Except Norm was softly smiling to himself, the curve of his lips visible to her in profile, illuminated by the light of his desk lamp.

She hesitated to snap him out of this trance. So she oozed into the pillows, moving an inch at a time, and lay in the near dark of the bedroom, gazing around without moving her head.

The last few times she'd stepped into Norm's boudoir she'd been too distracted to appreciate the details. Now, she did her girl snoop full throttle. But, like the rest of the apartment, Norm's bedroom appeared exceptionally tidy for a twenty-something guy. She was a fallen woman, after all, and had seen a fair number of twenty-something guys' bedrooms. They usually, at the very least, had a fine layer of clutter tossed about. Dirty clothes. Dirty dishes.

Unexplained dark stains on the floors. A huge stack of anime porn on the bedside table. Butt plugs on top of the dresser. And, worst of all, a life-sized cardboard cutout of The Little Mermaid with mysterious white stains all over it.

Lucy had seen it all, and, occasionally, run screaming into the night at the sight of it all.

But Norm kept his dirty clothes in his laundry hamper, seemed never to eat in his bedroom, but if he did, he took the dishes to the kitchen. And, so far, aside from the whole English major thing, he had displayed no strange sexual perversions of any kind. Or at least, her skin heated in memory, not any he wasn't willing to share with her.

Based on the living room's décor, she'd believed the bedroom would likewise be heavy with the Geek Chic but, like the usual single guy clutter, the geek chic was also lacking in Norm's bedroom. He had chosen instead to decorate his walls with dozens of picture frames of all different sizes and styles. Some were simple black frames. Others were clunky and huge, with sculpted skulls and snakes that stood out from the wall. Lucy cursed the dark and the glare off the computer that made seeing any of the pictures in the frames impossible.

The bedroom was tiny, but he had a good-sized closet with white sliding doors, which he'd left open so she could see the rows of jeans neatly lined up, the cuff of one lonely suit sticking out just over the edge of the door, and a swimming cap and goggles dangling on a hook by the wall. The comforter was striped in tasteful browns and blue-grays, his sheets smelling deliciously of fabric softener with a hint of that clean, sharp Norm-scent she loved so much. She had to watch out or she might accidentally smother herself with one of his pillows while huffing it, trying to get more Norm-scent into her senses.

Next to the bed was the real heart of the space: Norm's desk. Covertly examining his desk from the shield of her covers, it became apparent Geek Chic was not absent from his bedroom--only clustered in a central location. His desk was the one total explosion of all-out geekery in the room as far as she could tell. He had several clumps of action figures scattered across the surface. Han Solo in carbonite. Kirk and Spock. Thor and Loki. A *kaiju* monster from *Pacific Rim*. A giant Treebeard next to the printer, and the *Back to the Future* DeLorean on top of it.

But the real centerpiece of the desk set-up was the plush toy of the face-hugger creature from *Aliens* that coiled around the armrest then up to hover on the back of his desk chair, poised to attack. Most people would be unnerved to have something like that suspended above them, even the plush toy version. But Norm scribbled on, lounging in his chair, serene and unmoved by the plushie alien perpetually three seconds away from latching onto his face and impregnating him.

At least the face-hugger isn't over the bed. She huffed to herself. *And he objected to my Einstein socks. Hypocrite.*

Taking in the neatness of the space, the geeky toys, the photos, she had a strong impression that here was Norm distilled, as if someone had plucked out the core of his personality and made it flesh--or at least made it into a fully pose-able action figure. All his passions were here, his habits, his hopes, and she sensed this room was an intensely private place for him, a sanctuary. After all, not every girl would be willing to get down and dirty with a face-hugger alien so near. So she felt doubly, *triply* gratified to have been invited in.

"You can have the light on if you want." At the sound of his voice she jumped, then, abandoning her ruse of sleep, she sat upright and bunched the covers at her waist.

He remained perched over the pages, furiously scribbling as he spoke without turning. "Did I wake you up with the desk light?"

"No. How did you know I'm awake?"

His mouth twitched, then he leaned more intently toward the pages, saying in an offhand way, "You stopped snoring."

"I do *not* snore."

"Sure you do. Like a mouse. Mousey feet. Mousey snore."

She plucked at the covers, gathering a handful then dropping the fabric and smoothing it, twitching with guilt. "Did *I* wake *you* up?"

"I didn't really go to bed. I wanted to stay alert, check on Zack."

"You're a good friend."

He waved that away, finally dropped the pen, and swiveled the desk chair toward her. He leaned forward, clasping his hands between his knees, which *really* emphasized the nakedness.

She tilted her head to the side. "Mind you, I'm not complaining but naked. Why?"

He glanced down then laughed, rocking on his feet to make his chair pulse back and forth. "Curse of the writer. I got up to check on Zack, came back, started changing for bed, glanced at one of my manuscript pages and found a

171

typo. Before I put clothes back *on*, I had been sucked into my galley edits."

"Galley edits?"

He dropped his eyes and scratched the back of his neck. "They're, um, one of the final steps before my book comes out."

His book? Waves of surprise crested through her, hot, tingly, and exciting. After a long moment of blinking shock, she shrieked, "*Norman!* Your book is being published?"

He visibly swallowed. "Yeah."

"Bookstores and everything?"

"Yeah."

It finally sank in on Lucy that he appeared vaguely uncomfortable about the whole thing instead of bubbling with the same excitement she felt on his behalf. Granted, he'd lived with the news longer than her but where was the happiness? "Norm? Are we not excited about the book?"

He fluffed his fingers through his hair then dropped his hand limply so it slapped against his bare thigh. "I am. I just--It's…"

She waited for him to finish the sentence, but he didn't. A weighted silence fell instead. She smoothed the covers. What could have him so worried about his book?

She slithered forward to the foot of the bed, then flopped onto the mattress, resting her chin on her hand. "You forgot to put clothes on because you were writing?"

A sheepish expression crossed his face. "When I'm in a writing jag not much can snap me out of it. Zack has whole conversations with me before he realizes I'm not listening. Which is how the electrical bill managed not to get paid one month."

"Tell me about the book?"

He vocalized a small groan then drew his shoulders back, obviously stealing himself. "It's science fiction. I wrote the novel about three years ago and landed my agent, Paige Adams, a little while after that. She sold the book to my dream publisher, the novel will be out in a few more months and," he blew his breath out in a tense stream through his teeth, "I'm kind of freaked out about all that, truth to tell."

Lucy blinked. She knew he loved writing, but she hadn't realized he was so serious about pursuing a career. "You really do want to be Neil Gaiman."

He flashed her a self-deprecating grin. "I told you I did."

"What's the story about?"

"Which one?"

"Any of them. All of them." She pressed upward, folding her legs Indian style on the bed and clasping her hands in her lap, trying to telegraph through her posture and expression that she was deeply interested in this. And him.

So Norm told her his ideas, he talked about his hopes for the book, awards and great reviews, and the blurb-endorsement thingy he was hoping to get from a famous SF author. All of it. She burned inside, wanting all of this for him and so much more, wanting to pluck the moon from the sky and present it to him, just to make him light up like this again.

He had wheeled to fully face her in his desk chair, poised on the balls of his feet to rise and come to bed. Watching him, her chest constricted as if someone were trying to crush her under a pile of stones. This was all too close, too much, and she hopped out of bed, flicking on the light switch, banishing the beautiful intimacy of the darkness.

Avoiding the bed, she crossed to the wall where the largest cluster of picture frames hung. Clearly this was the family photo section, because there were a ton of pictures of people hugging and laughing and mugging for the camera who all resembled Norm an awful lot.

One picture caught her eye of three grown guys--one of them Norm--and one little boy sitting all clumped at the base of a Christmas tree. Each one of them had the same identical goofy grin as they gazed into the camera and--She blinked. Each of them, including the little boy, wore identical blue pajama sets with chipper polar bears cavorting on them. "Nice PJs."

The chair creaked as Norm crossed to stand behind her. His breath stirred against her hair as he gave a small laugh. "Oh. Christmas. Two? Three years ago? My mom gets me and my brothers identical PJ sets for Christmas Eve every year. We thought she'd stop at some point. No such luck."

He crossed to his bureau and selected a pair of gray sweatpants, sliding his legs into them, finally finished getting ready for bed after how many hours spent sitting naked at his desk? He jerked his chin toward the picture as he tugged the waistband to ride low on his hips. "It was awful the year Tommy was born because she had to find something to match in sizes for three teenagers in various states of growth spurt and an infant. We ended up with these horrible tapered green pants that made us all look like walking string beans."

Family Christmas. Norm spoke about the holiday in an offhanded tone, half-amused, fondly annoyed. Taking these memories for granted, taking his family for granted. She would kill to have ugly, green tapered PJs. To have even one more Christmas with her dad. To have even one more *minute*.

Wetness pooled in her eyes, so she swallowed and moved away from the family pictures, crossing to examine the toys on his desk instead. "I've never seen a man with so many toys so proudly displayed. Well, no, I have. But that was a porcelain doll collection, and that guy was a whole other level than you. Much more severe case of geekery-itis."

Norm crossed his arms over his chest. "Well, I won't give you the 'they're collector's items' spiel then. I just like them. I like movies. I like movie memorabilia. It's fun and," His voice went quiet, shy as he continued, "I look at them and remember all the great stories that have been told, and that makes me want to work. To tell my own stories, create my own characters for the fans to drool over."

He was so cute, so earnest, that she couldn't help herself. She padded over to him, and his arms fell open to hug her close. She pressed her face to his chest, his skin hot and smooth under her cheek. "You totally play with them when no one's watching, don't you?" she whispered.

The vibration of his laugh rippled against her body, and he lifted his hands away to hold them high in a pose of surrender. "You got me."

Yes, I do. And she would keep him, too, for all the precious time they had left together. She burrowed against him, and he squeezed her back, pillowing his cheek on her

175

hair. Norm was built for the long haul, and she was an emotional fuckwit who screwed everything up. It was only a matter of time until he got fed up with her and left.

But, until then, she had him. And she wasn't letting go.

Chapter Fifteen

In the morning, they showered together. The hot water and Norm's hands slick with soap combined to leave Lucy weak-kneed with a languorous sort of desire. Norm carried her to his bedroom after to "towel off".

A long, slow bout of sex followed with much giggling and kissing, then she had a mock-tussle with Norm about borrowing a shirt and sweats to drive home in. Norm finally surrendered an old yellow t-shirt from a water polo tournament and an absurdly comfy pair of gym shorts. His shirt smelled of the wood from his bureau, grainy and sweet, vaguely homey, and she covertly pressed the fabric to her nose for a quick sniff. Why did Norm have to smell so *good*?

Their goodbye at the front door was as prolonged as if she were going off to war, and so intense she nearly followed him back to the bedroom in a cloud of lust. At last, she managed to pull away and step into the gray light of the California morning, the fog lying thick on the road. "I have to make sure my apartment is where I left it. And I have to get some homework done today."

With obvious regret, he let her go.

When she stepped inside her apartment, the rooms echoed with their own emptiness. The place tended to get stuffy and hot at the best of times. Now, after being left to its own devices for two days, the heat in her cramped rooms hit her like a hot slap, sticky with sweat. After two days spent in the neatness of Norm's apartment, her own space became doubly depressing. Empty of company, cluttered with crap, and coated in a fine layer of dust she never had the energy to tackle.

This apartment had seemed like such a temporary set-up to her she never even bothered to decorate. No family photos. No posters. No action figures. No real furniture--except her ugly dark brown desk--not even a bureau for her clothes; what didn't fit in the closet she'd stuffed into two squat, plastic drawer sets from the hardware store. Even her books were still in the Xerox boxes from the move--*two years ago*. When she wanted to read something, she dug through the boxes to get it.

Well, the anonymity of her apartment she couldn't change today; the clutter and dirt she could. Lucy spent the morning neatening her room and scouring the flat spaces and floors of her apartment--the first time in recent history that she could remember doing so.

Scrubbing at a stubborn food spot on her stove, something hard and heavy cracked inside her, like a glacier breaking apart to reveal smooth, warm ocean in its wake. She felt lighter, happier than she had in years.

***

By the time Lucy saw Norm again at the staff meeting that day, he had finally arranged to have his car towed out of the Jezebel's parking lot to his apartment. After the brief conversation in which they exchanged this information, Norm carefully avoided Lucy for the rest of their work day. She did likewise. Their play-acting almost

178

became like a game to Norm: Who does a better job pretending indifference?

If only the lying were a game, Norm would have been much happier but, when Hank nearly caught them holding hands, Lucy froze up. She stayed all the way on the other side of the bar, and didn't glance at him again the rest of the evening.

When he noticed his teeth grinding in annoyance Norm forced himself to stop and take a calming breath. *You signed up for this, remember?* Dealing with Lucy's weird paranoia about Jezebel's was the price of admission to their relationship. And Norm had already decided to play. He just wished the rules of the game weren't so stupid.

"Hey, newbie." Norm turned slowly at the sound of Ronnie's syrupy rasp. She raised an eyebrow.

"Hullo," he said.

"A bunch of us are hitting the Dogs of War after work. Wanna come?"

It was on the tip of his tongue to say he had plans, but what if Ronnie had already asked Lucy and she'd made the same reply? Would he blow their cover? If they were the only people at Jezebel's bowing out would people add two and two together and--

Are you getting as paranoid as Lucy? "Sure," Norm said. "Great. Can't wait." He nodded, probably too enthusiastically judging by Ronnie's widening eyes.

"Great." She eased away from him, like a hiker retreating from a mountain lion. "Wait by the front door and we'll all walk over together."

"Great."

"OK." She vamped away to approach someone else with the invite.

179

Norm pinched his eyes shut and whirled toward the wall. *Dammit.* How long was Dogs going to take? How much perfectly good Lucy-time would he be losing out on? He scoffed at himself. *You can go a few hours without her, Norman.* Thinking of her, every adorable, enjoyable inch of her, he sighed. *Do I have to?*

"Hey." Lucy's breathy whisper made his body tense, prickling with pleasure. He faced her, biting his lip to keep from just beaming. "Hello."

She stepped close, keeping her voice low. "Ronnie cornered me into going to Dogs. I'm sorry. I'll get away and drive to your place as fast as I can. Can Zack give you a ride?"

His heart did a happy skip-step, and he finally allowed himself a smile. "Oh, no worries then. She cornered me too. We can go together."

Lucy froze, her throat moving as she swallowed.

He leaned back, clearing his throat. "But not *together* together. Just, you know, occupying the same space together." He drew his brows down, feeling awkward, frustrated. Why was this elaborate charade even necessary? He managed to bite that unwise rejoinder back, but only barely.

Maybe Lucy was right last night. Can you take much more of this?

But then she reached tentatively forward to tuck her hand into his. "After Dogs of War we will definitely be together. Brace yourself, Norman." She winked and took herself off to sling more shots.

Norm collapsed against the doorway, more stressed by their ten-second exchange than he'd been after several hours corralling drunks. *Brace yourself, Norman.*

***

The Dogs of War gathering was as loud as Norm had expected it to be. All of the bar staff who'd worked that night showed up. Even the singer, Mia, and one of her back up guys dropped in a while to shoot the shit and nom on the delicious hot dogs. Hank stopped by to finish off a Much Ado dog then lingered to steal chili cheese fries off Lucy's plate.

Lucy, dedicated to her Norm-avoidance policy, sat at the opposite end of the table from Norm and chatted with Ronnie and Hank most of the night. Norm spent his after-hours time bumping elbows with Eddie, a raucous, buff blond guy, and one of the other bouncers, Ben, who was a *super*-buff black guy. Norm twitched, uncomfortably sandwiched between their muscles in the extra chair that had been stolen from another table.

As the large group laughed and joked with each other, rehashing old times, reliving war stories, he felt almost as if he were slipping away, as if he were isolated in his own force field. And all the while he had to sit there and watch while the girl he was dating pretended that he didn't exist.

"You hear from Berkeley yet, Luce?" Eddie called down the table.

She hurriedly set her hot dog down to make warding gestures with her hands. "*Ssh*. Don't jinx it."

Ronnie scoffed, laughing. "We're not even allowed to say the name? Should we call it The School that Shall Not be Named?"

Lucy tipped her chin up, mock-stern. "Yes."

Norm laughed with everyone else, even as some small pain nipped at him. He noticed a distance from Lucy among the Jezebel's crowd, not like the one she kept from

181

him for appearances, but a shield she maintained with everybody. Wanting some privacy was fine, but Lucy *always* spun the topic away from herself, even when it came to relatively minor things. Hank watched her every time she did this, the manager's eyes narrowed, as if he were assessing Lucy, measuring her scores on a test.

Norm clenched his hands under the table, an insidious jealousy winding through his guts. He believed Lucy that there wasn't anything romantic between her and Hank. Norm even believed that Hank's obvious attachment to her was as platonic as she believed it to be.

But what got Norm really good and pissed was Hank's proprietary attitude toward her. When they'd all gone to sit, Hank had immediately slid in beside Lucy, isolating her at the head of the table, inserting himself between her and everybody else. He acted like a bird with one chick, helping Lucy keep herself somewhat apart from her co-workers.

Norm had already noticed sub-groups in the bar. Ronnie, Hank and Lucy were the top dogs, the triumvirate who ran the whole show. Mia and her band were their own autonomous division beneath that, funky and alternative in their ripped jeans and nose rings--in contrast to the more mainstream Dickies and bowling shirts worn by the rest of the staff. Eddie and Jenna, the dark-haired shot girl with curiously hard blue eyes, reigned over their own clique comprised of some of the other newer hires.

And Norm was the odd man out who belonged to no faction or fraternity as yet.

This became increasingly clear as the night wore on, and the others talked more and more to their own particular friends, which left Norm with no one at all to talk to. *Fan-fucking-tastic.*

Hank snagged yet another fry off Lucy's plate, laughing at her faux indignation as he did so. Norm took a vicious bite of his "Green-Eye'd Monster Dog." Some of the guacamole slid off the dog to plop onto the table. He cursed and swabbed at the spill with a fistful of napkins.

"You all right, newbie?" Ronnie hollered down the table to him.

Norm gritted his teeth, the muscles bunching in his jaw. That was another thing: *newbie, newbie, newbie.* All the fucking time. Did these people not know his fucking name? He tossed the crumpled mess of napkins onto the plate with his half-eaten guacamole dog and pushed to his feet. "I'm not feeling too great. I think I'll call my roommate to come get me. Night, everybody." He waved to the table at large. making sure to gaze right past Lucy, then scooted his way free through the narrow opening between Ben and Eddie's sizeable shoulders.

"Feel better, newbie," Ronnie said to his departing back.

He stiffened his spine but kept walking. Prickly and exasperating were Ronnie's default settings. He wasn't even sure she was aware what she was doing ninety percent of the time. the habits were just so ingrained. He pushed through the Dogs of War entrance and stalked toward Jezebel's, hands shoved into his pockets, shoulders hunched.

After a few paces he stopped and glanced at the Dogs, letting out a low growl of annoyance. *What are you doing?* Where was he even going? Zack was working tonight. Lucy was Norm's ride home. But how could he

183

announce that to a table full of their co-workers when it was a deep, dark fucking secret? A fucking secret about secret fucking.

He kicked a stray beer bottle out of his path so it rolled into the gutter. The bottle landed with a hollow thud that echoed his state of impotence when the glass didn't even smash. *Being the dirty mistress sucks.* Why had he agreed to this idiotic idea anyway? To save his job? *Really?* Or Lucy's? If she hadn't been so adamant, would he have even thought about trying to hide their relationship at work?

The clack of heels made him turn. Lucy approached him, her eyes bright with happiness in the darkness of the street. "Ready to go?"

That's it? That's all I get? He narrowed his eyes at her, waiting.

She took a hesitant step toward him, tilting her head in question. "Norm?"

He wanted to push the issue, he wanted to say he'd had two nights of this bullshit and he already knew that he was sick of lying. He wanted to tell her that he deserved better from her, that she was capable of better, of more. She didn't have to close herself off to the entire world just because life had been so cruel to her before.

But she took another step toward him, her face scrunched with worry, a wistful, somehow fragile smile wobbling on her lips. So he bit his tongue and held his hand out to her. "Ready." Her fingers slid into his and clasped firmly as they strolled the empty street. Everyone else had been mid-meal at Dogs, firmly entrenched. Which was probably why Lucy felt safe holding his hand.

"What did you say?" he asked.

"Hmm?"

"When you left Dogs."

"Oh, homework." She gave a careless shrug, and they walked on.

Their silence felt strained to him, but Lucy didn't notice as she sidled closer, pressing herself against his side. All her warmth pressed against him helped unwind some of the knots that he'd tied himself into during dinner.

"Did you finish your...what was it...gaily edits?" she asked.

A laugh instinctively stretched his lips. "Galley edits. Yeah. I did. Hopefully they won't find any last minute problems."

"Are you excited yet?"

"Sure."

Despite doing his best to make his tone un-encouraging, Lucy pressed on, "Your family must be really happy. Proud."

Proud. Oh, yes. *Only not.* He swallowed, his skin going clammy at the idea of his book out in the world where his family could see it, read it, comment on it.

"Are you OK?"

"Sure."

She stopped and moved to face him fully. "OK. You've got a ginormous vocabulary and I've gotten two 'sures' in the last two minutes. What's up? Is it about dinner?" She grabbed his hands, squeezing them. "I'm really sorry if I hurt your feelings."

He shook his head. The Dogs of War and the petty politics of Jezebel's were utterly dwarfed just then by the horrible image of his family seeing his book, *reading* his book.

"The book then?" She held onto his hands, his own human anchor as the night air burrowed under his jacket, flaying his skin and his confidence both. "Want to talk about it?" she asked.

He started walking again, tugging her along behind him by their linked hands. "It's nothing. I'm a little...My family will not like the book."

"Of course they will."

A voice echoed in his head, synchronized to the clack of Lucy's heels on the pavement. *Melodramatic crap. Cardboard characters. Why are you wasting your time writing this trash, Norman?*

A frenzied need seized him to talk about *anything* else. He draped his arm around Lucy and reeled her in tight to his body. "I've never asked but: *why* mechanical engineering? It's not the most typical career path for a woman."

She shoulder-checked him in amused outrage. "You freaking chauvinist caveman. There are plenty of female engineers."

Norm passed a hand over his face, rubbing hard. *Nice one.* "I said that wrong. I *mean*, what made you decide engineering was for you. I, for example, want to be a writer because, well, because the voices in my head tell me to--"

She snorted

"But really, I want to be one because my mom is a writer. She does narrative nonfiction, mostly, and political commentary, but she writes some fiction, short stories, a novella. And one magnum opus of science fiction thirty years ago. So: why mechanical engineering, Lucy?"

Lucy shrouded so much of herself; he wanted to ease the layers away to see more of the complexity in this vibrant, beautiful, brilliant woman he kept only getting glimpses of.

They'd reached the Mustang, and she released his hand and slid into the driver's seat. Norm plopped into shotgun as she slowly started the car, buckling up, futzing with the radio. Lucy took infinite care with each gesture because somehow, he wasn't sure why, his question had made her emotional.

After a long moment, she let out a ragged *hmph* and drove out of the parking lot. "The summer my mother left, my dad sold our house in San Diego and moved here to live with his mom, my grandma. I was bored out of my mind, and behaving badly because I...I wanted my mother back." Her face had tensed.

Bitterness coated his throat. "Did--did your mom ever try to come back? To see you?"

Lucy shook her head once, sharply, and the clot of bitterness grew to leave his whole mouth stinging with acid. "Nope." Lucy flexed her fingers so hard the steering wheel rubber squished. "My dad tried to paint her leaving in a positive light, like Mom loved me but she didn't feel equipped to be a parent. Reading between the lines, I think she was a party girl who got trapped by a baby."

Lucy tossed her hair, as if throwing away the painful memories. "*Anyway*, Gram's house was in a bad neighborhood and I didn't know any of the other kids, so that whole first summer I sat cooped up in the house, bored out of my mind. Finally, my dad found a stack of comic books and, since I'd been having trouble reading in school, he'd give me a quarter for every comic I read. The first ones I dug into were *Iron Man*, and pretty soon I forgot to ask for my quarter."

As she continued, more of her usual brightness shone through. "I loved the Iron Man suit, all the things he could do with it, all the ways he made the world a better place with technology. I liked the other superheroes, but Tony Stark made it seem like anyone, if they were smart enough, could be a superhero. Build a better future." She shot Norm a flashing, mischievous look, bold but somehow brittle with emotion, and his chest hurt with his feelings for her. "Now you know my secret, Norman. You want to be Neil Gaiman when you grow up? I want to be Tony Stark."

Norm, sensing the tenuous hold she had on her emotions, merely said, in a carefully light manner, "How'd you like the *Iron Man* movies?"

"First's one great. Love *Avengers. Iron Man 3* doesn't have enough of the suit. Robert Downey Jr. is purdy."

He fixed his face into a wan pout as he tried to coax a laugh out of her. "Am *I* pretty?"

"I confess my deep-seated childhood geekery to you and that's all you have to say?"

Norm shrugged, probably not quite casually enough. "Just checking that you aren't planning to leave me for Robert Downey Jr."

"Not tonight, babe." She snagged his hand again, clutching at him the whole way home. For his comfort or hers, he didn't know.

Chapter Sixteen

Norm's worries about Robert Downey Jr. decreased as the week wore on, but his worries about Lucy and their relationship didn't fully quiet. Nowadays, Lucy was too paranoid about Hank to do more than shoot Norm a quick wink or an illicit grin. Sometimes they'd make conversation of such studied politeness that if he were watching from the outside he would think they were ten seconds away from killing each other. Or fucking.

It shouldn't have been such a problem, but working in a bar consumed large portions of their lives. On any given night they both worked from about seven p.m. to three a.m., then slept from about four a.m. to at least twelve p.m. But if they stayed awake later than four a.m., which they usually did on nights they went home together--and Lucy went home with him every night for the next week--then they slept later and later. This meant they had less and less time before work to get out of bed. And less time to do anything as a real couple besides hit the sheets. In both connotations of that word.

His writing was suffering, too, because in a contest between tapping away at his computer or curling up with Lucy, Lucy won every time. No contest.

But if Norm kept sacrificing so much to be with her then he wanted to actually *date* her. To take Lucy to the movies and dinner and bowling and on a picnic and a million other interesting and fun activities that he kept thinking of but never had the time to execute. They didn't always have the same days off, and when they did both of them wanted to sleep and sleep together. Or Lucy had school. Or Norm had to work on his book. Or a million other excuses that left Norm feeling as if he were slowly morphing into a vampire--the totally nocturnal, non-sparkly kind.

Dollar Beer Night had rolled around again, and the theme of the evening was Game Night. Lucy was dressed to the nines, or dressed to the letters or something, as an anthropomorphized Scrabble board. The bodice of her dress was an imitation of the Scrabble board with lines of vaguely sexual or flirtatious words branching across her ribcage and stomach: *sexy, lust, tease, sensitive, kiss, lick, bite*...Just reading her clothes made him want to tear them off her as he remembered all the times he had done that or that or, ooh, *that* to the body encased in the silly Scrabble board costume.

He was the floater for the night, basically wandering the club acting tough and looming. Hank called this "establishing a presence." Norm called it, in the privacy of his own head, the worst job in history. Front door was good, even patio door most times, somewhere that he could be stationary and apart from the crush of sweaty, liquor-soaked bodies on the floor.

Lucy meandered into his orbit, and he instinctively redirected his steps toward her. A ship adrift seeking true north, he desperately needed a moment of her bright humor to wring the frustration from his soul.

As she saw him coming her lips softened from her usual fake, I'm-Having-So-Much-Fun Smile to her more natural, I'm-Happy-to-See-You-Norm Smile. His whole body heated, warmed back to happiness by this minute change of expression that was only for him.

As he strolled toward Lucy, a customer banged into him, nearly body-checking him to the floor because the woman hit him so hard. He instinctively caught her, supporting her weight as the woman melted against him.

"Hey, sugar," she slurred, her sweaty brown hair swinging to cover her face. He tried to set her on the nearby stool she must have tumbled off of, but she clung to him, pressing her body against his.

Norm stiffened his arms, keeping as much distance between them as he could. The woman's gaze roved over his body from toe to top in a glance that left him feeling sort of dirty. *How does Lucy deal with this everyday?*

The woman walked her fingers up his chest, like a sotted itsy bitsy spider. "Now here's a big ol'tree I'd like to climb."

A small scoff sounded behind him. He turned to see Lucy standing by the table with a fist stuffed in her mouth to muffle her giggles. He cast Lucy a beseeching *Help me* glance. But before Lucy could elbow her way through the lump of people separating them, another drunken woman teetered along and leaned over to yell into the first woman's face, "Alexa, come *on*. We're about to get the hot bouncer to give Elsa her shot."

Drunken Girl #2 managed to pry Drunken Girl #1, Alexa, off of Norm and haul her away. Alexa blew him a sloppy kiss in parting. Norm slowly retreated, scared she would chase him if he bolted.

"The key is not to let them smell your fear," Lucy hissed in a loud stage-whisper.

Lucy leaned in, sweet and cute and wonderful, and he actually ached with wanting to kiss her. Her eyes flickered, mirroring his own desire back at him, but then she gently twisted her arm free.

He narrowed his eyes at her and jerked his chin at the drunk girl's receding form. "Does that bother you?"

"The flirting? Of course it bothers me," she murmured. "You think I like other women crawling all over my man--"

Her man. That's nice. A dopey grin blossomed on his face.

"--trying to get him to go home with her? No. But what can I do about it?"

The grin fell off his face. "I dunno...maybe say, 'Back off, he's mine'?"

"Haha, Norman."

I wasn't joking. But this conversation was already killing his buzz and he *really* didn't want a fight tonight. He forced himself to give her a playful soft-punch on the shoulder. "You could just pull her hair, call her a whore, and get some sexy catfight action going on."

"Haha, Norman." Lucy, perhaps sensing his unhappy mood, flicked a mischievous gaze his way, nodding toward Alexa's drunkenly retreating back. "Gotta appreciate a woman who likes her men tall."

He shuddered, being the good sport, playing along. "No, I don't."

Teasing him, Lucy purred out, "Six foot four and worth every inch of the climb."

He restrained a laugh, shaking his head. "I'm the kind of man you can put on a pedestal without having to buy the pedestal." He reached out to smooth the wispy bangs away from her forehead.

"Luce, I need you." Hank's voice over Norm's shoulder made them both jump, and Norm let his arm twitch back to his side, his body burning with disappointment.

Lucy brushed past him to follow Hank, the tips of her fingers brushing over Norm's hand in passing. A small thrill blazed through him, like one of those frustrated lovers in a British historical movie. A repressed man confined to longing glimpses and illicit touches of the hand. *God, this is ridiculous.* All of Norm, everywhere, felt like hard rebar twisted into knots.

"Hey, newbie, come watch this." Ronnie tucked her gloved hand into the crook of his arm and dragged him with her through the crush of the crowd. Her face was filled with a glee that only filled him with dread. Ronnie could have a pretty vile sense of humor; anything that delighted her this much couldn't be good.

Ronnie possessed the same Zen powers as Hank and somehow managed to part the crowd before herself so they proceeded smoothly to one of the large booths in the back. Norm stopped short, his mouth falling open at the sight of Hank bent over a girl and delivering one of the injector shots. Lucy stood to the side, a hand flat over her mouth to stifle her laughter.

The table was filled with a gaggle of women toasting and falling all over each other with laughter. The woman

193

beneath Hank in the chair twitched, appearing vaguely uncomfortable after she had received her shot. Hank eased away, face utterly blank. Lucy moved in to ask if anybody else wanted one.

Ronnie giggled beside Norm with vicious glee. "I love when he has to do that."

Another woman, she might have been the girl who'd finally rescued him from Alexa, pushed forward and threw herself into the chair, sinking down as she shot Hank a come-hither smolder.

Hank braced himself for round two, and Norm watched him with pity. "I didn't know we did this."

"Not often, but sometimes the ladies want in on the shot action too. Not often enough for Hank to hire an actual shot boy, though. Which means this delightful task falls to one of the bouncers." She slapped Norm hard on the arm. "Something to look forward to, newbie."

"Great." He wheeled around in time to see the second woman receive her shot then immediately reel forward and spit the liquid out down the front of Hank's shirt. Hank stumbled back and toppled into Lucy, knocking her tray out of her hands to send her shots and the booze scattering all over the floor.

"Shit." Norm rushed forward along with Lucy to help Hank move away from the woman and collect the spilled shots off the floor. Ronnie, cursing under her breath, left to fetch a mop to clean the spilled booze up.

The girl covered her mouth with her hands in horror, her face flaming red. "I'm so sorry, but that drink tasted so awful."

"No worries." Hank grinned at her even as he pinched his bowling shirt with two fingers to hold the wet fabric away from his body. He pointed at Norm and Lucy then jerked his hand in that patented Hank *come-along* gesture. "Let's get Lucy's tray filled up."

Confused about why he was coming too, Norm nevertheless followed Hank to the back room.

"Lucy, can you grab the spare shirt out of my locker while Norm re-fills your tray?"

That insidious sizzle of jealousy wormed through Norm again. Lucy knew Hank's locker combo? Hank felt comfortable sending her to fetch him a new shirt?

Lucy briskly trotted off to obey and was the first one through the break room door. Norm started in after her then actually collided with her back as she stopped dead in the middle of the room. He gazed over the top of her head then jumped with shock.

Jenna and Eddie lay tangled together on the couch, her Monopoly costume pushed well above her waist as Eddie...passed go and collected his $200. The two of them were so hot and heavy, faces glued together in a hard, wet kiss, they didn't even notice Norm and Lucy.

Norm retreated, pulling Lucy with him, but after one step he collided with Hank's hard bulk.

"What the fuck?" Hank's low bass rolled through the room. Jenna and Eddie jerked in surprise on the couch. Eddie reared back, a look of horror plastered on his flushed face. He fumbled to zip his pants while Jenna yanked her skirt down. Norm jerked his head away, shielding his eyes until she was decent.

Hank rammed past Norm, stalking toward the couple on the couch. "How long has this been going on?"

Norm tried to tug Lucy onto the floor, but she remained rooted to the spot, her body rigid, her face

195

frozen in blank shock. Not wanting to leave her, he lingered, twitching with awkwardness.

Jenna confronted Hank, yanking the neckline of her Monopoly board into place over her impressive breasts. "None of your fucking business, Hank."

Hank puffed up, his rage lending him extra bulk that he didn't even need because he was already built like a damn wall. "It becomes my fucking business when you start *fucking* on my couch." His lip curled, disgust and anger knotting his face into a furious mask. "You're fired."

Lucy winced beside Norm, and he squeezed her forearm.

"Hank, *please*--" Eddie tottered forward, holding his pants up because apparently the zipper was beyond him in that moment. His spiky hair was tousled, half flattened on one side from the couch cushions.

Hank's arm swept through the air in a cutting motion to annihilate anything else that could be said. "Clear out your shit and get out. I'll mail you your checks. Don't ever show your faces here again."

Jenna stormed toward the door, tossing her long dark hair, and Norm actually had to tug Lucy out of the way so Jenna could make her furious exit. When Norm touched Lucy he found her shaking, actually trembling under his hand.

To quote Hank: What the fuck? He tried to lean down to see if she was all right, but Hank thundered past him. Norm had to lean back to make room for Hank and then Eddie as the disgraced bouncer chased after their manager, begging for his job.

Norm winced, and as the door swung closed he wrapped Lucy in a hug. What an ugly little episode to witness. Still, screwing on the couch was pretty heinous. No wonder Hank was pissed.

Lucy pushed away from Norm, dodging his hands when he tried to catch her. Dumping her soiled tray into the sink, she grabbed up one of the prepared spare shot trays. She snatched it to her like a shield. "I have to get back on the floor."

"Lucy--"

She shook her head, the muscles in her arms trembling as she clutched the tray. "Not now. Please."

He wanted to press the issue but she seemed so brittle, teetering on the edge of tears, so he moved aside. She immediately darted past him and was soon swallowed by the mass of bodies in the bar. Norm stared after her retreating form. She and Jenna had never seemed that close but, then again, watching anyone get fired wasn't exactly happy fun times--

That could have been you, asshole. That's probably what's got her freaked out. She believes she's seeing her own future. Hank's rage. Disgrace. Exile from the bar. Exile from her surrogate family.

He raked a hand through his hair and crossed back to the floor himself. But couldn't she see they weren't Eddie and Jenna? He would never, *never* be so stupid or unprofessional to hook up in the bar. On the clock, no less. He sincerely believed Hank wasn't pissed Eddie and Jenna were hooking up--he was pissed they were hooking up *on his couch*.

Everyone on the staff spent the rest of the night gossiping about the double firing. Apparently, five minutes after exiting the club with their pink slips, Eddie and Jenna had broken up in a vicious shouting match rife with

197

blame-casting. Norm couldn't help but wince when he heard this. Another bad omen for him and Lucy? Fired *and* broken up?

Hank stomped about the place for the rest of the night, snarling at one and all. Norm was about ready to snap himself, and Lucy's behavior only wound everything in him tighter and tighter. She spent the rest of the night in a strange fugue state, wandering aimlessly, smiling mechanically, and she didn't say anything or look at him.

Am I about to get dumped? kept circling round and round in his head.

After much thought of his during his grueling, draining, brutal bitch of a night at the bar wound up, he knew what he needed to do. He just had to nerve himself up to do it.

Chapter Seventeen

After work, Lucy seemed especially cautious about meeting him by her car. She kept darting nervous glances around, and when he finally slid into his seat she drove out of the parking lot before he had even buckled in.

He let several moments pass in strained silence before he reached over and caught her hand. She let him hold it, but she didn't squeeze back. She was stuck in that tense, high-tension state she'd been in ever since Hank had fired Eddie and Jenna.

Norm stared straight at her, making his voice calm and sure as he said, "Lucy, I want to go to Hank. Tell him everything."

The car jerked as she shot him a look of baffled horror. "*Tell* him? You saw what happened tonight. We agreed telling him was a bad idea."

"You said you didn't want to. I agreed to that, but now I don't know."

"What don't you know?" Her voice had gone stiff, chilly.

Norm pressed on, somewhat daunted but not defeated yet. "If he catches us then yes, he will fire someone. He's made that clear enough after tonight. But, I think, if we go to him and explain about our relationship--

we won't screw at work, we'll maintain our professionalism, I won't flip out if someone feels you up-- then I think he'll at least give us a trial period to see if it can work. Jenna and Eddie weren't fired because they were dating. They were fired for swapping fluids on the break room couch."

Lucy scoffed loudly, apparently code for *You don't know shit.*

He gritted his teeth, getting kind of livid himself. Why couldn't she understand this? "You were right before: Hank's not a bad guy. If we tell him, let him be a part of the conversation and help figure out how this can work, then he won't fire us. But, if he catches us out somehow, then you and I both know he'll make good and fire me."

She snorted, loudly. "Both of us."

"No, Lucy," he lowered his voice, trying to instill in her how serious he was. "You're one of his favorite employees. Hell, let's say it, you're like his precious baby sister. If, no, *when* someone gets in trouble for *this...*" He gestured back and forth to indicate the two of them together. "...it'll be *me*. Hank'll never fire you. He'll be pissed at you if he finds out, but he won't fire you."

"He *told* me he would. He straight out said he would a few weeks ago if he caught me lying."

"I think he was just trying to scare you. My ass is the one on the line here, and I don't really like it hanging out in the wind. Thank you very much."

Lucy jerked the wheel hard over in one swift, stiff movement to get off the freeway for his house. "No."

"No?"

She parked then wheeled toward Norm, her eyes blazing. "No, I don't want to tell Hank. No, I think you're wrong."

Norm braced his arms against the dashboard, every muscle in his body hardening with anger and frustration. "Are you ashamed of me?"

"*What?* No. Of course not."

"You won't tell your friends about me. Hell, you won't even go out with me."

Lucy sunk into her seat as she stared at him. "Norm, *what?* We are in a relationship."

"No. We're having sex. Lots and lots of fantastic sex, but we never get out of bed, we never do anything except each other." She winced but he pressed on, "The secrecy at work is part of that. Maybe if we didn't have to lie to all your friends we'd go out after. We'd hang with them. But you're so busy trying to keep me compartmentalized away from your work life that you shut me out of everything."

She shook her head, blinking in confusion.

He closed his eyes, clawing for patience as it speedily circled the drain. "What we have now is good, great, but it's not enough."

Her face pinched and her chin crumpled with emotion, which told him she must have understood at least part of what he was trying to say to her. But then she shook her head in a small 'no' and started the Mustang. As rejections go, that was pretty crushing. "I can't stay tonight," she said. "I need to be alone. To think."

Norm nodded. He moved stiffly to climb out of the car. Every muscle in his body felt heavy, weighted with the lump of depression sinking deep in his gut.

All he'd wanted was to open their relationship up, bring it into the daylight. But he may have ruined everything instead. And, in a choice between going on together as they had been or losing Lucy forever, he knew which one he would have chosen. *Lucy.*

When he touched the curb the Mustang snarled to life, and Lucy burned rubber to get away. As he reached his front door, he moaned and pounded his forehead against the wood twice in quick succession. "*Idiot. Idiot.*"

Once inside, he fell right into bed, but his body was on Lucy-time, which meant that when his body got home, it expected to be awake for several more hours...and inside her.

Tough luck, pal. Norm finally surrendered and trudged into the living room to watch mindless TV until he could sleep. He should have seized this opportunity to work on his writing, but the inspiration wasn't there, and his ambition had been amputated sometime in the past day.

Zack rolled in at the ass crack of morning in his rent-a-cop uniform and stopped short, arrested by the sight of Norm on the couch, still awake. And alone.

"Where's Supergirl?"

Norm shrugged, hiding a veritable geyser of emotion in that small gesture. "I told her I didn't want to lie to our boss anymore. She told me she needed time to think."

Zack plopped onto the couch next to Norm. "Ouch."

"Yeah."

"I'm sorry, man."

"Yeah."

Which was all that needed to be said. Zack sat with him in companionable, and silent, moral support, watching an orgy of action movies on TV as the ass crack of morning slid into the rosy cheeks of dawn.

Just when Bruce Willis was about to save his family and America from terrorists for good and all--yet again-- the low snarl of a motor ripped through the street. Norm perked up because the rumble sounded like Lucy's Mustang, but the car passed their apartment and he oozed against the couch feeling more pathetic than ever.

Not Lucy. Obviously. Stupid.

Zack fell asleep somewhere between Mel Gibson avenging his dead wife or dead kid or dead something and Bruce Willis blowing another building sky high. The low, nasally rasp of Zack's snore clawed at Norm, like someone taking a cheese grater to his nerve endings. He leaned over and shook his buddy awake. "Zack, it's OK. Go to bed."

Zack groggily stumbled to his bedroom. Norm resigned himself to more lonely wallowing with a bowl of popcorn and the canon of action stars from the 90s as his only companions. Bruce turned into Arnold turned into Keanu, and Norm fell into that numb state of funk where he was too tired to move, but had passed the point where he was tired enough to sleep.

He began muttering along with the TV, doing all the good lines in a vain act of self-flagellation to keep himself conscious. As he murmured, "Shoot the hostage," right along with Jeff Daniels, someone knocked on the front door.

Norm jumped, a tide of popcorn arcing out of the bowl and onto the couch. He sat there, blanketed by spilled snack-food, trying to kick-start his groggy brain into moving. As the person knocked again he at last managed to push himself off the couch and reach the door. He swung the door open, his nerves jangling, and found Lucy standing on his front step. She wore a pair of faded blue mechanic's overalls covered in car grease.

He managed to restrain himself from crushing her in a hug and settled on a stilted, polite nod instead. His fatigued body could manage all or nothing in the movement department, but not the nuances in between.

Lucy shot him a small, wobbly smile that made his heart flip and his stomach bottom out. She popped onto her toes and held her hands wide in a *ta-da* gesture. "Supergirl Auto Repair and Maintenance. We make housecalls," she chirped out.

Norm bit his cheek to keep from laughing and leaned against the door frame. He said nothing, merely raised an eyebrow. She was adorable, but he'd spent the last seven hours miserable and wallowing because she needed 'time to think'. She didn't get to pop in all perky and cute-like and skip right over the part where they talked about the Hank Issue.

She rested against the door frame beside him, her head tucked under his chin as she avoided his gaze. Her hair and body reeked of grease and gas, and her voice sounded small when she finally spoke. "Can we compromise? I will make a better effort to go out and do stuff with you, and you agree to hold off on telling Hank for at least a month. At the end of the month, we can revisit this and decide *together* if we want to keep quiet or tell him. Fair?"

It wasn't what he'd wanted, but this concession was obviously all he'd get and, after a night tossing in his cold, empty bed, he was ready to take what he could get if it meant he got to have Lucy. He tucked his fingers under her chin and titled her face.

As he met her gaze, her entire face tensed with worry. And regret. "You were right," she said. "About me. I do put my head down and sleepwalk through life most times." She bunched her hands into fists, gathering a wad of fabric in each hand so his shirt flattened across his chest as she tugged on it to emphasize her words. "But *not* with you. And I want to be better about that. I do."

She seemed truly sorry. *Now.* But what would happen in a month when the time came to do this all over again? Would she balk and run, or follow through like he wanted her to? And was waiting another month worth it to see if she meant to stick?

Norm almost scoffed aloud as he slid his hand along her jawline to bury his fingers in her messy ponytail. Yeah. It was worth it. Time with Lucy was worth about any price a person could name.

Even your heart? He swallowed the sudden sick lump in his throat. Obviously, after this last night's display, he would be totally wrecked if the thing with Lucy didn't work. But that was no reason not to try.

He dipped his head down and whispered, "Deal," against her lips. Then he kissed her and her mouth tasted sweet and soft. Still, the rest of her was so soaked in the smell of grease that he had to reel away from her after a long minute. "Why do you smell like the inside of an oil drum?"

"I told you I'd look at your car the other day, and I never finished the job." She looped her arms over his neck and draped herself against his body. "Fire your mechanic. The transmission's fine. Problem was your electrical

205

system. I replaced a few parts and the car seems to be running great now." She couldn't entirely bite back the triumphant smirk stretching her lips.

Norm blinked. "You fixed my car?"

She bobbed her head. Yes.

He bent and knocked her knees out from under her, swooping her into his arms and carrying her over the threshold. "Do you take checks or will my body be payment enough?"

Her fingers curled into his shirt collar, her knuckles brushing against his throat. "Your body, a shower, and pancakes."

"You drive a hard bargain." He bounced her in his arms to get a better hold, and she squealed so adorably he bounced her again.

Now she had both arms twined around him, her face buried against his neck. "I missed you."

Norm grinned as he kicked the bathroom door open, more than ready to assist his personal mechanic with her shower.

***

Sunday morning Lucy stirred, stretching in luxurious splendor against Norm's long, warm body in bed beside her. Sunday they both had off and she had big plans for that day, which mostly involved Norm, the bed, and nakedness. *Three out of three ingredients ready to go!*

The gray light of morning poured through the window. Too early, and she didn't know what had awakened her. Norm's palm slid along her arm, slow and tender, leaving a trail of goose bumps behind. Lucy rolled against him, her breasts brushing his body, his chest hair tickling against her skin. She propped her chin on his torso and reached up, tracing the line of his nose from brow to tip.

He twitched. "Are you trying to make me sneeze?"

She bounced her finger on his nose, squishing the cartilage. "You got a great nose, you know?"

"We do not speak of the nose."

She laughed under her breath and crawled up his body to perch with her face right over his. "I like the nose. It's, ah, what's that word? Patrician! Roman-esque. Stately." She dropped a quick kiss on the facial feature in question.

Norm snagged a kiss from her mouth too then reclined on the pillows, shaking his head. "The nose is a beak."

She was opening her mouth to argue with him when the sharp rap of knuckles on the front door made her jolt in surprise. Norm rolled away from her, scooping up a pair of sweats and a t-shirt from the floor. "Probably Jehovah's Witnesses or something. I'll tell them I'm busy fornicating then I'll rush right back."

Lucy burrowed into the covers, giggling as he trotted to the front. Dreamily floating toward sleep, she listened to the sounds of him flicking the lock, the front door creaking open. She waited for him to deliver the fornicating line but, after one tense, pulsing moment of silence, he yelled, "*Mom?!*"

Lucy bolted upright in bed, totally awake now. "*Shit.*"

Chapter Eighteen

Lucy flung herself out of Norm's bed, nearly doing a face-plant on his ugly shag carpet when her foot tangled in her underwear on the floor. She somehow managed not to fall and she used the momentum from her near-tumble to scrape her clothing from the ground. She dumped the pile on the bed and hurriedly sorted her things from Norm's, then skinned into her own clothes in record time. her overalls were still on the floor of the bathroom. Norm not having wanted them to stink up the bedroom overnight. She raked her fingers through her hair then surveyed the room, searching for her bag and it's so useful hair brush, but the purse was nowhere. *Crud. Must have left it in the living room.*

She hissed her breath out through her teeth in frustration then took a deeper breath in. *Still, of all the things to betray to this woman the fact that I'm shagging her son, bed hair is probably the least of my worries.* Lucy slapped her thigh, admitting defeat. She wasn't capable of climbing out the window and shimmying down the drain pipe anyway. *Does Norm even have a drainpipe?*

A meeting with Norm's mother was, therefore, unavoidable. *Dammit.*

Lucy pressed her forehead to the bedroom door and sucked in one quick breath to steel herself, then another. Her nerve endings on fire with anxiety, she pushed open the door and made her walk of shame toward the living room with head held high.

In her Jezebel's tank top and matching hot pants.

When weighing her options, appearing before his mother in her own revealing wardrobe--vs. Norm's pajamas or the stinky overalls--her own clothes, minimal as they were, had seemed the least of all evils.

Lucy entered the living room and Norm flashed her a wide-eyed glance, looking like a cornered animal. A really embarrassed, cornered animal. His mother pushed from the plush confines of the couch and nodded 'hello' to Lucy.

Lucy had to force her features not to betray her surprise. Norm's mother was *tiny*, pint-sized even as she stood in the shadow of her six foot four inch son. She was even a few inches shorter than Lucy, barely over five feet. A second look showed Mrs. Keane was in her early fifties but with a slim figure displayed by her jeans and slightly fitted t-shirt--a vintage *Return of the Jedi* t-shirt.

Lucy grinned. "Wow. I *love* your shirt!"

Mrs. Keane gazed down to make eye contact with the cartoon R2 and 3PO adorning her breasts then smiled back at Lucy. "Why, thank you. I probably shouldn't admit this, but I bought this shirt when the movies first opened."

On first glance, Norm's mother didn't resemble him in appearance much more than she did in height. Her face was round and full where his was long and lean. Her nose was small and cutely snub where his was large, long, and, Lucy chuckled inside, *Patrician*. But Mrs. Keane did have

209

the same eyes, big, round and colored a pretty burnt toffee shade. They probably had the same light brown hair, too, but hers was longer, of course, hanging to her shoulders in thick layers, and hers was darker, nature perhaps supplemented with the help of her stylist. She had a sort of pixyish look about her, which had probably been much more pronounced when she was younger. Even now, in her fifties, she moved with a sunny, bouncing energy.

Mrs. Keane stepped forward, extending her hand. "I'm Janet Keane. Norm's mother."

Lucy clasped the other woman's smooth, cool hand, blushing as she realized how long she must have been staring. "I'm Lucy. Lucy York." Lucy shot Norm a quick, questioning glance. Should she elaborate beyond her name? *Norm and I are coworkers? I'm a friend?*

I'm his girlfriend.

That last thought, scary and sweet, burned through her brain to sear the back of her skull, like a particularly bright flash on a camera. Her heart clenched with some strong emotion she didn't want to identify. She pursed her lips and said nothing.

Norm's mom--*Janet*, Lucy corrected herself--tipped her head to the side, a wry smile playing about her lips. "Honey, your shirt is on backwards." Which effectively settled the matter of whether they were pretending that his mother had done anything but walk in on Norm with a girl.

Lucy snapped her eyes shut in embarrassment so acute it hurt. "Just hell." Norm didn't help any when he choked back a laugh.

Janet leaned forward and patted Lucy's shoulder. "It's all right, mothers are people. I've even had sex a time or two myself." She slid a mischievous glance Norm's way. "And Norm is living proof."

"*Mom.*" He groaned, for all the world like a grossed out teenager.

Lucy blew her breath out on a gusty laugh. "Of course, Mrs. Keane."

"*Janet*"

Lucy nodded. "Janet."

Norm, all this while, had been hovering, shifting from foot to foot, watching their exchanges with bated breath. "Right. Lucy, I'm sorry, but I forgot I'm visiting an amusement park with my family today."

"It's my birthday," Janet said.

He cast her a glare of mild annoyance. "Don't make this sound worse than it is, Mom." He wheeled toward Lucy. "Her birthday is on Saturday. I *remembered* it was Saturday." He seemed concerned for Lucy to understand that he had not forgotten his mother's actual birthday.

"He just forgot he agreed to a family fun trip for today." Dimples appeared on Janet's cheeks.

"Yeah." Norm swung toward Lucy, his face apologetic.

She gasped in a quick breath, shaking her head, hiding disappointment. She'd been looking forward to a full day with Norm all week and now--*Non-productive, Lucy. Just get your shit and get out.* She ran her gaze all over the living room floor, desperately scanning for her purse, which had picked the perfect time to go AWOL. "Oh. Well then I'll get out of your way so you can get ready. I don't want to hold you guys up."

"*No.*" Both Keanes said the word at the same time, though Norm employed more force than his mother.

211

"Oh, come with us," Janet said. "It won't be only me and the boys anyway. My son Truman is meeting us there with his wife, and my youngest son is bringing a friend. And Hunter couldn't make it so we even have an extra ticket. Please, we'd love to have you."

Lucy did not miss the sly glance Janet slid Norm's way from under her lashes. Co-conspirator or puppet master?

Whichever it was, Norm leapt in support of the invite at once. "Yeah. Please, come. You have the day off. It'll be great." Without waiting for a reply, Norm grabbed Lucy by the hand and dragged her toward his bedroom. He called over his shoulder as he walked, "Mom, give us ten minutes and we'll meet you out front."

Lucy couldn't help but feel ambushed, and didn't know whether to be annoyed or flattered.

When they were safely alone together in his bedroom, she whirled on him, vehemently shaking her head. "Norm, I can't go. I have literally nothing to wear." She whipped her arm down in a large circle to encompass the skimpiness of her outfit. "And, as crazy as I am about you, even *you* cannot convince me to go to a family amusement park dressed in hot pants. In front of your mother."

"No, no, it's fine. You left a pair of jeans here the other day and I washed them for you. So no hot pants." He crossed to his dresser and yanked out an armful of clothes. He dropped the jeans into her arms with one hand while holding the other behind his back. "And, I have *this* for you if you don't want to brand yourself a Jezebel in the land of family fun times." He swung his arm forward and dropped a pale gray t-shirt on top of her folded jeans.

SAVE THE CLOCK TOWER blazed in bright white letters from the shirt, and she brushed her fingers fondly over the material. "You got me my own?"

"Yeah, so you wouldn't steal mine. I was also hoping to ransom my Batman t-shirt. A prisoner exchange, if you will."

"Norm, thank you." She paused. "But you're never seeing that Batman t-shirt again."

"I thought it was worth the effort. See, you have no excuses. You have to go."

She grimaced, her gut writhing with unease. "Do you really want to introduce me to your whole family already? I mean, so soon?"

"Ah, don't over-think, angel, just come with me." His voice turned cajoling, "When was the last time you visited an amusement park?"

"Probably with the robotics club in high school."

"See, you're overdue." He caught her hands and shook them slightly, as if he could jiggle her into submission. "We can do all the roller coasters: guaranteed to give you motion sickness or your money back. We can make out on that tunnel ride they have. I never got to do that as a teenager. It'll be *great*." He wiggled his eyebrows, horny guy leer appearing cheek by jowl with the breathless excitement of a kid.

Feeling her resolve bend, she tweaked his nose. "Yeah, don't hold your breath for that last one, babe."

"You'll go?"

Lucy nodded and knew it was the right decision when he scooped her up in a quick, hard hug that lifted her feet off the ground and sent her heart swooping.

213

An amusement park with the whole family was more than slightly intimidating but, after all, she'd promised Norm more dates, right?

***

She almost balked when they descended the apartment stairs to get to the car and she discovered she would be in the backseat. With Norm's little brother and his little friend. Trapped in a backseat with two rowdy twelve-year-old boys. Yeah, so *not* her idea of romance.

Norm leaned so his lips brushed her ear, causing shivers as he said, "I'm sorry. I promised Mom I'd drive. She hates parking at this place, and she gets easily frazzled."

Norm's mother materialized from the other side, and patted Lucy on the shoulder. "I'm sorry, hon, I'd give you shotgun but I get motion sickness if I sit in the back." She grimaced in embarrassment.

Lucy waved their apologies away and pinned a game smile on her face. It was the backseat. Not the end of the world.

She climbed in and nodded at the two boys. They had been sitting as far apart as the backseat would allow, each huddled over their own individual tablets. "Hi. I'm Norm's friend. Lucy."

The boy on her far side with the window seat was tall in a painfully skinny, stretched taffy sort of way that boys in the middle of growth spurts often got. He had dark skin and startling pale grey eyes and would probably grow into a handsome guy someday. The other boy was on the shorter, stocky side, with a cap of glossy black hair and his cheeks plump with baby fat. When he finally darted a nervous gaze at Lucy, he had the more masculine version of Janet's nose and the same brown eyes Norm and his mother both shared. She held her hand out to the dark-haired boy squashed in next to her. "You must be Tommy."

He clasped her hand briefly, young enough to be awkward at the unfamiliar adult gesture. "Tom."

The other boy glanced away from his game long enough to give her a wave. "I'm Franco."

She waved greetings to both but each boy had already resumed their interrupted video games. *Tom, eh?* Someone seemed to be edging toward contrary teenager-dom early.

The twelve year olds were polite enough to know not to crowd the strange lady in the backseat with them, but clearly they were not under any orders to make polite conversation. As Norm drove down the street to the onramp her nerves vibrated harder and harder inside her. Every pulse of her heart seemed to come from the space right behind her ear drum. Who knew family car trips could be so stressful to her?

It's because they're not your *family.* She swallowed a small knot in her throat and leaned forward to engage the front seat in conversation, since the back remained too enamored of their video games. "Is Mr. Keane meeting us there, too?"

"No. My husband couldn't make it." Janet let out a small, quick huff of annoyance and Tommy--*Tom* twitched beside Lucy.

Norm cast his mom a quick glance. "Dad's not coming?"

Janet visibly pushed aside her annoyance and waved her hand in dismissal. "Oh no. He hates amusement parks, sweetie, and he's finishing a paper on the significance of

215

makeup imagery and its relation to women's roles in *Hamlet*."

"Fun." Norm's voice was flat.

Lucy shook her head, gnawing at her lower lip. Crud, two minutes into the car ride and she'd already picked open one of the family's scars.

Janet glanced out the window, then gave a gasp of pleasure. "*Oh*, what a beautiful car."

Lucy grinned as they whizzed past her bright red beauty.

Tom whirled to gaze out the back window so he could keep the Mustang in sight. He didn't face forward in his seat again until they had rounded a curve in the street and the car passed out of sight. "That is one hot ride," he murmured, lifting the videogame up from his lap.

Rocking forward, hesitating, Lucy finally touched his arm to draw his attention away from the game. "That was my car."

The game dropped to his lap, completely forgotten as he whipped toward her with wide, shining eyes. "You own that cherry Mustang?"

"Yeah."

Norm half-turned over his shoulder. "She built it, too." The way his voice warmed with pride you'd think *he'd* built the Mustang.

"*You* built a *car*?" He gripped her arm in excitement then remembered himself and released her. He bounced in his seat, betraying that there was still some little kid left in him. His friend, Franco, just rolled his eyes.

"I built the car with my dad during the summer in high school," she said. "You like cars?"

216

Tom's friend snorted, which seemed to mean something along the lines of *Duh, lady.*

Shoving his game to the side, Tom whipped toward her and for the next thirty minutes he picked her brain about the Mustang. Once she'd demonstrated that she wasn't a one-trick pony, for the thirty minutes after that, he picked her brain about cars in general. Driving them, building them, he appeared determined to empty her brain of every last car related fact she possessed.

And she loved the whole conversation with Tom. A long time had passed since she'd had anyone to talk shop with. Janet beamed at the two of them as they chattered away together, and Lucy shook her head in awe. *Clever woman.* Janet had obviously commented on the Mustang on purpose to get Tom to open up. The woman really was a master tactician.

Tom, it turned out, was astoundingly bright as he asked her all sorts of car questions. *Runs in the family.* Lucy cast a fond glance at the back of Norm's head that he couldn't see.

Tom squirmed beside her. *Oops.* Backseat Etiquette Rule #1: *Don't ogle the older brother in front of the younger one.*

"Are you and Norm dating?" Tom dropped his voice low, like he didn't want the front seat to hear.

She nodded, scrutinizing him in confusion.

"Do you think you'll be hanging with Norm for awhile because--if you are--maybe...I could work on your car with you sometime?" Tom's voice had that cultivated air of indifference that pre-teenagers were so busy developing. She would have believed his indifference if not for the way his voice threaded high on the last word in vulnerable hope.

217

"Sounds fun." Inside, her stomach busied itself twisting into a rat's nest of tangles.

Janet leaned over the seat to pin Lucy with her affable gaze. "How long have you and Norman been...seeing each other?"

Norm froze in the front seat, maybe scared by what Lucy'd say, or maybe as uncomfortable as she was with the relationship interrogation.

"About two weeks or so." Not even that, she realized, counting back. Only about a week and a half. Their relationship seemed so new and shiny that she found it hard to believe a week had already passed.

Then again, it seemed equally hard to believe it had *only* been a week.

Janet's tone suddenly struck Lucy as odd. A question within a question. Janet wasn't just asking how long they'd been seeing each other. Janet was asking if they *were* seeing each other. Norm's mother was *really* asking if Lucy's intentions towards Norm were honorable.

Gulp. Her and Norm. The thousand dollar question, right? *What are we doing? Where is this going?* They'd barely started dating and already that question had become fully loaded, perilous.

If she and Norm were having a fling, fuck buddies, all in good fun, etc., etc., then she didn't have to tell Hank about the relationship--because the interlude would be over soon enough so what was the point of creating a lot of drama over something so trivial?

But if she and Norm were having a fling then she should dive out the car door right now and run for home--because obviously flings did not get to go on family fun days.

But if she and Norm were *more*, were heading toward some auspicious relationship milestone she couldn't even wrap her head around, then she had every right to her space in this backseat, sandwiched between two budding teenagers, staring at the back of her maybe-boyfriend's head.

But if she and Norm were *more*, then she should dive out of the car and run for Jezebel's to tell Hank about them right now--because Hank was her boss, but he was her family too, and he had a right to know about anyone important in Lucy's life.

And why, *why*, did she have to worry about so much five minutes into their relationship? She didn't even know his birthday yet!

She wanted to bunch her fists in her hair and scream just to purge some of the tension. Instead she sat straight and tall in the backseat, wrestling to keep the worries tearing through her skull from spilling onto her face.

Today is going to be a long day.

Chapter Nineteen

They rendezvoused with Norm's brother, Truman, and his wife outside the front gates. After seeing short, dark Tommy, Lucy hadn't known what to expect from Truman, but this other Keane brother was Norm all over again, only with slightly fairer hair and blue eyes. Other than that, Truman was essentially Norm Take Two: same nose, same ridiculous height, only Truman was skinnier which, oddly, made him appear taller.

Truman's wife, Alisha, was almost as tall as the older Keane brothers, at least six feet. Slim and leggy, she was a playful redhead with a bossy streak that delighted her husband if no one else. Lucy liked her--but she would never want to live with her.

Janet was the Queen of the Day and so dictated the agenda. Lucy braced herself for a day of tame rides and lots of shopping, but Janet surprised her by being a roller coaster aficionado. The woman got car sick but could handle three barrel loops, a two hundred foot drop and being shot backwards at 100 mph. *Go figure.*

The family spent the morning riding all the roughest, wildest rides in the park. One particularly violent go on the stand-up roller coaster rendered Lucy unable to support her own weight on her legs. Leaning on Norm as she staggered down the coaster's exit ramp, she finally asked to sit out the next bar brawl--roller coaster, that is.

"Oh, of course," Janet said, patting her own wildly matted hair into place. She leaned past one of her very tall sons and pointed to the brightly colored stalls around the corner. "Why don't you and Norm check out the carnival booths, and we can all meet again for lunch?"

Norm, not waiting to be told twice, snatched Lucy's hand and dragged her away. As soon as he seemed certain to be out of his family's view, he pulled her against him and kissed her in the shadow of the roller coaster.

Weird as the concept was when they'd already spent the whole morning together, but she *missed* him, missed having him all to herself. Maybe that was why she'd kept him chained to the bedroom, not to hide him away from the world, but to selfishly keep him all to herself?

Whatever. Didn't matter. She slanted her mouth against his, drawing her tongue slowly over the seam of his lips until he parted them and his tongue touched hers. He gave a small, quiet groan and she found herself pressed against the wall, Norm's body leaning over hers, deliciously *looming*, hard and hot. She threaded her fingers into his hair, drawing him closer, holding him right where she wanted him, feeling delightfully naughty the whole time, like two teenagers who'd snuck away from the chaperones.

Come to think of it, *she'd* never made out with anyone during the tunnel of love ride in high school either. Maybe now was the time to rectify that. She wrapped his calf with her leg, the denim of her jeans rasping against his, and he braced his legs to keep his knee from popping in under the pressure.

221

Things were getting really good when someone cleared their throat noisily behind Norm.

He eased away from her, a red flush creeping out of his collar to spread up his neck and into his cheeks. Lucy's face heated at about the same rate, probably leaving her as beet red as him. "Please, don't let that be my mother," he murmured. Lucy popped onto her tiptoes and peeped over his shoulder.

Not his mother, just a huffy grandmother with two giggling pre-teen girls in train. Lucy shot her an apologetic grimace and waved to the girls. Their giggles redoubled and the grandmother towed them away from the little corner of sin.

Norm turned back from peeking over his shoulder and met Lucy's eyes. She broke first, clinging to his shoulders as she collapsed in a fit of giggles, and he broke next, falling into her, vibrating with silent laughter against the top of her head.

Pinching laugh-tears from his eyes, he stared affectionately down at Lucy, and she warmed all over, but not from embarrassment anymore. A wicked grin curling his lips, he said nothing, only offered his hand to her.

Shy now, she slid her palm into his, and let him tow her over to the carnival booths.

"And now I shall display for you my manly prowess." He strolled toward one of the shooting gallery games, but she hauled hard on his arm to steer him in the other direction.

"Norm!" She pointed, giddy with the silly excitement that a girl could only get when her man was about to win her a cheap stuffed toy.

He craned to see the booth she was pointing to then huffed out a laugh. "OK."

The corner they strolled over to hadn't caught her eye because of the game played there but because of the prizes. Plush dollies of every Marvel Comics superhero: Hulk, Spiderman, Wolverine and the other X-Men, and, joy of joys, Iron Man. The booth housed a water gun game, where players had to shoot a target with the stream of water to power their little figure to the top first. This one was designed like a miniature race track where mini-horses passed each other in jerky gallops. A new race was about to begin, and Norm handed over cash to secure the last two seats in the race for Lucy and himself.

She blew her chance right out the gate when the water flicked on, and she was so surprised she let her gun veer sideways, totally missing the target. Norm was an expert, keeping his stream trained dead center, his tiny horse shooting to the top way ahead of all the others. Knowing she had no chance to recover her ground, she glanced sideways at their opponents: a couple of teenage boys more interested in ragging on each other's technique than winning, and a little girl, maybe kindergarten age, sitting on her dad's lap, her small hands wrapped over his where he gripped the gun for her. The girl and her dad were neck and neck with Norm on this last leg of the race, and the little girl bit her lip, her smooth child's brow furrowed in concentration.

Lucy smiled, reminded of her dad but, in the sun and comfort of Norm's company, for once, she wasn't crippled with pain by her memories. A tender warmth spread from her chest, radiating comfort. Maybe she'd reached a place

223

where she could remember her dad without having to mourn for him.

Norm glanced over and noticed the little girl, his gaze briefly slid over to Lucy then he refocused his attention on the water gun. A hairs breadth away from winning, he jerked his gun slightly off-center and the little girl won by a nose. She gave a crow of delight and the booth attendant presented her with her very own squashy red and yellow Iron Man doll. Norm beamed, clearly basking in his own chivalry.

Lucy glowed with pride in him but then winced as a high scream pierced her ear drum. She recoiled as the little girl let out another high animal howl of rage. She'd transformed at once from an adorable moppet to a snarling beast. "I *said* I *wanted* the pink penguin, Daddy!"

Her father shot a nervous glance at the watching crowd and made placating gestures. "But, sweetheart, you said you wanted to play *this* game."

"I don't *want* this doll." The girl threw her Iron Man at her father, the plush toy bouncing off his chest, and he caught it one-handed.

The father gave Norm and Lucy an apologetic nod as his daughter continued to shriek, sliding upwards toward a full scale tantrum. The much put-upon man yanked his daughter away. Eventually, he had to hoist her into his arms to restrain the pint-sized spitfire from bodily throwing herself to the ground.

Shaking her head in awe at the kid's lung power, Lucy pivoted on her stool and draped her wrists over Norm's shoulders. He smoothed his hand along her forearm, tilting his head apologetically. "That should have been your Iron Man."

Lucy snapped her fingers in an 'aw, shucks' gesture. She leaned in, feeling the heat of his skin inches from hers. "Doesn't matter. I already have the best prize in the park."

Norm ducked away from her kiss and scrunched his nose in a grimace. "Corny, angel. Sweet, but *tch* a leetle corny."

"Ah, shut up." She gripped the back of his neck and jerked him closer for a victory kiss.

The teenage boys behind them wolf-whistled, the booth attendant rolled his eyes, and Lucy just grinned against Norm's mouth, enjoying her prize.

***

On the car ride back, *almost* as late at night as Norm usually got home from Jezebel's. One by one, the rest of the car surrendered to exhaustion. Tommy's friend Franco fell asleep first with his head against the car window, then Mom snored softly in the seat beside Norm. Eventually, even Tommy slumped over sideways into Lucy, sleepily pillowing his head on her shoulder.

"Just push him over if that bugs you," Norm murmured, keeping his voice low to avoid waking anyone.

Hesitantly, looking nervous, Lucy hugged Norm's baby brother with one arm instead. Tommy was growing so fast, but he appeared more child than teenager in that moment, sweet and painfully young. As Lucy hugged him close, her affection for Tommy plain on her face, Norm's heart clutched with a rush of affection for her.

Being surrounded by people and yet totally alone created a special kind of intimacy between him and Lucy. That awareness charged the air as he looked ahead to the moment when he and Lucy would really be alone. He

225

stretched to glance at her in the rearview. "Is my baby brother putting the moves on you?"

"I wouldn't worry about that for a few years yet, Norman."

He wet his lips, his chest tight with sudden worry. "Did you have a good time today?"

"I did. You have a great family."

"Good." He forced himself to face front again, his hands clenching and unclenching on the steering wheel as he released the nervousness that had been building inside of him. He'd been a little worried that Lucy had been pretending all day, and when they were alone she'd let him know how pissed she was. "Good," he said again softly to himself, reaffirming it.

His family had wooed her well then. She seemed to like all of them, even bossy Alisha. His heart fluttered, like a startled bird trying to fly, as he realized he wanted Lucy to be a part of this. To be a part of his clever, loud, bossy, crazy family.

Too soon, Norman. He glanced into the rearview again as Lucy slowly lost out to the relaxing feel of a warm, sleepy child in her arms. Her head dipped to her chest in sleep, the soft blonde of her hair sliding down to hide her face.

He blinked. *Yeah. Much too soon.*

"I like her, Norm."

At the sound of his mom's voice he jumped. "Thought you were sleeping," he murmured, still quiet so as not to wake the people in the backseat.

His mom stretched then shot an uncomfortably keen-eyed gaze his way. "So, is it serious between you two?"

He had a hard time drawing his breath, but at last he let out a gusty laugh, trying to sound light-hearted but sounding simply panicked instead. "Please, don't let visions of grandkids start dancing in your head. We're just having fun right now." Not entirely true, but it seemed better than: *I'm dead serious, but she might be using me for my body. And my t-shirt collection.*

"Oh, hey, I forgot." Desperate to change the subject, he eased up and pulled his wallet out. He tossed it sideways to her and jerked his chin. "I have one of my cover flats in there."

His mom let out a tiny huff of annoyance--probably that he hadn't mentioned the cover flat sooner. She unfolded the wallet to slide out the glossy paper that had a mock-up of his novel's book cover. The publisher had sent them last week and a heady mixture of emotions had consumed him ever since. Crazy levels of excitement. Worry. And a bone-deep terror that sometimes made him long to yank the book from its publication spot and never write again.

"Have you told him yet?" he asked.

His mother's jaw clenched and she gave a stiff jerk of her head. *No.*

Relief flooded him along with a healthy dose of shame at that relief. He wasn't doing anything wrong having his work published, writing fiction. So why did his writing career still feel like a dirty secret?

His mother stared avidly at his cover. The image was a stylized white and gold hourglass with a long red crack running down the front. Very vintage Michael Crichton. Norm loved it. And he really loved the quote from one of his favorite SF authors saying, "Boy, can this guy write!"

227

"This is a great cover, honey." And she smiled, but the expression was wistful, her eyes sad.

He clutched the steering wheel and fought to keep his tone off-handed. "Mom, I could talk to my agent, Paige. Or my editor? You're an award-winning science fiction author. I'm sure--"

"We already talked about this. That's all behind me." She whipped her head sideways to cast him a pleading look, her face brittle, lined with weariness.

Reading the request in her face not to ruin Family Fun Day with this old wound, Norm bit his tongue and swallowed. Clutching his cover flat in her hands, she pretended to go back to sleep, and Norm pretended not to notice the falsehood in her snores.

Pretending not to notice was a finely honed skill in his family.

Chapter Twenty

Back at Norm's apartment he made his mother coffee for her drive home, and Lucy chuckled in memory at the last cup of coffee Norm had made for *her*. The door opened as he returned from seeing his family off. She dipped over the couch arm to see him. His face appeared preoccupied, frown lines knotting his brow.

"Hey!" she called.

His gaze crossed hers and she leaned over the chair arm, crooking her finger for him to come closer. "You owe me a day's worth of sexual debauchery, pal."

"Do I?" He prowled toward her, the air between them thickening with anticipation. She raised an eyebrow in challenge then fell back to sprawl across the couch. Norm, without missing a beat, stretched his full length atop her, pressing a knee between her legs to part them, the pressure of his thigh spreading a delicious heat where he touched her.

"Is Zack here?" she asked.

"His car's not. He must have been called in to work." Norm slid his hand behind her head, cradling it as he angled her face up to kiss her. His lips parted hers, his tongue massaging hers and coaxing a moan of pleasure out

229

of her. His thumb traced the edge of her jaw in small, tender circles.

She pushed him away carefully, her hands spread over his chest. "Norm."

"*Hmm.*" He nuzzled at her hair.

"Norm, I'm not good at this."

"Lucy, I know firsthand that you are."

Now she pushed him away in earnest, grimacing a little. "That is not what I mean. I mean *this.*" She flapped her hand back and forth in the narrow distance separating them. "Us. Relationships. I am not good at relationships. I haven't had a lot of practice. The longest relationship I ever had was twenty-nine days. The second longest was twenty-six."

"Oh-kaaaaay." The sound was a long, drawn out syllable, unsure, testing.

She sucked in a bracing breath then framed his jaw with her hands. "But you make me want to try."

His face split in a wide, goofy grin. Then he bent and kissed her again, groaning with pleasure when she stretched underneath him.

She slid her hands under the hem of his t-shirt, smoothing her fingers over the sculpted planes of his back then scratching as she worked south. The light material of his shirt fluttered over her hands, tickling as she moved. His muscles quivered under her touch, and he deepened their kiss, his tongue rubbing against hers, mirroring the subtle, almost instinctual movement of his hips. She flattened her palms against his spine and arched her body against the long curve of his. He slid his knee down and she moved her leg free, wrapping his waist with her legs and pulling his hips into the cradle of her own.

Norm broke the kiss when she moved against him. "Ah, not this time." He kissed her nose then gently eased her head onto the arm rest. He braced himself against the couch with one hand while the other hand glided over her body in a slow, torturous caress down her neck, tickling over her collarbone, out around the curve of her breast, over her ribcage, in to the softness of her belly then all the way to the button of her jeans. Lucy was fairly writhing beneath him by the time his strong fingers had worked their way that far south. She pushed her hips against his hand, and in one smooth twist he'd popped the button of her jeans. The quiet rasp of her zipper had Lucy nearly climbing out of her skin in anticipation.

He peeled the edges of her jeans away, loosening them on her hips without taking them off. She made a small mew of protest, which he muffled with a kiss as he slid his hand under the elastic of her panties to cup her. The tip of one finger worked gently at her folds, slicking over her, up and down in a gentle but firm pressure that made her muscles tense. Her breath left her in shallow, gasping pants. Strung taut, coiled with tension and heat and energy, all of her self seemed to be sliding down and narrowing, narrowing to that one tiny place where Norm's finger stroked the very center of her. He watched her, his gaze dark, liquid, then pushed one long finger inside all the way to the knuckle. He pressed against her clit and slowly rubbed.

She skimmed her hand along the braced muscles of his arm to shackle his wrist, holding him in place. In case he had *any* plans of moving anytime soon. He chuckled low in his throat, the laugh more vibration than actual sound.

231

Dropping a quick kiss to her lips, he slid another finger inside, stretching her, touching her deep, rubbing her nerves deliciously raw with desire and heat and *need*. She pressed her eyes shut, the muscles of her sex pulsing around the length of his fingers, echoing the gasping need that held the rest of her body poised, teetering. *Close. So close.* He increased his rhythm, rocking the heel of his hand against her and the cord inside her broke. She came with a quick, sharp scream, the world blacking out for a long, ecstatic minute. Her orgasm broke through her, leaving her shuddering and laughing and gasping in its wake.

While she was rolling in languid afterglow, Norm whipped her *Back to the Future* t-shirt off and tossed the garment aside, leaving her in a black lace bra she'd worn special for him. She peeled away his shirt and sent it sailing over their heads to join hers. He dipped his head and nibbled her skin, carefully grinding his teeth against the hardened bud of her nipple over the bra. His teeth and the fabric rubbing against her skin sent her writhing anew, her desire only magnified by the orgasm she'd already had.

He popped the front-clasp on her bra and peeled the fabric away to bare her breast. A look of almost pained pleasure crossed his face as he bent to kiss her nipple, whispering "Beautiful," across her skin as he licked and sucked. She fumbled for his belt buckle and jeans, her hands rough and shaky as she folded the fabric back and pushed her hands in, sliding over the curve of his ass to grab his lovely tight cheeks and hold him against her, straining her hips against his.

Which was when the front door banged open and the lights came on.

Norm stiffened above her, lowering his body to shield her nakedness. The muscles on his arms and chest stood out in sharp relief as everything in him went rigid with tension. "Zack," his voice was a deliciously low growl. "Turn around. Right now. *And go away*."

"He can't, newbie," Ronnie said in her husky drawl from the doorway. "He's got company."

Ronnie's voice made Lucy cold all over, and the delicious heat and friction in her body leached away, flash frozen to absolute dread. Norm's gaze whipped down to Lucy, his face scrunched with concern. Feet shushed over the carpet; high-heels clacked across the entryway.

"Hey, give him a minute, Ronnie."

"Why?" The redhead rounded the corner to the living room, and Lucy squeezed her eyes shut, her face blazing with mortified heat, her body cold with absolute dismay.

"*Zack, don't--*" Norm's arm flashed out, his body sliding over hers, then the soft fabric of a t-shirt settled over her chest, shielding her breasts if not her dignity from the horror of this moment.

"*Oh, shit.*" As the horrified exclamation broke from Ronnie, Lucy finally forced her eyes open. She met Ronnie's wide-eyed disbelief over the edge of Norm's bare shoulder. Yup. No way to pass this off as anything other than a Caught in the Act Moment.

Twice in one day. Lucy swallowed with difficulty, clutching the fabric of Norm's shirt protectively over her tits.

Zack, at least, had his back turned and his eyes shielded, but Ronnie remained too shocked for a long, impossible minute to remember those social graces. Finally, shaking her head, Ronnie wheeled away, her ankle

233

popping once beneath her as she teetered precariously on her heels. "Fuck. I am *so* sorry, guys."

Lucy seized the moment to whip Norm's shirt over her head without even clasping her bra first. She roughly pushed him off her and darted across the living room, snatching her purse then scraping her car keys off the coffee table.

"Lucy? *Lucy.*" Her name was a distracting buzz in her ear, insistent, desperate, too loud. She shook her head, jerking away from Norm's voice as she scrambled to get the hell out. To get *away.* Fortunately, they hadn't gotten to taking their shoes off yet, so she didn't have to pause for that.

A curious numbness settled over her, leaving her distant, detached as she collected her things at hyper-speed and hurried out of the apartment. It was over then. All done. This secret, beautiful, private thing she'd had with Norm had just imploded. Ronnie had caught them, she'd tell Hank, and it was all over. Everything was over.

"Lucy!" This was as she threw the door open and hurtled down the apartment steps, her sneakers dull thumps as she bounded to her car. She caught a quick glimpse of Norm chasing her, still shirtless, frantic. Then she was in the Mustang and roaring through the street, the panicked, too-quick rasp of her own breathing deafening in the quiet of the car, her own heartbeat making her ill with its frenzied rhythm. *One more night.* The words became a refrain in her head, a furious pulse at the back of her skull. *Just one more night.* If she had to lose Norm why couldn't the universe have given them one more night together first?

Tears clouded her eyes and emotion burned her throat. She sniffed and blinked the tears free to clear her vision. After a long, squinting minute she finally remembered to flick on the Mustang's headlights. *Idiot.* She parked at her apartment and raced up the steps, nerves jittery even after her long drive home. She slammed into her apartment then fell against the door, sliding with her back to the wood until she'd crumpled like a rag doll on the carpet. Drawing her knees close, she sunk her head between them, grasping her skull with her fingertips, trying to make her brain stop. Just stop.

Someone knocked on the door behind her and she nearly jumped out of her skin.

Adrenaline burned her throat, but she wobbled to her feet and peered through the peephole. *Norm.* She recoiled in surprise then flicked the deadbolt off and eased the door open.

Norm, panting and furious, his t-shirt on backwards, pushed into her apartment. "What the hell was that?"

She swallowed and shrugged. "Panic? 'Sheer, bloody panic, sir.'"

"This isn't fucking funny."

She fell against the door and it pressed closed under her weight. "You're pissed."

"*Yeah.* Why did you do that?" He paced her narrow living room, his long legs crossing the space in milliseconds so he kept having to wheel back and start all over again to keep moving.

Good thing I don't have furniture.

He stopped, his arms braced on his hips as he scowled at her. "You know, there was about a minute

235

there when Ronnie actually believed I'd been hurting you. *Forcing* you."

"Shit." Lucy squeezed her eyes closed, lifting her hand to her mouth. "I'm sorry."

"Yeah, and *then* I had to talk her into giving me your address because I don't even know where you fucking live."

Steeling herself, she let her hand fall and opened her eyes, meeting his furious gaze head on. "Norm, I am so sorry. I wasn't worrying about how things might look. I just had to get out of there."

He nodded, his head jerking hard up and down, every movement of his body charged with brittle energy. "Right. Because God forbid anyone find out about your dirty mistress." He jerked his thumb against his chest then let his arm fall limply to his side. His eyes were pinched and sad when they met hers. "Especially your friends. Wouldn't want them to know you'd fuck someone like me."

"*It wasn't like that.*" She rushed toward him, reaching for him, but he retreated, shaking his head, making a small warding gesture with his hand. She cleared her throat once, and was pleasantly surprised when her voice came out normal. "I freaked. I'm sorry. My tits were hanging out, your fly was open and we had a goddamn captive audience for the whole big show. Having Ronnie catch us is nearly as bad as Hank and I freaked out. Fight or flight--"

"And, boy, can you fly."

She bit her cheek, twisting the hem of her t-shirt. "I wasn't ready to tell people yet and now, twice in one day, we've been outed."

He snorted, leaning against the wall opposite from her and crossing his arms over his chest in a distinctly uninviting posture. "Nice word choice."

"I told you I'm not good at this stuff." She banged her fist against the door, making the wood rattle behind her. "I *told* you." Her knees buckled and she slid down again, curling into herself. She'd known this would come: the moment when she'd blow everything and drive him off. But this smash up had happened so quick. *One more night. Just one more...* she raked her eyes against the skin of her arm to brush away the tears.

The warmth of him reached her first as he crouched in front of her then a hint of lovely Norm-smell hit her, which only made her sobs redouble. Her chest ached as she hiccupped out a breath.

"*Hey, hey.*" Somehow he managed to get her unfolded from her hunched position by the door and settled into his lap. He curled around her, warm and hard and safe and Norm, and she clung to his t-shirt collar and cried, whispering, "*I'm sorry,*" over and over again until she was gasping and hiccupping too hard to form the words.

Something had broken in her, an inner dam that had held back a well of emotion, and Lucy wasn't sure what she was crying about anymore. Being caught. The fight. His family. Her dad. Everything collided together in a hurricane of wild, clamoring emotions. And it was all trying to burst from the broken places inside her to slosh out her eyeballs in a flood of tears.

Norm said nothing through the tumult, simply held her and made those soothing noises everybody makes when people cry. He was a bit more adept at comforting a crying woman than most guys of her experience, though.

237

Maybe his steadiness came from having younger siblings. A rational adult sobbing her eyes out couldn't be half as intimidating as a wholly irrational infant squalling for God only knows what.

Once her sobs subsided she pushed away from him, using the hem of her shirt, which was really his shirt, to pat the wetness from her cheeks. Norm took over, lifting the hem of the shirt he wore and flashing some belly as he swabbed at her cheeks and under her eyes.

That brittle, biting anger was gone from his eyes, and she sighed her relief aloud. "I'm sorry," she said one last time, slowly, calmly, and staring him straight in the eye so he'd know she was sincere and not just hysterical.

"OK." He smoothed one hand over her face. "We're OK. I am not a one-fight boyfriend here."

"'One-fight boyfriend'?"

"Those guys who decide that one fight means the relationship is over. Who cut and run instead of talking stuff out or trying to repair anything. One fight and they're out."

She voiced a small, bitter laugh. "In that case, I guess I'm usually a one-fight girlfriend."

"But not with me?"

"Not with you," she murmured.

He kissed her gently, quickly on the lips, and when he pulled back he pressed his forehead to hers. He kept his eyes shut tight as if maybe he could hold that moment forever if only he didn't open his eyes. *I know how he feels.*

Norm wasn't the most muscular man she knew, but he was the strongest. Her eyes prickled again, and she pushed away from him, murmuring, "Tissues."

At her kitchen counter, after blowing her nose on a rough paper napkin and disposing of it, she faced him. "I will try to be better. We will do stuff. Date stuff. And I will introduce you to my non-work friends, and I will hang out with your family. And I will not melt down or run away. And we will make this work." She clutched the counter behind her hard enough her fingers felt ready to snap with the tension. "I want this to work."

He stood in front of her, looming like he did, solid and real and everything she wanted. He hugged her, pillowing his cheek on her hair as he whispered, no louder than she had, "Me too."

Chapter Twenty-One

Over the next two weeks, Lucy made more of an effort not to hide Norm away from the world and Norm, for his part, fought hard not to push Lucy about moving the relationship further. He took her on a picnic in the Huntington Gardens. She made him try horseback riding in Griffith Park.

They also both worked on balancing their real lives with the crazy infatuation of their relationship. Lucy stopped skipping her classes, and Norm refocused on writing. Sometimes they just sat together in his bedroom, Norm pecking away at the computer on his next story, Lucy stretched out on the bed solving all the universe's problems with mathematics.

One weekend Norm quelled his nerves long enough to let Lucy read his book. The novel was a breathless page turner with time travel, a star-crossed couple and *dinosaurs* of all things. Lucy loved the book and, after much honest praise, she managed to convince *Norm* that she loved his book.

The next full day they both had off, they stayed in together at Norm's apartment and had a movie day, making the other sit through all the beloved films of their misspent youth. He made her watch *The Thing From Another*

World, which had a surprisingly sexy romantic subplot, and *Forbidden Planet*, which had a surprisingly sexy young Leslie Nielsen. She made him watch *Ladyhawke*.

"You know," he said after *Ladyhawke*, "that movie could have been a classic of American cinema but for the unfortunate disco score. Navarre is a total bad ass."

"Told ya you'd like it." She gave him a gloating nudge with her socked foot. The socks had robots on them.

He glanced to where she had her foot pressed to his thigh and tweaked her toe. "Nice robots."

"Nice giant, *warrior* robots," she corrected, which made him laugh as he padded barefoot to the kitchen to refill the popcorn bowl.

Spending all this time with Norm seemed so right, snuggling against him on the couch, strolling and laughing in the sun, kissing and touching in the dark. He was her lover, but, more than that, he was swiftly becoming the best friend she'd ever had.

Not wanting to be a one-fight girlfriend any longer, she ignored that insidious, nasty voice in her head telling her that it was only a matter of time until he left her. But believing in them was hard for her. They were swiftly approaching their one-month anniversary--an expiration date which none of Lucy's previous relationships had made it past.

The night of their movie day and two weeks after the whole caught-in-the-act thing, Zack managed to convince both of them to go bowling with him and Ronnie to make up for the "in flagrante delicto situation" as he called it.

Lucy had been diligently avoiding Ronnie at work while also watching for any signs of trouble from the Hank-quarter. After all this time, everything *seemed* quiet

241

there. Ronnie probably hadn't told Hank anything. But that didn't mean she wouldn't. Or that she hadn't been hinting to him.

Lucy and Ronnie were friends, allies at the bar when needed, even against Hank on occasion. But Ronnie had a ruthless side too and, for whatever reason, she never had particularly liked Lucy being Hank's favorite. The redhead also constantly needled Hank, tiptoeing toward the line without actually crossing it, but one of these days she would push Hank too far. And what then? Could Lucy depend on Ronnie not to sell her out to save her own ass? Ronnie was also a shit-stirrer by nature, and Lucy didn't know how long she could trust a perpetual troublemaker like Ronnie to sit on such a delicious secret.

And the fact Lucy was having all these horrible, mistrustful thoughts and worries about one of her best friends really wasn't helping improve her mood either.

Lucy and Norm arrived first at the bowling alley, and she headed straight for the bar to order a beer. When the drink came, she gulped half of it in one go to calm her nerves. And, hopefully, silence some of her roiling paranoia.

"Hey, slow down, sweetheart." His hand settled against her lower back, rubbing soft, soothing circles of warmth that helped more than the beer had.

"Sorry. Nerves." She wiped her mouth with her hand. "Besides, isn't bowling more fun when you're drunk?"

"I guess. But I think it's a sliding curve."

Zack hailed them from the front of the alley. Norm waved while Lucy pushed away from the bar counter more slowly at Zack and Ronnie's approach. The redhead shot past both the guys to hone right in on Lucy. She grabbed

242

Lucy's arm and tugged her away from the safety of Norm's shadow, bellowing, "Girl talk!" over her shoulder.

Ronnie hauled Lucy to the far corner of the bowling alley and settled her hip against an empty seat there. Lucy blinked, taking in Ronnie's street wear. She so seldom saw the busty redhead in anything but her shot girl clothes that seeing Ronnie in jeans and a pale green blouse was a bit of an adjustment. Of course, the jeans were skin-tight and the blouse was low-cut but still, the outfit was a whole new Ronnie. "You and Zack dating?" Lucy asked.

Ronnie lifted one shoulder in a casual shrug. "Nothing serious. He's cute, he's fun, and he's good in bed." Which effectively ended that conversation. Lucy braced herself as Ronnie leaned toward her, eyes narrowed. "So, you and the newbie."

"Norm," Lucy corrected again, without any heart. She fiddled with the buttons on her red cardigan, popping them open and closed, open and closed, as she avoided Ronnie's piercing gaze. "Please, don't tell Hank."

Ronnie let out a disgusted scoff. "Honey, as if I *would*."

Lucy blinked, totally confused. "But…" She cleared her throat, realizing just in time that she probably shouldn't say what she was thinking.

Ronnie glared. "What?"

The top button on Lucy's cardigan came off in her hand when she pulled it too hard. At last, she met her friend's gaze head-on. "You love getting me in trouble with Hank. It's practically your hobby."

Ronnie eased back, her eyebrows arched in surprise. "Honey, that's always nickel and dime stuff. He'd probably fire you over this." She squeezed Lucy's hand. "I'd never

243

do that to you, Lucy. I'm not telling anyone at Jezebel's about you and the newbie." She crossed an X-mark over her impressive bosom. "Promise."

Lucy nodded, and fought to control a sudden trembling in her gut. Norm was so, *so* wrong. Even Ronnie believed that Lucy's relationship with Hank wasn't enough to save her job.

Ronnie, perhaps in an effort to change the subject, wiggled her hips and settled herself more firmly on the back of the bowling seat. "Hon, I really dragged you over here to get the details. When did the thing with the newbie start? *How?* What's he like in bed?"

Lucy let out a quick laugh, all the Ronnie-related tension leeching out of her. Unfortunately, her perpetual dread about Hank finding out had only begun to grow.

***

"What are they doing over there?" Zack asked.

Norm narrowed his eyes as one red head and one blonde head leaned closer together, the blonde casting a shifty glance over her shoulder. Norm shrugged. "Plotting world domination."

"Should I be worried?"

"Probably. You're with the redhead. In the evil genius equation, Lucy's the genius, but Ronnie brings the evil. I'm convinced she eats her mates after she's done with them."

"You were right. She is one *scaaaary* lady."

"And?"

"And I like it." Zack grinned, showing every one of his very straight, very white teeth.

"Well, mazel tov."

"Don't pick out the china yet, Bates. We're just having fun. Not like you and Supergirl."

Norm tried to sound casual, dismissive even, as he said, "Me and Supergirl?"

"'*Wuv*,'" Zack declared. "'Twu wuv that will fowow you foweva...So *tweasure* your wuv--'"

Norm waved him to silence before Zack could finish the whole *Princess Bride* monologue. "Nah, man. We're just having fun." Norm's words were stilted, unnatural, a hollow echo of Zack's breezy assertion about Ronnie. "It might go somewhere, but I'm not worrying about that."

"Sure, Bates. Whatever you say." Zack slapped his shoulder and crossed to the cashier to pay for their bowling games.

In the far corner, Lucy laughed and shook her head, retreating from Ronnie. It took everything Norm had not to swoop in and draw her protectively against his side. Her eyes actually glittered with amusement as she came toward him. He kissed her quick then gazed down, his brows furrowing despite his best efforts not to frown. "What did Ronnie say?"

Lucy bit her lip, half-successful at hiding her laugh. "She wanted the deets on you, babe. I'll have to watch the two of you, I can see that. You might be next on her list of conquests."

"Saints preserve me." He hugged Lucy close as if for protection. She giggled, a happy burst of joy, and threw her arms around his shoulders. Hugging her waist, he straightened up and lifted her feet from the ground. She let out a small, delighted squeal, and cocked one leg in the classic kiss pose.

"Oy, Buttercup!" Zack hollered. "Let's get this game going. I want to score tonight." Ronnie swatted Zack's

245

arm, and he winced then gestured to the bowling lanes. "At bowling. I want to score at *bowling*."

"Uh-huh." Ronnie shook her head and sauntered past him, all her curves jiggling.

Lucy yanked Norm's eyes forcibly away from Ronnie's curves with one hand on his chin and made him look at her. "Did Zack just call me 'Buttercup'?"

Norm adjusted his hold, still not setting her down; he enjoyed holding her too much. "Maybe..."

Zack appeared at Norm's side. "Nah, man. *You're* Buttercup. She's Supergirl, remember?" He rolled his eyes, apparently at Norm's lousy memory. "Let's bowl, lovebirds."

"Just when I was getting used to being 'Bates'." Norm set Lucy on her feet with reluctance, but took her hand as he tugged her toward their lanes.

"Why are you 'Buttercup'?"

"Because my roommate is an absolute, complete, one hundred percent, Grade A jack-ass." *And he thinks I'm in love*. Norm swallowed with difficulty and held hard to Lucy's hand.

They played girls vs. guys and, through a combination of Zack being distracted by Ronnie's ass, and Lucy's apparent bowl-improving buzz, the girls wiped the floor with the guys. After the game, Ronnie dragged Zack back to her lair to inflict God only knew what torture on him. Zack bore the danger stoically, shooting Norm a quick wink as Ronnie hauled his poor carcass away.

Which meant Norm had the apartment and Lucy all to himself once more. On the car ride back, he drove his fabulous, running-just-fine-thanks-to-Lucy Toyota, while she snuggled against his side, only somewhat hampered by the gear shift. "That was fun," she murmured, her voice thick with sleep.

"No reason to be so worried about Ronnie?"

"No reason."

He awkwardly slung his arm over her shoulders but the angle hurt too much so he adjusted to keep her leaning against his side. She had both her hands wrapped around the one of his and ran her thumb along his skin, gently stroking. A shiver of happiness pulsed through him. *Zack's not wrong.*

Norm let out a long, slow breath. No way could he tell Lucy. Not yet. She was doing much better, but she still got skittish sometimes, nervous about the depth of their relationship. Nervous about her own feelings maybe?

He let out a small, derisive snort. He was *the guy* and he was expending all this time contemplating *feelings*? If Zack knew, Norm really would be stuck with the "Buttercup" moniker for the rest of his life.

"Hey, I was gonna work on the Mustang tomorrow at my place." Lucy sat up, blinking to awaken herself. "Can we go there instead?"

He lifted their clasped hands to kiss the back of hers. "OK. I can work while you work." He merged the car out of the far lane and into the middle since Lucy's exit was much farther down the freeway than the off ramp for his place.

"I promised Tom he could help. Do you mind if I invite him over?"

Norm tensed, hesitating. "Sure. That means we'll be seeing my mom, though. Tommy can't drive."

She rolled her eyes. "Norman, I like your mother."

247

"Right. Well, we'll have to make sure you have all your clothes on this time too." She slapped him in the gut. He caught her hand and, laughing, kissed her fingertips. "Don't assault the driver."

"No?" Her voice had gone oddly low, and she reached over to slide her palm along his thigh then down and in--

"Hey!" He jumped in his seat and plucked her hand away from his crotch. "Not that I don't appreciate the thought, but I can't multitask that well. Drive or receive handjob. Not both."

Lucy primly tucked her hands into her own lap. "I'll keep my hands to myself until we get to the apartment then."

"You do that." But he let his hand snake out, sliding under her shirt to fondle her breast.

"Oh, the driver doesn't have to keep *his* hands to *himself*?" She tilted back to give him freer access and shivered as he rolled her budded nipple between his fingers.

"Hell no."

Chapter Twenty-Two

At Lucy's apartment the next day, Norm stayed curled on her mattress on the floor, his back awkwardly propped against her wall while he typed on his laptop. Clinking and clanking sounds emerged from the parking area below. Maybe because her apartment was such a shithole, the landlord let Lucy work on her car there. Guilt perhaps. Norm tried to make himself focus on work, but couldn't help glancing again at Lucy's dark, sad little apartment.

There was no furniture. Not even a bed frame. No pictures. None of those small touches people put in a room to make it home. Clearly, this place wasn't Lucy's home but, if this cramped, dingy apartment wasn't it, then where?

Jezebel's. The thought came clearly to him, hard and hurting. Because if Lucy had so much invested with the bar, how could she ever really get invested in him? This apartment epitomized the perils of his relationship with her, its potential impermanence.

He slammed his laptop shut and grabbed Lucy's keys off the kitchen counter. Locking the front door on his way out, he padded downstairs to watch her work. Anything was better than being trapped in that apartment.

Lucy's laugh, vibrant and sunny, reached him and he redoubled his pace to the "garage" level. All the parking spaces were open air stalls with pull-down doors. Lucy was snugged in her own nook with the door open, her Mustang nestled in the corner.

Norm's littlest brother hunched next to her, rapt as they stared into the mysteries of the engine. Norm was surprised that Lucy hadn't let him know when Tommy arrived. The longer he observed them, though, heads bent together, he realized maybe she'd been sucked into car talk right away and had no opportunity yet to find him.

"Maybe something wrong with the camshaft lobe?" Tommy asked.

She shook her head, short blonde hairs sticking to her temples. "Nah. Cams don't generally make that rocking noise. Could be a rod or a piston, though."

Norm beamed at Lucy and his brother. "How's it coming?"

Both their heads shot up. Lucy's face lit with pleasure, Tommy's with a slightly surly disappointment. Norm paused seeing that, then had to bite back a laugh. *Riiiight.* Norm's arrival interrupted Tommy's quality alone time with Lucy. The kid was twelve; he wasn't blind. Also, in all fairness, Norm's arrival would probably dilute some of their arcane car talk into the more mundane English the rest of the world used.

Lucy, greasy, sweaty, and grinning, hopped over to give Norm a quick kiss on the lips. "Going great. Tom here's a natural."

Tom. Tom. Norm repeated it inside his brain in a fast, staccato rhythm to make the revised name stick. But...the kid had been "Tommy" for the last twelve years, *all his life,* so this sudden preference for "Tom" took awhile to get used to. "When did you get here?" Norm leaned around Lucy's lovely form to address his brother.

Tommy shrugged, giving an excellent imitation of the teenager he was not quite yet. "Mom dropped me off half an hour ago. She'll be back at seven."

It was just after four thirty. "Are we feeding you?"

Tommy shrugged again. Which could mean anything from *I don't care* to *Yes, please God, I'm starving.*

Surrendering. Norm tucked his hands under Lucy's chin, cradling her jaw--the only remotely clean part of her-- and tipped her face up. "You hungry?"

"Pizza? Round Table delivers here."

"I'll call. It'll probably take you and Tommy awhile to clean up. You should start now." Norm smoothed his thumb over the pert swell of her lip, too tempted by all that lush pink to leave her alone. She nipped the pad of his finger and darted her eyes in Tommy's direction as a warning. Duly chastened, Norm bent to kiss her forehead then started upstairs toward the dingy apartment to Google the local Round Table's number. Halfway up the stairs, he paused and called back, "What should I order?"

"A personal-sized pepperoni and black olives for me, with a coke," Lucy hollered. "Tom?"

Norm craned to listen, but could only hear some half-hearted muttering from underneath the garage. Lucy reappeared at the foot of the staircase, wryly amused. "Tom doesn't care. He'll eat what you eat."

Norm stamped up the stairs, distinctly disgruntled. *I should get anchovies, jalapeños and pineapple to teach the kid a lesson about apathy.* But then Norm would be stuck with that, too. The fatal flaw in his revenge plot. Alas, alack.

Tommy was essentially a teenage boy, he should be thrilled, *thrilled* at the idea of pizza. Especially because, Norm knew from personal, painful experience, that his mother was a vegan and did not stock such delicious staples of any normal kid's diet like coke, sweets, or pizza. Oreos, though, Oreos were vegan. But *then* she wouldn't keep anything but soy milk for her boys to dunk them in.

Her plan had backfired, though, because, in trying to raise her kids vegan, they'd rebelled as adults. Now Norm, Tru and Hunt ate like ravening pigs any junk food they could get their hands on. Like Meat Lover's Pizza. *Oh, yeah.* Norm's mouth watered, and he took the rest of the stairs to the apartment two at a time.

***

Since the weather was nice they ate dinner outside on the lawn in front of the apartment building. Plus, Lucy didn't have a dining table so, in a choice between eating on the floor in her dingy apartment or eating on the ground outdoors in the cool evening air, there was no competition.

They arranged themselves in a rough circle surrounding the pizza boxes. Lucy sat between Norm and Tommy, her legs tucked to the side and under her. She'd changed out of those adorable oversized mechanics overalls and into a pair of sweats and *his* Batman t-shirt. Now she was just taunting him.

He handed Lucy her small box off the top then popped the lid on the larger cardboard container. Heat noticeably rose from the pizza inside and he took a long whiff of the garlicky deliciousness with its spicy tomato sauce, oozing cheese melted to a delectable crispness, and the meat. Oh, the meat. As he lifted his first slice and took a bite he made a sound like Homer Simpson beholding a donut: something split between a groan, a gargle, and an orgasm.

Tommy reached past him to snag two pieces at once, and Norm stifled a triumphant 'Ha!' The kid could play it cool, but Norm hadn't totally lost touch with his youngest brother. *Oddly comforting idea.* As he swallowed his first bite, he jerked his chin at Tommy, motioning to him with his slice. "How are you doing in school these days?"

Tommy shrugged, his default gesture, and tugged at a stubborn string of cheese that stretched on and on before he finally surrendered and piled it on top of his slice. "Fine."

Lucy, perhaps sensing Norm's rising frustration, filled the breech. "Tom was telling me his new junior high offers metal shop." She cast an uncertain look at Tom then, when he continued munching on his pizza, she went on, "Your mom doesn't want him to take the class."

Norm blinked, lowering his own pizza to the plate. "Why?"

"Because she thinks I'll get hurt. She is being *totally* unreasonable!" Tommy abandoned his meal in favor of his grievance, his slice of pizza half sliding off his plate and into the grass.

Norm spoke slowly, carefully, certain he was on dangerous ground but unsure where the quicksand was hiding. "Hurt by the equipment?"

"Yeah. Or maybe by the other kids. She's got it into her head I'm a fifty pound weakling and all the other guys will gang up on me or something." Tommy shook his head in disgust. "Total whack-job shit--*stuff.*"

Norm bit his lower lip at his brother's slip-up. Wouldn't do to laugh, his mother would never forgive him.

253

"That's silly," Lucy broke in. "It's not the fifties for Chris--for goodness sake. *I* took shop and I'm a *girl.*" She scrunched her nose at Tommy, teasing him. The kid gave her a small smile and shook his head.

"Yeah, and she said I should take Yearbook or Band or some lame sh--*stuff* like that."

I took yearbook. I was in band. Norm fought not to bristle at his brother's disgusted tone. Tommy was wholly wrapped up in his grievance; everything that wasn't Shop would fall into "lame" territory. Besides, the kid probably didn't even know what extracurriculars Norm had indulged in. Steeling himself, Norm sucked in a breath. "I can talk to her."

He was unprepared for the change in Tommy. His younger brother leaned forward, his face avid, his eyes alight with hope. "Would you, Normal? Please?"

Lucy choked, but the noise suspiciously sounded like a laugh. "'Normal'?"

Norm rolled his eyes heavenwards. "Another one of my affectionate nicknames." He ruffled Tommy's hair. "Something *Tom-tom* and the others call me."

"Man, don't call me that." Tommy swatted Norm's hand away, but the kid was chuckling. Abruptly, he subsided, wheeling toward Norm with desperation on his face. "Can you talk to her tonight? I have to have my schedule for next semester turned into the office by the end of the week."

"Yeah. I'll do it tonight." Norm patted his kid brother's shoulder with gruff affection. "*Tom-tom.*"

***

Norm's mother arrived right on time at seven. The three of them had remained camped on the front lawn, laughing and shooting the shit. With Norm's promise to go to bat for Shop, Tommy had finally opened up a bit, talking about his friends--some of whom Norm remembered playing with Tommy when they were five, how he spent his time these days--video games seemed to be the primary pastime, and even, obliquely, Tommy hinted at a girl he liked.

Now the pressure was on Norm to hold up his end of the unspoken bargain. After his mom said a polite hello to Lucy, he dragged the woman who bore him toward the car while Lucy took Tommy inside to gather his backpack.

"What's up, honey?" his mom asked, warm but worried, eyes pinched at the corners. "Did you want to talk to me about bringing your brother over here without asking you first?"

"No--"

"Because he does like Lucy very much, and it's so nice to see him showing enthusiasm for something."

"Yeah, I wan--"

"You and Lucy aren't breaking up, are you? Oh, dear. I invited her to Sunday dinner."

"No, we--you did what?"

"Sunday dinner at the end of the month."

He rolled his eyes. "I know which Sunday dinner you meant, Mom. You invited Lucy?"

"Yes. Isn't that all right? I mean, if you aren't breaking up."

"We aren't breaking up. It's fine." Even as the words left his mouth, all his spit dried up. *Worry about it later.* Shaking his head, he refocused and stared into his mother's guileless brown eyes. The woman was a master tactician. Was this whole Lucy-dinner thing a ploy because she

255

suspected what he actually wanted to talk about? "Tommy told me about the Shop thing. Why won't you really let him take the class?"

"I'm worried he'll get hurt."

"Good. Then you can sue the school district and retire with the settlement."

"*Norman.*" She swatted his arm in rebuke.

He caught her hand and gently gripped her fingers. "Mom, you raised me too, remember? You encouraged me to join *water polo*, one of the roughest water sports in the world, and that includes swimming with sharks outside a cage. Those little water polo fuckers--*kids* sharpen their toe nails. When have you ever told us not to do something because we might get hurt?"

"Has it occurred to you my parenting style might have changed? That I'm getting soft in my old age?"

"No."

"Well…" She raked her fingers through her dark hair, fidgeting, avoiding his gaze. At last, as he remained silent, she broke. "It's not good for his college applications, *all right?*"

"Ma, he's *twelve.*"

"Uh-huh. And I began worrying about your future college at right about the same time. And the only reason you didn't go to Stanford was because you wanted to hurt your father. You had the grades. The extracurriculars." Her voice had gone wistful, her eyes gazing far off. "Truman and Hunter messed around too much as teenagers. They were smart enough, but no discipline." She adjusted her hold on her purse, tucking the bag close to her side, her whole posture straightening into one of rigid determination. "Tom has as good a chance as you did, and I won't let him jeopardize it by taking *Shop*."

It's not like he's taking a course in Advanced Leprosy, woman. "OK." Norm put his fingers to his eyes then pressed inward to wring the tension out. "OK. He's attending Grant Middle School, right? Like me and the others?"

"Yes."

"Why don't you see if he's willing to take a zero period PE, then he can take two electives like your oldest overachiever did when he was a kid." Norm laid his palm flat against his own chest. "One elective to make you happy and one that makes Tommy--*Tom* happy."

She hesitated, swaying indecisively on her heels, then *hmph*ed. "All right. Despite what you seem to believe, I am not Machiavelli and I do want my children to be happy. *All* of my children " She patted Norm's cheek, her skin smooth and cool. That same familiar flowery perfume she wore wrapped around him like a comforting Mom-hug.

Lucy and Tommy, probably having hovered in the apartment doorway for some time, appeared. "All ready," she chirped, her eyes bright, her face brimming with happiness. *Yeah, they were eavesdropping.* He grinned at her, but his sinking worry about family dinner returned.

Lucy gave his brother a quick hug, slinging her arms all the way to the backpack on his shoulders. The kid returned her a half-hearted embrace, which was like a bear hug from Tommy. Norm strode past his mom and grabbed Tommy as soon as Lucy released him. He hauled the kid close for a real bear hug then threw in an affectionate older brother noogie for good measure. Tommy managed to slide and wriggle away, giving Norm a quick shove in payback when he broke free. Norm threw his arm over Tommy's shoulder and leaned down. "I had to offer her a zero period PE and a second elective, but if you agree to those you can take Shop."

Tommy took Norm completely by surprise when he knocked into him, giving his ribcage a squeeze, then dashed off to his mom's car. Norm swallowed, his chest tight with sudden emotion.

Tommy broke in on Norm's little moment when he whipped back halfway to the car, and pointed at the pizzas. "C--can I take home the leftovers?"

"Yeah, Tom. Whatever you want." Norm shot his mother a glare over his brother's shoulder, and she raised her hands in surrender, circling to the driver's side. Tommy slid into the passenger with the large pizza box on his lap, no doubt staining his jeans with pizza grease in addition to the car grease and grass stains.

Lucy tucked herself against Norm's side and waved at the departing car. Norm tugged her closer, resting his cheek against her hair. The whole moment felt vaguely surreal, like they were The Brady Bunch or something, waving goodbye to all the folks at home after another madcap episode of family hijinks. He enjoyed the moment anyway, his whole body warming where he touched Lucy.

When she faced him, he waited for her to utter some saccharine sentiment to cap the interlude, to wrap the moment up in a nice bow. Instead, she wiggled her eyebrows at him and, voice low with promise, said, "You wanna go inside and get naked?"

He broke away at once, smacking her lovely ass as he raced for the apartment stairs. "Tag! You're it!"

Lucy, laughing wildly, hair trailing behind like a silky banner, immediately broke into a run to chase after him. Norm redoubled his pace to beat her to the front door, happier than he'd ever been in his life.

***

"Do you want to sleep over again tonight?"

He shook his head, his stubbled chin scraping against the softness of her hair. "My back is killing me from last night on this mattress. It's too small for both of us."

She stirred, her breasts rolling against him in delightful new ways every time she moved. "I can't go to your apartment tonight, Norm. I have class tomorrow, and I know I won't get out of bed if I go with you."

He sighed, his body cooling with disappointment. A night without Lucy in his bed was barely a night worth living through. "How's English going?"

"It's going. I'm doing better at keeping up with the reading. 'Cats of Ulthar' was great, by the way. Twisted, but great. And I've been getting better grades on my assignments." She pressed her hand flat against his heart and pushed upright so she could meet his eyes. "You really helped. Thank you."

"Welcome." He pressed his hands to her bare back to tug her down, and kissed her long and slow, everything in him aching with a sweet pain. She smiled down at him, her eyes bright enough to burn, that beautiful tangle of gold a curtain to shadow her face. He grabbed a strand and twisted it around his finger, keeping his tone conversational as he caressed her hair. "You know it was all a ploy to get you into bed, right?"

"Helping me with English?"

"Oh, yeah. I was faking the whole time. I don't even speak English."

"And how did that work out for you?"

"Pretty fucking well." He grabbed her close for a kiss.

She eased away after a moment and drew patterns on his naked chest with her fingertip, circling his nipple, tracing his collarbone, all tiny, tickling touches that made him twitch under her hands. "You and Tommy aren't as close as you and your other brothers."

Crap. Not a question. "Tonight was a successful evening for me and Tommy. Probably the first one I've spent with the kid since he learned how to talk."

She frowned and her small caresses stopped.

Worried, Norm pushed onto his side to sit up and explain things. "Lucy, I was in my late teens and early twenties when Tommy was a kid. I moved away to college just when he was starting elementary school. I haven't been the most attentive older brother."

Maybe deep down in his selfish heart of hearts he believed he'd already done his Big Brother time with Truman and Hunter. He knew all three of the older Keane brothers had painfully resented the screaming, red-faced little monkey his parents brought home from the hospital. The (eventually) adorable new baby took away their Mom's attention from them before they were quite ready to relinquish her. Tommy's arrival had also made their dad retreat even farther from the family, hiding behind his work more and more.

Norm scrubbed a hand across his face, realizing that he'd been quiet too long. "I love Tommy the same as Tru and Hunt. But there's never been any closeness between us, any common ground. Does that make sense?"

"Yeah." Lucy played with the edge of the blanket, avoiding eye contact. "I loved my Gran to pieces, but she never understood me. What I wanted. What I liked to do."

Norm nodded eagerly. "Tommy's like that. You said it before: me and my family are a bunch of English nerds. My mom's a writer, my dad's a freaking English professor. We Keanes all favor the liberal arts. Art. Music. Literature. Philosophy. We thought Hunter was the black sheep when he got a business degree, but Tommy's worse. He excels at math and science. All the subjects every Keane from the dawn of time onwards has had to wallow to get through. He's not even athletic the way me and my brothers were. I did swim and water polo. Truman ran cross-country. Hunter did a mix of all three. Tommy wants to play *football*."

Lucy giggled, probably at the horrified way he'd said "football." She quickly sobered, shaking her head. "Poor kid."

Norm caught her hand, clasping it over his heart. "Which is why today was so great. He's got an adult who understands his interests, who's encouraging instead of just blank with shock. Who can help *me* understand him better." He studied her hand, staring at her short fingers, her dainty palm, tapping the freckle he found along her life line.

She sank into his lap and tucked her head into the hollow of his shoulder. "Janet tell you she invited me to dinner?"

That hollow unease returned, bottoming out his stomach, leaving a bitter taste in his mouth. "Yeah," he managed to croak out. After clearing his throat, he tried

261

again. "You know you don't have to go to dinner. I don't mind."

"No, it's fine. I promised Tom I'd find him some car parts to practice with. Taking them apart, putting them back together, you know. Just scrap stuff, not anything off the Mustang." She tipped back, glancing at him, her brow lined again with worry. "Norm?"

He shook his head, and urged her onto the small, hard mattress, covering her body with his. "Family dinner with the Keanes. That'll be something to look forward to all week."

When she opened her mouth to keep asking questions, he covered her lips with his own, smothering her questions and his own painful worry in the heat between their bodies.

Chapter Twenty-Three

The day of the Keane family Sunday dinner dawned and Lucy was fairly twitching with anxiety. She broke a plate washing dishes that morning because her hands were shaking so badly. When she tried to finish some math homework, which should have been a breeze, she couldn't remember the right formulas.

The nerves were probably because she hadn't met a guy's parents since high school. Back then meeting the parents was kind of a prerequisite to dating. Yhey were the ones driving the car, after all--or threatening your date with bodily harm if he didn't have you home by curfew in Lucy's dad's case.

But she'd never actually Met The Parents with intent before. Tonight was huge. It said something about where Norm wanted this relationship to go. And, since Lucy had agreed to this, it probably said a lot about where she wanted the relationship to go. Her mind shied away from that thought, and her hands grew shakier and shakier by the moment.

Norm didn't help her nerves any. If possible, he seemed even twitchier than her. The drive to Santa Clarita from his place lasted an hour and, the entire time, he kept fidgeting: drumming his fingers against the steering wheel, bouncing his foot against the floor, flipping maniacally through every station on his radio, then, when they switched to his mp3 player, he rejected *every song* after two seconds. He could *not* settle down and relax. That made Lucy, already strung tight with stress, ready to snap. "Are we there yet?" she asked.

"You know you've asked that six times already?"

"So shoot me. I'm antsy. Hey, is my dress good?" She smoothed her hands down the dark pink skirt, hoping to distract him.

"You're beautiful." He didn't even glance at her, and his voice had a flat, distracted quality.

"Norm."

"*Hmm?*"

"What's wrong?"

"Nothing at all." But his eyebrows gave this the lie as they scrunched with tension.

He'd been weird about this dinner ever since she first mentioned the invite to him. She would worry he didn't want her to meet his family, but since she'd already met ninety percent of his family that seemed unlikely. So what had him so jittery? Biting down on another wistful noise, she tried again. "I'm excited to meet Hunter. What's he like?"

"He's the runt of the family. Well, he is until we see how tall Tommy gets. Hunt was the black sheep until Tommy came along too. He doesn't look like me and Tru. People never believe we're brothers."

"Hunter's the one who works for NASA, right?"

"Yup. In Procurement. Oh." Norm shot a quick glance her way. "Mom told me yesterday, Hunter's bringing his new boyfriend, so you won't be the only significant other on display today."

Lucy's heart warmed. "I'm significant?"

"You are to me." He caught her hand and dropped a kiss to the palm then curled his fingers around hers, sealing the kiss in.

Still glowing with happiness from his last remark, it took her a long moment to process the one that had come before. She blinked in mild surprise, pondering the boyfriend remark. In all the times Norm had mentioned his brothers, he'd never once mentioned Hunter was gay. Was that why he was so jittery? Was he uncomfortable with his gay brother? Or was he worried *she* would be uncomfortable?

Or was she way off base and something else altogether was bugging him? She restrained an urge to scream. She would just have to figure it out when she got there.

With that not so comforting thought at the forefront of her mind, she settled back to stare at the miles and miles of rolling brown hills that flanked the freeway heading into Santa Clarita. Out the corner of her eye, she caught Norm's hand snaking toward the skip button on the radio, and she slapped his fingers away. *Are we there yet?*

***

The old Keane family house was a large, upper middle class palace. Two stories, a sort of orangey-beige stucco, with a tile roof and a long driveway with a basketball hoop hung over the garage door. His old house lay on a street of other houses built along the same boxy, big, All-American architectural lines, with red tile roofs adding a sort of local SoCal flavor.

Norm parked and reached to get the store-bought cheesecake out of the backseat. Lucy, flustered and clumsy with nerves, flipped down the passenger side mirror to check her makeup and hair. The hair was fine. Hard to mess up a ponytail. She smoothed her side-swept bangs and tucked them behind her ear.

Normally, she didn't wear makeup in her day to day life. Ronnie had taught her how to do a respectable pin up look for her Shot Girl persona. Other than that, Lucy was clueless about makeup.

The night before she'd trolled the internet for casual makeup How To videos then experimented with layering a lighter and darker shade of brown together, brown eyeliner, and one layer of mascara on her top lashes. She'd debated between lip gloss and her normal cherry chapstick and, finally, settled on chapstick because lip gloss was too sticky for Norm. If there was ever a day she wanted Norm willing and eager to kiss her, comfort her, it was today.

Norm, in contrast, was distinctly dressed down for the occasion in a t-shirt and khaki cargo pants that, admittedly, did do nice things for his ass. And Lucy's heart rate. The shirt of the day was a red and black ringer tee with **"*EXPENDABLE*"** in big black letters across the front, a small Star Trek icon over the heart, and "*Tell my family I love them*" scrawled across the back. She coveted the shirt. The man did good shirt.

Norm waited for her at the bottom of the short concrete path to the door, so she slapped the mirror closed and flipped it into place against the car ceiling. "You'll be fine," she muttered. She blew out one last calming breath then hopped from the car to join Norm.

As she passed him on the path, he caught her wrist and tugged her back. His forearm circled her waist, the cheesecake box pressing coolly against her spine. He traced the pad of his thumb over her cheekbone, soothing and gentle. "You're wonderful," he whispered. "And I am crazy about you."

His words were less comforting than they might have been because he said them firmly, as if reminding her of these facts. Would something at dinner make her believe she wasn't wonderful and he didn't like her? She tensed up again. *How bad is this night going to get, Norman?!* She swallowed that hysterical question down, and smiled at him, the expression feeling wobbly and wan, precarious almost, on her face.

His lips brushed softly over hers before he broke away, towing her gently along the path to the door. The front was unlocked when Norm tried the handle, so he stuck his head in and called, "Hello!" Lucy trailed after him, clinging to his hand like she would a life preserver in the middle of the Antarctic Sea.

The interior of the house matched the outer in that it was beautiful, quietly elegant, but somehow homey, furnished with Southwestern art in warm creams and browns. Janet looped through enroute to the kitchen and nodded 'hello' at both of them. Her friendly greeting went a ways toward banishing Lucy's nerves, but still she scanned the whole set up, poised, waiting for the landmines to go off. Janet relieved Norm of the cheesecake and carried the dessert off to the kitchen to thaw.

The missing Keane brother, Hunter, stood in the living room and bustled forward to introduce himself and his hunky boyfriend. Lucy was curious about Hunter, but her attention was momentarily diverted; Hunter's boyfriend, Bryan, was a tall, beautiful Asian man with the best pair of cheekbones she'd ever seen. Hunter had good taste in men.

Forcing her eyes away from the pretty, pretty man, she examined Norm's brother. Hunter was a Keane brother more in the mold of Tom; short, dark, slim, with a thick cap of silky black hair. He was taller than his mother, but, other than that and his dark hair, he was the younger, male version of Janet, right down to the toffee colored eyes. Or, alternately, he was the older, taller, slimmer version of Tom. Hunter was attractive in the same geeky-cute way his brothers were, although Hunter skewed more toward the cute end of the spectrum than his brothers did at first glance. Now, of course, Lucy knew *she* was with the most delectable guy in the room. Including beautiful Bryan.

Norm glowered at her, perhaps sensing her budding crush on Bryan, and held her close. She tucked herself against him, pleased with how second nature touching Norm, being with Norm, had become. And how good it felt.

As they chatted with Hunter and Bryan, she kept darting her gaze over to Norm to catch his reactions. He appeared perfectly at ease and not at all uncomfortable with either his gay brother or the new, exquisitely beautiful boyfriend. Pressed to Norm's body, she could also feel how loose he was, relaxed. So he obviously wasn't hiding any inner awkwardness either. *OK. Hunter's not the landmine.*

Hunter took Bryan into the kitchen for a refill on their drinks, and Lucy tipped onto her toes to whisper in

Norm's ear, "Is Bryan the first boyfriend Hunter's brought home?" Maybe Norm wasn't uncomfortable about his own reactions; maybe he was worried about the rest of the family.

But Norm immediately scoffed. "Angel, Hunter introduced the family to his first boyfriend when he was fourteen. Hunter was bringing boys home before I was bringing girls home, and I'm three years older." Norm's lips quirked up, his pride shinning through. "He was the first boy at our high school to take another boy to prom. Can you imagine the kind of courage that took?"

Lucy bit her lip, unaccountably touched by this obvious pride in his brother. "Go Hunter." She hugged Norm, resting her ear over his heart and listening to the beat.

Truman and Alisha emerged from the kitchen, and Lucy took a brief moment to once again adjust to a blue-eyed Norman. The resemblance between the two eldest Keane men really was uncanny, right down to the big nose Lucy had grown to love so much. Alisha stooped her long form to reel Lucy in for a hello hug, which was nice. The four of them stood chatting for a while about odds and ends. Janet meanwhile clattered away in the kitchen, loudly conversing with Hunter and obviously pumping Bryan for information about his intentions.

Truman was working on a masters in English Literature at UCLA and Alisha was also a grad student there but in Anthropology. Lucy tensed. Was this the landmine? Was Norm scared she'd be intimidated by his family's accomplishments because Lucy didn't even have a BA yet? And wouldn't for another two years. But no, she'd met Truman and Alisha at the amusement park, talked to

269

them about their crazy academic accomplishments on the Ferris Wheel. Their academic pedigrees hadn't scared her off then. Intimidated her, sure, but they hadn't scared her off. So this couldn't be the landmine.

Crap. Where's the stupid landmine?! Lucy was so tense anticipating the explosion she was ready to curl herself around whatever when it *did* appear and let the damn thing go boom just to get the drama over with.

A side door opened off the living room and a ridiculously tall older man stepped out. He tugged the door closed then faced the company, blinking in obvious surprise at the crowd of people.

Norm's shoulders snapped back and his jaw clamped tight, his whole body bracing with an abrupt tension. "Hi, Dad."

Lucy stiffened too. *Hello, landmine.*

Chapter Twenty-Four

Norm's father stepped forward. "Hello, I'm Mike Keane."

She clasped hands with him. "Lucy York." As Mike's hand fell away from hers she had to blink and refocus her brain. Genetics was a weird thing. She'd never believed hands were that distinctive. Hands are hands. Basic, utilitarian. But Mike had the same hands as Norm. Long fingers, wide palms, a light dusting of pale hair on the backs and fingers. This funny sensation curled in her stomach seeing the hands she'd grown to know so well, hands that had touched her so intimately, not only on another man but gnarled and knobby with age.

The rest of Mike Keane was equally jarring to her senses. He was about as tall as Norm. They had the same lean frame, same arms, same legs, same big ears, the same long oval shape to the face. They even parted their hair to the same side, although Norm's shaggy brown mane was a far cry from the conservative business-like cut Mike favored. Mike's nose was Norm's all over again; his deep-set eyes had the same wide roundness, although small lines feathered away from the corners of Mike's eyes where none marred Norm's face. Mike's eyes were also the same

271

icy blue as Truman's, not the warm toffee brown that colored Norm's gaze.

Mike was at least ten years older than his wife, probably in his mid-sixties. His hair had gone white, but, if she had to guess, Lucy would wager Mike was the source of Hunter and Tommy's thick black hair. Maybe if she'd met Mike Keane as a younger man the difference in coloring would have helped soften the startling resemblance between Norm and his father. As it was, she couldn't help feeling like someone had cracked a window into the future.

So that's what Norm will look like in forty years. She shook her head, bemused, overwhelmed. *Good to know.*

Before Lucy had a chance to figure out *how* Norm's dad was the landmine the rest of the gang filed in.

Janet tottered out of the kitchen, shepherding Hunter and Bryan before her like a mother duck. A slightly buzzed mother duck. Hunter passed a beer with a slice of lime off to Norm. "Grabbed you one." Norm muttered fervent thanks to his brother, squeezed the lime into his beer, then immediately knocked back a long swallow. Hadn't this same man lectured her barely a week ago about hitting the booze that hard?

Janet sidled over to Lucy, two big glasses of margarita in her hands. She passed a frosted, green-filled glass to Lucy. "I thought you might like one, dear." Janet slurred her *m*-sounds and the wink she gave Lucy was a little spasmodic.

Unnerved, Lucy sipped. Immediately, she snapped her eyes closed in shock as a rush of alcohol flooded her system. *Whoa. Mama Keane pours with a heavy hand.* Lucy switched at once to simply cradling her margarita for

272

show. Just because she'd discovered the landmine didn't mean she could create her own disaster. Getting plastered at family dinner was not on the agenda. *Even if everyone else is.* She glanced around, noting everyone else's half-full or nearly empty drinks. Lucy was freaked out, but she still wanted to make a good impression. Especially on the imposing, coolly grave Mike Keane.

He chatted with the group--or maybe *at* them--as he discussed, *in depth*, the defects of a paper Truman had recently written about *The Canterbury Tales*. As she watched Mike, somber, serious and intellectual while surrounded by his own children for goodness sakes, she was reminded of that word she'd used to describe Norm's nose once. *Patrician.*

Yeah. Like some icy Roman politician. Mike Keane would've been right at home in a sober white toga, droning on about the higher principles of the Republic, unruffled, untouchable, so above it all.

When Janet was roped into a debate with Alisha about the latest drama on *Dancing with the Stars*, Lucy retreated to the kitchen. Keeping careful watch, she poured half her margarita down the sink then diluted the drink with water from the tap. If one sip of this monster had her thinking deep thoughts about Roman senators then she couldn't risk two sips of Janet's undiluted margarita mix. Passing out drunk under the dinner table was as bad as getting sloppy drunk. Lucy sincerely hoped to avoid either fate that night.

Tom revealed himself at last, emerging from some dark pre-teenager lair. He wore nice pants and a short-sleeved shirt with a collar and buttons, the most spiffed up she'd ever seen him. Norm's youngest brother let her reel

273

him in for a hug before he retreated, his eyes darting nervously over the group.

Following the path of Tom's gaze, glancing at the whole group, Lucy realized Norm was the only Keane male not in a collared shirt of some kind. His *Star Trek* shirt was great but appeared wildly inappropriate to her eyes when set in the midst of everyone else. Beautiful Bryan was even wearing a tie. *Freaking overachiever.* Lucy smoothed uncertain hands over her pink sundress but, thankfully, on closer inspection of their outfits, she noticed Janet and Alisha were both in sundresses like her. *So at least I'm dressed right.*

Why had Norm dressed so decidedly down when clearly these things had a dress code? *Oh, good, yet another mystery to unravel about Sunday dinner.* Lucy sucked up more of her diluted margarita, wistfully wishing she hadn't diluted it. She might need some liquid courage to get through this damn thing.

Tom stuck close to her side, a hunted look in his eyes, but his uneasiness might just be a younger person forced to mingle with his elders look and not an Oh-God-this-night-is-going-to-suck look like Norm's. She blinked at Tom then slapped her forehead. "Crap--*crud*, Tom, I left the parts for you in the car."

He shrugged. "S'OK."

She shook her head and set her margarita down then snatched a coaster at the last minute when she noticed them perched on the end table. "Keys, Norm?"

Norm took his face out of his drink long enough to fish his keys out. He paused, bouncing the weight in his hand then, instead of tossing them to her, he tipped his chin toward the front door. "I'll help you. Don't want you to get your dress dirty."

"No, but your t-shirt is expendable." She bit back a laugh, and Norm's eyes lit in response, the first Norm-like expression to cross his face since they'd walked inside. She almost groaned aloud in relief.

He hadn't been replaced by an alcoholic pod person then. She might have miscounted somewhere, but he seemed to already be on his third beer. *Great.* She didn't exactly want her *date* getting sloppy drunk or passing out under the table either. She jerked her head toward the door in a *come-along* gesture at him.

"Oh, I'll help you, Lucy. Norm can stay and chat with his mother." At the sound of Mike's voice, Lucy swallowed. She might be throwing herself over the landmine, after all. Mike plucked the keys out of Norm's palm and herded her toward the door. When she gazed over her shoulder, Norm had retreated to his drink again, gulping the beer down like it was going out of style.

The questions from Mike began as soon as they cleared the doorway. "So, Lucy, you and Norm are *friends*?"

The question lilted upward on an unmistakable note of hopefulness, the cadence of his voice hitting her like a slap. *He doesn't want me dating Norm.* Lucy now had her first inkling of why ol' Papa Keane was the landmine. But she couldn't tell if he was insensitive or just evil.

Just in case, she widened her eyes with fake obliviousness. "We've been dating for almost a month."

"How nice." The tone was flat, but the look in his eyes was distant, not filled with the cool meanness she'd expect from someone doing this on purpose.

275

She plucked the keys out of his hand with another one of those oblivious bright smiles she'd perfected at the bar. Popping the trunk, she hauled the box out then unceremoniously dumped the load into his arms. Snapped out of his reverie, Mike staggered under the weight then adjusted his hold. "And what do you do, Lucy? How do you keep yourself busy?"

Isn't Janet supposed to be the one grilling me? Isn't this women's work? Lucy clamped her teeth on her tongue and wheeled toward the house. "I work with Norm. That's how we met."

Hurrying inside before Mike, Lucy managed to dodge more questions from him. Shortly, he disappeared outside to grill dinner. Janet apparently relaxed her infamous vegan rules for company so the non-Keane members of the party were having burgers. But everyone named "Keane" was having a veggie patty. *Poor Norm.*

All the brothers offered to help their dad on the grill, but Mike just waved them away. As he disappeared outside, Lucy imagined the entire company breathing a synchronized sigh of relief. She *might* have been projecting, though.

Janet drifted by as Lucy clung to Norm's arm, trying to recover from her alone time with Mike. Janet patted both their shoulders. "Why don't you two tour the house? Norm hasn't shown it to you yet." Her eyes held some hidden emotion, tensing at the corners, making the crow's feet there more pronounced.

Norm walked away, guiding Lucy along by her elbow, but Janet stopped him and plucked his beer out of his hands. "Not in the office or the bedrooms, sweetie."

Lucy flicked a quick glance at Janet, searching for guidance as to whether this was a 'Take your man out back and sober him up' moment. But, if there was a hidden message in Janet's eyes, the meaning was all for Norm. She never glanced at Lucy as Norm yanked her away.

They retreated into the room his dad had emerged from, which turned out to be Mike's office. Norm moved to a far corner, sitting on the edge of the heavy dark wood desk there, a wary expression on his face.

Lucy paced the room, her body too coiled with tension to examine anything about her surroundings. "Why does your family do Sunday dinner every month when clearly you all *hate* family dinner? Christ." She threaded her fingers into her hair, tugging on the ends. No doubt mussing her ponytail.

Norm lifted one shoulder in a careless half-shrug, his gaze pinned to the tasteful beige carpet. "Told you you didn't have to come."

"Oh, hell, Norm." She paced over to him and forced his chin up so he had to look at her. "Sober the fuck up, pal. I need you here and you're letting me flounder around and drown. What is wrong with you tonight?"

His eyes slid up, finally meeting hers in a searing glance so edged with pain she actually hurt with him. "My family."

He slurred the *m*, which stilted Lucy's sympathy for him somewhat. She stepped away, folding her arms over her chest. "Bullshit. You weren't like this at the amusement park." She paused, sucking in a bracing breath. "It's your father, right? He's the reason this is some special kind of hell for you?"

Norm glanced away, his face slack, his eyes shifty.

277

"I'm driving us home tonight. *You asshole.*" She grabbed his shirt and gave him a small shake, livid and worried and churning inside. Norm was the calm one in their relationship, the one with his shit together. Seeing him fall apart like this, watching him tear himself apart made her gut hollow out with fear. Which was why she was a bit shriller with him than she'd intended. "What the hell, Norm? What. The. *Hell?!*"

He caught her fingers and wrapped them round with his own, pressing the bundle of their knit hands to his chest, over his heart. "I'm sorry, I'm sorry. My dad drives me nuts."

"I noticed."

"I'm sorry." This time, when he glanced at her he seemed like *her* Norm again, albeit a slightly looser version after all that beer. But his face remained rigid with strain.

She stepped closer, tilting so her forehead pressed against his. "Norman, I'm pissed but I'm not going anywhere."

His breath gusted out of him again and, when she eased back, the bleak, frozen expression had leeched out of his eyes. Some of the tension locking Lucy's muscles seeped away, and she tucked her fingers behind his neck and pulled him toward her for a kiss. She'd meant the kiss to be quick reassurance, but Norm cradled her cheek, and his mouth slanted open against hers. He kissed her deeply, thoroughly, desperately, and she clung to him, her fingers curled on his forearm, her heart throbbing at how torn up he was. *God, I love him.*

She broke the kiss and ducked her head away, her body flaming hot, burning all over with adrenaline. "You should, ah, um, show me the house. Janet might quiz me."

278

He nodded obligingly, and moved away from her to begin the grand tour. She plastered an interested expression on her face while all the time her heart was wailing, *Coward. Coward. Coward.* Each thought pricked against her chest, zinging into her with a twinge of pain like poisonous darts. *Goddamn coward.*

Chapter Twenty-Five

Apparently oblivious to her whirling emotions, Norm spread his hands wide to encompass the room. "This is my father's secret lair. We were never allowed in here when we were young, which meant we snuck in every chance we got. Tommy has finally met the minimum age requirement for admittance, I believe."

Shiny wood panels covered the room, which was also lined with bookcases stacked high with old leather volumes and battered paperbacks. Lucy lifted an old copy of *On the Road* off the shelf, and the book fell open, pages crossed with small notes and highlights, post-it flags fluttering from the corners of nearly every page. "Your dad is clearly a serious reader." That topic was safe. Her voice sounded normal to her own ears, even as her mind kept circling back and back to that quick, flashing thought. Love.

Love?

"He specializes in Beat Literature," Norm said, "but, these days, you have to have many disciplines if you want to teach and publish. There are too many players in the game for anyone to build a career on one specialty. Last year he taught a class on Post-War British Drama." Norm must have seen the lack of recognition on her face because he elaborated. "*Top Girls. Waiting for Godot. Rosencrantz and Guildenstern Are Dead.* That kind of stuff."

She crinkled her nose in distaste. "I had to read *Godot* in high school. A whole class on that stuff? Shoot me now."

"He's also a fan of Victorian Literature, one of the few genres which can rival British Post-War stuff for bleakness."

Lucy crossed behind the desk to read more of the titles and her eye was caught by the pictures in their matching silver frames placed at exact angles on the desk's surface. She leaned down to study one more closely, but Norm just picked the frame up and handed it to her. "My dad can pretend he lives in a museum. You don't have to."

The framed picture was a young girl in a cheerful pink bikini, actually a very similar shade to Lucy's dress. She blinked in surprise to find such a silly, bright picture gracing Mike's desk. The bikini was one of the old-fashioned, boxy styles girls wore in the 60s, and the bikini girl was delightful, beguiling, with shoulder length, shining brown hair, and huge brown eyes. Her full mouth curled with naughtiness which made her cheeks into ripe apples and gave her a pixyish appearance. The whole picture burst with joy and mischief and fun, the girl inside the frame a cheeky 60s siren enticing you into her world. "Your mom was adorable."

Norm grinned as she handed the picture to him, and stared fondly at the teenaged Janet. "That's why he married her."

"Why'd she marry him?" The question was out before Lucy had time to think it through. She winced and covered her mouth with both hands.

281

Norm had his back turned to her as he plucked another picture off the opposite corner. "She wanted a family." He handed the next frame across the desk to Lucy.

She peered down and recognized this photo as a shot from another family Christmas. All four Keane brothers wore matching PJs--red reindeer patterned this time. Using Tom as a carbon dating technique, this one was more recent than the one at Norm's. The family group was off-center and busily tumbling into a pile on the floor: Truman crashing into Norm, Norm half-falling over, Hunter clutching Janet as if to keep his balance, Alisha to one corner, a hand over her mouth as she laughed. Tom lay at the bottom of the pile, only his wide, surprised brown eyes showing over the top of the frame as Janet bent double, clutching his shoulders and laughing, too. Everyone's face was glowing, scrunched with amusement. Holding the picture, the small image exuded the same delight and luster as the one of young Janet.

If the boys' height was Mike Keane's legacy to his children, then clearly Janet Keane's was this pervasive sense of fun that radiated out from each of her sons. Lucy blinked, squinting at the frame. "Your dad took this?" This seemed like the kind of picture Mike would delete off the camera at once as "too silly" or something.

Norm shook his head. "We took this picture after presents last year when Dad retired here to get some work in before dinner. He wasn't even there." Lifting the frame from her fingers, he weighed it in his hand for a long moment before replacing the picture on the desk. "We set the camera on a timer to take three pictures back to back. I set the clock then ran to get into the shot and I knocked into Truman. He fell over and took Mom and Hunt with him. Each picture in the set gets progressively sloppier and sillier. We all ended up in a doggy pile on the floor. This picture is the last one in the set of three. The worst of the bunch. *I* keep them on my computer because they crack me up." Norm traced one finger over the edge of the frame then shook his head. "I wonder why Dad *framed* this one."

Lucy caught his hand and towed him away from the desk. "Wanna show me the bedrooms?"

He banded his arms around her waist. "Mom cleaned them out after we all left for college. No real relics of our childhood there. We can peek into Tom's, but his room's probably a disaster."

Tugging Norm toward the door, she shook her head. "We should get out there anyway. Your mom probably thinks we're fighting in here."

"Or fucking."

She gave him an extra hard yank toward the door and shoved him out first as a human shield for any parental displeasure. The rest of the group sat hunkered in the living room, variously draped or perched on the leather chairs and couch. Lucy sidled forward with Norm, both of them reluctant to rejoin the family fun until the absolute last moment possible.

"Here. Check this out." A few feet shy of joining the others, Norm dodged away to a far corner of the living room, leading her toward still more bookshelves overburdened with paperbacks. The books here were all genre fiction, though: Asimov and Tolkein. LeGuin and Bujold. Gaiman and Pratchett.

"No genre stuff allowed in your dad's library?" Lucy traced her fingers along the spines and found some of her favorite authors there.

Norm lifted his head high in a snooty posture of superiority. "Literary riffraff like this among the glitterati in Professor Keane's library? Perish the thought." He walked his finger along a row near the top then slid out an old paperback with a very cool spaceship on the cover hovering like a wall between the face of a beautiful woman and a superbly square-jawed man in a nondescript gray uniform. "*Choices* by J.B. Donovan" was embossed in flaking gold across the cover.

"*Janet.*" Norm poked the gold-embossed 'J' on the author's name. "Beatrice. Donovan."

His mom's book. "Donovan is her maiden name?"

"Yup."

"Very cool."

"Yup." Norm lifted the book out of her hands and slotted it into the empty place on the shelf, his face oddly tense. Lucy scanned the rest of the books, searching for more by J.B. Donovan, but the one book was it. *Why didn't she write anymore novels?* "Does your mom have an office too? She's still a writer, you said. Doesn't she work from home a lot?"

"Mom likes to write out on the patio when weather permits, and inside by the fireplace when it doesn't."

Right. Vivid and vivacious Janet Keane wouldn't want to be cooped up in a stuffy old office. So why had she chained herself in what appeared, from the outside at least, to be such a stuffy and joyless marriage?

Mike reentered and gestured for everyone to follow him outside. Lucy plucked her margarita from the coaster and took a sip of the watery, semi-warm beverage. As they arranged themselves outside around a large metal table, she noticed Norm had been arbitrarily switched to water by his mother. As he scowled and sipped his water, Lucy hid a laugh in her own glass.

Janet kicked off conversation at the table by asking Beautiful Bryan what he did for a living.

"I'm an aerospace engineer," was his reply.

Oh, good grief. Lucy barely managed not to slump in her chair. *Gorgeous* and *he's a rocket scientist?* Why did Hunter have to bring this particular great catch home the same weekend as her inaugural visit? Mike obviously regarded her much in the same light as something the cat had dragged in; maybe after the cat had thrown it up first. Now, with Beautiful Bryan and the Accomplished Alisha bookending her, Lucy felt more pathetic than ever.

Like clockwork, Mike wheeled on her with a false smile and narrowed eyes. "What is it *you* do, Lucy?"

She choked and coughed then glanced quickly at Norm for some kind of guidance. Did his family know about Jezebel's? That he worked there? That *she* worked there? Norm had his nose buried in his water glass, wan that the drink wasn't beer, and didn't seem likely to be coming out anytime soon. *Great.* So she slapped a big, shit-eating grin on her face and turned to Mike with as much confidence as she could fake. "I work at the bar with Norm."

"The *bar?*" Mike slid his eldest son a shocked glare that was hardly encouraging.

Lucy pressed on. "Yeah. Jezebel's in Hollywood. That's where we met. Norm's a bouncer. I'm a server." She snagged a passing platter and loaded her cheerful red

285

Fiestaware with salad. Lucy wasn't ashamed of her job, but explaining the intricacies of a shot girl career at family dinner was more of a tightrope than she wanted to walk. Especially with Mike staring at her like some kind of strange, grotesque specimen in a lab, revolting and captivating all at once.

She imagined she could actually hear the words flashing through his brain: *My brilliant son is working at a bar. As a bouncer.* Mike blinked once, tense and quick. *My brilliant son is dating this woman. A slutty bar waitress.* And each thought probably rained down on Mike like a physical blow; Lucy certainly felt pummeled just imagining the inside of his brain.

She scanned the rest of the group, but they all gazed in rapt fascination at their salads. Mike had obviously been the odd man out here, and the rest of the Keanes had known exactly where she and Norm worked, *and* what she did. *Janet probably keeps Mike on a need to know basis when it comes to their sons. Smart woman.* Although, this time Lucy wished Janet had done some prep-work on her husband *before* this awkward moment.

Ah, fuck Mike. "But Norm's book is coming out." Beaming, Lucy crunched her fork into the salad, loading the utensil with crisp greens and a juicy tomato. "Maybe he'll make enough on his writing soon to quit the bar."

"That trash." Mike's fork clinked loudly against his plate as he shuffled through his own salad. He gave a rude snort. "You could have gone to Stanford, Norman. Harvard. Gotten a PhD. Been well-respected in your field." Mike tried to pin Norm with his gaze, but Norm kept his eyes fastened in front of him. His whole body had gone stiff as he sat unnaturally straight in the chair.

Lucy wanted to squeeze Norm's hand, offer some kind of comfort, but they were on opposite sides of the round table, and footsie didn't seem like the best idea. She might catch Janet's foot instead. Or Beautiful Bryan's. *Awkwardness for everyone! Get it while it's hot!*

Janet opened her mouth, probably for another one of her brilliant tactical conversation changers, but Mike rode over his wife's words. "You are wasting your intellect writing *crap*. That paper you wrote on the Eucharist themes in *Merchant of Venice* as an undergrad was brilliant. Brilliant, Norman. Better than Truman's work, and he's the one who's going to get a PhD." Mike shook his head and hunched to pick at his salad.

Lucy paused, her whole body flash-freezing with horror. Her head, moving stiffly against her better senses, turned to join everyone else as they gazed with pity at Truman.

Alisha leapt from her seat and coiled around her man, scowling like some kind of tawny, enraged lioness. "Shut the hell up, Mike."

Lucy restrained an impulse to applaud. Daughters-in-law could probably get away with that kind of thing. Maybe-girlfriends would probably do better to sit on their hands and wait things out.

Mike blinked and a pained expression crossed his face. "I'm sorry, Truman. I didn't mean--" He threw his fork down with a clatter and whirled on Norm. "I only meant your older brother could be doing more with his life instead of writing those trashy novels and working in a bar."

287

And dating these trashy women, was kindly left unsaid, but the implication was heavy in the air as Mike's disapproving gaze flicked over Lucy then moved back to Norm.

Norm stared at his father, everything in him vibrating with tension. "You've never even read one of my books." The coldness in his eyes was enough to make Lucy recoil, and Norm's glower wasn't even directed at her. "You talked Mom out of writing fiction, and you sabotaged what could have been a great career for her. But *I* gave up pleasing you a long damn time ago so you can save your breath." Norm rose, muttered a violent, "Excuse me," and stomped into the house, slamming the sliding door behind him.

Lucy instinctively bolted from her chair to follow him but then turned back with her hand on the door and faced Mike. "You're an English professor. Right, sir?"

Mike leaned back in his chair, looking tired, looking old, his eyes narrowed in displeasure. "Yes."

"So you know books which were belittled in their time, written off as popular crap, as *trash*, went on to become some of the classics of literature. Classics which you study and write long-winded academic papers about, yes?"

His face had gone wary; his reply was slow. "Yes."

"Then maybe you shouldn't be so quick to dismiss what Norm writes, what your wife writes, as trash. Your field is all about knowledge, having an informed opinion. And if you're so quick to dismiss anything that's popular as crap without even reading it first to verify your hypothesis, well, people might decide you're not very good at your job. Sir."

And, by the way, fuck you very much. She gave a small toss to her ponytail and slid inside to search for Norm.

***

Norm hadn't stormed far, only into the kitchen. He spread his arms along the counter and braced himself against the granite. Rigid in every muscle, he tried to force the anger free from his body. *Forget him. Stupid old man.* But his father's words echoed so many of his own lurking, ugly doubts. Making a career in writing was hard, especially in this economy. He had a promising start, especially for being so young, but he could pancake any moment; he might *never* reach the point where he'd be making enough to quit his day job.

Gentle hands slid up his shoulders, and soon enough, small arms had coiled around his waist, warmth pressing all along his back from behind. "You are a brilliant writer," she said in her sweet, sunny voice, the sound sucking away his tension. She hugged his middle, her fisted hands pushing into his stomach. "Your book will kick ass. And so will every book that comes after it. And there will be *many* books that come after it."

He covered her hands where they lay over his stomach, leaning back against her warmth, against all the strength encased in that deceptively petite form. He swallowed, water pooling in his eyes.

"Truman's life." Her voice was muffled from where she had her cheek pressed against his shoulder. "The eventual PhD in Literature, the bookish, elegant wife, and so on, that was what Mike had mapped out for you."

Norm cleared his throat and wheeled about without breaking her hold. He looped his arms over her like that old London Bridge game and hugged her close. "Yeah. But when I declined that honor to, horror of horrors, write genre fiction, Truman took up the cause. Truman became the pleaser. The Golden Boy. And it doesn't even matter." He perched his chin on her head, the softness of her hair tickling against his skin. "My dad's an asshole, but he's not wrong. Truman isn't doing so well in his Masters program. So, even though he's sacrificing everything, stifling his own dreams to make Dad happy, it's not enough because he's failing."

"But could you have done it? Had the career Mike wanted for you?"

Norm blew his breath out through his teeth, bitter memories stinging his brain. "Yeah. I could have done it."

"You--you did get your BA in English. You were on that road for a time, weren't you?" She phrased it as a question, but her tone said she already knew the answer.

"Yeah."

"What changed?"

"I was writing my applications to PhD programs, I didn't even need to do a Masters first. My grades were so good, and all my professors loved me. But the applications. I kept putting them off and putting them off. I nearly didn't get letters of recommendation from my professors in time. And, you know me, I am not a procrastinator."

"Hell no, babe, you get things *done*."

"And then I invited Zack to visit me the weekend before the deadline." Norm shook his head, smiling a little as he remembered. "We got shit-faced drunk. Worse than we have ever been before or since. That was the first and only time I got sick from drinking."

"You didn't finish the applications."

"I landed in the hospital with alcohol poisoning. My dad came to visit. Said he could pull strings, lie to the admissions people, say I had appendicitis, my computer crashed. Whatever. He would do whatever he had to and I would get into Harvard for my PhD."

"You balked."

"I didn't balk, angel. I *ran*. That weekend made me finally realize that.. that everything I was doing, the whole projected course of my life, he'd mapped out for me when I was born. And the worst part, the insidious part, was how easy pleasing him was.

"I knew exactly what to do. PhD at Harvard. Teach English Literature. Tenure. Become department chair. Spend my life writing articles on the Eucharist in *Merchant* and makeup in *Hamlet*. Spend my life buried in books by other people while my 'hobby writing' languished unfinished or forgotten on my hard drive. Abandon every dream and desire of my own so I could do what *he* believed I should, what *he* believed was worthwhile."

Norm tipped his head, a strange cascade of regret and bittersweet triumph tumbling through him. "I could make him happy, but the cost would be everything I wanted for myself. Christ, even my personal life was mapped out. Marry young to some sober, elegant, career-minded intellectual who'd be good at networking--"

"Was there a candidate for that, too?" Lucy toyed with the hem of his shirt, tugging and plucking at the fabric as she avoided his gaze.

He tucked his hand under her chin and tilted her face up. "Yup. Pamela. My college girlfriend. She was this slick, sophisticated History major. A very cool brunette. Dad

291

loved her. Zack *hated* her. Never even gave her a nickname."

"Pamela? Horrible name. Sounds like lunch meat. *Pamela.* Pam. Bleck." Lucy's voice had gone small, listless, and her face was pinched.

Norm bit the inside of his cheek to restrain an unwise laugh. "Awful name."

"Were you two serious?" She caught her lower lip on her teeth, her large blue eyes wide, pleading.

Ah. Dangerous ground here. He chose his words carefully, picking through them like a debris field as he spoke, "I *believed* I loved her. I even asked my mom for grandma's heirloom engagement ring about two weekends before Zack's fateful visit." He fanned the pad of his thumb back and forth across the silk of her cheekbone.

She hummed and leaned in, her eyes fluttering closed. "I'm guessing ol' Pam split when you burned your PhD apps?"

"Oh yeah, I think she broke a heel running away from the ruins of my career in academia. Probably thought it was contagious."

"I like your contagion." Lucy popped onto her toes and kissed him. As she eased back, she smacked her lips. "*Mmmm.* Tasty."

He barely let a moment pass before he kissed her back, tasting the smile on her mouth. Everything in him arched toward her, reaching to wrap close around the wonder of her, the brightness, the beauty. Inside and out. Wanting to claim her, to have her always with him, close. And he wanted her to need the same from him. Like to like. Heart to heart. The two of them together, forging a--a *magnificent* life of warmth and happiness and affection. Him and Lucy, faithfully loving, joyfully living. Together.

His heart hurt with the wanting, pushing outward with a sweet, consuming ache that made his eyes prickle. He broke the kiss and pressed his forehead to hers, hissing in a breath. Then--hands clasped tight, voice calm, gaze steady on hers--he whispered, "I love you."

Chapter Twenty-Six

The moment stretched between them, a fragile cord unspooling like some kind of time lock that would never end. Lucy frozen, a shocked expression stamped on her face. Him staring at her, his whole body coiled with tension, watching, waiting, hurting.

"Norm?" *Dad.* Norm released Lucy and whipped away from her. He pooled his arms on the counter and dropped his head there. He didn't know if he was hiding from his dad or the rattled expression on Lucy's face but, whichever, *both*, he didn't want to deal with it now.

"Norm?" Dad's voice was closer, and when his sandals flopped against the tiles, Norm finally raised his head. Mike Keane gazed uncertainly between Norm and Lucy. Norm met his father's eyes with a hard-eyed glare, surrendering no ground, offering no quarter. And the old bastard could just get over it.

Mike faced Lucy, gently touching her arm. "Would you mind giving us a minute alone?"

"Of course." She fluttered away, her pink sundress a bright blur as she all but sprinted out of the kitchen. *Crap.* Norm watched her go, a part of him writhing in pain even as he regarded his father with cool eyes.

Mike paused and then, at the sound of Lucy sliding the glass door closed, he confronted Norm.

Norm held up one finger, forestalling whatever cruel, insensitive remark his father would say. "Fair warning. You can be snide and awful with me, but don't you *dare* look down your nose at her. She is smart and kind, and ten times more worthy a person than you will ever be, you bitter old bastard."

Mike recoiled, and sucked in a hard breath as if Norm had punched him in the stomach. Which, Norm had to acknowledge, he sort of had. He and his dad had argued before, but Norm had always pulled his punches, relented before emotional blood was spilled. But here, now, he wanted to lash his father with the fury inside him until his father understood what he'd done, what he was still doing to their family.

"Norm, I'm sorry." Mike leaned against the counter, tunneling his fingers into his white hair. "Those things I said to Truman, to your friend."

"Lucy."

Mike's head shot up then he nodded. "Lucy. I am sorry."

Norm hesitated, tilting his head to the side in confusion. *What the fuck?* Mike never admitted he was wrong. Norm opened his mouth, but then his father stormed away from the counter, throwing his hands high. "I don't know why you're wasting your time at a place like that bar. And with people like that."

"'Like that'? Like Lucy?"

"You can do better than her, son. You have done better than her. Pamela was--"

295

Norm pushed past his father, twisting so he wouldn't slam his shoulder into the old man.

Mike caught his arm, trying to haul him back, but Norm shrugged him off and stomped onto the patio, escaping into the sunshine and open spaces. He sucked in a breath then blew the air out in a long stream, feeling as if he'd expelled something clinging, toxic. The glass rattled behind him as his dad slammed the door to his study. A small, bitter smile curled Norm's lips. Right on schedule. Two hours of family time and Mike had already retreated to his lair.

Norm swallowed the sourness in his throat and stalked to the table. Everyone craned to scrutinize him-- except Lucy. He waved away any questions and fell into his seat. Reaching over, he ruffled Tommy's hair. "Did you get into Shop, squirt?"

Tommy batted his hands away, but grinned in relief, and launched into an excited monologue about shop class, cars, and machinery that gave the rest of the adults enough breathing room to regain their equilibrium. Although, after a quick glance at Lucy's pale, averted face, Norm wasn't sure he'd *ever* regain his equilibrium.

***

As dinner broke up, Lucy stayed with the women. Hunter carried Bryan off to safety as soon as propriety allowed and Lucy mentally wished them luck. Beautiful Bryan had a bit of a shell-shocked air about him, but endearing nonetheless with his gorgeous features. Hunter shook her hand and gave her a quick hug as they left. "I'm sorry we didn't get a chance to talk more tonight. Norm told me you're interested in engineering?"

She bobbed her head 'Yes,' her mouth too dry for speech.

"Have Norm schedule a visit to the lab soon. The project manager on the new Mars Reconnaissance Rover is a friend of mine. I'm sure she wouldn't mind chatting with you about the project, and I can give you a tour of the lab after."

She nodded again, numb as well as dry-mouthed. Too much. She wanted to retire and wallow into her pain, but these people, these good, wonderful people kept *talking* to her.

After Hunter's defection, Tom made to scurry to the safety of his room, but not before a ten minute round of grilling her with car questions about the parts she'd brought him. A tension headache had started behind her eyes and she was shaking pretty badly from, well, from *everything.* Still, she smiled at Tom and smoothed his hair down when he said goodnight. She cupped his cheek, still rounded with the fullness of childhood even as the rest of his body stretched and strained towards adulthood. Tilting forward, she planted a quick, affectionate kiss on Tom's cheek then roped him in for a hug. Poor Tom. Of all the casualties this evening, Tom was the most innocent. Being a twelve-year-old caught in the power plays of grown-ups couldn't be fun or healthy.

After Tom's retreat, Lucy stayed close to Alisha and Janet at the patio table, letting their affectionate, idle chatter wash over her, participating only when she had to, and only then in monosyllables.

He loves me. He loves *me…*She blinked free of her reverie to scan for Norm, but he had taken Truman aside after dinner and not reappeared yet.

297

When the darkness lengthened and it grew too breezy to stay outside, the three women stepped in and settled onto the white sofa set. After awhile, Alisha excused herself to find her husband and Norm. Lucy had noticed the half-full six pack missing from the fridge when she helped shove the leftovers away, but she said nothing to Alisha.

As the silence stretched between Lucy and Janet, alone in the living room, Lucy fidgeted in her chair more and more. Finally, she pushed to her feet and crossed to the pictures on the mantle. One in particular kept nagging at her, grating against her senses like a discordant note. She lifted the frame, not a plain silver one like Mike's, but a wide enameled one with a chunky, textured design, looping and curling in bright red tones.

It was another Christmas family photo, and she recognized the reindeer pajamas, so this was the same year as the one on Mike's desk. But this one was so different. Posed. Stiff. Everyone in the Keane family carefully arranged. The whole thing looked as carefully choreographed and staged as a ballet. Everyone in place, everyone adjusted to the exact right angles. The image might as well have been a photograph of a half dozen mannequins for all the life or vibrancy it projected. Hard to believe this had been taken with the same *people*, let alone on the same day as the other one.

One family photo with Mike in it, one not. If Lucy'd had to pick she would have guessed Mike would want this picture on his desk. The carefully regulated one, the proper and formal one where everyone was exactly in place. But he hadn't chosen this print--he'd chosen the silly picture, the one full of light and laughter. *The one he's not in.*

Sadness washed over her. Mike Keane was a man who didn't fit into his own family. A man who obviously liked the picture of his family better when he wasn't even in it. Maybe he *wanted* to be in the fun, silly picture, to bond and laugh with his family...but maybe he didn't know how.

Like me. She clung to Jezebel's because she didn't know anything else, didn't know any other way to live anymore. After the world she'd built with her father imploded, she'd inserted herself into Hank's. She didn't know if she had the strength to build a new life again. *This world, Norm's life, his family*--how could she ever teach herself to fit here?

Do you want to fit here?

Her throat prickled, tears stinging her eyes, and she slammed the Christmas pic onto the mantle.

Too much. This whole night was too much. Norm had tried to warn her, and she ignored him and now *this*. This huge black hole of pain and yearning gaping in front of her like an open wound.

Janet's palm settled lightly on Lucy's shoulder, and Norm's mother squeezed gently. Her smell was soft and flowery, that comforting feminine scent all moms seemed to have.

Lucy swallowed and shoved a grin onto her face through sheer force of will as she faced Janet. "You guys have such great pictures."

Janet grazed one finger along the top of each frame. Lucy followed the finger's progress and caught a glimpse of Alisha and Truman mugging in formal wear, probably on their wedding day. A larger frame with four cutouts occupied pride of place at the center of the mantle, four fat babies staring out at Lucy, indistinguishable one from the other in their pink roundness. Janet lingered over a small three paneled folding frame with a picture of all the older Keane brothers in caps and gowns. Norm had a horrendous shaggy beard in his, looking scruffy and a-dork-able and sexy as hell. *Oh, Norm.* Her heart clenched. She pushed the aching aside. *Later.*

Reaching the end of the mantle, Janet plucked the last frame off before Lucy could see the picture it held. "Did Norm show you my old bikini picture?" Janet asked, her dimples showing.

"You were a cute beach bunny."

"I was, wasn't I?" Janet let out a gusty breath and at last handed the mystery frame over to Lucy. "I suppose I can't complain about the silly bikini in Mike's office when I keep this one in the living room."

Lucy glanced down and frowned in confusion. The picture was Norm dressed in green fatigues and mugging for the camera. *Halloween sometime?* The best part was how he had his tongue all the way out, his features scrunched in a taunting, silly, *nyah-nyah* face at someone off camera.

Noticing a new detail, Lucy blinked. Black hair. The picture was too grainy to make out eye color, but she bet they were blue. *Mike.* This ridiculous, goofy picture was of a young Mike Keane. Who, if possible, even with his black hair, resembled Norm more closely even than Truman did. Lucy swallowed, unnerved. The reason she'd mistaken this for a photo of Norm wasn't only the uncanny physical resemblance, but also the luster of Mike Keane's expression, the mischief lighting his face. She ghosted one finger over his smile, seeing Norm reflected there.

300

This is why Janet married Mike. He made her laugh. Lucy swallowed, shaking her head in sadness. As far as things to build a life on, you could do worse. *So, what happened?*

Janet lifted the picture free of Lucy's limp hands. "I keep this because it reminds me how he was."

Norm's mother cradled the frame against her stomach, gripping the corners with her fingers, staring down at young Mike, but seeing farther than the picture, her mind obviously casting back to days long past. "We met as I was finishing college and he was a returning student on the GI Bill. Eleven years older than me. Bitingly funny. Dark. Moody. *Magnificent.* My mother begged me not to marry him." Janet laughed to herself.

She set the picture on the edge of the mantle with a small click, her hand lingering against the wooden frame. "I think even then I knew you couldn't burn that bright without flaming out but..." Shaking her head, she curled her arms across her stomach. "After we got married, he asked me to stop my writing *hobby.* Said a wife who wrote sci-fi potboilers was embarrassing at the English department dinners. And I loved him so much I agreed to quit." Her face flinched, tightening in wistful regret. "I switched to nonfiction, work that he approved of.

"We waited to have the boys until our careers were more settled. Until we could afford this place. But then once we had all this, his career plateaued. People got promoted above him. His grant requests were denied. Everything became a slog. Norm wasn't an easy baby and Mike began using his work to wiggle out of things. To escape. I...don't know when it got as bad as this, though." Janet shook her head and Lucy crossed to her, resting her hand lightly on the older woman's shoulder. Janet patted

301

her hand absently then retreated to the sofa, falling against the cushions and staring at the ceiling, her gaze blank, her pixie face wiped of emotion.

Chilled, sick to her stomach, Lucy stared hard at Mike Keane's picture.

Mike might be Norm's doppelganger, might conjure the image of Future Norm forty years down the line, but Norm's fate was not his father's and never could be. And Lucy, if she stayed with him for forty more years of love and jobs and kids and *life*, would not have the life Janet had lived through. In one month, Norm had been there for Lucy, supported her, cared for her more than anyone else she had ever met besides her own father. Norm was solid, and he would never withdraw like his father had because of life's disappointments.

No, not Norm...Lucy's heart froze, cold fear clenching her throat in a grip strong enough to strangle. Norm wasn't the potential Mike in this future scenario. *I am.*

Nausea boiled in her stomach. How many times had she abandoned Norm, withdrawn from him, hurt him, and they'd only been together a month? If they stayed together and Lucy didn't change, then she didn't need to worry about turning into Janet--she needed to worry about turning *Norm* into Janet. About condemning her dear best beloved geek to life as a sad figure, old before his time.

No. I'll leave him first. But just the idea of leaving Norm made her ache inside. No wonder Mike Keane had held so tight to his bright, beautiful bikini babe.

As the sliding doors opened, Lucy jumped. Alisha trudged in, dragging a tipsy Truman behind her, murder in her gaze. Norm followed behind, and Lucy's breath hitched in her chest as he stared at her--his love glinting

302

there in his gaze as a bold challenge. Every corded muscle of his body, every tick of tension in his movements, held that same questioning, demanding note: What are you going to do, Lucy?

What am I going to do? Sucking in a breath for courage, Lucy crossed to him, hand held out. "Home?"

Chapter Twenty-Seven

Lucy drove Norm to her apartment afterward because she needed to "pick up some things," whatever that meant. She didn't say anything else for the dark, hour long, interminable drive back from Santa Clarita. The whole evening had been a disaster of epic proportions that even the greatest Greek tragedian might have had trouble trumping.

Norm rolled his eyes at himself. *Overdramatic, Norman.* Still, that was how he felt. Like someone had punched a hole in his chest. *I shouldn't have said it.* Lucy was edgy, wary. He believed--he *knew* she had feelings for him. Strong feelings. But every time he pushed, she bolted. This was their pattern and he knew it, and he'd still pushed her. *And see how you are rewarded.*

Hunched over the steering wheel, her entire posture telegraphed her distraction. He flicked the radio on to break the silence and good old Steve Perry wailed over the speakers in his raspy power ballad voice, singing about loving with "Open Arms." Norm irritably flicked to a radio station playing nothing but Mexican music.

She parked at her apartment, blocking her Mustang in with his Toyota. Unwinding from her clenched position, she faced him at last. "Come inside a sec?"

He closed his eyes, his whole body folding over in weary pain. "Not tonight. I can't take anymore tonight."

She caught his hand, tugging until his fingers slid off the car door. "Please? I want to show you something."

He puffed out his breath and rolled out of the car, feeling like his bones had fossilized and he should be on display in some museum. Lucy let them into her apartment and crossed to her kitchen counter where a stack of mail sat. She plucked one large, 8 1/2 by 11 envelope off the top of the junk mail and carried the letter to where he waited by the door. "This came today."

He glanced at the address and blinked. "Berkeley?"

"Yeah. I didn t open it because...well, I wanted you here for this."

An irrepressible grin spread over his face, thawing away some of the chill that family dinner had left. "It's the Big Envelope."

"I know." She flapped her hands in a warding gesture, her eyes tense. "But don't jinx it."

He tried handing the envelope back to her but she clasped her hands together as she shook her head. "You do it. Please?"

Obligingly, he ripped the envelope open and pulled out the dark blue folder with the silver Berkeley seal stamped on the front. He read the first line of the letter and promptly dumped the whole packet into her hands.

Lucy sucked in a tense breath then looked down. Her gaze skittered across the paper, gradually widening with each sentence she read. Then, she finally tore her gaze away, her mouth splitting in a grin. "Berkeley, Norm! Berkeley!"

He caught her around the waist and spun her in a wide arc of joy, bouncing with her in his arms as the two of them chanted together, "*Berk-e-ley! Berk-e-ley! Berk-e-ley!*"

He set her down after a long minute and kissed her soundly on the mouth. She matched his fervor, her lips opening against his, greedily coaxing and keeping him pressed to her. She cradled his face, the acceptance letter crackling in her hand.

Even as he blazed with gladness for Lucy, a remote corner of his heart had chilled to solid ice. *Berkeley. She's leaving.* "Congratulations." He pulled away, hurting to have her, hurting to not have her, but giving her the distance she probably needed right now after everything.

Lucy surprised him, catching his wrists and holding him. "Wait." Slapping her acceptance packet onto the kitchen counter, she scurried into her bedroom.

Norm bounced on the balls of his feet as he listened to her thump and shuffle in her bedroom. Finally, after several minutes, she emerged with a large frame clasped to her chest. She wet her lips, her eyes settling somewhere to the right of his shoulder. Instinctively, he stepped away from the entryway and pushed the door shut.

She eased the obviously precious picture away from her chest, holding the frame out to him with shaking hands. "Your mom showed me a lot of your family pictures today. I thought it was fair to show you one of mine." She caught her lower lip with her teeth and gnawed gently, her gaze darting to him as he took the picture.

Norm glanced down and the air heaved from his lungs in one quick, painful breath. The picture showed Lucy in a light blue graduation gown unzipped to show her pretty white floral dress beneath. Her strikingly blonde hair

306

fell in fat ringlets and her big blue eyes were overly made-up, lined heavily with distinctly immature sparkly blue eyeliner.

An older man with thinning, faded blond hair had his arm thrown around her as the two of them beamed with matching smiles at the camera. Lucy's dad had been bigger than her, burly, with a full, square face, but he had her eyes, and he had her smile, and the two of them together made Norm hurt for her.

"This is the last picture I have of us together where he looks healthy." She'd retreated into the kitchen as if she couldn't bear to be too close to the picture, to even glimpse it. "Dad was diagnosed with pancreatic cancer a few months before that. It derailed my whole senior year." Her voice quavered, a reedy vibrato of grief. "I got accepted into a bunch of colleges, but I didn't go. I wanted to stay with him. He tried to talk me out of postponing college, but I knew he wanted me with him whatever he said. So I stayed."

She crossed her arms over her chest, her fingernails denting the flesh of her forearms. "Do you know the five-year survival rate for pancreatic cancer is less than five percent? My dad made it three years. He beat it the first time. He was in remission. We started to hope, I started to plan again, started taking classes at the community college, started thinking ahead to a time when he'd be healthy...then his screening came back. He died two and a half years ago."

"*Lucy*--" Norm took one impulsive step toward her, but she jerked her hand up to stop his motion, her face clenching with pain. She shook her head sharply, and Norm stayed rooted where he was, holding absolutely still.

307

The muscle in her jaw ticked for a few minutes then she continued, dry-eyed. "There's this magical thinking you get during the first year. After. Like you have this unspoken agreement with the universe that if you live through one year then everything will go back to the way it was. He'll come back. Somehow. You wait, and the one year anniversary comes, and the one year anniversary passes and it's not all magically better. The pain's still there. My dad isn't ever coming back.

"The couple years after the first are better, but it never goes away. My dad died when he was forty years old, Norm. I can go on, I can live, but he left me too soon and that doesn't get better. He should be here. He should be here." She slapped her hand onto her Berkley packet and brandished the papers in the air, her eyes shimmering with unshed tears. "*He should be here.*" Throwing the packet down, she leaned on the counter, her hands white-knuckling where she gripped the edge. Fat drops welled from her eyes, spilling over her cheeks, and her chin crinkled with emotion.

Norm strode over to her and enveloped her in his arms whether she wanted comfort or not. He cupped her head, clasping her to his shoulder as she cried into his shirt. Easing her to the ground, he curled over her smaller body and he rocked back and forth, soothing her, hurting for her, for what she'd lost.

Eventually, the sobs shifted into sniffles and she eased away, leaving the shoulder of his shirt damp against his skin. She scraped with her palms at the tear tracks but he took over, gently soothing the water away with the pad of his thumb. Her broken gaze flicked up to meet his, and he stopped, arrested by the intensity in her face.

"Norm..." Her voice quivered, hitched with the occasional sobbing hiccup. "I want to be with you, but it's hard--" She tilted back, her cheeks slicked with new tear tracks. "It's hard to care about someone again. It's so much easier to feel nothing at all. To share nothing. Do nothing." She gave a small, brittle laugh. "You scare the hell out of me." But she stared at him tenderly as she said the words, and her hand moved to clasp his.

He hissed in a slow breath. Lucy's admission wasn't an "I love you too," but it was something. Meaningful and precious in its own way. He squeezed his eyes closed and kissed her, tasting salt tears.

Lucy retreated to the bathroom to blow her nose and, when she reappeared, she seemed more herself, wan but not so fragile. "You want to go back to your place?" she asked, scrubbing at her nose with a wad of toilet paper.

"We can stay here."

"Norm, you hate my apartment."

He shot her a small, apologetic *so-so* head tilt then popped the apartment door open. She walked past him and clattered down the stairs. Back in his Toyota again, Norm cast about in his mind for something to break the dour mood between them. With a crow of delight, he remembered he had just the thing. Reaching over, he tugged the lever to pop his trunk. "I forgot something." He hopped out of the car to retrieve a small package from his trunk.

He dropped the parcel in Lucy's pink-clad lap and the crinkle of thick plastic filled the air. The present was still encased in its heavy-duty plastic shipping envelope so he had to loan her the serrated edge of the car keys before she could get into her present. He started the car as soon as

309

she handed him the keys, and he gladly sped away from the gloom of her hulking apartment building. Lucy yanked the plastic open, eviscerating the envelope and clocking Norm in the chest with her elbow as she did so. Finally, a square of folded blue fabric fell into her lap from the ruins of the shipping envelope.

She frowned and cast him a questioning glance.

"It's for the Career Day theme night at the bar that's coming up," he said. "I saw this online and thought of you."

She unfolded the costume and flattened the fabric against her body. His imagination cheerfully filled in exactly how hot she'd be in the revealing, undersized coveralls. Adorable and sexy. Lucy shook the envelope again and a faux-leather belt tumbled out loaded with plastic tools in primary colors.

Her distinct lack of a reaction made Norm stir uneasily. "It's a mechanic's uniform. Well, a sexy one. I wanted to get you a sexy engineer but, oddly enough, they don't make sexy mechanical engineer costumes yet, so this is the closest I could get."

"Oh."

He clenched his hands on the steering wheel. The costume abruptly struck him as silly, and he began babbling in his nervousness, "I know it's too cute and it's not really revealing enough for a shot girl and, you know, never mind, you don't have to wear it." He reached over to snatch back the costume but she recoiled against the door, clutching the costume to her.

"*Norm.*" She hadn't used that particular exasperated/amused tone with him in awhile--the two syllable version of his name: 'Nooo-*orm*'. The plastic wrapping crinkled as she clutched the tool belt to her chest. "I love the costume. It's fantastic. You're fantastic." She snaked one arm around his neck, kissing him heartily on the cheek.

At least she loves something tonight. He winced then pushed that pain away, far down deep. It was too soon. She hadn't said the words back, but that didn't mean she wouldn't. They were on an OK track. It would be fine. Everything would be fine.

Until she goes to Berkeley and leaves you.

He pressed his teeth together hard, crushing the steering wheel with his fingers. *Jesus. What kind of jerk are you that you can't be happy for her? Not everything needs to be about you, Norman.*

"Hey, Norm?"

He shot her a quick, happy grin to dispel any hint of brooding from his heart. "Yes?"

"I want you to call your dad tomorrow and make things up. Don't apologize to him just…smooth things over."

"No."

"*Norm.*"

"*No.*" He braced his arms against the steering wheel, concentrating painfully on his driving.

"He's your dad."

"You don't understand."

"He's your dad. He's your dad and he's here and he's alive."

Norm winced, guilt coating his throat. Guilt about what he wasn't quite sure. That he had his dad and Lucy didn't? That he would fight with his dad when she couldn't

311

even talk to hers? But his situation was different. It just was.

"Lucy…don't you…I mean, isn't your perspective slightly skewed on this one? My dad isn't like your dad. There were no Mustangs and Iron Man comics with Mike Keane. Mostly there were a lot of closed doors and *'do you boys have to be so loud when I'm working?'*"

"He does love you." She touched his arm gently, like she was scared he'd recoil. Her voice dropped to a small, thready whisper. "I know I'd give anything, *anything* even to fight with my dad again. My perspective may be skewed but that doesn't mean I'm wrong."

Norm sagged. "I'll call him."

"Tomorrow."

He *tsk*ed in annoyance then nodded at last. Only a few hours into love and he was already whipped. *Oh, please, you were whipped from the beginning.*

"Do something else for me?" she asked.

"*What?*"

"Tell him you love him. People…people don't say that to their parents enough."

Meaning she believes she didn't say it to her dad enough. Hell. Norm wanted to bang his head against the steering wheel, just to refocus the pain somewhere else for a little variety. But, as he was going 80 on the 5, that didn't strike him as a good idea. Instead, he slid his hand out and caught Lucy's, tangling his fingers with hers. "Lucy, your dad knew you loved him."

She squeezed his hand. "OK. So make sure *your* dad knows."

"Little hard ass." He blew his breath out through his teeth. "*OK*," he blurted out, then, more gently, "OK."

312

**

When they got to his apartment, Norm was quieter than usual, listless and solemn. Lucy swallowed panic. This was about what he'd said to her. Before. In the kitchen. Her mind shied away from even thinking the words again.

And now there was the Berkeley thing complicating everything too. She wanted to go, burned to go, but she wanted Norm too. Wanted him near her on some deep, nameless level of need, a place as primal as hunger or thirst. Or breathing.

But couldn't she have NorCal *and* Norman? He was a writer, not a bouncer. And he could write anywhere. If she asked him to go to NorCal, wasn't there a good chance he'd go with her?

Maybe if you could tell him what he wants to hear. She swallowed. Needs *to hear.* Her heart fluttered, bursting with affection for him, but naming it, saying it, scared her out of all proportion. She'd hoped telling Norm about her father would help, would show she wanted him in her life, but Norm, however he tried to hide his feelings, was seriously hurt that she hadn't said the three words back.

They were quiet as they padded hand in hand to his bedroom, partly because of a sleeping Zack, partly because the air between them remained too charged, too perilous for words. As if saying something, *anything,* might be the spark that ignited the dangerous potentialities choking the air. Alone in his room, Norm crossed to the bed before her and she closed the door with a click.

He sat on the end of the bed, bending to toe off his sneakers and peel his socks away. His face was pale, his movements slow and too careful, like he had to concentrate extra hard to make his fingers work.

313

Everything in him seemed drained, sucked dry by the emotions of the day.

I can't tell him how I feel...

But I can show him.

Lucy went to him and gently pushed him down with a hand on each of his shoulders. She traced her fingers over his body, stroking the corded muscles of his arms. Sitting straight on the edge of the bed, his body tightening with sudden tension, he leaned back under her touch. She moved between his legs, his thighs bracketing hers.

She held his gaze and slowly, carefully lifted the hem of her pink party dress over her head. His hands trailed after hers, finding the skin as she uncovered it inch by inch, skimming her body in the ghost of a caress. She stood before him for a long minute in just her panties then leaned forward and grabbed the hem of his shirt. Obligingly, he lifted his arms as she peeled the garment away. His broad hands settled under the curve of her breasts, cradling her ribcage, his thumb stroking the tender skin there until she shivered.

She sank to her knees in front of him and worked his belt loose. Ruthlessly dealing with the belt and zipper, she peeled the pants away and his erection nudged free of the slit in his boxers. He tilted his hips and she slid the pants and his boxers down until he had carefully kicked his legs free. Standing again, only the barrier of her underwear remaining, he slowly lifted his hands. He didn't immediately reach for her panties; instead he smoothed his hands over her stomach, around her side to the small of her back. She trembled and leaned into his touch, her body going warm and melting as he traced a path over her skin.

He hooked his thumbs in her cotton panties and slid them off, his fingers tickling over her legs, guiding the undergarment on its path. Then he let her panties fall and gently raked his fingertips along her legs until he clutched the curve of her ass, pulling her toward him. He slithered farther onto the bed as she set her knees on the mattress to hover over him, the bare tip of him just shy of impaling her. Norm's hands traced gentle circles over her flesh, by turns tender and rough, but all of his touches plucking at that strung cord inside her, slicking the place between her legs with a damp, aching heat. He reached for the nightstand, foil crinkled, and she eased away from the nearness of him only so he could sheathe himself with the condom. Then, as soon as he'd moved his hands away, she sank onto him, taking him far inside her, wanting him there touching the very core of her body.

She moved slowly, biting her lip to choke back a moan at the exquisite, luxurious slide of their bodies together. She pinched her eyes closed, climbing, climbing toward that beautiful blackness at the tip of her ecstasy.

His hands traced over her body, palming her breasts until she arched higher. As his hands slid over her lushness, pebbling her nipples, her whole body tingled with a decadent warmth. Then, still rubbing the nipple between two fingers, he threaded his fingers into her hair and coaxed her to him for a long, slow kiss. When he broke it, he cradled her head, holding her face close to his. "Look at me?" he whispered.

She blinked her eyes open, holding his gaze as she continued to rock against him, to coax as much of that luscious, coiling, crackling sensation out from where their bodies joined.

315

Making love. The phrase had always sounded so silly to her, syrupy and vaguely old-fashioned, but she understood it now, understood the sweet ache of joining emotion to sex, intimacy on intimacy, yearning and wanting. Need. Absolute and all-consuming.

Each movement between them, each touch, was powered with a strange new potency. As if every other moment of intimacy between them had been veiled by some thin, invisible barrier that had now disappeared. Lucy had undressed in front of Norm many times before, but she'd never felt so naked.

He found her rhythm, matching it perfectly, doubling the sensation, hitting a sweet, tender place inside her that seemed to press as deeply into him because he threw his head back on the pillow, the cords of his throat standing out with tension. He looked at her again, and held her close to him, close enough so she breathed his breath as the pleasurable wave raked over her body. A thousand pinpricks of satisfaction exploded both her body and mind as the thread inside her snapped, and she had to break their locked gaze to squeeze her eyes shut and scream her ecstasy. He redoubled his rhythm beneath her and tumbled over the edge a few seconds after she did, his breath hitching as he came.

She returned to herself, slowly blinking, the bottoms of her feet tingling from the strength of her orgasm's aftershocks. Breathlessly laughing, she clasped him with her muscles down there and he twitched beneath her. She rolled off him, sweaty, dazed, and smiling from the bottom of her soul.

He tumbled off the bed to deal with the condom. Lucy curled on her side, oozing into the pillows as her body went liquid, sliding into an almost-sleep where everything became distant, coated with a gauzy barrier that made it not quite real. The bed tipped as Norm sat. "Lucy?" He gently rubbed her arm, but she was too tired to stir, to speak. Giving an amused grunt, he settled his full weight on the bed and stretched out so his body warmed her all along her back. He draped his arm over her waist and molded himself to her curves. After a long moment, he murmured, "I love you."

Her eyes shot open and she pressed them to the very edges of her eye sockets trying to catch a glimpse of him out of the corner. But he was too far behind her, so she couldn't know if she'd been meant to hear that or not.

Chapter Twenty-Eight

The next day Norm had no need to call his father to patch things up because Mike Keane arrived on his son's doorstep just as Norm, Lucy and Zack were sitting down for post-coital pancakes. Well, post-coital for Norm and Lucy. They were just pancakes for Zack.

Norm held the door open and gaped as his father stood there on his front doorstep. Mike glanced down, shaking his head. Finally, patience clearly breaking, Mike threw his hands wide and said, "Can we talk, Norm?"

Norm, wary and unsure, stepped outside to join his father on the landing, gently closing the door behind him.

Mike faced away, clutching the iron railing that ran the length of the apartment's outdoor landing. "I came to apologize for yesterday. Your mother and I...we had a long talk." He gave a small laugh. "A *long* talk."

Norm winced in unwilling sympathy. Behind his mother's sweet gamine face lurked the whip-hard tongue of a termagant. Even when you knew you deserved every barbed word she threw your way that didn't make the dressing-down any less painful. Violently squashing his sympathy, Norm folded his arms and waited for his dad to continue.

"We're..." Mike swallowed and his eyes twitched with tension. "We're starting couple's counseling, and I'm going to see someone on my own, too."

Norm blinked, shock whipping through him, leaving his conception of the world scrambled. Mike Keane in *therapy*? Norm craned around, searching for the Four Horsemen.

"Your mother says I try too hard to live my life through you boys. Through you. And it's not healthy or fair." Mike's voice was slow, measuring, still unsure. But when his gaze crossed with Norm's there was real pain there. "What I said last night, to you and to Truman. I never wanted to be that kind of father. I'm...I'm sorry. I really am."

Prickles started along Norm's arms, like a limb waking from sleep. "Did you tell Tru?"

"Talked to him before I came here." Mike snorted. "Alisha nearly punched me in the face."

Norm bit back a laugh. The door opened, and he stumbled as the thing propping him unexpectedly swung inwards. Lucy poked her head out, her hair tousled, her face fresh-scrubbed and beautiful as a new-minted sunrise. "Hello, Mr. Keane."

Mike dipped his head in greeting. "Lucy." He hesitated, clearing his throat. "And call me Mike, please." He cast Norm a small, worried glance then refocused on Lucy. "I wanted to apologize to you for my behavior yesterday. Also, what you said about the books...you were right. It was intellectual bigotry, and I should know better."

Lucy waved his apology away and beamed, brightening the already bright California day.

319

Norm raised an eyebrow. *What the hell did she say to him?* Mike drew himself up with dignity. "I hope you'll send me a copy of your book when it comes out, Norm. I would love to read your novel."

Norm's mouth fell open and a riot of emotion blazed through him, like he'd been kicked in the gut. Lucy caught his hand, clasping his fingers while Norm just stood there, flabbergasted and reeling. If Norm hadn't already loved Lucy this moment would have sealed his fate forever. *What did she say to my dad?*

"We're having pancakes with Zack," Lucy said. "Want some?" She swung the front door open wider in a *please-come-in* gesture.

Mike shook his head, already half-turning away. "Oh no, thank you, I have work--" He broke off, his gaze darting to Norm.

Norm, after years of practice, managed to keep his face impassive. *I knew it! I knew he couldn't change!*

Mike hesitated, poised on the tips of his toes to leave then, smiling shakily, Norm's dad brushed past him to step inside the apartment. "Pancakes sound great."

Norm blinked, frozen out on the landing, staring after his father in absolute shock. Lucy dipped out of the apartment and grabbed his wrist, hauling him inside. Her grin was smug as she towed him after her to the table.

Norm stared at the back of her head and his heart clenched with love, with pain. But he set that aside as he fell into his seat while his father settled more composedly into the chair beside him. Calmly turning toward Norm as if he stopped by for pancakes and chitchat every morning, Mike Keane said, "Please pass the syrup, Norman."

***

During breakfast, Mike made stilted conversation, asking the three young people about their lives. Zack had grown up with Norm, so Mike managed to fill several conversational lapses by asking Zack about his folks and his sisters. Zack slid Norm a wide-eyed stare halfway through breakfast and Norm returned a sympathetic nod. It was like someone had replaced Mike Keane with a pod person--a socially inept pod person--but one that obviously wanted to make things work with his son.

Mike managed not to say anything obliviously cruel or unforgivable over the whole course of the meal and, as his dad was leaving, Norm actually walked him out. They shook hands then--heart fluttering with a fragile, wary hope--Norm reeled his dad in for a quick hug. After freezing in surprise for a long moment, his dad hugged him too, even patted him gently on the back before padding down the apartment stairs.

Norm started inside, then, remembering his promise to Lucy, he tilted over the railing, hoping to catch his father before he reached his car. Mike was almost onto the street. "Hey, Dad!"

Mike wheeled back, sending Norm a questioning glance.

Norm hesitated, swallowing with uncertainty. *Aw, screw it.* He sucked in a rousing breath then bellowed, "Love you, Dad!"

Mike stepped back as if the words had physically collided with him, but then a slow smile spread over his face, showcasing a set of laugh lines that bracketed his eyes and mouth which Norm had never noticed before. "Love you too, Norm." Mike waved a hesitant, somehow gentle goodbye then walked off to his car.

321

Norm stood outside a moment, heart stretching with a hard-edged hope. It was only a beginning, and a fragile one at that, but still. *Still.*

As he pushed the apartment door open, he laughed happily and bounded into the kitchen. He half-pulled Lucy out of her chair and kissed her soundly on the lips. When he broke away she sank into her seat, blinking and smiling dreamily.

"Hey, Bates," Zack said. "Pass the maple syrup."

***

At work that night, Ronnie cornered Lucy in the back room. "Berkeley, Luce? Congrats!" The Amazonian redhead enveloped Lucy in a hug.

Lucy sidled away. She hadn't wanted to make a big announcement about that yet. Or ever. "How'd you find out?"

"Zack sent me a text."

"You two going strong, then?"

"Nah. But we're cordial."

"*Berkeley?*" Hank's voice from the doorway made Lucy freeze, all her muscles tensing up. "You got into Berkeley, Luce?"

She wheeled to face him, sweat popping out on the small of her back. She'd been avoiding Hank lately and had hoped to continue the pattern tonight. Unreasonable or not, she felt like she had a scarlet 'N' emblazoned across her chest, proclaiming to anyone who cared to look what was going on between her and Norm.

Hank reeled her in for a crushing hug, lifting her off her high-heeled feet. When he set her down his dark eyes shone with happiness for her. Feeling like a liar and a traitor, Lucy smiled back. He gave her a small pat on the arm. "We are having a party to celebrate this, kid. This Wednesday. Two hours before opening. Ronnie?" He glanced over at the redhead.

Ronnie shot him a dry glance. "I'll take care of it."

Hank gave Lucy one last beaming grin before he sauntered out of the room.

After he'd left, all of her insides seemed to turn to lead, dragging her down. *A party. Crap.* And there went her resolve not to cold shoulder Norm anymore, not to push him away. He worked front door most nights so she usually just avoided the front door, and thereby killed any attempts on his part at fraternizing. But at a party there would be socializing and mingling. She'd have to cold shoulder him again, hurt him again to keep their cover. And, after telling her he loved her, he probably didn't give a damn about keeping their relationship under wraps anymore.

*But...*She was going to Berkeley. She only had a month or two left to work at Jezebel's, and she didn't want to risk that time by pissing off Hank. And if she and Norm came out Hank *would* fire them. She was sure of that in her bones. How could she have the party, not hurt Norm with her cold shoulder, and keep Hank in the dark all at once?

I can't. She glanced desperately at Ronnie. "Don't tell Norm about the party."

Ronnie's eyes widened. "What? Why? Did you two--"

"We're fine." Lucy pressed a hand to her throat, her own pulse throbbing under her fingers. "But it'll hurt him to be at the party and get ignored by me--"

"So don't ignore him, dummy."

Lucy shook her head, her bangs falling over her eyes. "*No.* I don't want to get fired if Hank figures it out. I've only got a few more months here anyway. We can keep the secret that long. We have to."

"You're nuts."

Lucy squeezed the other girl's forearm, pleading with her eyes. "Please, Ronnie?"

Ronnie *tsk*ed but nodded. "It's your party, fuck up your life if you want to."

***

Over the next two days, Lucy was jumpy and nervous at work, at Norm's, even alone in her apartment. She kept second-guessing herself. Invite Norm. Don't. Tell Hank. Don't. Everything in her was stirred up and riled. A foaming cloud of indecision cloaked her, making her hands tremble and sweat soak through her clothes at regular intervals.

The day of the party she woke up at Norm's. As soon as she rolled over to say good morning, he frowned. "Are you OK? Did you sleep?"

"Yes." She popped upright and turned her back to him, tunneling her hands through her snarled hair. "I just have a test today I'm worried about."

He banded an arm around her waist from behind and dragged her close for a quick, sleepy hug. "Well, good luck, angel."

"Thanks. See you later."

He waited expectantly, watching her. The same watchful waiting he'd done ever since Sunday night. His sadness made her want to scream and cry, but anytime she opened her mouth to force the words out they wouldn't come.

Norm collapsed against his pillows and rolled away from her. This was the first time he hadn't kissed her goodbye. Fear, cool and heavy, knotted in her chest but she pushed the feeling away and set about gathering her scattered clothes. From his slow breathing, Norm had immediately fallen back asleep. She dressed quickly and slunk out of the apartment back to her own place, worried and unhappy.

Class that day passed in a blur. She had three reviews for her finals, and if she understood two words her professors said all day it would have been a miracle. Her brain kept circling back to the impending party, her heart shadowed with dread that, one way or another, she was being very, very stupid.

***

The party was fun enough. Cheap store-bought cake. A sizeable gift card Ronnie had cobbled together after taking collections from everyone at the bar. Except Norm, of course. Lucy's eyes brimmed at the huge total on the card. The staff of Jezebel's took care of their own, and they would send her into the world in fine style. She clasped the card close and beamed through her tears.

The party didn't get *too* mushy. Hank donated one bottle of champagne the dozen or so staff had to all split between them because he didn't want anyone sloshed for their shift. The event was a quick party, haphazard, simply something to show how proud they all were of her. Lucy smiled her way through the whole thing, even as her heart ached that Norm wasn't there.

Close to opening time, the party wound down and everyone switched over to Clean-up Mode, picking up cake plates and forks, retrieving the plastic cups and dumping them in trash bins. Someone wrapped Lucy's cake in foil for her to take home, and she slipped out to

325

her car to stow the dessert in the backseat. She *should* stow the cake in the fridge of the back room but she was scared Norm would see it and ask questions.

People had already asked questions during the party, but Ronnie--a good friend if unwilling accomplice--had pawned them off by saying Norm was too new. He didn't know Lucy that well so why would he want to come? Ronnie had also taken the precaution of not inviting the other two newbies who had replaced Eddie and Jenna. During this discussion, Hank had shot Ronnie an unhappy scowl but then he was distracted by the presentation of Lucy's cake.

All in all, everything had gone fine and, even as Lucy's gut roiled with guilt, at least her sickened terror had pretty much cleared away with the last of the incriminating party supplies. Unfortunately, people had been too stubborn to empty the trash can in the middle of the party. The stupid bin was filled to bursting with blue and gold paper plates and napkins emblazoned with "Congratulations" and a jaunty black graduation cap and tassel. All she needed was for Norm to find one of these stupid things somewhere in the bar. Lucy maniacally scanned every corner of the club, rounding up any and all strays from the other trash bins.

Satisfied she'd finally found them all, she stuffed the last of the party supplies into the already overfull trash bag then yanked its ties closed. Ronnie had to hold the edges of the can for her while Lucy pulled the bag before they could get the stupid thing free. Ronnie jerked her chin toward the back door. "Want me to take the bag to the dumpsters?"

"Nah. You start in on making the shots." Lucy wasn't usually a controlling person but this she needed to see

326

done for herself. She hauled the too-full bag out to the dumpsters and glanced over as a car drove into the lot: Norm arriving in the Toyota for his shift. She swallowed her unease and waved.

Hurriedly, she hoisted the lid on the dumpster. The damn thing stuck. She pushed harder, her heart strangling in her throat. *No.* He couldn't see this stuff. *Not now. Not after everything.* Gravel crunched behind her, Norm's familiar even tread.

His breath stirred her hair as he reached around her to lift the dumpster lid. "Let me help you with that, little lady."

She curled her mouth into a smile and wheeled to face him, her hand at her waist in a posture of annoyance as she said, "'Little lady'? Really, Norman?"

He chuckled as he bent to grab the trash bag. Lucy barely stopped her instinctive rush to take the garbage from him. Instead she eased away, forcing her body to relax even as her eyes nervously tracked every movement of the stupid black bag. The bag itself wasn't incriminating. She was fine.

When he lifted the trash, though, she noticed a hole in the bottom as a white plastic fork poked through. As Norm struggled to lump the thing over the edge of the tall dumpster, the hole widened before her horrified eyes.

The bag split in a fluttering spill of paper and plastic cups. Norm cursed and recoiled to avoid the flood of garbage. Lucy stayed rooted to the spot, mouth open in horror, the evidence of her selfishness pooling over her Come-Fuck-Me heels.

He started to laugh then paused, his eyes widening as his gaze raked the pile of trash. He flicked her a glance

327

from under his brows then slowly, deliberately, bent to pick one of the paper plates free from the pile. He pushed to his feet, his brows furrowed with anger as he stared at the plate. "Good party, Lucy?"

Chapter Twenty-Nine

"Norm..."

He threw the party plate down and wheeled away. She could only see him in profile, the muscle in his jaw ticking for one long, tense minute before he whipped back. "This is stupid, Lucy. I deserve better than this." He kicked at the pile of party mess.

She stumbled toward him, shuffling her way through the sea of plates. "I know. I'm sorry, Norm. I'm so sorry."

He crossed his arms over his chest at her approach. She hesitated then gently rested her fingers on his forearms. His muscles were like steel beneath her fingers. Unyielding. The expression in his eyes was the same.

"I..." She blew her breath out on a sigh, her heart hammering, her nerves jangling with real fear. She started again, "I thought it would be easier not to invite you than having you there and pretending. Easier for both of us."

"It's been a month, you know."

"What?"

"A *month*." His nostrils flared with anger, and he jerked his chin violently in the direction of the club. "Ready to tell Hank about us?" She instinctively recoiled and he let out a small, bitter laugh. "Fine, Lucy. That's just fine."

329

Lucy glanced at him, hope rising in her throat until she could barely get her words out. "It's OK?"

He half-turned his head to avoid meeting her gaze, and the tendons on his neck stood out. His words when they fell were stark, clipped. "No, Lucy. This doesn't come close to OK. This is not in the same fucking solar system as OK." He stalked to the side, presenting his back to her. "It's not OK. I'm just not talking about it anymore. I'm not putting myself through this anymore." His voice cracked a little.

Tears filmed her vision over and his face blurred. She stumbled one step toward him, but he retreated, which hurt more than a slap. He turned to face her fully, planting his feet as if bracing for a physical onslaught. She blinked and the tears unspooled down her cheeks, leaving hot wet tracks, but she could see him again, see the way his face seemed chiseled into hard lines by his anger.

She swabbed at her face with her thumb, wiping the water away. "Norm, I care about you."

He shook his head once in quick, brutal denial. "Not enough. Not enough to want me with you. Not enough to choose me over this place." He jerked his chin at Jezebel's.

"I didn't choose anything. I just--"

"Yeah. You did." He flicked her a careless salute and breezed past her toward the door. "Have a nice life. Congrats on Berkeley."

She ached at his coolness, hunching over in pain at the casual way he'd ended everything. She'd stretched herself for him, not far enough maybe, but she *had* tried her best to show him what he meant to her. And now he was walking away like their relationship hadn't meant anything. Like it *had* only been about sex.

He had his hand on the door, ready to go inside and leave her life forever.

All her emotions, guilt and fear and sadness, boiled inside like a sickening geyser. "You said you loved me!"

"And you didn't say it back." He pushed the door open and slipped inside.

As the door swung shut, Lucy's knees gave out and she collapsed to the ground, feeling like she'd just watched her whole future walk away from her.

***

Norm pushed the back door closed then fell against it, pressing his skull against the puckered, rusty metal. Wetness prickled in his eyes and his throat was thick with emotion, but he managed not to give in, not to descend into a rubbery, sobbing wreck. But, inside, his heart broke with a crack that echoed through his whole body.

It was better this way. It was. Norm knew his own worth, knew what he wanted, what he needed from the relationship. And Lucy, as much as he--as he cared about her, was not able to give him that. Clearly. *No hard feelings. Moving on with my life. Yada. Yada.*

He clenched his teeth, wrestling against a burst of pain. Leaving her was the right thing to do. Norm had to walk away. She had to *choose* him, to open her life, to let him be a part of it...or their relationship was no good.

He slapped at his eyes with his palm, dashing away any betraying moisture as he grimly padded through the club to run the front door. Time to search for a new job so he could get on with the rest of his life. Without Lucy.

***

Ronnie took Lucy home that night and held her while she cried herself sick, clutching Norm's Batman shirt like a kid with a safety blanket.

Ronnie stroked her hair, crooning comfort like Lucy's grandmother had when she was younger. "It'll get better, Lucy. A day at a time. Get through it. Soon enough a week will pass, then a month, then one day you'll realize you've lost count. One day you won't even remember the last time he kissed you, or what day you broke up. One day, this pain won't matter anymore." Ronnie's voice was rough, hoarse from some strong remembered emotion. And Lucy didn't believe she was remembering her week of sexy fun times with Zack.

Lucy sniffed and clutched Norm's shirt. The fabric still smelled faintly of him, that sharp, clean, delicious Norm-smell. Her pillow was damp with tears under her cheek so she shifted to find a dry spot. "I'll remember what day we broke up. We just had our one-month anniversary. One month. This was like every other guy I dated. One month and I drove him away. Even Norm, wonderful Norm, couldn't stand me." She rolled her face into the pillow, her sobs redoubling, her whole body vibrating with a throbbing, empty pain.

Showing her first sign of wearing patience that whole long evening, Ronnie clicked her tongue. "Well, you could try getting him back."

"I screwed it up. He hates me." Lucy sobbed the words out, repeating them endlessly throughout the course of the night, whipping herself with them again and again. *My fault. My fault. Too late.*

Ronnie sighed then resumed patting her hair and making soothing noises.

332

***

Lucy filed Ronnie's advice away, though, picking the idea up and turning it over again and again throughout the long, miserable days that followed. It was the worry stone she used to rub her thoughts against, trying to smooth them out.

Bitterly, she reflected that if her life were a romantic comedy and Doris Day or Meg Ryan or Reese Witherspoon or someone were playing her, the plucky blonde heroine would have some brilliant flash of inspiration right about... *now,* and the whole thing would be fixed in the next fifteen minutes as she did the standard RomCom Run on her way to accomplish whatever Grand Gesture was needed to win her love back.

Unfortunately, nothing occurred to Lucy. No gimmick. No grand gesture. No public declaration she could make that would pierce the cloud of Norm's disappointment in her. And, besides, emotionally drained to the dregs, bloated and nauseous from too much junk food, she was in no condition to RomCom Run anyway.

She punched her pillow and snagged a bag of chocolate donuts, dragging the sweets closer. Fuck Doris Day. Bitch didn't know shit about love.

Chapter Thirty

A week passed and Lucy was pretty sure she aged a decade. She certainly put a decade's worth of mileage on her stomach lining as she stuffed herself with every niche of junk food imaginable. Ronnie had been right insofar as Lucy had managed to survive each day, day after day for a week. But Lucy didn't know if that was progress or penance.

She saw Norm every day at work. Had to pass him to get inside and clock in. Well, not totally true, Lucy could have gone in the back door. But something, maybe a hidden masochistic streak, made her walk in the front door every day for work. Even when she'd parked in the back.

On deeper reflection--and Lucy had done a lot of deep and dark reflecting for the past eight, interminable, lonely days--she figured it was a more simplistic urge than that, though.

She missed him.

She missed the sly and subtle flirting they'd done at work, she missed driving home with him afterward, fighting over the radio and laughing and dissecting their days, she missed kissing him and holding him until they were both languid and sleepy, she missed rolling over in bed and seeing his face and that beautiful Patrician beak of his. She missed the Bad Pick-Up lines game. She missed his laugh and his silences and his fingers tapping away at the keyboard while she worked on her math homework.

She missed all the grand, great, small, important and insignificant accumulation of details that had built up over the past month and molded together into their relationship, their life together. A life she'd trashed by being too chicken shit to fight for them. To go to Hank and say his rule didn't apply for them and if that wasn't OK then fuck you very much, Hank, and fuck this job too.

Rumor around the bar said Norm was scouting for other jobs, which meant he'd quit soon then Lucy would never see him again. Part of her believed that was just as well. The two of them mingling together was like pieces of bone from a bad break, grating and painful every time they rubbed against each other. Better to amputate.

"Oy, kiddo, planning to do any work tonight?"

Lucy blinked and broke eye contact with her own reflection to glance at Ronnie hanging through the half-open bathroom door. Ronnie was dressed as an airplane pilot in a dark blue and gold dress for the Career Day Theme Night. She had enough cleavage to hide a small animal in, and her name tag proclaimed her a "Captain of the Mile High Club." Lucy blinked again, having already forgotten Ronnie's opening remark. "What?"

"Your shift started ten minutes ago. Planning to hawk some shots tonight or do you want me to fly this boat alone?"

Lucy wet her lips nervously, bobbing her head 'yes.' She felt so oddly detached lately. Numb seemed an understatement. It was like she'd died and her body kept

335

walking, talking, and no one noticed. The Zombie Shot Girl.

Grabbing her tray off the top of Ronnie's then smoothing a hand down her own costume--the sexy mechanic uniform--Lucy wandered onto the floor.

Not Lucy's most successful night ever. Her bright, cheerful smile, a smile she'd spent years cultivating and perfecting, a smile she could usually fix on her face better than something stuck there with Superglue, kept slipping, cracking into a frown. And the bar patrons were noticing. Lucy, usually one of the most popular shot girls in the bar, was now the stinky kid on the playground. No one bought from her.

To make matters worse, Norm wasn't safely hidden at the front door taking cover, he was floor staff tonight, wandering through the crowd, "establishing a presence" and looming, always *looming*. When he did venture near her on his rounds, he swung past the periphery of her section, never even getting close enough to make eye contact with her, let alone speak.

Norm was making one of those circles now, carefully swinging wide of her. But then the party of bachelorettes at Table #2 closed on him, a frenzied gaggle like piranhas feasting, pawing at his shirt and giggling. Lucy instinctively stepped forward to extract him from the nice, horny drunk ladies.

The Bride to Be caught sight of her and beamed, frantically signaling Lucy closer.

Bemused, Lucy pressed forward, but slowed her steps to a hesitant crawl as she tried to evaluate the situation. The Bride to Be, face red with drink and a cheap tiara on her head with "BRIDE" in pink letters, was having none of Lucy's dawdling. The woman wheeled toward her, flapping her arms in a stern *come-here* gesture. Lucy hurried forward and slapped the smile onto her face while carefully avoiding eye contact with Norm. At Lucy's approach, Norm tried to wriggle his way free, but two of the bridesmaids had their arms locked around him. He wasn't going anywhere.

"What can I do for you ladies?" Lucy asked.

The women giggled some more and exchanged furtive glances. The bride leaned close for a conspiratorial stage whisper heavy on the spit and not so heavy on the whispering. "You know that shot thing you do where you straddle the guy? Well, when I came here for my friend Elsa's bachelorette we had one of these hunky bouncers do it for her." The bride licked her lips and cast a quick, predatory gaze at Norm. Lucy, mouth agape, instinctively followed her gaze and found her eyes locked with Norm's.

His face went blank. A hot burning filled her cheeks. She made quite a business of arranging her shots, ducking her head to avoid another such look.

"Well?" The bride jiggled her arm, pinching the flesh.

Lucy blinked. "I'm sorry. What is it you're asking for?"

"I want to buy one of your shots." The bride whirled and leveled her finger at Norm like Death marking his next victim. "And I want him to give it to me."

"Me?" Norm squeaked.

Lucy bit back a laugh at his discomfort. *It's not like they want him to strip.* Norm scowled, but the corner of his mouth quirked with amusement. Her breath hitched at that sweet, familiar sight and her heartbeat quickened when he

337

didn't immediately glance away but held the look, held the small, tentative grin.

The bride gave Lucy's arm another bruising shake. "Well?" the woman demanded.

"Ah, well…" Lucy spotted Hank striding toward them, the crowd parting easily for his bulk. "Well, we do sometimes do that for special occasions. Hank over there would be more than happy to give you the shot."

The bride raked her gaze over Hank's form in a rapid-fire assessment before she whipped away. Her face had wrinkled into a grimace of intense distaste. "That gym rat? No thank you." The woman sidled toward Norm, trying to do one of those sexy hip-wiggle walks and only tottering precariously forward on her heels instead. "Why would I want that gorilla when I've got Stretch here right in front of me?" She blew Norm a sloppy kiss.

Norm's face became a study in astonishment, and Lucy hurt on his behalf. Was it so incomprehensible someone would find him more attractive than Hank?

The bride, meanwhile, slid her hand under the hem of Norm's shirt. He caught her wrist and gently plucked her fingers away from his body. He smiled politely as he did it, trying to preserve that we're-all-friends-here-good-time vibe the bar fought so hard to cultivate. If it had been her, Lucy would have slapped the guy's hand away and stalked off. She opened her mouth to say as much to Norm, but he brushed past her, fumbling for the shot tray with a muttered, "Let's get this over with."

Lucy hesitated then gave a brisk nod, snapping her mind back to business. She signaled the bride to take her seat. "Sit. Keep your hands down and tilt your head." The bride obeyed and soon enough was arranged, properly if not decorously, in her seat. Lucy wheeled to coach Norm. He had a Jell-O injector clutched in a taut grip like a doctor about to administer adrenaline.

She bit her lip to restrain a laugh. "Put one leg on the chair and inject the booze into her mouth. Then get the hell out of Dodge before she can cop a feel." Unable to help herself, Lucy winked. "Show some cleavage and she might tip better."

He snorted, slid a small grin her way, then stepped past her to finish his task.

"Hey, Lucy," Hank called her.

She hesitated, torn between chaperoning Norm's first run as a Shot Boy and seeing what Hank wanted. But Norm seemed fine looming over the bride. Intimidated, sure, but still competent.

She walked toward Hank and raised an inquiring eyebrow.

He jerked his chin toward Norm and the bride. "Shot Boy? I was on my way."

"She asked for him."

For one moment, something flashed across Hank's face. Hurt? Annoyance? *Jesus, is Hank actually pouting about not being chosen in favor of Norm?* Lucy shook her head in disgust. "Was that all?"

Hank folded his beefy arms over his chest. "You and Norm. There've been some weird vibes this week."

And only a week ago that statement would have sent her heart with fear. Now that remembered fear seemed so stupid. Now she lifted an indifferent shoulder and said nothing. Unless they were screwing in the bar their relationship really wasn't Hank's business.

339

Lucy swallowed, her eyes stinging with sudden emotion. *Jeez, and it took you a damn month and losing Norm to get there? Dammit, Lucy.* She wanted to barf or punch something. Hank, by preference. Or herself. She wasn't picky.

Hank's mouth curled at one corner with mischief, apparently from watching Norm administer the shot.

Lucy wheeled back. The Bride to Be had locked her arms around Norm's back and wasn't letting him up. To keep his balance he had to straddle her in the chair, and he had his knees awkwardly bent to keep himself up and off the woman's lap. Lucy surged forward to end things but Hank caught her elbow. "He's fine."

Anger blazed through Lucy. "If that was one of the girls you'd do something right now."

"He's not a girl."

"So letting him get groped is OK? Fuck you, Hank." Lucy ripped her arm free and pounded toward Norm.

In a flash, the bride progressed from drunken hugging to full on groping. The woman slid her hand between Norm's legs and rubbed over his package before moving to grab his balls. Norm jumped a foot, his face flooding red as Lucy's vision did the same.

Rage pounded in her veins. "*Get your hands off my boyfriend, you bitch!*" She charged in and slapped the woman's hand away with a loud *smack*. Norm, his family jewels secure now from pilfering, toppled free, falling over sideways in his haste to get clear.

The bride pushed to stand and knocked her chair over in the process. She planted her feet, squaring up to Lucy. "Who you calling bitch, skank?"

The woman was taller and beefier than her, but Lucy had fury on her side. "You, you damned sexual pervert."

"*Lucy*," Hank said, his voice a low growl of warning behind her.

One of the bridesmaids rushed forward. "Hey, you can't talk to Alexa like that. She's getting married in the morning."

Lucy wheeled toward that woman and jerked her finger back at the bitchy bride. "Then why the hell is she groping my boyfriend *tonight*?" Lucy folded her arms, glaring at the bride again. "In fact, if she's such a fucking blushing bride, why is she groping my boyfriend *at all*?"

The bride adjusted the strap on her neon green dress and titled her chin up. "I was just having some fun."

"Yeah, well now you can take the fun somewhere else and get your ass out of this club."
Lucy jerked her thumb toward the exit.

The women chattered indignantly amongst themselves for several moments until a wall of solid heat stepped up behind Lucy. Hank's voice so close was more a vibration through her body than an actual sound, "Go on. Get out. And don't bother coming back here for your next bachelorette party," he said.

As the bride straggled past, Lucy, still fuming, muttered, "Bitch."

The woman wheeled and slapped Lucy hard across the face.

***

"What the hell, Lucy? I mean WHAT THE *HELL*?"

Lucy winced as Hank's voice bounced around the small confines of the office, each word pummeling her.

341

She let the ice bag over her cheek fall away into her curved palm and met his furious gaze with one of her own, if not calm then at least as steady as she could make it. "You should have done something about Norm."

"I see that now."

"No, I mean before that bitch slapped me."

"At least you didn't hit her back."

"I don't need an assault charge. Even if she deserved a good slap." Lucy glanced down, studying the condensation on her bag. "You should have helped him. That was shitty, Hank."

Hank hissed his breath out and finally paused in his pacing to rest his hip on the edge of the desk and face her. "You and Norm."

"Yeah."

He passed his hands over his face, rubbing hard. "You and *Norm*?"

"*Yeah*. Until I screwed it up because I was scared of what *you'd* think."

"What *I'd* think?"

"Yeah." She fell against the couch. "You with your stupid no-dating rule. You with your never liking anyone I date."

Hank visibly ground his teeth. "If anything, after tonight it should be very clear to you why bouncers and servers shouldn't date." He adjusted his weight and the desk groaned in protest. "I do like Norm, though."

Too late. She sniffed and shook her head. "Doesn't matter anyway. He dumped me."

Hank collapsed next to her on the couch, and gently lifted the ice bag away so he could clasp her hand. "I'm sorry, Luce. He's an idiot."

She shook her head, her throat thickening with tears. "No. I deserved it. I lied to him and I shut him out of my life. He *does* deserve better than that. Better than what I gave him."

"You did the best you could." Hank stroked his hand down her hair, gently squeezing the back of her neck.

She leaned over to rest against his shoulder, and he slung his arm over her, the weight heavy and comforting but poignant too. "That's just it, Hank. I didn't. Because I was too scared to try. Because I don't want to get hurt again." She stared him straight in the eye. "But the only way you get the big rewards are if you take the big risks, throw yourself into the breach and pray for the best."

He frowned, dark brows drawn together, not getting it.

Lucy hurt for her friend that he couldn't understand, but she knew what *she* had to do. She tossed her ice bag onto the small table then pushed to her feet, a new resolve pulsing through her. "But the biggest thing, the most important, is trusting the other person not to hurt you. You have to believe they deserve your heart, that they'll take care of you, love you." She grinned at Hank. "And I just realized, Norm is the most trustworthy person I know."

***

Slightly off-kilter after her meeting with Hank, the rest of Lucy's life loomed before her, a precipice that seemed to look down on a far green land if only she could get there. *All you have to do is jump.* She swallowed and tugged her gym bag free of her locker, clearing out a few other odds and ends from the small cubby. *Jump, eh?*

343

But would she fall or fly? She padded quickly to the parking lot, shoving the door open so hard the metal banged against the side wall as she stepped through.

Norm wheeled, straightening hurriedly from where he'd been bent under the hood of his car. He saw her and his face tensed. "Oh, uh, hi."

Her breath stalled somewhere in her chest. *Fall or fly. Doesn't matter. You're going to jump anyway.* She straightened, using the door frame to support her suddenly unsteady weight. "Hi."

The air seemed to thicken, charged with all the tension and trauma of the last week. Last week? Hell, the last month. Lucy's tongue felt weighted, heavy in her mouth with all the things she wanted to say to him. But her thoughts were too disordered, all trying to crowd out at once until she ended up tongue-tied and silent.

But then, realizing what Norm bent over his exposed engine meant, she shook her head slowly, laughing as she paced closer. "You need a new car, Norman."

He folded his arms across his chest and dryly raised his eyebrow in challenge. "Uh-huh. Something wrong with the electrical system, eh?"

She unlocked her own car and held the passenger door open. "Get in the car, Norman."

"Is this an abduction?"

"Yes, and I've got candy. Let's go." She waved at the car, but he'd tensed again, his expression hesitant. "Please, Norm? I want to talk to you."

He shuffled one step closer, slowly, carefully, as if measuring the distance between them to the most precise inch. He studied her for a long moment then circled the long way around the car so he didn't have to pass behind her. He climbed in and instinctively tossed her textbooks into the backseat as he had many times before.

Lucy slid into the driver's seat, her nerves crackling with unease. Norm paused halfway into his seat and tugged a black garment from under his butt. She blushed as she recognized the Dickies jacket she had never given him back and had, in fact, been wearing on the sly ever since, even after their break-up. The Norm-smell. It was a hard habit to kick.

Norm shot her a narrow, inscrutable glance then tossed the jacket in back too.

She started the car and cranked the stereo. She wanted to talk to him, desperately, but everything in her head was whirling too fast for her to settle on the first word to set the flow moving.

After driving for ten minutes in silence, Norm flipped the volume down on the music and murmured, "This song is stalking us." These were the first words he'd uttered since they left the parking lot. Which, she supposed, was fair. She had said she wanted to talk to him. Not make him talk to her.

She blinked and refocused on what he'd said. The song? She turned the radio up to make out the song's melody then restrained a bark of laughter. The mp3 player was on a shuffle, and of all the songs for its microchip to randomly select…"The song *is* stalking us," she told him, making her voice solemn.

"Isn't this the one that was playing the first time you drove me home?"

"Yes. 'Faithfully.' Last time it was the Steve Perry version. This is a duet cover." The song wound on, but this duet version didn't have the loneliness of the original.

Instead of one voice wailing high in lament, two voices worked together building the melody, creating a moment of hope together: *We can make this work.* Lucy swallowed.

"I've never heard this version," he murmured.

"It's on my mp3 player. I own both versions but, honestly, I like this one better." She darted a look his way, unsure how such a dire confession would go over.

Norm thumped the dashboard. "*Blasphemy.* Pull over. I'm walking."

Calling his bluff, she drove to the side of the road. "OK."

"All right, I'll let it slide. This time."

"Huh. That's what I thought. Don't be criticizing my music, babe."

He flinched at her use of 'babe', and Lucy sighed. Every word between them, even the inane chitchat, was so fraught, so loaded right now. Like playing Russian Roulette with words--and whoever lost had a hole blown through their heart instead of their head.

She drove on, her fingers flexing spasmodically against the steering wheel, creating a steady chorus of *squish, squish, squish* noises until Norm reached over and covered one of her hands with his, tensing it around her fingers in a small, reassuring gesture. She blew her breath out and stopped torturing her steering wheel.

All the tension in her rocketed into overdrive as she parked at Norm's building without having said a single solitary thing to him that she'd wanted to. He shot her a small, sad smile and jerked his thumb toward the apartment building. "Can I make you coffee?"

"I'd like that." Feeling fragile, her eyes prickled. *I'd like that a lot.*

Inside, things were just as uncomfortable, with Norm hovering on the edge of the living room as she sat and cradled her coffee without drinking. If she drank the coffee she d finish it, and then she'd have to leave.

His weight settled next to her, and he pushed her mug away from her, urging her to face him with his hands on her shoulders. His face drooped a little, making him look suddenly sad. Crestfallen. "Lucy, I'll quit. It's fine. I will appease Hank's wrath. I don't mind."

She gaped, momentarily pole-axed. That's what he believed all her tongue-tied tension was about? Working herself up to ask him to quit? She blinked and recovered, covering his hands, holding them in place against her shoulders as she shook her head. "You don't have to quit. I did."

"What?"

"I'm going to Berkeley this summer. Find my apartment, try to get an internship. I love Jezebel's, but I'm ready to move on."

Norm's face erupted in a bright, spontaneous grin, but his eyes were wistful and sad. "Wow. Lucy. I'm happy for you."

She wet her lips, nerving herself up. "Norm, you don't have to quit but...will you?"

"Why?"

She cradled his cheek, rasping the pad of her thumb against his stubble. "I want you to come with me. To Northern California."

Norm swallowed, and the muscles bunched in his jaw. "As a roommate?"

She let her gaze wander to his mouth, and traced the Cupid's bow of his top lip with her fingernail. "And a bed

347

warmer. And my boyfriend." She darted her gaze over to meet his and shook her head. "God, that's such a stupid, small word for what you mean to me, but it's the only one I've got at the moment."

He caught the hand she had clasped to his face and gently pulled her palm away, but he wrapped it in both of his, replacing the warmth he'd removed. "You've used that word a lot tonight. Even in front of Hank. I can't remember you ever using it before."

"I mean what I'm saying. I want to be with you."

He pinched his eyes closed and let out a long sigh then he dropped her hands.

Her eyes brimmed at this rejection. "Norm?"

But then he fished something out of his pocket and placed it in her hand. Lucy uncurled her fingers from the cool metal object and found herself holding a spark plug. The spark plug from a Toyota. A spark plug she was infinitely familiar with, having spent a lot of time with her face shoved inside Norm's engine. Keeping her tone carefully neutral, she asked, "How did you know which part to pull, Norman?"

"I texted Tommy. He sent pictures."

She gaped at him and slammed the part on the table. "You dirty rat. Car trouble, my ass. *And* you maligned my abilities as a mechanic."

"I wanted to see you tonight. To talk. And I didn't know if I could get you alone any other way."

She wrinkled her nose, delighted but not wanting to show it. Yet. "Uh-huh. What did *you* want to talk about?"

"If you wanted to make that boyfriend title present tense again instead of past."

348

Happiness welled inside her until her eyes had flooded with it. "I'm so sorry about the party and the lying. I'm sorry I hurt you at all. Ever."

He shot her a glance out of the corner of his eye, keeping his tone casual as he twirled her coffee mug. "You know, no one's ever defended my honor before. I'm all a-twitter with gratitude." He leaned toward her mouth, the couch creaking with his shifting body.

Her breath hitched in anticipation, aching for him, but she eased back, knowing there was one last thing to say. "I love you, Norman."

"I know," was his soulful reply.

She scoffed and poked him in the gut. "Now is not the time to play movie quotes."

He grabbed her hands and held them against his chest. As she thrashed to free herself, he held first one clenched fist to his lips then the other, kissing her knuckles. "I'm sorry," he said. "And I'm sorry about this week. I was hurt and pissed and--"

"Norm?"

"Yeah?"

"Shut up and kiss me."

He cupped her face with both his hands. "I love you, Lucy. I'll go with you wherever you want. Berkeley. Dagobah. Wherever. If you're there, I'm there. You got me. I'm yours."

Lucy gasped as a soft, pulsing heat spread all through her. *Mine.* "And I'm yours, Norman. I'll tell whoever you like. Hank. The bar staff. The--the Pope, the President. You name 'em, I'll find 'em and declare my love for you. You can get that in writing if you want."

349

He shook his head, his gaze tender. "I've got everything I want. But thanks."

Eyes damp with tears, she threw her arms around his neck and kissed him. He caught her to him, cupping her head to hold her close, his other arm sliding around her waist to drag her into his lap.

When they both came up for air, she planted a chaste kiss on his lovely big nose, shooting him a flirting look from under her lashes. "Was that an earthquake, baby, or did you just rock my world?"

He blinked and then, catching on quick, he shot her a sultry smolder in return. "Is there an airport nearby or is that my heart taking off?"

Her heart almost burst then with love for this sweet, silly, wonderful man, and she brushed her hand over his hair, tracing her fingertips over the beloved lines of his face. "You know, Norman, life without you would be like...a broken pencil."

"How so?"

"Pointless."

He laughed and kissed her, and she grinned and kissed him back, falling into his heat and love and light, reaching for him, dragging him against her body, folding up her future in a tight embrace.

Thanks for reading *Love's Last Call*. I hope you enjoyed it!

• Would you like to know when my next book is available? You can sign up for my new release e-mail list on my website www.bethmatthewsbooks.com.

• Reviews help other readers find books. I appreciate all honest reviews, whether positive or negative.

• If you'd like to read an excerpt from *A Midsummer Night's Fling*, my contemporary romance featuring reunited lovers, backstage romance, and a fun SoCal setting, please turn the page.

• If you're a fan of romantic fantasy, you might want to check out my fantasy releases, writing as E.D. Walker, available now:

- *The Beauty's Beast,* the tale of a cursed werewolf knight and the lady who loves him.

- *Heir to the Underworld,* the Greek Gods are feuding with the Celtic Gods, and one fierce modern teenager find herself stuck in the middle.

A Midsummer Night's Fling
Another contemporary romance by Beth Matthews
Available now!

She can't forget him...
After dating her childhood sweetheart Max on and off for years, aspiring actress Nicola Charles is finally ready to move on. It's time for her to focus on her stage career and stay away from Max—before he can break her heart again.

He's never stopped loving her...
Max regrets hurting Nicola, but he wants another chance. So when his play loses its leading lady, giving Nicola the part seems like the perfect opportunity to win back his old flame.

But the course of true love—and a theater production—never do run smooth.
As Max fights to reignite Nicola's love, the onstage antics can't rival the bedlam backstage: a neurotic cast, a prickly crew, and an evil diva of a director who's got designs on Max. Nicola and Max are battling to keep the drama onstage, but Max can't help wondering if their romance will end with the last performance. Or have the two of them finally captured what they've dreamed of all their lives?

Chapter One

For Nicola Charles, the yellow water was the breaking point.

She had already spent several hours working her way through five years of dust as she sorted all her worldly possessions. With her throat parched from that uncomfortable effort, she'd staggered past her friend, Cassie, to get a drink from the kitchen sink.

When Nicola turned on the tap, a long pause ensued followed by several ominous spit-takes from the sink. The faucet finally shot to life with a stream of dark yellow water.

Nicola stared for a long moment then said to Cassie, conversationally, "I'm moving." With a firm hand, Nicola flicked the tap off and retreated from the sink.

Her friend Cassie, sitting cross-legged on the floor, didn't even glance up from the old clothes she was sorting. "You just got here, Charlie-girl."

"My water is *yellow*."

Cassie shot her a bright, shit-eating grin. "Welcome back to California, Ms. Charles."

"Is it too late to go on tour with *Oklahoma*?" Nicola kicked her way past a graveyard of empty boxes to reach her bed where yet another box lay half sorted.

353

"Don't whine," Cassie said. "It's unbecoming in a woman your age."

"What, they revoke your whining rights when you hit twenty-nine?"

"Yes." Cassie lifted a sweater with a sailboat on the front and held the garment against her own chest, evaluating its merits. "Why is all this stuff so dusty?"

"I haven't touched it in five years." Why had Nicola even bothered storing this junk while she was on tour? All this crap was just an annoyance now.

She flung a stack of old script pages into the trash then reached into the moving box for her next armful. Her fingers bumped something metal, and her heart twisted as she realized what she was holding. She pulled the gold-framed photo of her and her ex out of the box.

Max. The name tore its way out of her back-brain, half sigh, half groan.

Stupid Max. She scowled at his blond handsomeness, at the grin on his gorgeous face, at the strong arms draped around her in the picture. Max: the mistake she had made at sixteen. And nineteen. And twenty-five. And --

She scowled at herself in the picture too. Five years younger. Five years dumber.

With an inner wrench, she tore her gaze off the frame and slapped the picture face down on the bed. She whirled toward Cassie. "This is what happens when you box up your life and ignore it for five years."

"What happens?"

"You outgrow it." Nicola restrained an urge to throw that golden frame across the room. *Stupid Max.*

Cassie cocked her head to the side, black hair sliding over one pale, tattooed shoulder. "If you don't want any of this, why did you pay to keep it in storage while you were on the road?"

Because it was easier than sorting through all of this. The photo frame seemed to pulse behind Nicola. The telltale snapshot. Five years ago it had been easier to package up all of her old life and forget it while she escaped unhindered into a new one.

Cassie was still watching her, so Nicola shrugged and said, "Storage seemed like a good idea at the time."

"Uh-huh. No more tours? I thought you were up for *Anything Goes.* What happened there?"

"I'm sick of touring. I want to stay in one place for more than six weeks. You know how it is. You gave it up too."

"It's because my roommate on that last tour was so annoying." Cassie winked.

Nicola stuck her tongue out. "I'm not the one who snores."

Cassie flapped her hand, brushing aside this inconvenient truth about herself. "Do you have any auditions out here yet?"

"I've got my feelers out."

"Like a giant fire ant."

"Sure." Nicola put her pointer fingers on each side of her forehead and wiggled them like antennae, crossing her eyes at Cassie.

But her friend was not to be distracted; Cassie's face was gently compassionate. "Nothing?"

"I've got prospects." Nicola popped the lid on yet another banker's box to avoid her friend's sympathy. Things would turn around. *Soon. Soon. I'll get a job soon.* This was the national anthem of the actor's life.

355

"What's the picture of?" Cassie asked, nodding toward the frame on the bed, obviously hoping to break the depressed silence with a new topic.

Nicola snatched up the infamous photo frame. "Doesn't matter." Without letting Cassie see the picture, and without glancing at Max, Nicola hurried to the kitchen trash and dumped the photo in with her empty pizza box from the night before. The picture thunked heavily into the bottom of the bin. "I'm done with the past!" Nicola proclaimed, flinging her arms wide in triumph.

Someone rapped on the door. Nicola jumped at the sound. Cassie raised a questioning eyebrow.

"Probably the landlord." Nicola crossed to the door and yanked it open.

"Hi, Nicci," Max said.

At the sight of him, her blood rabbited through her veins with a dizzying, painful thrum.

Max.

Max?

Here?

She stared at him in simple, stupid shock, worried he was some kind of stress-induced mirage.

But no, he was real enough -- all six foot three of him standing on her doorstep.

Max. *Here.*

He was still spectacularly good-looking. Handsome, chiseled face. Thick, waving blonde hair that had grown long enough to brush over his ears and forehead. Strong jaw with a scruff of stubble inching into a full-blown beard. A sensuous, mobile mouth. Piercing, sea blue eyes, and those damn laugh lines around them that added an extra layer of charm to his every smile.

Just your basic All-American, Grade-A, prime beefcake demi-god.

Noting her prolonged perusal, a lop-sided grin tucked itself into the corner of Max's mouth.

The smile -- that same teasing grin he'd always used to charm her out of being mad at him -- that *stupid* smile broke his spell. "You always did have impeccable timing," she said.

And then she slammed the door in his face.

Cassie blinked. "That wasn't very neighborly."

"What?" Nicola shook her head, dazed. She recognized Cassie had made sounds, was looking at her, expecting her to say...something. But communication, processing words, parsing social cues, the basics of human discourse...these skills all deserted Nicola as she stood with her spine pressed against the front door.

"Charlie?" Cassie asked.

Nicola winced as a knock sounded through the door, the noise loud and right behind her ear.

"Nicola, please open the door," Max said. "I only want to talk to you."

Cassie padded to the door, shoving Nicola to the side so she could peer through the peephole. When Cassie eased back, she shot Nicola an *atta-girl* grin. "Are Jehovah's Witnesses getting cuter or has it been too long since I got laid?"

Nicola smacked her friend's arm and retreated, her heart hammering as if a grizzly bear stood behind the front door and not her incredibly hunky -- and annoying -- ex. "That's not a J-dub."

"Selling subscriptions for the evening post?" Cassie asked.

357

"No."

"Girl scout cookies?"

"I wish."

A furrow appeared between Cassie's eyebrows. "Are you all right? Should we call the police?"

Nicola pressed a hand to the knot under her sternum and waved that offer away.

Just the sight of Max could *still* drive her crazy? Unfair, but all right. Anyway, she could definitely hide that fact from *him*. Maybe she'd botched her opening move with the whole door-slamming thing, but she could recover. She was a professional actress! This sort of thing was her bread and butter. Or would be if she ever got another acting job.

She sucked in a deep breath and fumbled for the doorknob, turning it as she whirled to peer through the crack she had made between the door and the jamb.

He beamed at her, big and handsome as he ducked down to lean against the door so their faces were close.

Too close. She let the door fall open wider and stepped back. "Hello, Max."

His grin inched up a notch, laugh lines crinkling. Those damn laugh lines. "Nic, I've got a proposition for you -- "

She slammed the door.

"I'm confused," Cassie murmured.

"Me too," Max said through the door.

Nicola stalked into the living room, digging into a box at random. "*'I've got a proposition for you'?* Who does he think he is?"

"Who is he?" Cassie asked.

"Five years and he uses that *cheesy line*!" The sparking

anger inside Nicola made her yell the words loud enough so she could be certain Max had heard her.

"*Hey!*" he called through the door. "That was not *cheesy.*"

Cassie paused, squinting back and forth between Nicola and the front door. "Um."

"Nicola!" Max pounded on the door.

Glowering, Cassie pounded right back at him, the flesh of her arms jiggling from the force of her knocks. "*Watch it, buddy, or I'll call the cops!*"

Observing her friend's furious performance, thinking of Max baffled on the other side, and realizing her own irrationality wasn't exactly mature, Nicola pressed a fist into her mouth, hoping to stifle the giggle that bubbled up. But then Cassie turned to face her and Nicola burst out laughing, defeated by her absurd situation.

Cassie's lip curled, flashing her dimple, then she was laughing too, crumpling to the floor and resting her forehead against her knee as she gasped.

"You guys are laughing," Max said through the door, sounding disgruntled. "At me."

Still laughing, wiping her eyes, Nicola opened the door, facing Max. "And me."

He glared at her, brawny arms folded. Although the door was wide open he did not step inside.

Somehow the laughter had worked the tension inside her loose, and Nicola wasn't worried about seeing him anymore. "What's up, Maxim?"

He grinned at the use of his old nickname and for a flash, one searing moment, the years peeled away. He was a cocky seventeen year old playing Romeo, making goofy faces at her, trying to get her to break character while they

359

performed the iconic balcony scene together. Something in her heart trembled at that memory, stumbling toward darkness, and she braced herself, pulling her gaze from his face.

Her mood must have been contagious. He shifted on his feet, and she could actually hear the grin leave his face as he angled his body toward Cassie. "Hello. You do a very intimidating yell."

Cassie sidled forward with her hand out. "You do a fine knock, my good man." She darted a questioning glance at Nicola, which Nicola chose to ignore. "I'm Cassie Xu."

"Max Fiesengerke."

"Fiesengerke?" Cassie asked, blinking free from her starry-eyed adoration of Max. "Isn't that the name of that actor?"

Trying to be stealthy, Nicola turned her back to Max and made a throat-cutting-shut-*up*-Cassie motion with her hand.

Cassie burbled on, oblivious, "The guy in that pirate movie."

"Orlando Bloom?" Nicola chirped out, hoping to derail this topic.

Cassie sent her a *WTF?* face. "No, the other pirate movie. *Fortune's Fool.*"

"Peter Fiesengerke," Max said through gritted teeth.

"Yeah. I *love* him. Are you guys related?"

"That would be my brother," Max said in a dry, dead tone, like the butler in a gothic novel announcing the Master had died of a bad case of bloody murder.

Nicola pressed a palm to her aching forehead. Landmines carpeted the ground where she and Max walked together, and poor Cassie was the innocent pedestrian who'd stepped right on top of one.

Cassie, catching on quick, puffed out a small, "Oh."

"Cass, do you mind leaving us alone for a sec?" Nicola asked.

Judging by how Cassie fled into the bathroom and closed the door: she didn't.

"Why are you here?" Nicola asked Max, keeping her voice quiet but sharp.

He retreated a step, and any lingering warmth in his voice faded. "I wanted to offer you a job."

She frowned as she stared at his handsome, now expressionless face. *That's it?*

They hadn't seen each other in five years. They'd been childhood sweethearts, best friends, he'd been *inside her,* and his big opening salvo after years of estrangement was a *job offer?*

She slammed the door in his face.

If you enjoyed this excerpt,
A MIDSUMMER NIGHT'S FLING is available now!

ABOUT THE AUTHOR

Beth Matthews (a.k.a. E.D. Walker) is a Southern
California girl, born and raised. She's a total geek, a movie
buff, and a mediocre swing dancer. She lives in sunny
SoCal with her boyfriend and two of the neediest
housecats on the planet.

For more information on Beth Matthews, please poke
around her website www.bethmatthewsbooks.com.

Or, you can just email her at:
beth.matthews.books@gmail.com

But, however you connect, she's always happy to hear
from readers. ^_^